These vi...
t...

Wed in White

Marrying Marcus
"Strong, rich characters; heart-tugging
moments; and a wonderfully appealing
hero come together in this keeper
by Laurey Bright."
—*Romantic Times*

First Time, Forever
"Cara Colter takes two wounded, sensitive
people and creates a great story about the
importance of family and love."
—*Romantic Times*

*Celebrate the joys of first love with
these two unforgettable stories!*

Wed in White

Laurey Bright & Cara Colter

*M&B™ and M&B™ with the Rose Device
are trademarks of the publisher.
Harlequin Mills & Boon Limited, Eton House,
18-24 Paradise Road, Richmond, Surrey TW9 1SR*

WED IN WHITE © by Harlequin Books SA 2007

Marrying Marcus © Daphne Claire de Jong 2001
First Time, Forever © Cara Colter 2000

ISBN: 978 0263 85848 8

10-1007

*Harlequin Mills & Boon policy is to use papers that are
natural, renewable and recyclable products and made from
wood grown in sustainable forests. The logging and
manufacturing processes conform to the legal environmental
regulations of the country of origin.*

*Printed and bound in Spain
by Litografia Rosés S.A., Barcelona*

MARRYING MARCUS
by
Laurey Bright

Laurey Bright has written more than sixty books, sometimes under the name Daphne Clair. She lives in New Zealand where she creates the stories of contemporary people in love that have won her a following all over the world.

Chapter One

Anticipation sizzling in her blood, Jenna Harper scanned the passengers from the recently landed Los-Angeles-to-Auckland flight. Backpackers in jeans and boots, business people in tailored suits, parents with tired-eyed children, a middle-aged couple whose grandchildren swarmed to them as they appeared from the customs area.

Among those waiting at the arrivals gate, Pacific Islanders in flower-patterned prints, and an Indian woman's butterfly-wing sari, created splashes of early-morning color.

By Jenna's side her best friend, Katie Crossan, shifted impatiently from one foot to the other. Katie's sister, Jane, hitched her youngest into her arms while her husband restrained the older two, who were becoming restless.

"When's Uncle Dean coming?" the four-year-old demanded.

"Soon," his grandmother assured her.

The entire Crossan family had turned out to welcome Dean home. Even Marcus, his elder brother.

Jenna wondered if Marcus would have come if Katie hadn't begged him to drive her and Jenna to the airport at Mangere.

He stood a little aside from the rest of the tightly knit group, taller than any of them, including his father. Dark hair was ruthlessly combed back from his angular, intelligent face; his hands were thrust into the pockets of gray-green trousers, which he wore with a cream shirt.

He turned his head a fraction and caught Jenna looking at him. One black brow lifted slightly, and then a corner of his long, firm mouth. His storm-cloud eyes were disconcertingly penetrating.

Jenna gave him a nervous smile, flicked a strand of fine, light-brown hair from her cheek to behind her ear and looked away, searching the next wave of arrivals.

Marcus was older than Katie and Dean, the twins who were born when he was nearly six and Jane five.

Katie and Jenna had agreed that although they'd miss Dean like crazy, the scholarship that had taken him away for four years to America would give him the chance to move out of Marcus's formidable shadow. But the waiting had been hard.

Marcus saw him first. "Here he comes."

Katie broke away from the group, shrieking Dean's name before her arms circled his neck and he caught her, swinging her off her feet.

The children, suddenly shy of this stranger, hung

about Jane, impeding her and her husband as they too pressed forward.

Jenna couldn't help a smile of pure joy, bubbles of it bursting inside her like champagne, but she made herself wait. As soon as the family greetings were over, Dean would look for her. And she enjoyed just drinking in the sight of him.

He was not as tall as his brother, but his hair was nearly as dark and had a nice wave. His features were regular and his eyes a warm blue. Film-star looks. And when he saw his family, his face showed unashamed affection that to Jenna's eyes made him even more handsome.

Mr. Crossan gave him a quick hug, Mrs. Crossan wiped a tear after hugging him in her turn, the three children clustered around Jane as she kissed her younger brother's cheek, and her husband clapped him on the shoulder.

Jenna took a step forward, then halted when the tall, tanned blonde behind Dean, whom she had assumed was another passenger patiently waiting for the family to move out of the way, went to his side. Unbelievably he turned to put an arm about her.

It was like a slow-motion movie. Jenna's mouth dried, her blood froze. She was almost suffocating, standing immovable as a puzzled hush settled on the group just yards away.

Dean smiled down at the girl and said happily to his family, ''This is Callie—we're getting married.''

Chapter Two

The world stopped for Jenna, although all about her people were moving, calling out to others, hugging and kissing, helping to push carts piled high with luggage.

The family came to life. Katie squealed, punched Dean's chest. "You didn't tell us!" His mother gave Dean another hug, embraced the girl and kissed her cheek. His father shook her hand, then Dean's.

Dean hadn't even looked at Jenna.

Everything around her faded and turned gray, and the jumble of sounds became muffled. She was numb.

A hard hand closed about her arm, so tight that it hurt. And she was glad, because she needed something to persuade her she could still feel. Marcus's deep voice next to her ear said, "Do you want me to get you out of here?"

Yes, she thought, but said thinly, when her woolly tongue found itself, "No." He couldn't abandon his family. "Of course not. You...h-haven't said hello to your brother."

She dragged her eyes from Dean and saw that Marcus was looking extremely grim, his gaze on his brother's face not welcoming at all. He returned his attention to her. "Neither have you. Are you up to it?"

Overwhelming embarrassment and panic gripped her. Maybe she was going to be sick. Afraid to open her mouth again, she tried to nod.

"You look as though you're about to fall over," Marcus said bluntly.

Jenna gritted her teeth, forcing out words. "I won't." She held her breath, hoping to bring some color into her cheeks.

The group around Dean was surging toward her and Marcus. He didn't let go of her arm as Dean saw them and bounded over, abandoning the baggage cart.

Jenna molded her lips into something approximating a smile and instructed herself to breathe again. Marcus had moved ahead of her, his free hand outstretched so that Dean had to stop and take it, giving Jenna a little more time.

Marcus said unemotionally, "Hi, Dean. Congratulations. And welcome home."

"Thanks." Dean's other hand gripped his arm. "You haven't changed a bit, Marc."

Behind him, Katie shot Jenna an anxious look. Then Dean turned to Jenna and held his arms wide, eclipsing his sister. "Hi, Jen! Sweet of you to turn out at this time of the morning. How are you?"

He hugged her, not seeming to notice that her own

arms hung lifelessly at her sides. "You have to meet Callie," he said.

She supposed she did.

Stepping back, she almost collided with Marcus, her shoulder touching his chest, but he didn't move. And neither did she, buttressed by the solid feel of him right behind her.

She turned the hurting smile to the girl's face. "How nice to meet you."

"You too." Callie had a warm American accent, a genuine smile. "I've heard a lot about you."

What? her mind asked frantically. What did Dean say about me? Did he tell you I've been stupidly in love with him since we were children? That I thought he would come back and marry me? That next to Katie and his mother I thought I was the person he was closest to in all the world?

"Katie's best friend," Callie said, "and room-mate—except here you call it a flatmate." She screwed up her nose and laughed. "Isn't that right?"

"Yes." Jenna couldn't say any more. She wanted to scream, cry—run. Pride kept her upright, smiling.

Callie looked at Marcus. "And you're Marcus," she said. "The big brother." She gave him a frank, open look, her eyes wide and candid, and the smile turned from friendly to appreciative. "He's told me all about his family."

"And yet he hasn't told us a thing about you," Marcus said.

Callie laughed again. "He wanted to surprise you."

"You are certainly a surprise." Marcus paused. "A welcome one, of course. I hope you'll enjoy New Zealand."

"I'm looking forward to it, and to getting to know you all. Oh—and Jenna too."

The afterthought was kindly meant, Jenna knew, but it made her conscious that she wasn't really family, she didn't belong.

Jane's children had commandeered the baggage cart, and one of the bags slipped. While Callie helped to reorganize the luggage, Jenna blindly turned away, following an instinct to flee.

Marcus was in her way. His fingers circled her arm again for a second. "Just stay here." His voice held a note of command.

She stood there while he exchanged a few quick words with his parents and Katie, who threw her friend another worried glance.

Then Marcus was back at her side, his hand on her elbow. "Come on."

She didn't ask where they were going, so relieved that he was taking her away from this nightmare that she didn't care. "Katie...?" she said feebly as he whisked her across the polished floor.

"There's room for her in Mum and Dad's car, and she won't want to be separated from Dean. That's something Callie will have to get used to—how close the twins are."

And of course with Callie sharing the back seat, there'd be no room for Jenna.

Dean's parents expected him to stay at their home, just half an hour out of Auckland, until he'd settled. They hadn't been expecting him to bring a fiancée, but there'd be no problem putting up an extra person in the big house where they'd brought up their family—the house Jenna had known almost as well as she knew the much smaller home she'd shared with her mother next door.

In the parking area the cool air chilled her, although the gray morning sky was turning to blue, with high white clouds drifting across it.

Marcus guided her to his sleek maroon car and opened the door for her. He didn't speak again until they were on their way out of the airport complex, driving between green fields gradually being overtaken by new buildings.

Then he said, "I told the family I'd join them later. Have you had breakfast?"

"Breakfast?" Jenna repeated vaguely.

"Something to eat. What most people have in the morning."

"No." She and Katie had been too rushed and too excited to eat breakfast at that early hour. She didn't see what relevance it had.

"Neither have I," Marcus said. "We'll stop on the way."

Jenna didn't argue, although she had never felt less hungry. Like his younger siblings, she'd developed a habit of listening to Marcus.

When they reached the outskirts of the city he found a restaurant and ordered juice, toast and pancakes for two, and made Jenna drink hot, strong coffee. With sugar.

"That's better," he said, after she had eaten two slices of toast and pushed the empty coffee cup away. "You're beginning to look human again."

"I'm never at my best in the morning," she said.

Marcus gave her a thoughtful look. "I'm sorry, Jenna."

She gazed down at the white ceramic salt cellar on the table—shiny and smooth. "Thanks," she said, "for breakfast." And for rescuing me. Stopping me from making a complete fool of myself. "I'll pay my share."

"Don't be silly." A lean hand caught hers as she made to open her purse. "I'm paying." He removed his warm, strong fingers from hers and took out his wallet.

In the car she said, "Maybe I should just go home."

Katie had taken it for granted that Jenna would spend the weekend with the Crossans. It was lucky, she'd said, that her twin had chosen to fly in on a Saturday. They needn't take time off from work.

Jenna had thought it lucky too. Now she wished she could plead pressure of work, an emergency, any excuse not to be there.

His hand on the ignition key, Marcus turned a searching look on her.

"An engagement is a family affair," Jenna suggested, her voice strained. "And I'm not family."

Gently he said, "It smacks a bit of sour grapes, you know. Do you want to make us all feel guilty?"

"No! We—you've all been looking forward so much to having Dean home again. I want everyone to be happy for him and...and Callie."

"Very noble." His tone was extremely dry. "I suspect you'd like to slap him silly, really. I know I would. I felt like thumping him at the airport."

Jenna blinked up at him, surprised that Marcus should feel so strongly on her behalf. "I don't suppose I'd be missed," she said.

He made a small, scornful noise in his throat. "You
know better than that. Of course you'd be missed."
He paused. "If it's what you want, I'll take you back
to the flat and tell the family you're not well." But
he sounded reluctant.

They'd guess that the only thing she was nursing
was a broken heart...wouldn't they? And if Katie did
believe in a sudden sickness, concern about Jenna being ill and alone would spoil her delight in her
brother's return.

She chewed her lower lip, undecided. "I suppose
your whole family is sorry for me."

"Katie might be. I guess you've told her how you
feel?"

After a moment Jenna shook her head. "Not really.
I mean...not in so many words." She'd assumed that
Katie knew—but then she'd assumed Dean felt the
same. And she'd been totally, unbelievably wrong. "I
thought everyone knew." She lifted her eyes to his
almost accusingly. "You did."

His mouth moved in a slight smile. "I don't think
my parents have recognized yet that you and the twins
are actually grown up. They've never taken your ad-
oration of Dean seriously. And Jane has been pretty
much occupied with her own family for the past few
years. I take it you haven't been exchanging love letters with my little brother?"

She'd always signed her regular letters with "Love,
Jenna." And Dean had sent his love in return when
he wrote, but his much-less-frequent letters were addressed to both Jenna and his twin, and when he
phoned the flat, whichever of the girls answered the
phone called out to the other, and they'd eagerly

swapped the receiver between them and passed messages until Dean had to hang up.

Jenna had never minded sharing. She'd been grateful that Katie didn't either. Twins, even nonidentical ones, enjoyed a special bond. She understood that. Did Callie? She said, "Not love letters, exactly."

She and Dean had known each other so long there was no need to express their feelings in extravagant words. They would have felt silly doing it.

"Dean isn't cruel," Marcus said consideringly. "But he's not always terribly bright about people's feelings. Probably he just never noticed. The consequence of growing up together. He didn't see what was right under his nose practically all his life."

If Marcus was right, staying away today would only fuel any suspicion that might enter anyone's head—including Dean's. Or Callie's. Somehow that would be worse than anything.

His voice became brisk. "How are your acting skills? You used to be pretty good as a kid. Especially if it was a question of saving young Dean's bacon."

But Marcus, she recalled, had always seen through her subterfuges on Dean's behalf. As he'd seen through her today and stepped in to avert what might have been a dampener on the family reunion, an embarrassment to everyone.

When she remained silent, he added, "It's entirely your choice, but if you come along I promise I'll make it as bearable as I can—and we'll leave early."

Jenna took a deep breath. "I'll come."

She couldn't read the look he gave her. His mouth was very firm, his eyes dark and probing. Then he put out a hand to squeeze hers before starting the car.

* * *

It was just as bad as she had imagined.

Marcus parked in the asphalt area in front of the sprawling old house with its gabled windows, the walls and decorative trims freshly painted in honor of Dean's return. Brushing past scented lavender and frilled pinks in pots at the side of the steps, they went in the big front door that was expectantly open and through the wide hallway.

The adults were sitting around in the family room with cups of tea and coffee, while the children darted between the chairs and chased one another in and out of the French windows opening onto the tree-fringed lawn and the fenced pool.

Marcus explained their delayed arrival by saying he'd needed something to eat after being dragged out of bed at some ungodly hour at his younger sister's insistence and then stuck at the airport for nearly an hour.

"You could have eaten here," his mother chided.

"I was too hungry to wait." He smiled at her. "And going without breakfast didn't do Jenna any good, either."

Mrs. Crossan gave her a sympathetic look. "You are a wee bit pale." She dropped her voice and murmured anxiously, "You're not upset about Dean's engagement, are you, dear?"

"I think it's wonderful," Jenna lied valiantly. "Callie's beautiful, isn't she? And Dean looks so happy."

"Well, yes." Mrs. Crossan's eyes turned to the couple, and Jenna saw the smile she couldn't help. "They are very happy."

Dean and Callie had freshened up, and Callie

looked even more gorgeous than she had at the airport. Dean hardly took his eyes off her for long enough to wave to his brother and throw a careless "Hi, again!" at Jenna.

She should be glad he didn't look at her too closely, but instead she felt a jealousy so strong and painful she had to bunch a fist at her midriff to stop it hurting so much.

Marcus's fingers closed over hers and pried them apart. "Is there coffee on?" he asked no one in particular. "Let's get some, Jenna." He hauled her with him into the big, sun-filled kitchen.

"We just had coffee," she said as he dropped her hand and went to the machine in a corner of the counter.

"Have some more. Or can I get you something stronger?"

Jenna shook her head. She needed her wits about her. "No."

He pulled two mugs from hooks under the cupboards and filled them, stirring some sugar into hers. "Here."

Katie came in, a pile of cups and saucers in her hands. "Are you all right, Jen?"

Trying not to sound too hearty, Jenna injected a faint note of surprise into her reply. "I'm fine. Are you pleased to have your brother home? Don't answer that. Silly question."

Katie grinned, obviously unable to suppress it. "I never realized how much I missed him." The grin fading abruptly, she added, placing the cups on the counter, "Callie's a bit of a bolt from the blue, though.'' Her eyes worried, she asked, ''He…he hadn't said anything about her to you, had he?''

''Not a thing.'' Jenna made her voice cheerful. ''If he'd told anyone it would have been you.''

Marcus interjected, ''A whirlwind romance? If even you didn't know anything, Katie…''

''He did mention her a couple of times, but I never twigged she was anyone special, and he hadn't said anything about her recently. He says he was scared she'd turn him down, and he didn't want to come home and have us all know he was nursing a broken heart. She only agreed to come to New Zealand with him a couple of weeks ago, and he decided to keep it secret until they got here, so he could see our faces when he gave us the news.''

Thank heaven he hadn't seen hers, Jenna thought. She curled her hand around her hot coffee mug, ignoring the discomfort.

Katie added thoughtfully, ''And I have a suspicion he was afraid she might change her mind before he got her on the plane.''

Jenna forced a smile. ''Well, it's a nice surprise, isn't it?''

Dubiously, Katie agreed, ''I suppose so. Are you sure you're okay with it, Jen?''

Hoping she looked bewildered and innocent, Jenna said, ''Of course. Dean's very happy. And I'm happy for him. Aren't you?''

Hesitantly, Katie said, ''I thought it would be you and him. Even when we were kids you said you were going to marry each other.''

Jenna's laugh should have earned her an Oscar.

"We were—what?—eight years old? Come *on,* Katie!"

"Sometimes when we were older it kind of looked like you were more than friends."

Jenna had thought so. They'd exchanged kisses from time to time. She'd imagined that, like her, Dean was keeping their relationship on the level of a warm, intimate friendship while they both worked hard at their degrees and were too young and impecunious for marriage.

After they'd graduated, the scholarship had come up for him to study in America. He'd asked Jenna's opinion, stressing how long he'd be away from home, and she'd somehow concealed her panic and dismay and said of course he must take it, a chance like that wasn't to be missed.

The kiss he gave her then was definitely not a brotherly one, and she'd seen it as a promise, a pledge, an unspoken commitment to a shared, if deferred, future.

She'd held on to that memory for four years. And now she wondered if Dean even remembered it. Certainly it had held none of the significance for him that it had for her.

Painfully putting her newfound insight into words, Jenna said, "We grew out of it. If there'd been anything serious, Dean wouldn't have left me to go to the other side of the world for years. Would he?"

Marcus added, "Wishful thinking, Katie. Very nice for you, to match your twin and your best friend, but in real life our childhood sweethearts grow up and marry other people."

"Did yours?" Katie asked, temporarily diverted.

"Of course," Marcus answered. "And I didn't lose a moment's sleep over it."

Katie switched her attention back to Jenna. "Have I been daydreaming?"

"I won't lose a moment's sleep," Jenna echoed Marcus, trying to sound as convincing.

Either Marcus had sown the seed of doubt, or Katie decided to take her cue from Jenna's denial. "Well, that's a relief," she said. For a long second her eyes rested thoughtfully on her friend, before she began stacking cups and saucers in the dishwasher.

Jenna and Marcus finished their coffee, and all three of them rejoined the others. Neighbors dropped in to say hello, and a cousin phoned inquiring after the traveler. Dean invited her and her parents and boyfriend to come over.

A party atmosphere developed. Some of the guests sat out on the tiled patio, and children were allowed to jump in the swimming pool in its fenced enclosure at the back of the house. Jenna talked and laughed and even conducted a conversation with Callie and Dean, finding that Callie was exactly what she looked like, a golden California girl. She'd been studying at the same university as Dean, although they had met only a few months ago.

"And when he opened his mouth and I heard that cute accent," Callie confessed, her hand caressing Dean's arm, "it was love at first sound."

"She thought I was Australian," Dean teased, grinning adoringly at her. "I had to educate her about the difference between Kiwis and Aussies."

"It took him all night." Callie swept him a flirtatious look.

"Slow learner." Dean shook his head, returning the look.

Jenna's smile felt set in concrete. She didn't think the two of them would have noticed if everyone else in the room had disappeared in a puff of smoke.

Marcus laid a hand lightly on Jenna's shoulder. "Dad says you haven't seen his latest acquisition," he said. "He wants me to show it to you."

Gratefully she followed Marcus to the back lawn, where a shade house was tucked into a corner screened by pink-flowered manuka shrubs. Mr. Crossan was a keen amateur orchid grower, and when Marcus ushered her into the shade house, they were surrounded by pots and hanging baskets of the exotic, distinctive flowers.

The air was cool here, and the bark chips that covered the ground muffled their footsteps. A damp rich smell pervaded the glassed-in area.

Jenna walked along the narrow space between the tiered benches holding rows of orchids, many of them smothered in blossom. Delicate, spidery varieties and large opulent ones were ranged along both sides, the flowers spilling over their pots, some almost to the ground. "Which one are we looking at?"

"The pink one over here." He guided her to it with a hand lightly on her waist and stood behind her as she studied the pale, frilled blooms, flushed with gold at the throat.

Tentatively she touched a fingertip to a delicate petal. "It's very pretty."

"It's called Puppy Love," Marcus told her, slanting her a rather dry sideways glance. "Personally I prefer the more sophisticated varieties."

Staring down at the plant, Jenna blinked away tears. Puppy Love. A fragile flower. And though orchids lasted longer than other flowers, there came a time when they too withered away and died.

She turned away from it, and Marcus moved to let her pass him, returning along the row. "We needn't hurry back." He strolled after her, hands in his pockets. "No one will miss us for a while."

No one would miss Jenna. Self-pity threatened to overwhelm her. But they'd miss Marcus for sure. Marcus was a dominant figure in any gathering, not only because of his height. There was a quiet air of confidence and authority about him that even his family acknowledged.

Maybe it came from being the eldest. Jane was nearly his own age, but having two much younger, mischievous siblings might have given him an exaggerated sense of responsibility.

She halted before a plant exploding with extravagant bronze blooms. They blurred before her eyes, and she bit down fiercely on her lower lip, squeezing her eyes shut, taking a long, deep breath.

Marcus said, "One of Dad's prizewinners. Magnificent, isn't it?"

"Yes." Her voice was husky, but his casual tone steadied her. "What...what's it called, do you know?"

"The name should be on a marker in the pot." Marcus leaned across to part some spiky leaves, and his sleeve brushed her arm. "Dark Delight."

As he drew back he slanted her a swift glance, and his hand briefly rested on the skin of her arm, a comforting caress. His breath stirring her hair, he said, "It will get better, you know. Hard to believe right now, maybe, but I promise you it's true.''

She gripped the edge of the bench in front of her. ''I don't want your sympathy, Marcus.'' It would be too easy to turn and let him take her in his strong arms and hold her while she wept out her bewilderment and heartache. She had to get through this day without cracking, in order to keep her pride, at least, intact.

''Sorry.'' As far as the space would allow, he moved away from her.

''I didn't mean to seem ungrateful.''

''I'm not looking for gratitude, Jenna.''

''You've been awfully kind.'' She blinked the tears away and managed to face him.

A strange expression crossed his hard features, almost as if he shared her pain. He lifted a hand, and his thumb wiped an escaped salty droplet from her cheek. ''It will soon be over.'' His thumb strayed to her abused lower lip, where she had bitten into it. Unexpectedly he dipped his head and pressed his firm mouth gently to hers.

Chapter Three

It lasted only a second, but a faint warmth seeped into her cold heart, and when he stepped back, saying, "Can you stand to go back inside?" she nodded, feeling somehow stronger, braced for the fray.

Jenna helped Katie and her mother rustle up an impromptu meal. Some visitors had drifted away, but there was quite a crowd around the big table in the spacious dining room, and Jenna's lack of conversation went unnoticed. Marcus took a seat next to her, shielding her from Callie and Dean on his other side.

After the dishes were disposed of, Marcus found Jenna hanging up a tea towel in the kitchen, carefully straightening the edges. "Anytime you want," he said, "we can go."

Thankfully she took the hint. Steeling herself, she parried Katie's suspicious surprise that she'd decided to go home after all, using the excuse that this was a family occasion, and repeated her congratulations to Dean and Callie.

Within minutes she was releasing a sigh of relief as she fastened her safety belt.

Marcus started the car and edged out of the driveway. "You can let go now, if you want," he said.

Cry, she supposed he meant.

Although she'd been fighting tears for hours, now the urge to weep had left her altogether. She sat dryeyed and silent beside Marcus all the way back to the city. The sunlight dancing on the water of the west harbor as they sped alongside it seemed to mock her bleak mood of despair.

Leaving the high speed zone, Marcus glanced at her as he eased off the accelerator. "Will you be all right on your own?"

"I won't slit my wrists," she promised.

He smiled. "I know you wouldn't. If you'd rather come to my place, I have a spare room."

She shook her head. "Thanks, but no. You've been great, Marcus."

"It doesn't cost me anything, and much as I'd like to wring his neck, I couldn't allow Dean's homecoming to turn into a disaster."

He might have been sorry for her, but his main concern was his family. Because she was close to his brother and sister, Jenna too had always come under his protection, but she guessed that if she threatened their happiness he'd sacrifice her without a second thought.

Which was right and natural. Only it didn't make her feel any better.

Marcus said, "It's a pity your mother's so far away."

For the past three years Jenna's mother had been

living in Invercargill, at the other end of the country, with her second husband. "I'm too old to run to my mother," Jenna said.

She'd learned early in life that running to her mother didn't solve anything. Karen Harper loved her daughter, but at times her own problems had been too overwhelming for her to cope with Jenna's, as well.

Marcus cast her a glance. "If you do need someone to run to," he offered, "I'll be around."

She managed a pale smile. "Thanks, but I don't think so."

"Independent little cuss, aren't you?"

"I've always tried to be."

"Had to be, I suppose. It must have been tough, losing your father so early."

"I never really knew him—I only have a few hazy memories. It was hard on my mother, though. I'm glad she's found someone else."

"We promised to keep an eye on you, you know, when she went to live down south."

Jenna had been just short of twenty then, still at university and living in a students' hall. "I don't think she meant me to be a lifelong burden on your family."

He turned the car into the quiet suburban street where she and Katie lived. "You're not a burden, Jenna. You're a friend. And that's going to make things difficult for you over the next few months, perhaps. You won't confide in Katie, will you?"

She wasn't sure if it was a question or a disguised warning. "No." It was going to be difficult enough for Katie, adjusting to a stranger having a claim on her twin. Knowing that her closest friend carried a torch for him would add extra stress.

"Here you are." The car stopped outside the building. "I'll come in with you."

"You don't need to—"

He ignored that, and it was just as well. When she opened the door of the flat they were greeted by disaster. Water was dripping from the ceiling and running down the walls, spreading a huge dark stain across the carpet.

"Hell!" Marcus surveyed the mess. "It's either a burst pipe or someone's left a tap running in the flat above you."

It was hours before it was all sorted. The upstairs owners—away for the weekend—were tracked down, a key located, the forgotten tap turned off. And then came the cleanup.

Marcus stayed despite Jenna's protest. He made phone calls, shifted furniture, helped her mop up water, and tracked down a carpet-cleaning firm who sent a couple of men who moved more furniture and set huge electric fans about the place to dry out the carpets they'd lifted and folded back.

Over the roar of the motors Marcus said, "Well, that settles it. You'll have to come to my place after all."

"I don't know if—"

"You can't stay here," he said. "Is all you need in this bag?" He lifted the tote that she'd previously put essentials into, assuming that she would stay the night at the Crossans'.

"I'll just change my clothes," she said, capitulating. Her cotton trousers and shirt were wet and grubby. "I won't be long."

One thing about the past few hours, she'd scarcely had a chance to think about Dean and his bride-to-be.

Marcus's apartment was a direct contrast to the cheery muddle Jenna and Katie lived in. The main room was large and airy, the sofas long and luxurious and precisely aligned about a solid rimu coffee table that held one elegantly formed pottery dish. Theirs was invariably cluttered with magazines, paperback books left open and facedown, junk mail, the TV remote control, probably an opened snack food bag and quite likely a hair dryer and bottles of nail polish.

Marcus's books and magazines were arrayed on shelves, probably in alphabetical order, Jenna thought, and there wasn't a sign of clutter.

The spare room he ushered Jenna into was equally sparse and neat. "The bed's made up." He placed her bag on the end of it. "Make yourself comfortable. I'll give Katie a ring to let her know you're here and break the bad news about your flat."

She unzipped the bag, shook out the skirt and top she'd packed, and hung them in the empty wardrobe to get the creases out.

Shutting the door, she caught her reflection in the mirror on the outside. Her face looked lifeless, her mouth pale and tremulous. Rummaging in the bag, she brought out a lipstick and swept a little color over her lips, then rubbed at her cheekbones with her knuckles. At least she could make an effort not to look like a Victorian maiden about to go into a decline.

In the living room, Marcus was replacing the receiver on the phone. "I'll have a shower and get out of these clothes." He still looked remarkably well groomed, despite the wet patches and dirty splashes on his shirt and trousers. "Are you hungry?"

She hadn't thought about eating. Marcus was probably starved. "I could cook something while you're in the shower, if you have anything…"

"I'll take you up on that. Raid the freezer. Use whatever you want."

Forty-five minutes later they sat down in the dining area to honey-glazed chicken with rice and peas. "This looks great," Marcus told her. "And it deserves a good wine to go with it."

He poured a New Zealand Chardonnay for them both and smiled at her as he sipped at it, but he didn't offer a toast.

Apparently having a broken heart hadn't destroyed Jenna's appetite after all. She ate everything on her plate and finished the wine in her glass.

Marcus refilled it. They didn't talk much, and when he pushed away his plate she said, "I didn't make a dessert, but you have cheese in the fridge."

"I'll get it and put coffee on." He cleared their plates and returned with a couple of cheeses and some crackers on a ceramic square. "Coffee coming up. Do you want more wine?"

"Why not? I'm not going anywhere."

Marcus filled her glass again, and she lifted it to her lips. She could feel the alcohol-induced flush on her cheeks.

Slicing himself a piece of cheese, Marcus shot her

a quizzical look. "It's not the end of the world, you know."

Unaccountably irritated, she said resentfully, "I don't need you to tell me that!"

"Okay." He held up a hand in a gesture of truce. "Take some time to wallow in your misery. But remember there's a life out there waiting for you."

And she'd already wasted four years of it. "You're right," she said, and raised her glass. There was no point in dwelling on what might have been. "Here's to the future," she said resolutely.

Marcus matched her gesture, giving her a look of approval.

Jenna drained her glass. "Is there more of this?"

He hesitated, poured some for her, then emptied the remains into his own glass.

By the time they left the table, the world looked a whole lot better. Marcus vetoed her feeble effort to deal with the dishes, and when she yawned, he said, "You've had a long day. Bedtime, I think."

"Yes." She blinked at him, not moving, and yawned again.

Marcus gave a low laugh and stood up, grasping her hands to haul her to her feet. The room tilted, and when he released her hands she clutched at his arms to steady herself. "Ooh! Too much wine."

"Very possibly," he agreed, and slid an arm about her waist to guide her. "Come on."

In the spare room he led her to the bed, switched on the bedside lamp and stripped back the covers for her. "Can you manage now?" he asked, straightening. "You know where the bathroom is."

"Yes. Thank you, Marcus."

"You might not be thanking me in the morning."
He surveyed her with critical amusement and a hint
of tenderness. "Good night, Jenna."

He bent and brushed his lips over hers—a fleeting
kiss of friendly comfort, but enough to upset Jenna's
already precarious balance, and as he lifted his head
she swayed, so that instinctively he put his arm about
her waist again to steady her.

She leaned against him, thankful for the solid feel
of him, and her hands slid around his shoulders. She
raised her face, found his mouth with hers and kissed
him with fervor, her eyes closed, fiercely shutting out
all thought. She didn't want to think, only to feel
something other than grief and humiliation.

And Marcus, perhaps understanding her need, returned her kiss beautifully, satisfyingly. He put his
other arm about her and brought her closer, making
her feel warm and wanted. Like a desirable woman.

But then he drew back, and his hands left her waist
to curl about her arms and hold her away. Although
his eyes glittered disturbingly and there was a flush
on his angular cheekbones, his voice was steady.
"Enough. Get some sleep, Jenna. I'll see you in the
morning." Then he walked to the door and shut it
firmly behind him.

Jenna slept surprisingly well but woke with a
leaden feeling in her chest and a slight headache.

A hangover, she supposed. All that wine last
night...

She closed her eyes again. That only brought the
memory more vividly to her mind, and she groaned.
She and Marcus, of all people, locked in a passionate

kiss. What had possessed her? And now she was going to have to face him. She could hear him moving about already, the bathroom door closing, his footsteps in the passageway.

No use cowering in bed, he would probably come and rout her out of it, anyway. Reluctantly she threw back the covers and got up.

By the time she'd showered and dressed, the aroma of frying bacon was wafting through the dining area. Trying to look casual and unembarrassed, she went to the kitchen where Marcus was standing at the stove, breaking eggs into a pan. "That smells good."

He turned and smiled at her. "Good morning. I heard the shower and figured you'd soon be ready for breakfast."

"Can I help?"

"Make toast if you like. The bread's over there."

It wasn't until they'd finished eating and she'd had her second cup of coffee that she gathered the courage to say, "About last night…I'm sorry."

"What for?"

"For being so…stupid. I'd had too much to drink or I wouldn't have…"

"Kissed me?" His lips curved. "I wondered if you'd remember. You needn't apologize, Jenna. It may have escaped your notice, but I enjoyed it." He paused. "I thought you did too." His eyes held a question.

Heat burned her cheeks. "I would never normally have—I didn't mean to—"

"No need to explain." He stood up abruptly. "Want to help me get these dishes out of the way?"

Later he took her back to her flat.

"I'll try to get it looking a bit less like a disaster area before Katie arrives home," she said. "It will give me something to do."

"She won't be here for a while. I told her there was no point while the carpet's still drying."

"That's okay. I can do with some time alone."

He gave her a sharp look but didn't argue. "Let me know if you need anything," he said. "I'll be home. And if your place is still in a mess, you and Katie can both sleep at mine tonight."

After he'd left her she picked her way around, flattened some of the carpet that had dried, moved the machines to where they'd do the most good, and cleared paths through piled furniture to beds and the kitchen.

Remembering the orderliness of Marcus's apartment, she was spurred into an orgy of tidying and cleaning. So when Katie arrived she was on her knees, head and hands deep in a kitchen cupboard while she wiped down the shelf from which she'd removed all the pots and pans.

It wasn't until she emerged and sat back on her heels, wiping a strand of hair from her eyes, that she realized Katie wasn't alone.

Dean grinned down at her. "What are you doing?"

"What do you think I'm doing?" she asked crossly. Yesterday she'd dressed carefully, if casually, and put on makeup, and he'd hardly glanced at her. *Now* she was a total mess and he was looking her over as if he'd never seen her before. "Where's Callie?" she asked him.

"Jet lag caught up with her and she couldn't stay

awake. Marcus said you'd had a flood here, so I thought you girls might need some help.''

He didn't look jet-lagged. He looked wide-awake and heartbreakingly handsome, and she wished he were anywhere but here. ''There isn't much we can do,'' she said, ''until the cleaning firm has been in again and fixed the carpets back in place, once they're dry.''

''You look busy.''

''I just had this urge…I'll be finished here in a few minutes.''

She hoped they'd go away, but instead the two of them stood about the kitchen talking, and helpfully handed her things to put back in the cupboard.

Afterward they all sat drinking coffee, and it was almost like old times until Dean pushed back his chair, saying, ''I'd better get back. Callie should have woken by now.'' Apparently he couldn't bear to think of her spending any waking moment without him.

When he'd left, Katie gave Jenna a searching look. ''Are you really okay?''

''Tired, after spending half the night getting rid of the flood, but otherwise I'm fine.'' Without pausing for breath, Jenna asked, ''How did you get on with Callie?''

''You can't help liking her…''

''That's good,'' Jenna said enthusiastically. ''It's important that you two get along. Not that Dean would have picked a girl you wouldn't like.''

Katie hesitated, then refrained from pursuing the subject. ''I'm sorry you got stuck with the cleanup here. I would have caught the first bus back, but Marcus said there was nothing I could do that the two of you hadn't done already.''

''He was right, there was no need for it. Marcus was great.''

''He's good in a crisis, our big brother. And I suppose he thinks of you as another little sister.''

''I suppose,'' Jenna agreed, but the memory of last night's kiss surfaced with sudden clarity, and unexpectedly she felt her cheeks flush.

Katie noticed. Her eyes widened. ''Jenna...? You and Marcus aren't...? When he said you were staying the night I didn't think he meant—''

''Of course not!'' Jenna denied quickly. ''He gave me his spare bed, that's all. He said we could both stay tonight, by the way.''

Katie regarded her fixedly for a moment longer, then shook her head slightly as though dismissing the thought as fantastic, and looked about them. ''Mmm. It's still a bit of a mess, isn't it? Just as well you did leave early yesterday.''

''Yes, the water would have done a lot more damage before anyone noticed it. The upstairs neighbors were away for the weekend.''

As if on cue there was a knock at the door, and Jenna hurried to open it, revealing embarrassed neighbors bearing apologies and a placatory gift of wine. She made sure that Katie had no more opportunity to question her about the night she'd spent at Marcus's apartment.

A couple of weeks later Mr. and Mrs. Crossan held an engagement party for Dean and Callie. Katie arranged to spend the weekend at her parents' place helping with the preparations. Casting about for an excuse not to join her, Jenna said the house would be full and anyway she had some work to get through. But of course she'd be at the party. Marcus had offered a lift.

She did sometimes bring work home from her job copy-editing documents for university staff members. It was a plausible excuse, and she made sure that Katie saw her working over a pile of papers on Friday before Dean came in his parents' car to pick up his sister.

That week Jenna had bought a new dress and spent a very expensive session with a hairdresser, who put some subtle highlights in and gave her a new, short and sassy style.

When she met Marcus at her door on Saturday night, he looked over the low-necked bright pink dress and high-heeled shoes and said, ''If you want to show Dean what he's missing, that'll do it.''

''It's a party,'' Jenna said defensively. Marcus looked terrific, she thought with mild surprise. She'd never taken much notice of what he wore, but he presented a picture of casual male elegance in a natural linen shirt, darker trousers and a light jacket.

On the journey they hardly spoke. Marcus seemed preoccupied, and Jenna was tense. On their arrival he opened the car door for her and briefly took her arm. ''I'll take you home whenever you've had enough.''

''I'll be fine,'' Jenna said, tilting her head and straightening her shoulders.

She felt an inevitable pang when Dean greeted her with a hug and a kiss on her cheek, but kept the smile on her face as she turned to Callie and handed her the gift-wrapped parcel containing a carefully chosen set of crystal wineglasses.

Callie looked radiant and Dean more handsome than ever. Jenna was glad that Marcus soon guided her away from them to get drinks. He handed her the gin and lemon she asked for, murmuring, "You'd better have something to eat too. There are nuts and dips over here." He guided her to the table.

"Don't worry." Jenna took a taco chip and dipped it in guacamole. "I won't get drunk and molest you again," she said before nibbling at the chip.

Marcus lifted a brow. "You disappoint me, Jenna. I was looking forward to it."

Her eyes widened. Was Marcus *flirting* with her?

His teasing smile said he was. Then he gave a soft laugh. "I told you I enjoyed that kiss. Is it too much to hope for a repeat performance?"

Flustered, Jenna stammered, "Yes…I mean, you know I was…I wasn't myself that night. Katie says you're like a big brother to me."

"Katie says a lot of very silly things," Marcus pronounced. He watched her take another nibble at the chip and lick at a little guacamole that had escaped. "I think I should make it clear," he said, "that I don't regard you as a sister."

Disconcerted, for a brief moment she felt hurt, then she saw his eyes momentarily shift and realized that Dean was watching them. Marcus looked back at her and inclined his head close to her ear. "If you want a smokescreen, I'm available."

Light dawned. He was pretending to be attracted by her so that Dean and anyone else with an inkling of her real feelings for him needn't think she was a discarded wallflower.

Her pride rebelled. "You don't need to do this, Marcus. Like I told you, I'm a grown-up."

"I'd have said you had a bad case of arrested development, myself."

Her eyes widening at his slightly waspish tone, she said, "What?"

"You've been in a state of suspended animation ever since Dean went to the States. When are you going to wake up and smell the flowers?"

"I haven't sat at home pining," she protested, stung by his portrayal of her languishing for love. "I've got an interesting job and plenty of friends— I've even dated a bit."

"You haven't had a serious relationship, have you?"

Astounded, Jenna snapped, "That's none of your business!"

Marcus laughed aloud, the sound deep and full-throated. It transformed his face, relaxing the seemingly harsh planes of nose and cheekbones and bringing a warmer look to his eyes. She saw Dean turn again and regard his brother curiously.

"I don't see what's funny," she hissed at Marcus.

The effort he made to control the curve of his mouth belied any implicit apology. "You just reminded me so much of the way you used to be as a kid."

"Short-tempered?" she asked suspiciously.

Marcus shook his head. "You were such a little thing, but stubborn as a baby donkey. Loyal to a fault and aggressive in defense. No one could put you

down. And woe betide anyone who attacked one of
the twins.''

"A little monster.''

"Not at all. The loyalty may have been misguided
quite often, but it's an admirable trait, if irritating at
times. And the aggression mellowed as you grew
older.''

"I was pretty insecure when we arrived next door.
I guess I was overcompensating.''

After her father's death, her mother's world had
crumbled and she could hardly rouse herself to care
for a bewildered and frightened six-year-old. Jenna's
father had been a farm worker trying to save money
for his own herd when the tractor he was driving
rolled down a hillside and killed him.

They'd had to move out to make room for her father's replacement, and her mother had taken another
cottage offered by a neighboring couple at a low rent
for six months. "Until you decide what you're going
to do,'' the wife said.

They didn't realize that Karen, sunk in grief, was
incapable of making decisions.

Jenna remembered the day she'd taken charge of
her own life. Karen was standing with a butter knife
in her hand, halfway through making Jenna's school
lunch, but had apparently forgotten what she was doing.

"The school bus will be here soon,'' Jenna had told
her impatiently. She'd had to go into Karen's room
that morning and wake her to get breakfast.
"Mummy?''

Her mother seemed deaf. Jenna realized she was

silently crying, tears dripping down her cheeks, oblivious to everything except her own pain.

It was the loneliest moment of Jenna's short life. Lonelier than when she'd watched her father's coffin lowered into the ground and dimly, frighteningly, known she would never see him again.

She took the knife gently in her small, capable fingers and said, "It's all right, Mummy. I can do it myself."

From then on she'd got her own breakfast and lunch, whether Karen was up or not, and caught the school bus on time every day.

After the six months were up, they moved to a dispirited little town that had once had a dairy factory and was now struggling to keep any population because the factory had closed and there was no work. But rent was cheap.

There was a new school too and Jenna, starting in the middle of a term, was an outsider. She suffered loneliness and some mild bullying, learned to stand up for herself and in time made a few friends.

She patiently reminded her mother when it was time to do the washing or cook dinner, or if they needed more groceries. For two years she looked after her mother as much as her mother looked after her.

Then one day Karen looked about at where they were living as if she'd never seen it before and said, "We're moving out of here."

They'd shifted to a pleasant dormitory village where half the population commuted to Auckland every day. Where people grew roses and hibiscus and mowed the lawns every week. Mrs. Crossan wel-

comed them from over the fence and invited Jenna
for a swim and to play with the twins.

She thought she'd loved them both from that very
first day.

Chapter Four

"What's the dreamy little smile about?" Marcus's voice intruded on the memory.

"I was remembering when I met Dean and Katie." Marcus must have been there in the background too, she supposed. But she'd naturally been more interested in the twins, who were her own age.

"That accounts for it," Marcus said dryly.

She recalled only a day full of sunshine and childish laughter, playing tag across the green grass and climbing into the wide, cradling branches of the old puriri, swinging thrillingly back to earth by way of the sturdy rope that hung from it. And her mother looking almost relaxed, acting like the mother she had been two years ago, smiling as she spoke with Mrs. Crossan and watched the children splash about in the pool.

Marcus's voice interrupted again. "Losing a youthful dream isn't the end of the world. One day you'll find it doesn't hurt anymore."

"Is that how it was with you?"

When he didn't answer, frowning as though at a loss to know what she meant, she reminded him, "You told Katie your childhood sweetheart married someone else."

"Oh, that." He looked slightly rueful. "It just shows, you see. I'd completely forgotten."

"I think you made it up," she accused.

"Not at all. When I was eleven I was madly in love with a girl in my class. A plump child with apple cheeks, and braces on her teeth. I thought they were incredibly sexy."

"Sexy?" Jenna nearly choked on her drink.

"Eleven-year-old boys tend to be into hardware. Airplanes, motorbikes and girls with a mouthful of gleaming metal." He looked blandly solemn.

"Did you ever get to kiss her?"

"Hell, no. I worshipped her from afar—well, two desks away—for six months, then we left for different schools the following year and I never saw her again."

"That's sad." Jenna made her eyes big and sorrowful.

"A tragedy," Marcus agreed. "Romeo and Juliet all over again."

Jenna giggled, startled that she still remembered how to laugh. The cold leaden lump that had taken the place of her heart began to melt around the edges.

Marcus was right, she would get over her shock and secret grief. Gratefully she touched his arm. "Thanks, Marcus."

He shrugged her off, looking faintly irritated. Then, as if to make up for it, he took her hand, his fingers curving about hers in a strong clasp. "You've nothing to thank me for," he said in a rather gravelly tone. "But I'm monopolizing you. We'd better circulate."

Later in the evening Jenna was placing a platter of rock oysters garnished with lemon slices and parsley on the long supper table, when Marcus appeared at her side.

"Looks good," he commented. "Shall I save you some before they all go?"

"Thanks." Jenna threw him a smile and hurried back to the kitchen to help Katie and Mrs. Crossan.

When all the food was laid out and everyone milled about with filled plates, Marcus appeared again at her side, holding a large platter piled with savories, seafood and chicken wings.

"I thought we could share." He leaned across her to snaffle paper napkins and forks from the table. Looking about, he added, "There's nowhere to sit. Let's take it outside."

He led her into a broad passageway where a few people stood about with plates and forks. "Hold this for a minute."

Jenna stood with the loaded plate as he disappeared, to return in a few minutes with an opened bottle of wine and two glasses.

Outside, light spilled from several windows, but the perimeter of the lawn was cool and dark. Marcus made unerringly for the big old puriri tree that had been there since before the house was built.

Guessing his objective, Jenna followed. She recalled when his father had built the wooden seat around the tree. And the summer that Marcus had helped the younger ones erect a rickety tree hut in its gnarled branches. They'd used it for several years before they became too old for games and it fell to pieces.

Jenna's mother, helped by Mrs. Crossan's practical brand of sympathy, had gradually emerged from the half world she'd been living in, fighting her way back to a normal life. She'd found a job working for a publishing house, first part-time in the office and later full-time in charge of distribution. Mrs. Crossan had promised to keep an eye on Jenna after school.

Once, when Jenna was thirteen, Karen had considered moving to a shoreside suburb closer to her office in Auckland, but when she suggested it Jenna had dissolved in angry tears. All the insecurities and misery of the two years after her father's death rose to the surface in furious, door-slamming, hysterical protest. The subject was never mentioned again.

Jenna sat on the worn, smooth wood of the seat, placing the food between herself and Marcus. A breeze stirred the leaves overhead, and she rubbed at her arms.

"You're cold." Marcus stripped off his jacket and draped it around her shoulders, ignoring her protest. The satin lining was warm, and a faint woodsy aroma mingled with the smell of the fabric.

He poured wine and handed her a glass.

"What do you want?" he asked, indicating the plate.

Jenna peered down at the indeterminate mass. "I can't see what's there."

"Oyster?" He handed her a fork.

"If I can find them."

Marcus speared into the mound of food. "Open your mouth," he said.

She obeyed, and he slid the pungent morsel smoothly onto her tongue. He watched her for a moment before taking another for himself.

Her eyes becoming accustomed to the dimness, Jenna hunted for the pearly glow of the oyster shells and began to help herself. When all the oysters were gone, she had a chicken wing and a savory pastry, leaving the rest for Marcus while she sipped at the second glass of wine he'd poured for her.

"You don't eat enough," he said.

"I've just pigged out on oysters."

He made a derisory sound. "Hardly a meal."

"I'm fine."

He finished a couple more savories and wiped his fingers on one of the napkins, then put the plate aside and leaned against the puriri, draining his wine.

A moth fluttered by on pale wings and disappeared into the darkness. As Marcus topped up Jenna's glass and refilled his own, a burst of laughter floated from the house.

"Should we go back to the party?" Jenna asked.

"There's no hurry. Are you warm enough now?"

"Yes, but you..." She touched the jacket he'd given her.

"Don't worry about me."

In the house the laughter died, a gradual hush taking its place. One voice—Mr. Crossan's—was audible, followed by a round of clapping.

"They're making speeches," Jenna said. Congratulatory speeches. Dean would be expected to say something too, about his engagement, his fiancée. "You should be there." They'd be looking for him.

His hand closed over hers, checking her movement to get up. "You don't want to be there, do you?"

Jenna didn't answer, and he said, "Neither do I. Let's finish our wine."

They did so in silence punctuated distantly by Dean's friends indulging in some good-natured heckling, further laughter and applause, some raucous cheers. Then the buzz of talk began again, and unconsciously Jenna breathed a sigh of relief.

Marcus drained his glass and turned his head, took her glass from her and placed them both beside the bottle at his side. "Are you okay?" he asked.

"Yes." She stood up, so quickly that the jacket slipped from one shoulder.

Marcus got up too, made a grab for the jacket and briefly grasped her bare shoulder before he pulled the garment around her again.

He didn't immediately move away, instead standing with both hands clasping the lapels. His lips brushed her forehead, and to her dismay she felt tears well hotly in her eyes. She choked back a sob.

"Jenna," he said. His lips found a trickle of moisture on her cheek. "Don't." The admonition came out in a soft growl.

Men hated women's tears. She was embarrassing him—and herself. "S-sorry," she whispered, gritting her teeth. "Just leave me alone and I'll be all right." Closing her eyes tightly, she willed the tears away.

"I can't do that." His long fingers curved about her nape, his thumb absently moving over the skin just behind her ear.

He altered his grip, turning her face up to his. He kissed her wet eyelids, and then she felt his warm, velvety mouth on hers, parting her lips just a little, with a sureness and tenderness that was electrifying.

She made a muffled sound of surprise, and for a split second he seemed to hesitate, but then his arm came about her waist inside the shelter of his jacket, while the hand on her nape shifted, lazed down her throat and splayed across the bare flesh exposed by her low-necked dress.

Jenna's heartbeat accelerated. Heat suffused her body. Her bewildered mind was telling her this was crazy, but her body wasn't listening. It was listening instead to the steady beating of Marcus's heart against her breast, and his quickened breathing. It was inhaling the clean, masculine scent of his skin and tasting his mouth as it moved gently on hers, making the kiss deeper, more intimate, more exciting. She didn't realize she'd wound her arms around his neck until the jacket fell from her shoulders to the ground.

As the cold air played about them, she involuntarily shivered, and Marcus abruptly lifted his mouth.

He slackened his hold and put a few inches of space between them. She heard him take a long, harsh, unsteady breath.

"I didn't mean that to be quite so…enthusiastic," he said.

"I got a bit carried away myself." She felt disoriented, as though she'd stepped out of a familiar door and found herself in a foreign country. "And I didn't mean it, either."

"I'm well aware of that." He stooped and picked up the jacket, holding it out to her.

Jenna stepped back. "It's all right." She was hot all over now. "It's...uh...time we went in, anyway."

The sound he made might have been an attempt at a laugh. "More than time, I'd say." He seemed to hesitate, though. "I guess that was hardly fair."

Fair? It had been...overwhelming. And a distinct shock.

"Still," Marcus said, flinging the jacket over his shoulder and pushing a hand through his hair, "you know what they say."

"What?" She was trying to absorb what had happened here, scarcely listening.

"About love and...never mind," he said after a tiny pause. "It had the desired effect, anyway. Stopped you crying."

It had done that, all right. Jenna cleared her throat. "A bit drastic, wasn't it?"

"It was only a kiss, honey." His manner was casual now, as if a kiss—that kiss—were nothing.

For the first time she wondered just how much practice he'd had. Jenna had met some of his girlfriends. She had no idea if he'd been serious about any of them, but he was certainly much more experienced than she was, although she'd kissed a few men in her time. Maybe kisses didn't mean much to him.

"Well," she said, trying for flippancy, "you know how wine affects me. And you did ply me with drink."

"You're not drunk," he said with a hint of asperity. "If you were, I wouldn't have touched you."

He'd warned her he wanted to kiss her again. Only she'd thought that was for his brother's benefit, to make her laugh and look as though she were enjoying the party. And maybe to reassure her that she was attractive to other men.

Not that she doubted he'd enjoyed the kiss. Nor could she deny that she had, too.

Still nursing the pain of her unwanted love for Dean, how could she have responded to another man like that? Surely she wasn't that shallow?

Sex, she assured herself as they walked back to the house. She'd been deliberately keeping it in the background for four long years, and now her hormones had decided enough was enough.

And maybe they were right. She had no one to be faithful to. What reason did she have to be celibate any longer? Only her outdated principles, a romantic notion that she wanted to wait for the ultimate commitment of marriage, and innate caution.

For a second she toyed with the idea of turning to Marcus and saying, "Take me home with you. Take me to bed. Make love to me."

But of course she couldn't. It would be totally outside her normal behavior, and in the morning she'd be bound to regret it. And they were both staying here for the night, Marcus in the room he'd had as a boy, and Jenna in Katie's room. She didn't want to think about where Dean and Callie would sleep.

And, anyway, she and Marcus—impossible. She was too close to his family. How would they react if they found out? There'd be complications, repercussions. Nothing would ever be the same. She might lose the nearest thing to family that she had.

The thought stirred a faint echo of atavistic panic, similar to her feelings when her mother had suggested moving closer to the city, and later when Karen had told her she was remarrying and moving to Invercargill to be with her new husband, a publisher she'd met at a conference.

That time Jenna had hidden her feelings better, knowing it was unfair to expect her mother to forgo a second chance at happiness, when she herself expected to marry within a few years.

Karen had given Jenna the option of going with her and continuing her studies in the south, but after agonizing months of indecision, she'd chosen to stay in Auckland. She wouldn't be a third wheel in her mother's marriage.

Marcus opened the back door and switched on the light, making her blink as he closed the door behind them and looked at her narrowly.

She'd been crying, and then been very thoroughly kissed, and probably looked a fright. Raising a hand to her hair, she smoothed it behind her ear. "I need to tidy up."

She scooted by him and ran up the stairs. At the top she glanced over her shoulder and momentarily paused. Marcus was standing at the foot of the staircase, with a look on his face she had never seen before. Intent, hungry, almost predatory.

Then he smiled, and the look vanished. A trick of the light, she told herself, the angle of his head making those high cheekbones seem more prominent, his narrow nose hawklike, the gray eyes darker, deeper set. She turned away and scurried toward the bathroom.

* * *

Somehow Jenna made it through the rest of the party and even slept afterward. Maybe the wine helped.

Katie was still sprawled on her stomach with her face buried in the pillow when Jenna got up and slipped into the bathroom for a shower.

She emerged, her damp hair tousled, a large towel wrapped about her, to find Marcus lounging against the passage wall, arms folded over his bare chest. He wore nothing but a pair of black satin athletic shorts.

She'd seen him in less. They had swum together with his brother and sisters every summer for years, nor was this the first time they'd bumped into each other coming to and from the bathroom.

But she'd never really noticed that his square shoulders, narrow hips and long, lean legs were perfectly proportioned for a man, or that his arms were so muscular.

Nor had she ever felt so conscious that she too was wearing very little. The towel was large and enveloped her quite modestly, but when his eyes took in her bare shoulders and legs, although his face remained impassive, she felt her body tingle in instinctive, primitive response. Clutching the towel tighter, she was glad he couldn't see through the concealing bulk of the cloth.

Marcus straightened. "Good morning. I heard the shower stop and figured you'd be out soon."

"It's all yours," she said, sidling from the doorway.

"Thanks." He moved toward it. As she turned away he said quietly, "And…Jenna?"

Reluctantly she faced him again. "Yes?"

"Thanks for last night."

That threw her completely, bringing warmth to her cheeks. "I should be thanking you for taking pity on me."

Marcus frowned. "Is that what you think I was doing?"

"What else?"

Another door opened and Dean stumbled into the passageway. "Hi." He peered at them blearily. "Anyone in the bathroom?"

"I'm using it," Marcus told him. "I won't be long."

Jenna said brightly, "Good morning, Dean."

As Marcus entered the bathroom, Dean grunted at her and retreated again into the bedroom behind him. She heard his voice saying something indistinguishable behind the closed door as she turned toward Katie's room.

Jenna was making coffee and toast when Marcus came into the kitchen. He was the only naturally early riser in his family, and this wasn't the first time they'd shared breakfast before the others got up.

"Just like old times." Marcus echoed her thoughts as they sat at the breakfast bar. He reached for a slice of toast and spread it thickly with butter.

Jenna pushed the marmalade toward him and bit into her own toast so she'd have an excuse not to reply. This wasn't like old times, it was...different.

She watched him spoon into the marmalade and dribble some onto his toast. His hands were broad and the fingers long. A man's hands, with a few dark hairs curling about the wide silver strap of the watch on one wrist. Last night that hand had been warm on her skin while he kissed her.

Hastily she dropped her gaze to her distorted reflection on the surface of her coffee.

She hadn't really looked at Marcus since he'd been a gangling sixteen-year-old with a fuzzy dark growth on his cheeks, and limbs that seemed to have outgrown his thin body. She'd seen the changes in him then, realizing that he was turning into a grown-up, and wondered what it felt like. But she hadn't known how to ask him.

She couldn't remember noticing when the process had completed itself, the gradual transformation from skinny boy to well-built man.

By the time Jenna hit adolescence herself, he'd seemed very much an adult, one she saw less and less of as he went to university, gaining a commerce degree, then worked in England as a security guard for a year before coming back to New Zealand.

With a friend he'd set up a small factory making security gates and doors. As the business expanded they moved to bigger premises and branched into burglar alarms, locks, armored transport. The company was well-known now.

Katie had told Jenna with pride that her brother had "made his first million" some years ago. Since then his picture had been in the business pages of the newspaper more than once. He was a success.

But to her he had been simply Katie and Dean's brother.

Marcus got up with his empty cup in his hand. "More for you?"

Jenna handed him hers and watched as he refilled

them. He put hers in front of her and reseated himself. "You don't have a hangover, do you?"

She shook her head. She'd been very careful after that episode under the puriri. He was right, she had not been drunk when he kissed her, and she hadn't wanted to run the risk of being so later. If she could behave that way when she was sober, what might she do after having too much to drink?

"What are you thinking?" he asked.

"About what I've been doing with my life." She had friends she liked being with, and her job at the university was stimulating, often challenging, sometimes hectic, the pay enough to cover her half of the rent and everything she needed.

She was good at what she did, but had never been ambitious. While Marcus had been forging a business and Dean studying to further his career, and Katie climbed to the rank of supervisor in her office, Jenna had waited like Sleeping Beauty for Dean to return, a fairy-tale prince carrying her off to happy-ever-after.

Arrested development, Marcus had said. She winced inwardly. She'd put her life on hold for a stupid, adolescent delusion.

"You think I've been silly," she said.

"I never said that."

"It's true."

"We all make mistakes." He paused. "I've made some pretty major ones myself."

With exaggerated gloom Jenna said, "You're just trying to make me feel better."

He gave her one of his rare, restrained grins. "Dead right. Is it working?"

"Tell me about your mistakes."

"Uh-uh." He shook his head, then said, relenting, "I suppose not kissing Essie Ramsbottom was a mistake."

"Essie…?"

"Braces," he explained succinctly. "Now I'll never know what it would have felt like." He waited for her tiny spurt of laughter. "And I suppose," he said slowly, "kissing you was a mistake. But I can't say I regret finding out what that was like."

Jenna looked away. "Forget it," she muttered.

"Oh, I don't think so."

He was leaning back in his chair a little, one hand resting negligently on the table, the other tucked into the belt of his moleskin trousers. His jaw looked strong and uncompromising and his eyes oddly considering.

Chapter Five

A strange sensation feathered its way up Jenna's spine. It wasn't fear—of course she wasn't frightened of Marcus, that was unthinkable. But she couldn't help remembering that moment last night when she'd seen him looking up at her from the foot of the stairs. "What do you mean?" she asked cautiously.

The disconcerting expression vanished, and he leaned forward to pick up his cup, then looked at her again, and now his eyes were light and unreadable. "I try to learn from my mistakes," he said. "What about you?"

Warily she sipped her own coffee. What had she learned from four years of wasted time? That she ought not to waste any more, was the logical conclusion. "Maybe I should go away," she blurted.

"Away?" he queried sharply.

"Australia? Or Invercargill, maybe." Where her mother was.

"Running to Mummy after all?" His jaw tightened. "I thought you had more guts than that."

She said defensively, "It's just a thought. I don't need anyone to tell me what I should or shouldn't do."

"That's the girl!"

"And I'm not a girl." He'd begun to make a habit of harping on her childishness.

A gleam of sympathy lit his eyes. "No, you're a very attractive young woman, Jenna. With intelligence and grit, when you care to use them." He looked at her surprised and self-conscious expression and added, his eyes glinting wickedly, "And a sinfully sexy mouth."

She opened it, trying to think of an answer, some snappy comeback, but nothing useful came to mind. Then to her relief they heard footsteps descending the stairs and heading rapidly toward the kitchen, and Mr. Crossan came in, rubbing his hands and demanding a cup of coffee.

Despite his earlier appearance upstairs, Dean and Callie were the last to come down for breakfast, pink-cheeked and happy and slightly sleepy. Replete with love.

Don't think about it, Jenna scolded herself. And tried not to.

By lunchtime the remnants of the party were cleared away, and everyone picnicked in the kitchen. The men leaned against the counters, the women squeezed around the breakfast bar. Nobody could be bothered setting the dining table and carrying the various dishes of leftovers through.

Callie picked up a cold chicken wing and said to Jenna, "You grew up with Dean and Katie, didn't you?"

"Mmm-hmm." Jenna bit into a leftover sandwich. It had tomato in it and the bread had gone soggy.

"So you're old friends. You'd have some stories for me, I bet." Callie cast a cheeky glance at her fiancé, standing beside Marcus. "Katie's too loyal to her twin to tell tales."

Jenna swallowed, the soggy bread forming a lump in her throat. "I wouldn't dare," she said. "Dean knows too much about *my* childhood." The last thing she wanted was to be drawn into recounting Dean's youthful peccadilloes to Callie.

"Too true." Dean grinned. "No use pumping Jenna, love."

Katie said, "Ask Marcus. He was always pulling the three of us out of trouble."

"Marc?" Callie appealed to him. "What about you? My folks told Dean all the embarrassing things I ever did as a kid. They even showed him my baby pictures!"

Marcus smiled at her. "If it's baby pictures you want, I think Mum's got one of him naked on a rug."

"Ooh!" Callie rounded her eyes and mouth. "That I've got to see! Is there one of you too, Marc?"

Marcus and Dean both laughed, and Marcus shook his head.

Jenna was fighting a suffocating anger. Callie was just having fun, not flirting with Marcus. *Marc.* Jenna had never shortened his name. In fact, Dean was the only person who did.

And of course that was why Callie did it; she wouldn't know that Marcus didn't like it.

Not that he seemed at all bothered now, smiling at Callie as if they'd known each other forever. As if he didn't care what she called him so long as she smiled back at him.

Unfair, Jenna reminded herself. Marcus, like the rest of the family, wanted to make Dean's fiancée feel she belonged.

Jenna wasn't even sure why she was angry. Perhaps an oversensitivity to Dean's feelings, to any sign that Callie could possibly be interested in another man.

And Dean's feelings were none of her business.

The others were laughing, Dean protesting at the idea of their mother dragging out baby pictures, Marcus saying his were of no interest to anyone.

Jenna caught Katie's eyes, thought she saw a hint of anxiety in them, and realized she was the only one not joining in the banter. Making herself smile, Jenna turned to Callie. "I've got a picture of them both skinny-dipping," she remembered.

Katie squealed. "Oh, you've still got that? Callie, you've got to see it!"

"Little sneaks," Dean accused his sister and Jenna. "Peeping Thomasinas. Baby voyeurs."

Jenna had been given a camera for Christmas when she was twelve, the year she was invited to join the Crossans on a lakeside camping holiday. At that age Dean's mates had regarded hanging about with girls as suspicious. When he and a young friend went off for a swim with Marcus to supervise, the two girls had secretly followed, gleefully concealing themselves behind the scrubby manuka and orange-flowered flax that fringed the narrow shore at a secluded part of the lake, snapping the boys when they stripped and ran into the water naked.

Marcus was looking át Jenna, his head cocked slightly, one eyebrow lifting. She stared defiantly back at him. "I'll find it," she said, "when I get home."

She knew exactly where it was, in a camphorwood box that held her most precious possessions. Her parents' wedding photo and a picture of herself as a baby, held in her father's arms. A gold-and-pearl tiepin that had belonged to him. The wedding and engagement rings her mother had given her when she married again. Photographs of Katie and of Dean, with or without other members of his family, some with Jenna herself.

Marcus turned to tip the dregs of his coffee into the sink. She wondered if he was embarrassed at the idea of the photograph being resurrected. He'd been older than the other two, a teenager, physically developed.

Not that there was much to see in the photo. He'd had his back to the camera, but she remembered watching him shuck off his jeans, and how she'd felt herself flushing behind the camera, a strange little wiggle of guilty excitement in her stomach as he straightened and the muscles of his flanks and thighs tautened before he followed the two younger boys into the water.

Callie smiled at her mischievously. "I'll look forward to seeing it sometime."

Already Jenna regretted the rash offer.

* * *

Marcus dropped both girls off later in the day, accepting Katie's offer of a coffee.

He didn't stay long, and while Katie cleared the cups away, Jenna followed him to the hallway. "I could say I've lost that photo," she offered quietly, "if you don't want Callie to see it."

His hand on the door, he turned to look at her. "It doesn't bother me. I'm surprised you've kept it all this time."

When she didn't say anything, he gave a low laugh. "Of course, Dean's in it. How many pictures of him have you kept?"

"I've got pictures of you all." Though his guess was too close for comfort. "You must have photos of me somewhere." If he ever kept family photographs.

For an instant his eyes glazed. "I have… somewhere."

"There you are, then."

"Where are we, Jenna?" he said, his voice somehow deliberate.

She blinked, not understanding. "It was a rhetorical remark. I didn't mean anything."

His short sigh sounded impatient. "Yeah, I know. I guess it's too soon."

For what? But she didn't ask, some instinct making her keep her mouth shut.

"One day," he said with suppressed force, "you'll have to come out of that cocoon you've wrapped yourself in. It'll be interesting to see what emerges."

He opened the door and let himself out, then snapped it shut behind him, leaving her staring at the smooth, painted wood.

He hadn't even said goodbye. And he'd seemed unaccountably angry.

With her? She hadn't done anything...

She trailed back into the kitchen, scowling.

Katie turned to her from the sink and covered a yawn with her wet hand. "Early night," she said.

"Mmm. Me too. Shall I dry those?"

"Leave them to drain." Katie let the water gurgle out and dried her hands. "Are you okay, Jenna?"

Jenna swallowed an unusual urge to snarl at her friend. Her concern was wearing, but she meant well. "A bit tired, like you."

She was glad, a little later, to go to her own room and be alone at last. Wearing the big T-shirt she slept in, she slumped down on the bed, then got up and went to the secondhand rimu wardrobe that stood in a corner of the room and opened the deep drawer at the bottom.

With the camphorwood box in her hands, she climbed into bed, holding the box on her lap for a minute or two before opening it.

The bulky envelope was at the bottom. She put the box aside on the night table and sifted through the photographs in the envelope.

There it was. Two young boys in the water, thigh-deep and splashing each other, laughing. And Marcus—his dark head half-turned so that his face was in profile, his already broadening shoulders tapered to narrow flanks, his long legs fuzzed with hair.

She looked at Dean's laughing face and felt a melting, asexual fondness for the child in his innocent boyhood.

But also in her vision was Marcus, unaware of the

camera, standing tall and straight and strong. Again heat flooded her face, and guilty excitement burned as it had when she'd clicked the shutter that day. An excitement she'd put down to the fear of discovery.

This had never happened before, all the hundreds of times she'd looked at the photograph. She'd always focused her attention on Dean, cutting Marcus out of her consciousness along with the other boy, whose name she didn't even recall. As she'd cut out—buried in her subconscious—the memory of that emotion, because it embarrassed her.

She had refused to recognize it then, but she was no longer a young girl barely embarked on the journey to womanhood and alarmed at its physical manifestations. Now she knew what the feeling was. It had been there again last night, in the garden when Marcus kissed her. When she'd kissed him back. Desire.

For a couple of weeks Jenna deliberately avoided Marcus. Time to regain a sense of perspective, she hoped. To suppress newly wakened emotions that were unsettling and somehow, she sensed, dangerous.

It wasn't too difficult at first. Marcus always made himself available when his family needed him or they had a special occasion to celebrate, but he was the most self-sufficient of the siblings, and sometimes Katie didn't see him for months.

When Katie told her one evening that he'd phoned and was on his way over, Jenna said she had to return some overdue library books and planned to have supper in town with a friend from work. She quietly called the friend and made the arrangement, leaving

Katie with a cheery, "Bye. I might be late home—
say hi to Marcus for me."

She hadn't seen him in sixteen days when she answered the phone and his deep, distinctive voice said,
"Jenna."

"Hi," she said, and quickly added, "I'll get Katie
for you."

Afterward Katie said, "I don't know why he called.
It's not like Marcus to phone just to chat."

In the first weeks after Dean went overseas Marcus
had been around to their new flat quite often, keeping
an eye on his little sister, Jenna had guessed, in case
she pined for her twin. Gradually the visits had tailed
off as Katie became accustomed to Dean's absence
and she and Jenna showed they could manage on their
own.

Maybe he was afraid Katie was feeling left out now
that Dean was engaged. Jenna herself was alert for
signs of distress or disappointment. But Katie seemed
fine with the situation. She talked on the telephone
almost every evening to Dean and lunched with Callie
while Dean was being interviewed for a job. They
even arranged a girls' night out, taking in a romantic
film and ending the evening with decadent desserts at
an all-night café.

Katie took it for granted that Jenna would come.
"And Callie will stay the night. She doesn't mind
sleeping on the sofa. It's okay with you, isn't it?"

Jenna said of course it was all right. And she went
along for the evening, unable to think of an excuse
that wouldn't renew Katie's suspicion.

At least during the film they didn't have to talk,
and at the café the music was too loud for real con-

versation. Back at the flat, Katie remembered Jenna's
offer to show Callie the nude photo of Dean and Marcus.

"I lost it," Jenna said without even thinking about
it, then felt a stab of guilt. She didn't normally lie,
but it was too late now to take it back. "Sorry."

Katie looked at her rather oddly, and Callie seemed
disappointed but soon got over it. She and Katie were
still chatting and laughing long after Jenna went to
bed.

Jenna recognized to her shame that she was jealous,
and wondered if she had been subconsciously hoping
that if Katie and Callie didn't get on, Dean would
change his mind about marrying the American girl.
She decided to stop looking for signs.

Katie wanted to spend the next weekend at her parents' home, cajoling Marcus into taking her. Jenna
declined to go, saying vaguely she had things to do.

"What things?" Katie demanded.

Jenna waved a hand. "Oh…you know. Lots of
things that need catching up on. Write to my mother,
mend some clothes—I haven't a decent thing to wear
to work on Monday. Tidy my room."

"Wash your hair?" Katie suggested dryly.

"That too." Jenna flashed her a guilty smile. "It's
been a busy week at work, and I've got a bit of a
headache. Much as I love you all, I just don't feel up
to this."

After a moment Katie shrugged. "I suppose we're
a bit much, en masse, if you're feeling under the
weather. Will you be all right on your own?"

"Of course. It's just a headache, nothing major."

She swallowed some aspirin and was sitting conscientiously on the sofa with a little heap of mending when she heard the discreet toot from Marcus's car outside and Katie went bounding past her toward the door. Marcus didn't like being kept waiting. "Bye," she said breathlessly.

"Give everyone my love," Jenna called. She heard voices and the slam of the car door, but minutes later the burr of the bell sent her to the door.

Marcus was on the tiny porch. "Katie says you're not well," he said.

He seemed to loom over her, a bulky figure with the lowering light behind him. She blinked up at him. "It's only a headache."

"Is that true, or an excuse?"

Jenna sighed. "Does it matter? Actually it is true, but it's nothing to worry about."

"Can I get you anything?"

"I've got aspirin, thanks."

He hesitated, looking as though he might argue. "You know where we are if you need anyone."

"Sure, but I won't."

He nodded, and she stayed in the doorway until he'd joined Katie in the car and started the engine.

Jenna was sorting through her wardrobe on Saturday afternoon when the doorbell pealed.

The bed was covered in clothes, and she had to pick her way over a litter of shoes, boots, balled pairs of socks and boxes of assorted junk. She brushed dust from her loose shirt, worn over old shorts, and tried to tuck in strands that had escaped the band she'd hurriedly twisted round her hair.

By the time she opened the door, Marcus had his finger on the bell again.

"What are you doing here?" She had assumed that, as he had taken Katie, he too would be staying for the weekend.

"And hello to you," he returned. As she remained staring at him, he said with a hint of impatience, "Ask me in, Jenna."

She stepped back so he could come past her and shut the door. Then she led the way to the sitting room.

Turning to face him, she asked, "What do you want?"

Marcus seemed to be looking at her with unusual attention, focusing on her face as if he needed to read something there. "A drink would be nice," he answered her. "You look all right. How's the headache?"

"Gone. Coffee, beer, lemonade? The only choices we have, I'm afraid."

He opted for beer and followed her into the kitchen. She made herself a shandy to keep him company, and they went back to the other room. "Did Katie send you?" she asked.

"No."

He waited for her to sit on one of the mismatched easy chairs before he took a seat on the sofa.

Jenna found she was tongue-tied, and Marcus was in no hurry to start a conversation, sipping his beer and wiping a line of froth from his upper lip without even looking at her.

When he did, his gaze seemed critical. "Katie thinks you're losing weight."

Under the baggy shirt he wouldn't have been able to tell, but his scrutiny made her self-conscious.

"Not much. I've been working hard."

She'd been keeping herself busy, trying not to leave too much time for thinking—for regrets. And hiding her feelings from Katie, maybe not altogether successfully.

"There are other ways of forgetting," Marcus said, "besides working yourself into the ground. More pleasant ways."

"I don't think hitting the bottle did me much good."

"I wasn't thinking of that."

His eyes held something that to her intense chagrin made her blush. She thought of claiming she didn't know what he meant, but he'd see through that instantly.

Fortunately he didn't appear to expect an answer. He got up, and Jenna tensed, but he walked away from her toward the window, looked out as though searching for something to interest him, then turned, his half-full beer glass held in one strong hand.

She noticed that his knuckles were white, but his face seemed emotionless. He gulped some more beer. His throat was taut and lightly tanned, the Adam's apple not prominent, but she saw it move as he swallowed.

Lowering the glass, he said, "You've never thought of any man but Dean, have you?"

"Not seriously." She had found other men fleetingly attractive, but she'd regarded herself as taken. So none of those attractions had come to anything—because she hadn't let them.

"You can't have him," Marcus said.

It was brutal, and unlike him. She felt herself pale. Her head lifted. "You don't need to remind me." It wasn't as if she'd tried to take Dean away from Callie. She'd actually bent over backward not to hint at her pain and disappointment.

"So is there anyone else on the horizon?"

Jenna's eyes widened. "There's hardly been time for that!"

"You do know other young men."

"Of course I do. Friends."

"Friends can become lovers."

"I don't need a lover!"

Marcus's mouth moved in a strange smile. The glint in his eyes made her uneasy, sending a weird little hot shiver up her spine. "Are you sure? You could have fooled me," he said, "the night of the party."

She recalled that in a moment of temporary insanity she'd thought of asking him to take her home, take her to his bed. Maybe he'd guessed. "I shouldn't have had so much wine."

He finished his drink in one movement. "But perhaps you need a friend more, right now."

"I'm certainly not ready for...for anything else!"

Marcus came closer to put his glass down on the coffee table in front of her, finding a clear space among the magazines and junk mail, beside a saucer crumbed with the remains of potato crisps. Straightening, he shoved his hands into the pockets of his dark trousers, regarding her narrowly.

"Do you always react like that to a couple of glasses of wine?"

"Throwing myself at the nearest male? No. And I wish you wouldn't keep bringing it up!"

He lowered himself again to the sofa, smiling at her now, disarming her completely. "I don't mean to give you a hard time," he said. "We've known each other so long, Jenna, I hate to see you unhappy."

"As you told me," she said, trying to believe it, "I'll get over it."

"Then let me help."

"How?" she asked starkly. "What can you do?"

"I can give you a social life apart from my family, for a start."

"I have other friends."

"Mostly they're Katie's friends too, aren't they?"

"Yes." Even people they met separately tended to become mutual friends. They liked the same people.

Marcus nodded. "And Katie will bring Dean and Callie into that circle. You need to break out of it if you're ever going to live your own life."

Jenna protested, "I'm not dependent on your family for everything." She had even dated occasionally, mainly because when Katie was dating someone she worried about Jenna sitting at home on her own.

"It wouldn't hurt to broaden your horizon."

"You think I'm narrow and dull." Indignation stirred.

Marcus laughed. "Not at all. But I think there's a world out there you haven't even begun to explore. And I'd like to show it to you."

Maybe her doubts showed. "Come on, Jenna," he urged. "What have you got to lose?"

"Why are you doing this?" she asked. "What's in it for you?"

He gave her a long, assessing look that held a germ of exasperation. "I'm helping out a friend," he said. "And I think it could be…rewarding."

"I never had you pegged as a do-gooder."

His brows shot up. "I'm not looking for a halo. Something much more…temporal."

"Like what?"

A different smile lurked in his eyes. "Let's take it one step at a time, shall we?"

Jenna moved restlessly and gulped down what was left of her shandy. A faint stirring of something curiously like anticipation shivered through her. After all, what did she have to lose? Except time spent moping around wishing for what might have been. Self-pity had never appealed to her. "All right," she said recklessly. "Let's."

He didn't move, but she had the impression he'd just released a pent-up breath. "Good," he said. "What would you like to do tonight?"

"Tonight?"

"A film…a show…dinner? What about a comedy club? You could do with a good laugh."

"I suppose," she said, lifting a shoulder. Already she had cold feet. More strongly she said, "Yes. That sounds like fun."

He stood up. "I'll pick you up around seven."

She trailed him to the door, where he turned to face her. He lifted a hand and just touched her cheek with his thumb. "Don't look so worried," he admonished. "It will be all right, I promise."

The silly thing was, Jenna thought as she closed the door after him, she believed him.

* * *

She did have a good laugh. Not all of the acts were truly funny, but there were enough humorous one-liners and witty monologues to keep the audience amused most of the time. She had never seen Marcus laugh so often.

Afterward they had a snack and a drink and then he delivered her home, leaving her at the door with a swift peck on her cheek. "I'm picking up Katie from home tomorrow," he said. "I don't suppose you want to come?"

"No." It was a relief to be frank, even blunt. She didn't want to see Dean with Callie again, to have to pretend it didn't matter. With Marcus she didn't need to put up a smokescreen.

"I didn't think so," he said. "I'll be in touch."

He was, less than a week later. When Katie handed her the phone and said, "Big brother wants to talk to you," Jenna tried to appear nonchalant.

A friend had loaned him a yacht for the weekend, he said, and he planned to spend a couple of days cruising about the Hauraki Gulf. "I'd like you to come."

"Just me?" Jenna asked involuntarily.

It was a moment before he answered. "You know what a poor sailor Katie is."

While still at university he'd bought, for what he said was a "single verse rather than a song," a small boat of his own, run-down and shabby. He'd spent every weekend he could spare from studying on scraping, repairing and restoring it, with occasional assistance from his younger siblings and Jenna.

Dean and Jenna had learned to help sail the boat

and loved it, but Katie spent most of the time hanging
over the side until Marcus took pity and returned her
to dry land. She never did acquire sea legs, and after
several attempts had given up. Marcus sold the boat
when he went overseas.

"He's got a boat for the weekend," Jenna relayed
to Katie when she had hung up. "He needs someone
to crew for him."

Katie shuddered. "No wonder he wanted to talk to
you."

They left on Saturday morning, a perfect day, with
a brisk breeze that filled the sails and scattered the
few ragged clouds hanging over Rangitoto, the island
volcano in the gulf.

The clear air, the wind in her hair, the water hissing
under the hull as they skimmed the jade-green surface
were wonderful fresheners. Scrambling to adjust the
sails, taking a turn at the tiller, obeying Marcus's
crisp, decisive orders, Jenna felt more alive than she
had in weeks—maybe years.

When they anchored in a sheltered bay in the lee
of a hillocky island, where woolly white sheep fled
across close-shorn green paddocks, she was aching
and sunburned but almost happy.

They swam in cool, clear water, Marcus in a fast
crawl away from the boat and back again, while Jenna
floated lazily on the surface and occasionally dived to
the sandy bottom. Shell fragments glistened red, orange and pale gold on the sea bed, and tiny shimmering fish darted away from the human intruders and
from a hungry gannet plummeting with folded wings
into the sea. Afterward Jenna roughly dried her hair,

then wrapped the towel about her waist over her swimsuit. Marcus had stripped to a pair of shorts.

"You're burned," he said, running a finger across her bared shoulders. The salt water drying on them stung. "Hang on a minute."

He disappeared below and came back with a pink plastic bottle, unscrewing the cap. "You should use more sunscreen," he scolded, turning her with a hand on her arm.

"I thought I'd used plenty." And he'd made sure she wore a hat all day, even clamping it more firmly to her head when the breeze had threatened to blow it away.

"This should help."

She shuddered as cold moisture hit her hot skin. Then his hand was smoothing it across the bones, down her arm, onto her back where her skimpy top had bared it to the merciless rays.

He anointed the other shoulder, his palm moving hypnotically over her skin. It was both soothing and disturbing. Another shiver passed over her body.

"Turn around," he said.

She did, and their eyes met before he dropped his gaze. She felt her breasts peak under the flimsy cloth covering them, and held her breath.

"Here," he said, passing her the bottle. "You can do your front."

She took the bottle from him, and he stepped away.

"Hungry?" he asked.

She was ravenous, Jenna realized, smoothing lotion down to the top of her swimsuit. The pulse in her throat was jumping. She breathed out carefully, steadying her nerves. "I could probably eat one of those sheep,'' she told him, ''if there's no horse available.''

Marcus laughed, and the tension eased. ''We wouldn't be popular. I don't think we're allowed to light fires on the beach, either, but we could grill some chops and sausages in the galley and eat on deck.''

While he cooked the meat, Jenna made a salad and sliced bread. Marcus found glasses and took out a bottle of wine that he'd chilled in the compact fridge.

Jenna eyed the glass he handed her as they sat on the gently rocking deck, watching a distant sunset wash the sky a pale pink and set the sea shimmering with golden light.

''I promise I won't get you drunk,'' Marcus said. ''You should know by now I prefer my women to know what they're doing.''

''Your women?''

He glanced at her, his eyes crinkling. ''Figure of speech.''

''I'm your crew,'' she reminded him.

He smiled. ''I don't get my crew drunk, either. Bad for discipline.''

''Are there…have there been many women?'' She shouldn't ask, but the words were out before she thought better of them. ''I mean—''

''I know what you meant.'' He seemed to consider the question, and she wondered if he was doing the mental arithmetic. ''Very few, as a matter of fact,'' he said, and looked at her. ''Do you want an exact figure?''

''No,'' she disclaimed. ''I don't know why I asked, I shouldn't have—''

"Because you wanted to know."

He almost seemed to be pleased about it. He picked up his fork and said, pointing to her steak, "Eat that before it gets cold."

Chapter Six

They lay at anchor overnight, sleeping in narrow bunks only a few feet from each other across the width of the cabin. Marcus sent Jenna down first, descending himself twenty minutes later, by which time she had slid into her sleeping bag.

"Want the light left on?" he asked.

"No. I don't mind if you do, though."

He shot her a teasing look, and she added hastily, "I mean, if you want to read or something."

He switched it off, and she heard him undress in the dark, and the bunk creaking faintly under his weight.

"Good day?" he said quietly.

"Yes," Jenna answered. "Thank you, Marcus."

The bunk creaked again as he shifted his weight. "You don't need to thank me. I've had a great day, and I'm looking forward to tomorrow."

Maybe Marcus needed a break too. Once Katie had

asked him why he didn't take more time off, and he'd told her that no one stayed at the top by slacking. Besides, he enjoyed being "hands on" rather than leaving the running of the business to someone else.

After an early breakfast they sailed out of the cove. Jenna wore a T-shirt to ensure that the burn didn't get worse, and Marcus made sure she used sunblock every hour. He'd insisted on applying more salve on her back while she held a towel around herself before she dressed.

When they anchored for lunch he took out the pink bottle again and said, "Take off your shirt."

"I'm not wearing anything under it!" Jenna protested. Her bra straps would have irritated the tender skin.

The only visible craft was a sailboat cruising near the horizon. Marcus glanced at it and cast her a quizzical look. "You hold the front," he said patiently, "while I get some of this stuff on your back."

She was being prudish, but he hadn't seen her topless since she was ten. She probably felt more shy with Marcus than she might have with a total stranger.

Jenna crossed her arms under her breasts while he pushed the shirt up and over her shoulders. The cold splash of the lotion made her flinch, and he said, "Sorry."

"No," she said. "It feels wonderful."

Marcus laughed quietly, smoothing the cool liquid slowly into her skin. He paused to get some more, then his hand cupped one shoulder, shaping it to his moistened palm. "Considering that you have a picture of me in the nuddy," he said, "I feel I'm being short-changed here."

"We were kids." She and Katie had been, anyway.

He didn't answer, gently massaging her shoulder, his palm gliding over the heated flesh.

Jenna closed her eyes. He applied the stuff to the other shoulder, then ran his hand across her back again. For a moment it rested there, his fingers spread between her shoulder blades. The sun was warm on her bent head, and she heard the slap-slap of the water against the boat, and the soft sound of Marcus's breath as it stirred the tendrils of hair at the nape of her neck.

She felt his lips briefly touch the skin just behind her ear, and it electrified her whole body.

Then he removed his hand, saying briskly, "There you are," and pulled down the shirt.

By the time Jenna had adjusted the shirt and turned around, he had his back to her while he put the bottle of lotion away.

When he returned her to the flat, it was getting dark. Katie met them at the door and insisted on Marcus coming in for a meal.

After they'd eaten they sat around the table with a bottle of wine, and then coffee, talking. It was quite late before Marcus pushed back his chair and said he'd better be going.

Jenna yawned and began to get up too, wincing when her sore shoulder rubbed against the chair back.

"What's the matter?" Katie queried.

"A bit of sunburn."

Marcus said, "Have you got something for it here?"

"Yes, calamine," Jenna said.

"Get Katie to help you." He turned to his sister. "She needs someone to do her back."

Katie did it for her before they went to bed, and again the following morning. Marcus phoned Jenna in the evening. "How's the burn?"

"Settling down nicely. It was worth it."

He laughed. "Want to try it again?"

"Sunburn?" she parried.

"You know what I mean."

"Sailing?"

"Not necessarily."

When she didn't answer, he said with slight impatience, "A date, Jenna."

He hadn't used the word before.

"What did you have in mind?"

"If you're free we could go to a movie tomorrow evening." He paused. "Bring Katie along if you like."

Katie, who had handed the phone to her when Marcus asked for Jenna, gave her a surprised look when she relayed the invitation.

"I forgot to tell you. Dean and Callie are coming over," she said. "Dean's got another job interview, and Callie's going to look for a place for them to live in the city, so they're coming for dinner afterward. But there's no reason you shouldn't go," she added. "Have a good time."

When Marcus brought her home after the film, he glanced at the familiar car parked in front of his, and said, "Do you want me to come in with you?"

"I'm sure Dean and Callie would like to see you."

She waited for him to close the door. "Did you know they were going to be here tonight?"

"Should I have?" His hand at her waist urged her toward the flat.

"I just wondered," she said, "if you'd invited me out tonight to be kind."

They stopped on the porch. It was dark, the street-light not reaching there. "I asked you out because I wanted to spend time with you!" he said rather force-fully. "I hope you accepted for the same reason."

"Of course I did," she said quickly. "I mean, I enjoy doing things with you, Marcus."

"I'm glad to hear that. And it's mutual. So...let's have no more of this stuff about you being some kind of personal charity of mine."

Inside the flat Dean had his arm about Callie on the sofa, while Katie sprawled across one of the big old armchairs.

The greetings over, Jenna poured coffee for herself and Marcus. He gave the other chair to her before perching on the wide arm, his hand resting behind her.

"How was the job interview?" Jenna asked Dean.

"I think it's in the bag." He looked pleased with himself. "And Callie found a great apartment today. If I get this job we can afford the rent."

Katie said, "Have you set a wedding date?"

"Not yet." Dean glanced at his fiancée. "Callie wants her parents here for it."

Marcus looked from him to Callie. "Of course she does."

"There's no hurry," Callie said.

They chatted for a while, and then Dean made a

reluctant move. Marcus got up too, and as they were leaving Callie said brightly, "Why don't we all go out together sometime? The five of us."

Dean and Katie agreed in chorus, "Good idea." Marcus lifted an eyebrow at Jenna.

She managed a smile. "That sounds like fun."

"Marcus?" Katie turned to him.

"We'd enjoy that." Casually he hooked his arm about Jenna.

She saw Dean's look of surprise, and Katie's eyes flicking from her to Marcus.

"Dean?" Callie prompted.

"Sure." He dragged his eyes from his brother.

Marcus loosened his hold and kissed Jenna quickly on her mouth. "Good night." His wave included Katie before he turned away to follow the other two out.

When Katie shut the door and turned, obviously bursting with curiosity, Jenna shrugged and answered the unspoken question. "We're...friends. I suppose we're sort of dating," she mumbled.

"What happened on that yachting weekend?" Katie demanded.

"Nothing! Honestly."

Katie looked fascinated. "You know, I sometimes thought Marcus kind of fancied you, after he came back from overseas. He used to look at you a lot when he thought no one was watching. But I asked him once, and he just laughed and reminded me you were the same age as me, as if it had never crossed his mind that you weren't his sister. And you never said anything...you would have, wouldn't you? I mean, if he'd made a move..."

"He didn't. We're friends," Jenna repeated. That

was what he'd said, wasn't it? That she needed a friend.

"Sure." Katie was unconvinced. "Okay."

They all celebrated Dean's job acceptance with dinner at a Turkish restaurant that Katie had discovered when she was dating her last boyfriend.

Instead of chairs, they were seated on a low, curved divan. Katie and Callie giggled as they arranged themselves against the piled silk and velvet cushions, and Callie pulled Dean down beside her. "This is wonderful," she said. "So-o over the top."

"They have belly dancers later," Katie told her. "The men will enjoy that."

They ordered exotic dishes and shared, sampling each other's and making recommendations.

Marcus offered Jenna something dark and prune-like, holding it by one end between his thumb and forefinger.

"What is it?"

"I've no idea, but it's good. Maybe a fig?" He slipped it between her lips and it was, as he'd said, very good, sweet and syrupy. Marcus watched her, and unexpectedly reached out and ran his thumb over her lower lip, leaving a trace of the syrup before he withdrew.

Instinctively Jenna licked at the sticky sweetness. Her eyes locked with his, and a jolt of sexual awareness coursed through her, leaving her breathless and dizzy.

Marcus's eyes had darkened, and she could see a tiny muscle twitch near his jaw. Then he smiled and, without taking his eyes from her, snaked his arm along the padded back of the couch, letting it lie there, his fingers just touching her shoulder.

"Nice?" he said softly.

Jenna couldn't speak, managing a jerky nod instead, and some sort of smile. That light touch scorched. She couldn't recall ever being so acutely aware of another human being. When his thigh brushed against hers she bit down hard on her lip.

This is Marcus, she said to herself, dazed. *Marcus.* She'd never felt like this about him—about anyone, even Dean.

He'd already turned away, finding another delicacy to tempt her with. This time she forced herself to laugh and shake her head. "I'll feed myself, thanks. I feel decadent enough as it is."

Marcus slanted her a smile. A knowing smile, as if he knew what he'd done to her. He turned to the table but didn't take away his arm, and when the lights dimmed and a burst of music announced that the dancers were about to begin, he sank back on the cushions and closed his hand over her shoulder, bringing her into the curve of his arm.

She glanced at him a couple of times while three women in their glitter and draperies gyrated and twisted and twirled. When one of them caught his eye and danced closer, her stomach muscles rippling amazingly, he gave her a coolly amused smile. But most of the time he watched with detached interest. Katie and Callie were both teasing Dean, whispering comments while he pretended drooling fascination.

Afterward Marcus took Jenna and Katie home, declining Katie's invitation to come in. She nipped inside, leaving the door almost closed, and Marcus gave a low laugh. "My little sister trying to be tactful."

"I told her we're just friends." Jenna was flustered.

"Did you, now?"

"You said…"

"I know what I said." He put a hand on her arm and made her face him. "But one day," he said with deliberation, "I intend to make love to you, Jenna."

Her breath stopped. The change of pace was too sudden. "You're taking a lot for granted, aren't you?" She'd stepped on a nice safe merry-go-round, and it had turned into a switchback railway. Hearing the panic in her tone, she brought it down half an octave. "I never said I'd sleep with you! I don't know if I want to!"

"There's no rush." He moved his hand to tip her chin and make her look at him. "What's the problem?"

"One step at a time," she reminded him frantically.

He looked at her consideringly. "Yes. Which implies moving forward. I'm a patient man, Jenna. More so than you know, but I won't mark time forever. Living on hopes and dreams isn't my style."

Without waiting for a reply he pressed his lips briefly to hers, and then he was gone.

Katie had a new boyfriend. When Dean and Callie moved into their flat and threw a housewarming party, Jason drove the two girls along to it, although Marcus had offered.

He was there, of course, and so were his parents.

Jenna knew most of the people present and was able to give a passable imitation of enjoying herself.

The guests milled about in every room and on the small deck and lawn outside, and some were dancing in the living room, which was almost devoid of furniture. Dean and Callie still had to get around to acquiring some.

Halfway through the evening, while Jenna was chatting with Mr. and Mrs. Crossan and Marcus had gone to get drinks for the two women, the phone rang and Callie disappeared into the bedroom to talk with her parents.

Dean, his eyes bright and cheeks flushed, appeared at Jenna's side. "My fiancée's deserted me temporarily," he said. "Dance with me, Jenna."

Giving her no chance to refuse, he put his arm about her and urged her in among the dancers. "Enjoying yourself?" he asked her.

Jenna smiled widely. "It's a great party." The other guests obviously thought so.

"What gives with you and old Marc?"

"What's Katie been telling you?"

His grin teased. "She thinks there's something going on."

"What's it to you?" she asked involuntarily.

He grinned. "I guess I just want everyone I love to be as happy as I am."

Jenna made her voice sound light. "That's nice."

"I'm a nice guy," he said modestly, and moved in, twirling her exuberantly, retaining his hold on her hand when they faced each other again. "Aren't I?"

He was, she knew that. Blind to a lot of things, but nice. He deserved his happiness. For the first time she felt genuinely glad for him, a rush of affection burying her hurt. "You're really in love with Callie, aren't you?"

Foolish question, but Dean didn't seem to mind. "I'm crazy for her," he said simply. He put his hands on Jenna's waist, moving gently to the music. Suddenly sober, he said, "Thank you, Jenna, for sending me to America."

Jenna blinked. "Me? Sending you?"

"You were right, it was too good a chance to pass up. Not that I ever thought I'd meet someone like Callie." He gave her a lopsided, almost embarrassed smile. "Remember when we were kids and we said we'd marry each other?"

A lump in her throat, Jenna nodded.

"You were the first girl I ever kissed."

"You were the first boy..."

"Yeah, I know. Y'know, while we were at university I wondered sometimes if we'd end up together after all. But...obviously you weren't thinking along the same lines."

Jenna's mouth opened. "O-obviously?"

"You were dead keen for me to take the scholarship. Well," he added as if it were self-evident, "you'd never have let me go away for four years if you were serious about me." He grinned again. "I can hardly bear to be without Callie for four minutes!"

An exaggeration, she was sure, but when Callie emerged from the bedroom a few minutes later looking pink-eyed, Dean excused himself, went straight to her and gave her a hug.

Still dazed from the irony of his revelations, Jenna

rejoined the elder Crossans. Marcus handed over the drink he'd fetched for her, and for the rest of the evening stayed at her side. Around midnight, after his parents had departed, he suggested, "I'll drive you home whenever you're ready. Katie looks as though she's happy to stay on until dawn."

Katie was energetically dancing with her handsome, laughing partner. Watching them, Marcus said, "What do you think of this guy Jason?"

"He seems nice. They have the same sense of humor, but they hardly know each other yet. He was nervous about meeting her family." They'd been joking about it in the car.

"Are we so formidable?" Marcus looked across the room at his parents.

"*You* are," Jenna said involuntarily. "I think as kids the twins and I were more afraid of you than we were of your parents."

He looked at her with skepticism. "I never lifted a finger to any of you."

She shook her head. "No, only you were bigger and...somehow you always seemed..."

"Bossy?" he suggested wryly.

Jenna laughed. "I know we said so. You felt responsible for us, didn't you? Protective."

"You were so much younger." He looked rueful.

"But we're all adults now." She looked again at Katie.

Marcus did too, and then back at Jenna, his gaze disconcertingly level.

Something about that straight look disturbed her equilibrium. Her eyelids fluttered, and she had to make an effort to meet his gaze.

"That's what I'm hoping." Marcus lifted the glass in his hand and tossed off his drink. She was already holding an empty glass. "Let's dance," he said abruptly, taking her glass to deposit it with his on the nearest flat surface.

Someone had turned up the volume on the stereo system, and the noise level had risen to where people having a conversation had to stand close or shout above the music to be heard.

But as he took her hand to lead her in among the couples wiggling their hips and stamping their feet in the center of the room, the track came to an end and was replaced by a slow, dreamy number.

A few people stopped dancing and went to refresh their drinks, but the others wrapped their arms about each other and began swaying to the new rhythm.

Marcus's arms came about her, and automatically she rested her hands on his shoulders. She lifted her face and found him looking at her almost somberly, his eyes very dark and enigmatic.

They stared at each other for a long moment, swaying in time to the music, their feet hardly moving. Then he shifted his grip and brought her closer, his hands sliding to her hips, his shaven cheek rasping gently at the tender skin of her temple.

She wondered if he could feel the hurrying pulse there, and if her scent was as alluring to him as his was to her. He smelled male and exciting, under the soap and clean clothing.

When the music picked up a faster beat and the other couples broke apart, he didn't release her. Instead he said in her ear, "Shall I take you home?"

A rush of panic made her stiffen. She pulled away,

not looking at him. "If you've had enough of the party I'd appreciate a lift, thanks."

Coward, sneered a tiny voice inside her head. She tried to ignore it.

"Fine," Marcus said, his voice clipped. When she dared peek at him his face was rigidly controlled.

Outside it was cooler. She had worn a thin dress, and she hugged herself as they hurried to Marcus's car.

"Didn't you bring a jacket?" he asked her.

"I didn't think it would turn cold. I'm all right, it's warmer in the car."

It was only a ten-minute drive, and he didn't speak again until he drew up at the flat and accompanied her to the door.

He followed her into darkness, and she fumbled for the hall light and switched it on while he closed the door. "It's late," she said.

"Not too late." As she started down the passageway his hand on her arm stopped her, turned her to face him. "What are you scared of?"

"I'm not scared."

Marcus gave a short, unexpected laugh. "What you always declared when Dean dared you to do some silly, dangerous prank. I'm surprised you survived childhood." He paused, but she was staring stubbornly at the open neck of his casual shirt.

"Look at me, Jenna."

She pulled a careful breath in through her nose and looked up into his eyes. They were steady and searching and stern.

Jenna swallowed, and when she spoke her voice came out husky. "What do you want, Marcus?"

His lips curved very slightly. "If you're really an adult, not a little girl any longer, surely you know."

She felt her eyes go wider at his blunt challenge. But she didn't trust her own reactions to him. They were too new, and too disturbing. Surely unreal. "A woman who's been in love with a man for years can't just *not* be in a matter of weeks, even if she's...in lust with someone else." She might as well admit it. He must know, anyway.

"In lust?" His tone was peculiar. "Is that what you call it?"

Pulling away from him, she said, "You're an attractive man, Marcus, you must know that."

"Thank you. Then why do I hear a *but* coming?"

Difficult to express her conflicted feelings of physical fascination and emotional rejection, her muddled thoughts. "You're the nearest I've ever had to an elder brother."

"I'm not your brother!"

He'd stepped out of the role, and it unsettled her.

Until recently she had known what place each of the Crossans held in her life, and where she stood in theirs. Since Dean had brought Callie home, all those relationships had radically altered. Jenna no longer held the position in his heart that she had always imagined. Katie was growing closer to her future sister-in-law, with the inevitable consequence that Jenna sometimes felt left out. Jenna herself had withdrawn from the family circle to some extent, not being a natural masochist. And now Marcus wanted to be her lover.

"Everything's changing," she muttered, reluctant to admit how much it frightened her, throwing her back into childhood nightmares where people she loved abruptly disappeared or turned away from her, and familiarity turned to strangeness and loss.

"That's what life is about, Jenna," Marcus said patiently. "Things change. You can't lock yourself away from it, a lone princess pining in her tower. People move on, they leave the past behind, take chances and accept risks, forge new relationships. Make love."

"But I don't want—"

"You do!" He took a step toward her, and she involuntarily moved back. Then she found herself trapped against the wall, with Marcus standing over her, his hands flattened on either side of her while his eyes held hers in thrall. "You do *want*," he repeated. "You just admitted you want me."

"Don't bully me, Marcus!"

He wasn't touching her. "I'm trying to shake you awake, Sleeping Beauty. Fighting through the thorny hedge you've grown around your dreams. Tell me, has Dean ever even kissed you?"

"Yes, he has!" she claimed hotly, his weary, contemptuous tone sparking her temper. "Lots of times."

The first had been a clumsy adolescent experiment when they were both thirteen, resulting in more embarrassment than pleasure. The last was lingering and tender and poignant, before he went away.

She supposed that what she had seen as a pledge, he'd known was a goodbye to young love, because realistically the scarcely budding romantic component of their almost lifelong relationship wouldn't survive four years of separation.

Marcus's jaw tautened. She thought, and it gave

her a perverse satisfaction, that he'd received a small shock. "You've never slept with him," he said flatly.

How would he know? She gave him a silent, stubborn look, and his eyes narrowed, speculating.

He said softly, "You've never slept with anyone, have you?"

"You don't expect me to answer that!"

Unforgivably Marcus laughed. "You don't need to, little virgin," he taunted her. "It's written all over you." His voice altered to a kinder tone. "Maybe I should have taken that into account. But if you've been saving yourself for Dean, what are you going to do now?"

"I'm not going to sleep with the first man who offers!" Jenna flashed.

His mouth thinned. "I haven't suggested that."

"You said you wanted to have sex with me."

He looked as though he was going to deny it. She wondered if he was going to tell her no, she'd got it wrong.

"I want to make love with you," he said slowly, at last. "And you want it too."

"I don't love you!" she cried. "Not in the way I love—loved Dean." This wasn't love, this tug of desire, of physical need, that sometimes shook her to her core. It was too elemental. Too scary. She thrust that thought away, not wanting to examine the implications.

Marcus went lynx-eyed. "Past tense," he insisted, "or present? Let it go, Jenna. Dean's committed to Callie. He's madly, deeply in love with her."

"I know!" There was anguish in her voice. "I accept that."

"Then why can't you accept this?" he demanded, and hauled her into his arms.

Chapter Seven

It was in a strange way both like and unlike the other times Marcus had kissed her. The same rush of pleasure, unexpected and overwhelming, invaded her body.

But there was another element in the erotic charge of his lips forcing hers apart—a ruthlessness that was new and alarming, as if he were determined to blot everything else from her mind, her heart.

Her head fell back, and he shifted one arm so that he held her securely in the curve of his shoulder.

He seemed intent on demonstrating to her an unleashed sexuality, freed from the consideration and tenderness he'd shown her previously.

Not that he hurt her, he was far too skillful for that—but this was no gentle caress of comfort, no restrained if passionate exploration. It was a no-holds-barred, primal sexual revelation. A brazen assault on her senses.

At first she was shocked, as much by her own instant response as by the power of his arms holding her and the near-aggression of his kiss.

Fire licked through her veins, setting her alight, and as his complete lack of inhibition transferred itself to her, she kissed him back recklessly, her mouth as hungry and seeking as his, wanting the taste of him, arching her body over his arm at her waist, letting him take her with him to another plane of intense arousal.

She clung to his shoulders, the taut muscles bunching under her hands.

He pushed her to the wall, and his hands were on her breasts, shamelessly possessive. Her body was no longer her own, but an instrument of pleasure brought humming to life by his hands and his mouth, strung so tightly that when his fingers found a way inside her dress and touched bare skin she shivered with delight.

Marcus lifted his mouth then, his breathing harsh. "Jenna," he muttered, "this is torture. We need a bed."

Oh, yes! her mind said, before he eased away from her, leaving a cold gap between them. He still had a hand on her breast, the other resting on her hip.

Outside a car door slammed, and Jenna stiffened, pushing away his hands, turning her horrified gaze toward the door.

Katie?

Quick footsteps, and the door of the adjoining flat opened and closed. Jenna slumped with relief, and Marcus gave a smothered, unsteady laugh. He reached for her again, but she evaded him, turning blindly to enter the living room, fumbling for the light. It dazzled her eyes, the room swimming before her.

When he followed, she whirled to face him, and his eyes, dark and glittery, went to the bodice of her dress. The neckline was half off her shoulder, the lace of her bra showing.

Hastily Jenna pulled her dress into place, and ran her tongue over throbbing lips. She felt disheveled and disoriented, tiny shudders like miniature after-shocks attacking her.

Marcus moved toward her, and she stepped back with a wary little shake of her head.

His face became shuttered. He stopped inches from her, and they stared wordlessly at each other.

His mouth twisted. "I suppose it was too much to expect the walls would tumble so easily."

"You're not *that* irresistible." Jenna felt a need to attack while she gathered some kind of defenses. He was a formidable opponent, and he didn't play fair. Bewildered, she realized she was thinking of him as the enemy. Marcus, her friend—her protective, slightly bossy, almost-big-brother. Until now.

The sound he made wasn't quite a laugh. "I think I proved my point, at least."

He'd certainly proven that he could make her want him—make her almost fall into bed with him. A myriad of thoughts, half thoughts, chased each other through her mind. And a formless, barely acknowledged fear that she couldn't name or understand.

Distractedly, she thrust her fingers into her hair in a useless attempt at tidying it. Making a decision to give up Dean and her dreams of a future with him was one thing. Having a steamy affair with his brother on the rebound was something else entirely. She couldn't trust these bewildering new emotions at all. Aloud she said, "This can't be real!"

Marcus's hands lifted, then fell to his sides. "It felt real to me. More real than your girlish romantic fixation on my brother."

That was cruel. She turned away from him, swallowing hurt. The coffee table as usual was a mess. Like her life, she thought, suddenly irritated. They really ought to tidy up.

Marcus said, "I don't mean to hurt you, Jenna. But I'm getting a little tired of waiting for you to emerge from your cozy dream world."

She faced him then, her eyes hot. "You think I'm a fool. But I'm not so stupid or so juvenile that I don't know the difference between love and…lust."

He just looked at her for a moment, then he laughed. "Lust?" he echoed harshly. "That's the second time you've said that. I suppose it was lust that made you kiss me just now as if your whole life depended on it."

Jenna shrugged, looking away and down.

A hard hand came under her chin and forced it up. "Maybe I don't care. Whatever it was, it's pretty potent. You lit up for me like a Roman candle."

"Fireworks don't last," she said. "They're all flash and burn and then…ashes." She pushed his hand away, but he grabbed at her wrist and held it.

"*That's* what you're afraid of? That it might all turn to ashes?"

"It's bound to eventually," she reasoned. "Isn't it?" All his other girlfriends had disappeared from his life, hardly impinging on his family, seldom mentioned. Katie had been through a number of boyfriends too, some of them looking serious for a while. A couple of times Jenna had comforted her friend while she wept for the ending of another relationship.

She'd thought herself lucky, secure in her certainty of Dean's steadfast love.

Now she knew better.

"If you and I were sleeping together," she said, "your family would know. We couldn't keep it a secret from them."

"So? They like you. Katie would be thrilled to bits."

"And what about when it ends?" Suppose they rejected her, out of family solidarity or embarrassment, or because it would be socially awkward to include their son's ex-lover? Especially if he'd acquired a new one. The ramifications could be endless. And heartbreaking. At the mere possibility of being shut out of their lives, all the fears and dreads of her childhood insecurities returned to haunt her.

If the Crossans rejected her, she'd be alone in the world. Even the thought of it made her shiver inwardly. She could feel again the intense, frightened loneliness she'd experienced at six years old, when she'd realized she could rely on no one but herself.

"I've no intention of letting it end," Marcus said.

"All your other affairs have. There'd be too many complications. I couldn't bear to lose my relationship with your family, Marcus." And if Marcus walked out of her life... Her heart quailed. "Or your friendship."

He took her hands in his. "You'll never lose that,

Jenna. It's yours for keeps. And I'm sure you won't lose Katie's, either...or Dean's. If that's what's bothering you, there's a very simple solution.''

Jenna shook her head. She couldn't see it. "It's too risky..."

"Listen," he urged. "I want much more than a few months of sharing your bed. And I know you need more than that. It wasn't Dean you wanted so much as what he symbolized for you—family, permanence and security, and those I'm more than happy to offer you. Marry me."

At first Jenna thought she hadn't heard correctly. She'd been about to argue with his assessment of her love for Dean, but his final words drove everything else out of her head. She froze, showing no reaction at all.

Marcus was studying her intently. "Well?" he said, when the silence had stretched to almost five seconds. "Will you marry me, Jenna?"

Somehow she unglued her tongue from the roof of her mouth. "You don't want to get married! I mean...you've never shown any inclination to—"

For a split second he looked as though he might argue. Then he said, "Don't you think it's time I did? Most of my friends are married or with partners."

"I thought you were quite happy."

"Did you?" His voice flattened. "Well, perhaps there's been something missing from my life that you didn't know about."

A wife? She looked at him and realized that although she'd known him for so long, there had always been something about Marcus that was hidden from her. She'd put it down to his being older, but the gap wasn't really so huge now. Yet he'd still seemed a little aloof. She knew him less well than she did any other member of his family.

And now he was proposing the most intimate relationship of all between man and woman.

His glance slipped over her, a crooked smile on his mouth. "I want you very much, Jenna, and I would love you...to be my wife."

Assuaging a sexual urge, however powerful, didn't seem sufficient reason to make such a binding commitment. "If you're doing this to get me into bed—" she started, before his look stopped her, sending a tremor of trepidation through her.

"You know," his voice was deceptively gentle, "I find that somewhat offensive."

"I'm sorry." She knew he wasn't that crude—or that desperate. He genuinely liked her, and maybe that was enough for him. Not for her. "I can't marry a man I don't love!"

He regarded her narrowly for a moment, and shoved his hands into his pockets. His tone became crisp, almost businesslike. "You love my parents, don't you?"

"Yes, but that's diff—"

"What about Jane?"

"I'm very fond of her."

"And Katie."

"Of course!"

He paused. "And you dote on Dean. Are you saying I'm the only member of my family you don't love?"

"You know it's not the same!"

"So you do love me."

"In a way, of course—"

"A way that includes sex—lust—whatever you want to call it. An adult emotion, Jenna, not a rosy adolescent illusion. And I love you..." Again he paused. "I'd say we have a pretty sound basis for marriage."

"It's crazy," she said. Her head spun, and pulses throbbed at her temple and throat.

"Why? Every day people who were perfect strangers months—even weeks or days ago—promise to love and cherish each other until death. We've known each other nearly all your life. No nasty surprises, and certainly no hostile in-laws."

His reasoning was cogent. She didn't expect to love again as she'd loved Dean. Marcus aroused sexual feelings she hadn't even known she was capable of. And they had lots of things in common.

He had put his finger on the most persuasive argument of all—the promise of cementing her place in his family, strengthening the bonds that were so important to her.

"Children," she said. Was she really seriously considering this? "Do you want children?" If there were children there would be no question of divorce. She'd never do that to a child. And she was sure Marcus wouldn't, either.

"I hope we'll have them," he said. "You like kids, don't you?"

She had always assumed one day she'd have a family. But not without benefit of wedlock. She wanted her children to have a father, one who was committed to them for life.

Everything he said made sense, and yet...

He reached for her, drawing her closer, his hands
gliding up her arms and over her shoulders to hold
her head. His lips met hers in a long, tender, drugging
kiss, utterly different from the heart-pounding rage of
passion earlier. "We have more than sex," he told
her. "Though that's important, and I want it, with
you. If you hadn't shown me you want it too, I
wouldn't have forced the issue. Oh, I know," he said
as she opened her lips to speak. "Your heart belongs
to Dean. I can live with that until you get over it. One
day you'll find you have your heart back—a bit
bruised perhaps, but yours again. Because he doesn't
want it."

She wasn't sure which came first, the hard pressure
of his lips on hers or the sound of Katie's key in the
lock.

If he heard it Marcus took no notice, nor of her
hands pushing at his shoulders. He was intent on pry-
ing her lips apart, exploring her mouth with his.

Katie's voice said, "That's Marcus's car outside,"
and then, closer, "Are you two still...ooh, sorry! Are
we interrupting something?"

She was standing in the doorway of the living
room, with Jason behind her. Marcus at last loosened
his grip on Jenna, though he still had his arm about
her as he turned to his sister.

"You are," he said calmly.

"We could go out and come in again?" Katie offered, her eyes avid, an intrigued, pleased smile on
her mouth.

"No," Jenna said. "I'll walk Marcus to the door."

"You're leaving?" Katie looked up at her brother.

"It seems so." He followed Jenna as she escaped his light hold and passed the other two.

Jenna opened the door for him, and a couple of small moths fluttered into the hallway. Marcus stopped, looking down into her upturned face.

He was right, she thought. Dean didn't want her, but Marcus, for whatever reason, apparently did. And her stupid, disillusioned heart would mend one day.

He lifted one hand and grasped the door behind her. It seemed neither of them knew what to do next.

"Think about it," he said, and bent his head to hers, but the kiss was so quick she hardly had time to respond. "I'll call you tomorrow."

He kissed her again, this time more lingeringly. Then he left her, and she waited until he'd driven off before she closed the door, and discovered that her knees were shaking.

After leaning on the door for a few seconds, she made her way back into the living room. "I'm going to bed," she announced, pretending not to notice the enthralled interest on Katie's face.

It was barely fifteen minutes before she heard Jason depart, and seconds later Katie opened Jenna's bedroom door.

"You can't be asleep yet," she declared.

Jenna sighed and struggled up, switching the bedside light on.

Katie grinned at her and sprawled across the end of the bed. "Come on, what's going on between you and big brother?"

"He asked me to marry him."

Katie's mouth opened on a strangled squeak. "He

did? I can't *believe* it!'' She flung herself across the bed to hug her friend.

"I hardly believe it myself,'' Jenna muttered.

"You'll be my sister-in-law!'' Katie said excitedly. "Well, I always thought you would be, but that was when—'' She broke off and hugged Jenna again. "I told you he fancied you! You said yes, didn't you?''

"No, not yet.'' She mustn't let Katie's enthusiasm influence her decision.

"Why not?'' Katie clapped a hand over her mouth, her eyes rounding. "Oh, sorry. We interrupted, didn't we! The air was positively sizzling tonight when we walked in.''

"It's all right. Probably just as well. It gives me time to think.''

"About what? I know you, Jen. You wouldn't kiss a guy that way unless you meant it. When did you realize you were in love?''

She couldn't tell Katie they weren't in love, really. "I suppose tonight,'' she said reluctantly.

"The family's going to be so rapt!'' Katie said. "You'll be legally one of us. Can we tell Mum and Dad tomorrow? Or does Marcus want to do it?''

"I haven't said yes,'' Jenna reminded her.

"Of course you're going to say yes! You and Marcus—it's perfect! I don't know why none of us realized before. You're both a bit reserved and serious, deep waters and all that, and you like heaps of the same things! He's always looked out for you, but you were the one who stood up to him when we were kids. He needs someone he can't push around. You're obviously made for each other.''

"We are?''

"Totally. But I guess you know that. Wait till I tell Dean!"

"You can't!"

"Well, not until you've said yes, I suppose," Katie sulked. She gave a little bounce on the bed, sitting up. "Phone him."

"Phone Dean?"

"Marcus, you idiot! Phone him and put the poor man out of his misery. He'll be home by now."

She bounded into the sitting room and came back with the portable receiver in her hand, thrusting it at Jenna before sitting cross-legged on the bed.

Her delighted enthusiasm was hard to resist. Apparently it didn't occur to her to give Jenna privacy. "Go on," she urged, and reeled off the number.

Why not? Jenna thought recklessly. Of course she wasn't doing it simply because she didn't want to disappoint Katie. There were lots of other, better reasons. If all the Crossans felt as Katie did, and Dean was going to marry Callie anyway, why shouldn't she accept Marcus's proposal? It was probably the best offer she'd get.

Nearly perfect, in fact, except that he was the wrong man. Which he knew and didn't seem to mind. It wasn't as though she would be doing it under false pretences. He himself had used the incentive of a closer tie to his family, knowing what a tempting bait that was for her.

As if in a dream her fingers pressed the buttons. She lifted the receiver to her ear and heard the ringing tone. Maybe he wasn't home yet after all.

Then his voice said, strong and deep in her ear, "Hello?"

"Marcus?" Her hand was shaking and damp. She licked her lips.

"Jenna." He waited.

She looked up at Katie who nodded vigorously, both thumbs held up, a huge, encouraging smile on her face.

Jenna cleared her throat. "I just want to say...the answer's yes."

For a minute she was afraid he hadn't heard. Then she heard him let out a breath. "Thank you," he said. "Thank you very much, darling."

Darling. Strangely, her heart seemed to melt, turning to a warm little mass. "Thank *you*," she whispered, "for asking me."

He laughed rather unsteadily. "That's very sweet. I thought you'd be in bed by now."

"I'm calling from there."

He made a soft, indefinable sound. "I'll let you sleep then. And Jenna...?"

"Yes?"

"I love you. I'm glad you called."

"I...I love you too," she said, conscious of Katie shamelessly listening. It wasn't a lie. As he'd pointed out, there were different kinds of love.

Marcus bought her a solitaire diamond set in a narrow hoop of gold. Later she phoned her mother with the news while he sat at her side.

"She's pleased," she said, handing him the receiver. "She wants to talk to you."

He took Jenna's hand in his free one, playing with the new ring on her finger while he spoke to her mother. "Yes," he said. "Thank you. And I'm a lucky man…. We haven't discussed the date, but very soon."

Jenna looked up at him, her eyes widening, and he went on talking to Karen. "I thought we'd have it here in Auckland, if you don't object. Of course we'll consult you about arrangements. My mother will be delighted to help…. Sure…here she is again." He handed the receiver back to Jenna.

After she'd hung up he said, "Do you want a big affair with all the trimmings?"

"No!"

"Sure?" His look was penetrating.

"Absolutely."

"That's good, because I'd like to do this quietly. And quickly."

"Quickly?" Her heart skipped a beat.

"I don't see any reason to wait, do you?"

Jenna swallowed. "I suppose not."

"Are you having second thoughts?" He looked grim, his hand tightening fractionally on hers.

"Are *you?*" she asked him.

"No. I know what I want, Jenna."

Jenna sat in silence for a second or two. For so long a time she had wanted Dean. It was difficult to break the habit. But she must move on—*had* moved on.

She'd agreed to marry Marcus, who wanted her in a way that Dean never had.

And she wanted him in the most fundamental, physical way, at least. He was an attractive, sexy man with his own successful business, and she knew he was decent, hardworking, kind. What more could any woman ask for?

She lifted her head. "I said I'd marry you. I won't go back on it."

"Good." She saw him relax. "Will a month give you enough time to get a dress and do whatever else you need to?"

"A month?" Her eyes widened.

"Why not?"

"Dean..." she said feebly "...and Callie."

Marcus's face had gone taut and narrow-eyed. "What about them?"

"We shouldn't steal their thunder. I mean, getting married before them. They were engaged first."

Katie had suggested a double wedding, to Jenna's dismay. Marcus had retorted curtly he had no intention of sharing his wedding day with anyone except his bride.

His eyes held hers, seeming to search the depths. "They haven't set a date," he said. "And I don't feel inclined to hold back until they do."

He held back in other ways during the next four weeks. Jenna had capitulated on the date after Katie told her that Callie and her parents were still discussing whether the wedding would be in America or New Zealand. "Her parents would like to give her a traditional wedding over there, and naturally Callie wants her friends around her. Mum and Dad are happy to have it here, but either way one family's going to have to travel."

Compared with the logistics of that wedding, Jenna and Marcus's was an exercise in simplicity. Katie helped Jenna choose an off-the-peg white silk dress trimmed with teardrop pearls. Marcus booked a chapel close to his parents' home, and the guest list was limited to the families and about twenty friends.

Marcus hired caterers, vetoing his mother's offer of doing the food herself. "I said a small celebration," he told her, "not a cheap one. And I want you to enjoy yourself, not be worrying over heating savories and whipping cream."

Katie was Jenna's only attendant, and Dean waited beside his brother at the altar. There was no way Marcus could have asked anyone else.

Escorted down the aisle by her stepfather, Jenna kept her gaze straight ahead.

When she raised her eyes to his face, Marcus looked serious and tense, but his lips moved in a slight smile as the celebrant began the marriage service.

Jenna spoke her responses in a voice that shook only slightly. Marcus made his firmly, but when he placed the ring on her finger she noticed his were trembling, so that he fumbled a little before slipping it over her knuckle.

He lifted back the short veil and kissed her, his lips warm and somehow reassuring. His hand was firmly wound about hers as they went to sign the register, and when they walked back along the length of the chapel.

Dean slapped his brother's back and kissed Jenna briefly on the lips. She hardly felt it. Katie hugged her exuberantly, and her mother, smiling mistily, came to kiss her cheek, followed by Mrs. Crossan.

There were photographs and congratulations and, back at the Crossans' house, a babble of noise, lots of champagne, more congratulations and a few short speeches.

She was aware of Marcus at her side, taking her arm, seeing that she had a drink, making her eat something. But everything was a blur until they left the house and ran to his car.

They hadn't escaped a hail of confetti. Jenna flicked it from her sleeves and shook out her skirt, and once he was sure they hadn't been followed, Marcus stopped the car and brushed some from his shoulders, then ruffled his fingers through his hair, scattering tiny rounds on the floor of the car.

"There's more," Jenna told him.

"You do it." He bent his head for her, and she reached up to pick out the stray scraps of color. His hair was soft and warm against her fingers.

"Thanks," he said when she sat back. "My turn."

She felt the light touch of his fingers in her hair, moving through it. When he was done he smoothed it back over one ear and his hand curved about her nape while a thumb stroked her cheek. "All right?" he asked quietly.

"Yes."

He studied her face. "Not nervous of me, are you, Jenna?"

Jenna bit her lip. She felt tense, and foolish. "Not of you."

"Of this whole business?" he guessed. His thumb moved over her mouth, and a pleasurable sensation uncurled in her midriff.

Marcus said, "I won't hurry you. We're married. There's a whole lifetime ahead of us."

He leaned forward and gave her a quick, reassuring kiss. Then he released her and restarted the car.

Chapter Eight

During their short engagement Marcus's kisses had been passionate, his caresses sometimes intimate. But he had stopped their lovemaking short of consummation, leaving Jenna tense and dissatisfied.

She supposed he was respecting her virginity, and she had always intended to be a virgin bride, but she sometimes wondered if he was deliberately keeping her in a state of suspense so she wouldn't want to delay the wedding. The breathtaking speed with which he'd arranged everything indicated that he might not be sure she'd go through with it.

Well, she had. And now, as he'd said, they were married, with a lifetime ahead of them.

But first there was tonight.

Marcus had booked them into a city hotel where they would stay before flying to Rarotonga in the Cook Islands for a week.

The room wasn't the honeymoon suite, but it had

a magnificent view of the blue-green expanse of the
Waitemata Harbor—and sported a king-size bed. A
small table flanked by easy chairs held a foil-topped
bottle and two glass flutes.

Jenna averted her eyes from the bed and went to
the windows. Dusk was falling. Lights flickered on
along the water's edge and outlined the ships tied up
at the wharf, reflected in wavy lines that appeared to
plunge into the restless sea.

Marcus came to stand beside her, an arm about her
shoulders, and they watched in silence as more lights
winked on and the water darkened. A few pale stars
jeweled the sky.

He moved his hand to the back of her neck and
began massaging it. It was soothing and yet erotic.
She tipped her head forward, allowing his clever,
strong fingers to ease away the tension that had held
her all day.

"I thought we might ask room service to send up
a meal," he said.

"Mmm. All right." When his fingers stilled on her
nape, she tipped her head back against his hand.

He dipped his head swiftly, his lips meeting hers
as he stepped close and angled her to him.

Jenna answered his kiss without pretence, her lips
parted and eager, and after a few moments she turned
to him, her arms sliding around his shoulders. He
went momentarily still as if taken aback, then his fingers were in her hair and the kiss became deeper, their
bodies pressing close.

Marcus lifted his head, and his hands skimmed
down her back, closed about her hips to put an inch
or two of space between them. His eyes were very

dark, and a layer of color outlined his cheekbones. "About that meal," he said, his voice low and rasping.

"What meal?" Jenna's arms were still loosely hooked about his neck, and she sent him a calculatedly provocative look.

Marcus appeared slightly dazed. "The one I thought we'd have with the champagne." He indicated the bottle on the table. "Before…"

"Do you plan to get me drunk again?"

His mouth curved in a bemused smile. "A bit more relaxed. I thought you were scared."

A tremor of nervous excitement fluttered in her stomach. "There has to be a first time."

The smile became strained. "It doesn't have to be tonight," he said gravely. "Not if you'd rather wait."

Something melted warmly inside her. Despite his haste to marry her, and the desire he hadn't tried to hide, he was still prepared to let her set the pace. That was a gesture of chivalry she hadn't expected, and yet it was characteristic of Marcus.

She touched her tongue to her lips. "I don't want to wait. Do you?"

His chest moved on a harsh breath. He tightened his hands again on her hips and brought her close to him. "In the stupid-questions department, my darling wife," he said, "that takes first prize."

She was laughing when he kissed her again, stifling the laughter with his mouth, and she wound her arms about him and clung while she kissed him back without inhibition, teasing him with her tongue and her teeth.

He drew away, breathing hard, and looked down at

her with narrow, glittering eyes. "Who taught you to kiss like that?"

"You did," she taunted breathlessly. "Are you complaining?"

"Hell, no!" Without warning he picked her up in his arms and strode to the bed, lowering her onto the cover.

She kicked her shoes to the floor. Marcus sat on the bed and bent to remove his shoes and socks, threw off his jacket and unbuttoned his shirt, discarding that too.

Jenna watched, her heart beating fast and hard, a delicious desire suffusing her body.

Marcus stood up and went back to the table, dispensed with the foil top and the cork on the bottle, and poured champagne into the flutes as vapor curled from the neck.

He carried the glasses and bottle to the night table by the bed and put them down. "Move over."

When she had, he turned back the bed covers and stacked a couple of pillows, inviting her to lean on them while he dealt with the other half of the bed.

He settled beside her and handed her a glass, clicked his against it. "To us."

Holding her eyes with his, he half emptied his glass. Jenna sipped at hers, the crisp, tart bubbles bursting on her tongue.

And then Marcus closed the few inches between them, and she felt his tongue on her lips, tasting the champagne.

She made a small, startled sound, and he drew back. "You don't like it?" He looked at her questioningly.

"No! I mean, it's not that."

He smiled slowly. "You do like it?"

She had to swallow some more of the champagne before answering. "Yes."

"Good," he said. "Tell me if I do anything you don't like." And he lowered his head again.

He dipped a forefinger into his glass and touched it to the hollow at the base of her throat, and she felt the coolness before he bent forward again and licked the wine away.

Jenna's lips parted and a wild heat flared in her cheeks. His eyes gleaming slits, Marcus kissed her again, deep and demanding, pressing her back against the pillows. The glass she held shook so much that some of the liquid spilled over her hand.

When they surfaced from the kiss he looked the way she felt—dazed and aroused. A trickle of champagne moistened his shoulder, and a lone droplet ran down to his chest. Daringly, she leaned forward and captured it with her tongue.

Marcus sucked in an audible breath. He downed the remainder of his drink in a single swallow and placed the glass on the night table. With an air of determination he began to undo the buttons on the front of her shirt.

The lace cups of her bra barely covered half her breasts, leaving the rest exposed to his gaze. Her heart thumped as he looked his fill before tracing the outline of the lace with a fingertip. He pushed the shirt from her shoulders and she helped him get it off.

Then he snapped open the fastener of her pants, and unzipped them.

"Lift up," he said, and she helped him peel off the pants.

Underneath she wore a minuscule garment that matched her bra.

"Very nice."

Jenna gulped down some more of her wine. She was both nervous and fascinated.

Then he leaned over and kissed her again.

A sweet tension began to build inside her. Her head buzzed. She tightened her fingers on the glass in her hand and made a frantic little movement.

Marcus withdrew his mouth from hers and took the glass, placing it beside his own, then he was shifting her farther down the bed, kissing her again, his hands making wonderful magic. And she reciprocated, finding his body unfamiliar but increasingly fascinating.

At last Jenna made an inarticulate sound in her throat. Marcus lifted his head. "Yes?"

"*Yes.*" She could hardly get the single word out.

He smoothed her tumbled hair and kissed her forehead. "There's nothing to be frightened of."

Jenna wasn't frightened; she was desperate for him. And desperately grateful for his careful initiation.

It was both strange and exciting. When he glided home, the fragile barrier stopped him, and she saw his cheeks tauten. He stilled, waiting for her, breathing cautiously.

Jenna moved tentatively, then as the barrier frustrated her she set her teeth and took the initiative.

It hurt, and she cried out softly in pain.

"I'm sorry, darling," she heard Marcus say. "If you want to stop…"

Fiercely she shook her head, and closed her teeth on her lower lip.

The barrier was gone. The hurt lessened. And soon she was soaring, and knew that he too had reached the pinnacle, holding her tightly while they both shuddered into quiescence, panting against each other.

He turned to her and kissed her deeply. Then his lips left hers and he said, "Are you all right?"

"Perfectly." She hung her arms about his neck. "Are you?"

"Need you ask?" He kissed her again. "I knew you could be a wonderful lover, but I didn't expect it to be so fantastic the first time."

"Neither did I," she confessed. "Thank you, Marcus."

"Don't say that. Thank you for marrying me, Jenna. And for being so courageous and utterly beautiful. You were stunning."

Jenna was glad she had pleased him. She felt nicely floaty, and when he withdrew from her she experienced a sense of loss.

Later they showered and decorously sat down to a room service meal and more champagne.

And still later they were back in bed and in each other's arms.

That was how they spent most of the next week, between walking along white coral-sand beaches and snorkeling in sparkling clear water, dining on exotic coconut-flavored dishes and watching the Cook Island dancers who provided entertainment at their hotel.

The dancing was sensuous and flirtatious, the men half crouching and slapping their brown, muscular

thighs together as they circled the women, who se-
ductively swayed their hips, eyes demurely downcast,
while the wooden drums that accompanied them kept
up a clamorous rhythm.

Marcus hired a motor scooter, the chief form of
transport, and they circled the island, Jenna clinging
to him with her arms about his waist. He drove up
through coconut and taro plantations to the hilly interior, and they walked under tall yellow-flowered hibiscus trees and raggedy-leaved banana trees with
huge dark-wine velvet flowers and found a secluded
little glade where moss cushioned their bodies as they
made love sheltered by a circle of close-growing
trees.

"This is a slice of heaven," she breathed afterward, as she lay in Marcus's arms, watching the lat-
ticework of leaves overhead shift against the sun. Distantly she could hear the waves breaking on the reef
surrounding the island. Close by the palms shivered
and swayed. "It really is a tropical paradise."

"Paradise is where you make it," Marcus replied.
"But..." He looked down at her, smoothing a strand
of hair from her forehead. "I'll never forget this. I
want to make you happy, Jenna. And keep you happy
forever."

On their last night on the island, when the guests
were invited to join in the island dancing, Marcus
surprised Jenna by pulling her to her feet. Laughing
at her protest, he put his hands on her hips and challenged her to imitate the women dancers, while he
followed the men's example.

At first self-conscious, she soon picked up the

rhythm and began to enjoy herself. The drumbeat became faster and faster, a frenetic, dazzling display,
and when it stopped she was breathless.

The dancers left to a storm of applause, and a three-
piece band began to play a jazz tune. Instead of lead-
ing her back to their table, Marcus folded Jenna into
his arms and moved to the music among other couples
taking the floor.

Tonight Jenna had worn one of the hand-dyed cotton sarongs sold in the local markets, knotting it about
her waist so that it fell to her ankles, teaming it with
a white cropped top. Marcus's hands were on her
skin, a thumb subtly tracing the groove of her spine.

His chin brushed her temple, and his thighs flexed
against hers. The lights dimmed and she closed her
eyes, enjoying the spell cast by the tropical night, the
music, and the man holding her.

She felt alive and content—more so than she had
in years. For a long time she'd been in a sort of suspended animation, waiting for her life to take up
where it had left off.

And now it had taken a different direction. She had
woken from a dream and found reality infinitely more
exciting and satisfying.

Tightening her arms about Marcus's neck, she laid
her cheek against his shoulder. When the music
stopped he didn't let her go immediately, but murmured, ''Shall we go now?''

''Yes.'' She wanted him. Wanted his hands on her
body, his mouth on hers, wanted him inside her again,
taking her to heights of pleasure that seemed to grow
more intense every time they were together.

The hotel was all on one level, its guest quarters

individual thatch-roofed units secluded by tall, grace-
fully bowed palms, heavy-scented frangipani trees
and glossy red-leaved shrubs. Low lights among the
shrubbery lit the path back to their unit.

Inside, screened windows allowed the scent of the
frangipani to perfume the bedroom, and through the
lattice of palm leaves a full moon lit the wide bed,
turning the sheets blue-white.

Jenna was admiring the moon framed by the big
window when Marcus came up behind her and linked
his fingers at her bare waist. He kissed her neck, and
Jenna leaned back against him.

He turned her and backed her against the wall and
kissed her until she was dizzy. When he began tugging at the knot of the pareu, Jenna reciprocated by
undoing the buttons of his shirt. She pressed herself
against him and felt with triumph the surge of his
response.

Naked, they fell on the bed together, and within
seconds her small cries of fulfillment were joined by
his low groans of satisfaction.

In the aftermath she turned to him, his sweat-
sheened body lit in restless bars of moonlight as the
palm tree outside whispered harshly in the wind. His
face was in shadow, but he wound his fingers into her
hair and kissed her again.

Jenna rested her head against his shoulder and felt
him let out a long breath. Her skin tingled, and her
limbs were twined with his. She turned her head to
kiss his salty skin, and his hold on her tightened. She
felt remarkably content, happier than she could ever
remember. She had never been so close to another
human being.

* * *

It was a night she was to remember for a long time. Something magical and intimate that they shared before returning to New Zealand and a different kind of reality.

Reality now was going back to work and spending the days apart from Marcus. But it was also settling herself into his apartment and into his lifestyle.

He made room for her clothes in his bedroom. She found space for her toiletries and makeup in the bathroom, and filled his kitchen cupboards with condiments, spices and ingredients that he'd never bought himself.

"I generally eat out or order something in," he told her the first time he came home to find her preparing a meal. "You're working too. There's no need to rush home and make dinner for me."

"I like cooking." Jenna opened the oven to insert a tray of duchesse potatoes. "If you don't want me to—"

"I didn't say that. Only it wasn't my intention to turn you into a housewife."

"You're not turning me into anything," Jenna said firmly. "Pass me that glass bowl over there, will you? I need it for the salad."

He passed it, and left to change out of his business suit into casual slacks and a T-shirt.

Over the filet mignon and fresh vegetables she'd prepared, he said, "This is great. I'm not much of a cook myself."

Jenna looked at him curiously. "You made me breakfast when I stayed here, the night the flat was flooded."

"Ah, breakfast is different. On weekends I often do bacon and eggs."

For two? Unreasonably, Jenna was pierced with jealousy, wondering how many women had sat at this table after a night of passion—how many had shared his bed.

Don't be silly, she admonished herself. He didn't marry any of them, did he?

He had married her—Jenna. Because he was ready to settle down, and preferred to do so with someone he'd known for years.

It sounded sensible—and boring.

"Do you like being married?" she asked him.

"I like being married to you, Jenna." He paused. "Do you like it?"

"Yes." She liked being with him and certainly was never bored. Besides having a quiet sense of humor and a kind heart, Marcus was an inventive, exciting lover. Jenna knew she had surprised and delighted him by matching his appetite, if not his expertise. They challenged each other to new heights of pleasure, often until they were both exhausted. And he was always careful of her pleasure as well as his own.

She glanced away from the rather penetrating look he was giving her. "You're a very considerate husband, Marcus."

He stood up abruptly and started clearing away plates. "I guess that's my cue."

Jenna hadn't realized what a full social life Marcus had. There were dinner parties and weekend yachting parties, and business occasions when Marcus asked her to accompany him.

His friends seemed happy to welcome Marcus's wife. His business partner's wife in particular was warm in her congratulations. As she and Jenna renewed their lipstick in the ladies' room after a restaurant meal with potential clients, she said, "Marcus has been wrapped up in the business far too long. It's time he had a real relationship."

"He's had girlfriends," Jenna ventured.

"Hmm." Angela Travers tossed her dark curls, her normally soft, pretty mouth thinning. "None of them were what he needs." She took a tissue from a box on the counter and blotted her lipstick.

"What do you think he needs?" Jenna asked.

"Someone who puts him first," Angela said frankly. "Who truly loves him and isn't just using him, who won't let him down."

Feeling a pang of guilt, Jenna said, "Has he been let down?"

Angela hesitated. "I don't know for sure. I've always had a feeling that he's hurting deep inside. And that none of those women he's been with have helped much. You've known him forever, haven't you? I thought you'd know."

Jenna shook her head. "He's older, and when we were kids the gap seemed huge. Since he left home I've only seen him at family gatherings, really. Until recently, that is," she added hastily.

"But you do love him?"

"I've always loved him." It was true, although of course it was different from the way she'd felt for Dean.

Different, but...? All that angst over Dean now paled into a fuzzy memory. Teenage romanticism,

Marcus had scathingly called it. Puppy love. Could he have been right?

Apologetically the other woman said, "I have no business cross-questioning you. It's just that Ted and I are very fond of Marcus, and we want him to be happy."

"So do I." She owed him that.

"Of course you do." Angela squeezed her arm. "I shouldn't be butting in. Put it down to the wine. I've never had a good head for alcohol."

Chapter Nine

They were invited to have dinner with Dean and Callie.

"How do you feel about that?" Marcus asked, studying her face.

Jenna shrugged. "We can't say no, can we?"

He didn't answer for a second. "I suppose not," he said finally. "We'd better accept, then."

Katie and Jason had been invited too, and the twins kept the conversation lively, each capping the other's jokes with some quick-witted reply. Callie smiled a lot, although she was quieter than usual.

Watching Dean as he laughed at something his sister had said, Jenna smiled too. She loved them both, and that would never change, but with a sense of relief she realized that her feelings for Dean had radically altered. Affection was there, but there was no tearing heartache and no longing for a closer tie.

It was over. Dean was someone she was close to

but not intimate with. And compared with his older brother he seemed very young.

A new sensation of lightness and freedom washed over her. She was happy, almost wildly so. When Dean made some silly pun and Katie groaned loudly, Jenna capped it with one of her own, her eyes dancing, and the three of them were soon off into a teasing, laughing round of quip and counter-quip that had Callie giggling, Jason grinning in a slightly bewildered way, and Marcus's eyes moving from one to the other of them while his mouth curved and his cheek creased in amusement.

Dean poured more wine, and Callie said, "It's great that you all get on so well together."

"We've been friends forever," Dean said. "I'm glad Marcus had the sense to marry Jenna. The best thing he ever did."

"I concur with that," Marcus said lazily.

"Thank you, Dean," Jenna said graciously. "I'm glad too."

They grinned at each other, and the bubble of happiness inside her seemed to swell and burst in a rush of affection for him, unmixed with any sexual feelings at all. He was her old playmate again, and she was glad to have him back. Laughing from sheer exuberant relief, she turned to Marcus, and saw his eyes narrow. The laughter died and she gave him a radiant smile. How foolish she had been to imagine that her puppy love was the real thing. Now she knew what a pale imitation it had been of grown-up, lasting love. She couldn't imagine being married to anyone but Marcus.

When Callie got up to clear the plates and bring

the next course, Jenna followed her into the kitchen, offering help.

"You could cut that into wedges." Callie indicated the cheesecake on the table. "I'll just put some fruit salad in a bowl."

"This looks good." Jenna found a knife and began slicing.

"I bought it," Callie said, seeming embarrassed. "I'm not much of a cook." She took a can of fruit salad from a cupboard.

"The chicken was delicious," Jenna assured her.

Callie wrinkled her nose. "The rice went gluey."

"It was fine. No one complained, did they?"

"You're all too polite." Callie wrestled with the can opener. "Oh, heck—I can't even open a can!" Frustratedly she banged it on the counter.

"Let me help." Jenna abandoned the cheesecake and picked up the opener, making sure it was firmly seated before turning the wings. The wheel cut into the metal and soon she was removing the top.

"Thanks." Callie took the can and emptied it into a bowl. "At home we had an electric opener." She sniffed.

"You can buy them here." Jenna looked at the other girl's downbent head. "Are you all right, Callie?"

Callie sniffed again and dashed a hand across her eyes, but it didn't stop the tears Jenna saw spilling onto her cheeks.

She put an arm about Callie's shoulders. "Callie?"

"I'm all right." Callie grabbed a paper towel from the wall dispenser and dabbed her eyes and nose. "I *love* Dean,'' she said fiercely. ''Only sometimes I miss home. You won't tell him about this, will you?''

''Does he know how you feel?''

''He knows how I feel about him.''

''If you miss your home so much, shouldn't you tell him?''

''I don't want him to know what a baby I am.'' Callie squared her shoulders. ''If I carry this, can you bring in the cheesecake?''

''We should have Dean and Callie round to our place soon,'' Jenna said later as Marcus drove the car into the garage.

He pulled on the hand brake and switched off the lights. ''You wouldn't mind?''

''She needs friends.''

''I would have thought you'd be the last person on earth…''

''You want your brother to be happy, don't you?''

''Of course,'' he replied shortly. Pulling the key from the ignition, he got out of the car.

Inside, Jenna prepared herself for bed, pleasantly filled with food and wine and the memory of an enjoyable evening, except for Callie's sudden revelation of her homesickness.

Marcus hadn't come into the bedroom, and as she was about to climb between the sheets, she wondered what he was doing and returned to the living area to find out.

There were no lights on, but in the darkened living room he stood, a dark, shadowy figure at the window, looking out at the lights of the city.

''Marcus?''

He turned at the sound of her voice, and she saw the faint gleam of a glass in his hand.

She went to join him, the satin of her nightgown sliding against her thighs as she approached. "What are you doing?"

"Having a nightcap," he answered, adding after a second, "Do you want one?" He sounded remote and polite and she couldn't see his face.

"No, I've had enough alcohol tonight." He had drunk very little, pacing himself because he was driving. Marcus had never been a heavy drinker.

She stood at his side, watching the winking lights, while he tossed off the remainder of the drink and put down the glass on the sill. A spatter of rain hit the window, and ran crookedly down the pane, picking up diamond points of lights on the way. Jenna felt goose bumps on her flesh and crossed her arms in front of her.

"You're cold." Marcus put an arm about her, rubbing his slightly roughened palm over her suddenly cooled skin.

"Not really."

The rain outside intensified, blurring the view, all the lights running together like an abstract painting. She looked up and saw Marcus's face in profile, jutting against the window, strong and impenetrable. She did feel cold, then. Cold and shut out.

"Marcus?" She said his name again, and he turned slowly, as if he'd just remembered she was there.

"What is it, Jenna?" he asked gently.

He must have heard the troubled note in her voice. "Nothing," she said. "Are you coming to bed?"

"Are you inviting me?"

Her heart quickened. "Do you need an invitation?" She paused. "You know you're always welcome."

"Always?"

She had never refused him unless for obvious reasons. "Of course. Surely you know that?"

"Men don't always know for sure. Women can pretend."

She'd never have thought Marcus was lacking in confidence. She tried to see his face, but it was too dark to discern his expression. "I don't pretend," she said. "I wouldn't. And besides, there's no need."

"You don't...fantasize?"

The only fantasizing she did was when he wasn't around and she was thinking about him. "Do you?" she asked point-blank. Did he see some film star or pin-up in his mind when he was making love to her?

"Why would I want to?" he said, turning to bring her into the circle of his arms. "When the embodiment of all my fantasies is right here?"

An extravagant thing to say, that would please any woman. She didn't know why it caused her a slight pang. Perhaps because she couldn't quite believe it. To banish the small doubt, she lifted her face to him in invitation and slid her arms around his neck. "Thank you, Marcus."

Their lips met in a long, increasingly passionate kiss. Through the thin satin gown she felt the heat and hardness of his body as he crushed her closer, and their breathing quickened. They didn't even get as far as the bedroom before he had discarded his clothing and pulled off her nightgown. The sofa was wide and soft and Marcus arranged the cushions for her comfort. In the darkness, with the rain beating on the windows, they came together, and Marcus muttered hoarsely, urgently, "Say my name, Jenna. Tell me you know who I am."

Almost lost in sensation, too caught up in the whirlwind to wonder why he needed this, she gasped it out, and heard him groan aloud when they reached at last a mutual fulfillment.

As they lay panting in each other's arms for minutes afterward, Jenna asked him, "Did that feel like pretending?"

She felt the heave of his breath, followed by silent laughter. "No," he said before he picked her up in his arms and carried her to their bed. "It felt like...nothing else on earth."

It wasn't the first or the last time they had not bothered with a bed. They had made love on the couch, on the floor, once in an armchair, even in the kitchen and bathroom, and a few times in the car when they'd been too impatient to wait until they were home after a night out.

Sometimes it seemed to Jenna there was a kind of desperation to their lovemaking that gave her an uneasy feeling. It was almost as if it was their only sure avenue of communication.

They had agreed that there was no need to prevent pregnancy. But despite their very active sex life, four months into their marriage Jenna's cycle was as regular as ever.

Marcus's mother chuckled when Jenna mentioned the fact. "Not everyone gets pregnant at the drop of a hat, you know. If you go more than a year or so it might be wise to get a doctor to check you out. Meantime the best thing you can do is relax. I'm sure Marcus doesn't mind.''

But there were odd occasions when she caught him watching her as if waiting for something. Maybe he felt more strongly about having children than he was letting on.

Then Katie phoned her at work one day, sounding agitated. ''It's Dean,'' she blurted, and Jenna's heart stopped for an instant. ''Callie's left.''

''Left?'' Jenna was dazed. Callie had left Dean?

''He's devastated,'' Katie told her. ''He's a mess.''

''Where is he? And where's Callie gone?''

''Home. Callie, I mean. Back to America. Dean spent the night at the flat with me. I'm worried about him, Jenna. Can you help?''

''What do you want me to do?''

''Jason and I are having dinner at his parents' place tonight. It's all arranged and I don't want to let him down, but I hate the thought of Dean going home to that empty house after work.''

''Don't worry, Katie,'' Jenna said immediately. ''I'll see he isn't alone.''

She was waiting outside his place when Dean turned up. He looked at her dully, without surprise. ''Katie told you,'' he said.

''Yes.'' Jenna touched his arm. ''I'm so sorry.''

He opened the door, taking it for granted she'd come in. He looked worn and pale, his mouth set in a stubborn line. ''It's nice of you to come, but I don't need a nursemaid.''

''I'm not a nursemaid, I'm a friend. And your sister-in-law. Next best thing to a sister.''

He managed a wan smile. "Can I make you a drink? I'm heading for the whiskey myself."

Jenna forbore to ask him if that was wise. If he wanted to drown his sorrows, she guessed he was entitled.

"Gin and lemon?" he asked her, and she nodded.

She sat on the sofa while Dean paced the sitting room, glancing out the window to the street, picking up books and ornaments and putting them down again as if he didn't know what to do with himself between gulping at his drink.

"Do you want to talk about it?" she asked quietly.

A photograph of Callie, laughing into the camera, stood on top of a bookcase. Dean picked it up and stared down at it. "Am I an insensitive sod, Jenna? Should I have noticed she was unhappy?"

"She wasn't unhappy all the time."

He brightened a bit. "She wasn't, was she? I mean, she can't have been pretending every time we…" Then he looked grim again. "But it was a tug-of-war between me and her old life. And I lost."

"Did you fight over it?"

He shook his head. "No. We cried over it." He looked embarrassed and buried his nose in the whiskey glass. "I took her to the airport," he said, lowering the glass and staring moodily into it. "Still hoping she'd change her mind."

When Jenna returned to the apartment, Marcus was on the sofa, a stack of papers on the coffee table before him, a pen in his hand and an empty shot glass at his elbow. He wore his business shirt but had unbuttoned the collar and rolled up the sleeves.

His gaze was alert and questioning. "You look whacked," he said. "Do you need a drink?"

"I've had enough to drink, thanks."

Marcus's brows went up. "Is that so?"

Not as much as Dean, whom she'd left curled up on the sofa where he'd finally collapsed. She'd removed his shoes and thrown a light blanket over him before leaving.

"A couple of glasses of gin and lemon," she explained, "with Dean. You got my message?" She'd left a message on the answering machine to say where she was, but with Dean listening in she hadn't gone into detail about why.

"How is Dean—and Callie? Is something wrong?"

"She's gone," Jenna told him. "Back to America."

His stillness was almost frightening. He might have been turned to stone, not even blinking as his darkened eyes bored into hers. "She's left him?"

"She was homesick. More than Dean ever realized, I think. He's terribly upset, and Katie was meeting Jason's parents tonight."

Marcus was scrutinizing her face. "So you went to comfort him."

"He needed someone." Jenna's eyes filled with tears. She was tired and wrung out after being supportive and sympathetic for hours while Dean talked and cried and finally drank himself into temporary oblivion. His shock and bewilderment and self-blame had made her own heart ache.

She wiped at the tears with her hand. Marcus didn't move, so she said, "I'm going to bed."

In the bathroom she splashed cold water on her

eyes and blew her nose. Poor Dean. And poor Callie. She felt wretchedly sorry for them both.

She was in the bedroom when the sound of breaking glass made her start. Marcus must have dropped something. She put on a silky nightgown and got into bed. She desperately wanted Marcus beside her, his warm, hard body close to hers. She wanted to make love to him, to feel his mouth on her lips and her body, his thighs strong and muscular between her own.

But by the time he slid into the bed beside her she had long been claimed by sleep.

In the morning she was lethargic and depressed. Marcus too seemed almost morose.

There was something wrapped in newspaper on the counter, and when Jenna picked it up Marcus said quickly, "Careful—I should have put that in the bin."

She looked at him.

"I...dropped a glass last night," he explained.

Dimly she recalled hearing the crash.

Marcus was putting folders into his briefcase when the phone rang and he handed the receiver to Jenna.

"How was he?" Katie asked.

"Sleeping like a baby when I left," Jenna reported. "Pretty cut up, actually. He'd had a lot of whiskey."

Marcus stopped by her and gave her a cool kiss on her cheek. He spoke into the receiver. "Jenna has to go to work, Katie. Why don't you phone Dean?"

"I have, and he's not answering," Katie said crossly.

Marcus had straightened. "What did she say?"

"He's not answering his phone," Jenna relayed. To Katie she said, "He's probably gone to the office."

"Or he's sleeping off the hangover," Marcus suggested.

Katie said, "Maybe I should go and see if he's all right. I'll be late for work, but—"

"Hang on." Jenna put her hand over the receiver and caught at Marcus's sleeve as he made to leave. She and Katie both had bosses to placate if they were late; he didn't. He *was* the boss. "Could you go round by Dean's place," she pleaded, "and make sure he's okay?"

Marcus frowned. "He isn't a child. And he's not the type to top himself over a broken love affair."

"Katie's worried."

He took the phone from her. "Katie? I'll call in and see Dean before I go to the office, okay? Though it's my guess he'd rather be left alone.... Yes, I'll let you know if I think he needs you. Yes...promise."

Hanging up, he gave Jenna an exasperated look. "Personally I should think the last thing he wants is a lot of women fussing over him."

She was home earlier than Marcus that evening, making dinner as he arrived.

"I saw Dean," he told her. "He's sorry for himself and he had a hell of a head, but he went to work. He'll get over it."

Jenna had to remind herself that Marcus wasn't as callous as he sounded. He might be less openly emotional than the twins, but he was fond of them. When his family was in trouble he always came through for them.

She set the table in the dining area in the living room and turned on the light. As she was returning to the kitchen, a glint of something bright made her bend down, finding a tiny sliver of glass. Picking it up cautiously, she noticed that the door was scratched, a new scar on the lower part of it marring the varnish. For a second or two she studied it, puzzled.

She recalled that Marcus had dropped a glass last night—so he'd said.

But if he'd dropped it on the carpet in the living room, it wouldn't have broken. And if he'd been in the kitchen she would hardly have heard it so clearly from the bedroom.

Surely he couldn't have *thrown* it at the door? That would have been most unlike him. And why would he do such a thing?

A hissing noise and a pungent smell from the stove reminded her she'd left a pot of vegetables on high. She rushed to save it, and by the time she'd disposed of the glass, rescued the vegetables and cleaned up the mess they'd made, Marcus had emerged from the bedroom.

Halfway through the meal she remembered. "Where did you drop that glass?"

"What glass?"

"You said you dropped a glass last night."

"Is it important?" He picked up the one in front of him and took a sip before putting it down again. "I'm sorry if it was a special one."

"No, but…"

"You can always buy more," he said.

"Yes, I know." He set no limit on her spending, although she still used her own money to buy her clothes and cosmetics. "It's not that. I just wondered how you broke it. There's a mark on the door."

Marcus frowned. "Is there? Where?"

She pointed. "It's not very obvious, but…"

"Never mind," he interrupted. "We can get it fixed."

That wasn't the point, but he said, "Have you heard from your mother lately? She promised to send a newspaper article she thought would interest me."

Not wanting to nag, or make a mountain out of what was surely not more than a molehill, Jenna let the subject of the broken glass die.

Three days later a handyman fixed the door and it looked as good as new.

Over the following weeks Katie and Jenna did their best to make sure Dean didn't have too much time to brood. Not the kind to slink off and lick his wounds in private, he accepted invitations and hid his feelings behind a show of his usual effervescence.

Jenna asked him round for dinner, along with Katie and a few other friends. She and Katie asked him to take them to a craft show out of town that Marcus didn't want to attend, and Katie persuaded him to drive her to their parents' place for a Sunday lunch. When Marcus had a boat again for a weekend, Jenna suggested that they invite Dean along. Shrugging, Marcus agreed. "If you think it's a good idea."

"He needs to be kept occupied," she answered. "And he likes sailing. We can tell him we need an extra pair of hands."

Maybe he knew they didn't, but Dean came along anyway, and she thought he enjoyed himself. She took careful note so that she could report back to his sister, who she knew would call the next day to ask how he had seemed.

"It will take time," Jenna warned her. "We can't expect too much too soon."

"There's a pop concert in the Domain next Saturday," Katie said. "We'll take him to that."

They did, although Marcus refused to accompany them. "Not my favorite group," he said. "I didn't think it was yours, either."

It wasn't, but Katie seemed to take it for granted that she would go, as she assumed that if she wasn't available to entertain and distract Dean, Jenna would be.

Sometimes Jenna noticed the droop of his shoulders, or caught him in an unguarded moment, his mouth turned down and his eyes distracted, and a little reflection of his hurt tugged at her heart. Then he'd look up and smile at her, and she'd smile back, not letting on that she knew his casual, laid-back air hid very real pain.

Katie knew it too. She worried that Dean had lost weight, that he wasn't eating properly. She wondered aloud if she should get in touch with Callie and tell her how much Dean missed her, that he still loved her.

"For God's sake," Marcus said irritably, strolling into the living room one day as Jenna was lending a sympathetic ear to his sister, "let the guy sort himself out in his own way. He won't thank you for trying to solve his problems."

"We just want to help him," Katie said. "Don't you?"

"I don't see there's much we can do. If he really wants Callie—"

"Of course he wants her!" Katie was shocked. "He loves her!"

"Then why isn't he on a plane to the States?" Marcus asked bluntly.

"It's not that simple. He's got a job here to hold down," Katie protested. "He can't work in the States without a permit and Callie—"

"It seems to me that two people who really love each other should be able to work out some kind of compromise."

"Like what?" Katie challenged.

"Like making a commitment to Callie spending time with her family a couple of times a year. Like marrying her and then looking for work in the States. Like putting himself out to make her so happy with him she won't miss her own people as much."

Katie sniffed. "It's easy for you to say. You have plenty of money."

"Dean knows he only has to ask and he can have a loan anytime. And I didn't say it would be easy. Loving someone was never meant to be easy. Real love demands sacrifice and pain and damned hard decisions. It's gut-wrenching and soul destroying, and there are times when it seems more than a man can take. But you'll do anything, put up with anything just to be near the person you love, even if it hurts like hell. And you'll even give *that* up if necessary to give her her heart's desire."

Jenna stared at him, and Katie was openmouthed too.

Marcus clamped his lips into a line, and color appeared on his cheekbones. "If he doesn't love her that way," he said, "then he doesn't deserve her."

After he'd left the room, Katie looked at Jenna and lifted her brows interrogatively.

Jenna shook her head, as bewildered as his sister, and perturbed. She had never heard Marcus speak with such passion. Who was the woman who had inspired it? Her hands unconsciously curled in her lap. Her back went rigid. A fierce flame of jealousy ignited inside her.

Marcus had never pretended he felt anything that strong about her. She couldn't reproach him for deceiving her, because he hadn't.

Chapter Ten

Jenna broached the subject obliquely with Katie. "I know Marcus had girlfriends before me," she said, as they washed up after the family had come to dinner one night. "Was he serious about any of them?"

"Hard to say," Katie answered thoughtfully. "He didn't bring them home often, and you know Marcus—he's always played his cards close to his chest, especially about his personal life. Still," she added cheerfully, "I'm sure you've nothing to worry about. I shouldn't think any of them are likely to crawl out of the woodwork now, and if they did, he wouldn't look at them. He's much too...well, honorable, and apart from that, he loves you."

"I know," Jenna hastened to agree, taking the latter part of her friend's assurance with her customary grain of salt.

"Is there a problem?" Katie asked.

"No." Jenna shook her head. "Except one of his

friends said...she thought someone had hurt him.''
She remembered his assurance when they were in his
father's orchid house that the pain would pass, she'd
get over it. Had it passed for him? Had he really got
over his mystery lover?

Katie said, ''Everyone's been hurt at some time. I
shouldn't think my big brother is the type to let any
woman blight his life...although,'' she added
thoughtfully, ''still waters run deep and all that.
Maybe he just wouldn't admit it. You probably understand him better than any of us.''

''Because I'm his wife?''

''Well, that, of course,'' Katie agreed. ''But you
and Marcus are alike in so many ways. I guess that's
why you fell for each other.''

Jenna blinked.

''Sort of enclosed and intense. Not like Dean and
me. We're all on the surface. Everyone knows when
we're happy. And when we want to hide something,
we just apply another glossy coat that looks like the
same thing to most people. I mean, look at him now.''

Jenna nodded. She and Katie knew Dean was covering up, and sometimes he let the cheerful mask slip
with them, but outsiders would be fooled by his de-
terminedly cheerful, outgoing manner. They would
think his broken engagement was a minor glitch in a
carefree life.

Katie said, ''I can tell with Dean. But I never know
what Marcus is thinking, even though he's my
brother. And you're more like him than I ever realized.... I thought that we knew all about each other,
though you don't blab about everything to me the way

I do to you. I know you have more secrets than I do. But I never suspected you had a thing for Marcus.''

''Maybe,'' Jenna said, thanking her stars that she'd never felt it necessary to tell Katie she'd been in love with Dean, ''I didn't know it myself. I was so accustomed to thinking of Marcus as a surrogate big brother.''

Katie nodded wisely. ''I guess that's why. And he was waiting for you to grow up.''

''That's what he said,'' Jenna admitted dryly. ''Several times.'' Sometimes she wondered if even now he regarded her as truly grown-up.

It was true that Marcus seldom showed his feelings openly. She was pretty sure that if she asked him point-blank who the woman was, he would deny there had ever been any such person. It was all in the past anyway, and although she was his wife, it didn't seem she had any right to probe into his previous love life.

She couldn't help noticing that he seemed to be preoccupied these days. Sometimes she found him staring at her frowningly, seeming deep in thought, but if she queried him he'd say, ''Sorry, I was thinking about something else.''

Maybe, Jenna deduced, he was as worried about Dean as she and Katie, although he seldom mentioned the subject. One Sunday she came upon him standing idly at the sitting room window, hands in his pockets and his shoulders uncharacteristically hunched.

''Marcus?'' She crossed the room and hooked her hand into his arm. ''Are you thinking about Dean?''

In profile his face looked hard and shuttered. It was a moment before he turned to her, pulling free. His eyes seemed oddly unseeing. "You could say so. Although you and Katie do enough of that for all of us."

"You're in a bad mood," she said. "Do you have business worries?" He never talked much about his business, but lately he'd spent a lot more time at the office than previously.

"Business is booming," he answered. Catching her hand in his, he looked down at it, then bent his head and dropped a kiss on the back. "I'm just a moody critter." He gave her a slightly twisted smile. But his eyes didn't match it.

"No, you're not," Jenna argued, then hesitated. "You would tell me if something was wrong, wouldn't you?"

He didn't answer at once. "That would depend on what it was. If there was nothing you could do about it, then very likely not."

"But we're married!" Didn't that mean they should share their troubles? Support each other in adversity?

"Yes," he agreed in a strange tone. "We're married. We've burned our boats, haven't we?"

"For better or worse," she agreed. His phrasing had seemed a little odd, though. She studied him seriously. "I really did mean that, Marcus." And she knew *he* had. Marcus would never go back on his solemn vows. "You're not sorry, are you?" she asked anxiously. He had seemed so sure, overriding her misgivings.

"How could I be sorry? Are you?"

Jenna vehemently shook her head. "Of course not. You're a wonderful husband." She reached up to give him a light kiss, but as her lips touched his he hauled her closer into his arms and kissed her properly, leaving her breathless.

When their mouths parted, he said, "Let's go to bed."

After the barest hesitation Jenna said, "I can't. I'm sorry, I promised Katie. We're going over to Dean's this afternoon. I came to ask if I could have the car. You did say you had paperwork to do."

"So I did." He swung both her hands in his. "I could do it tonight." His brows rose interrogatively.

Regretfully Jenna shook her head. "If I don't go, Katie will have to get a bus, and you know how they are on Sundays."

"Damn my family!" he said quite forcefully. "I think you spend more time with them than you do with me."

Not true, and it wasn't like him to exaggerate. "I owe them a lot."

"You don't owe any of us anything!" Marcus told her. "Except possibly my mother."

"Well…anyway, I promised," Jenna reiterated.

He looked at her rather keenly. "You never go back on a promise, do you, Jenna?"

"Not if I can help it. Neither do you."

He still held her hands. She felt his grip tighten slightly. "You didn't marry me because you felt you owed the family, did you?"

Astonished, Jenna said, "No!" Clumsily, because his probing eyes made her feel self-conscious, she added, "I married you because you asked me and…and I wanted to. And you were right—I…I do love you, Marcus."

He dropped her hands and cupped her face with his. "Thank you." His lips brushed against hers and lingered for a moment. "I'm counting on that."

When she came home later, he was deep in papers and using his laptop computer. He looked up rather remotely when she stopped to say hello, then his eyes focused on her and he said, "You look tired. What have you been doing?"

"Cleaning," she said. "It's amazing how quickly a place can get quite filthy. Katie told Dean he's living in a pigsty. It was only a slight exaggeration."

Marcus frowned. "Why doesn't he do his own cleaning?"

"I think he's too depressed to see the point of it. He did help once we got going."

"You two spoil him."

"He's going through a bad time."

"We all go through bad times. He'll work it out if he's left alone."

"That might be your way of coping," she pointed out, "but it isn't Dean's."

"Maybe," Marcus conceded. "You think I'm a heartless sod, don't you?"

"I know you're not. But you're stronger than Dean. I don't think you understand him the way…"

"The way you do?" Marcus supplied. Then he gave a short, harsh laugh. "You don't seem to have understood him as well as you thought, in the past."

Jenna flushed painfully, disconcerted at the oblique reference. It wasn't like Marcus to be callous. "I was going to say," she continued with dignity, "the way Katie does."

"Really?" He was regarding her with something

akin to disbelief. ''And does Katie think he needs you as well as her to hold his hand?''

''Well, you seem to have been too busy to do it!'' Jenna flashed, not that she could imagine Marcus holding his brother's hand exactly, but in the last few weeks he'd certainly been unavailable to his family on a number of occasions, pleading pressure of work. ''You could at least show you care!''

To her surprise he looked uncomfortable for a moment, before he came back with, ''Dean knows I care. Surely he doesn't need my shoulder to cry on too.''

''What have you been so busy with lately, anyway? I've hardly seen you myself.''

Marcus asked, ''Do you miss me? Most of the time you're either with Dean or discussing his troubles with Katie.''

Jenna gulped. Maybe it seemed that way to him. ''That isn't true,'' she defended herself. ''If you were home more you'd know.''

He gazed at her. ''Point taken,'' he said slowly. ''I'm sorry if you've been feeling neglected.''

''I didn't say that! I know you have a business to run.''

''I also have a marriage to protect.'' He seemed to be looking at her rather carefully. ''Burying my head in the sand—or work—isn't going to do any good, is it?''

Not sure what he meant, Jenna said, ''Our marriage isn't in any danger, Marcus. Just because I've been spending time with Dean...'' Surely he wasn't jealous? ''I mean, that's not an issue.''

''I'm glad to hear it.'' For a moment he seemed to be contemplating her, his eyes dark and strangely cool, almost analytical. Then he said abruptly, "You'd better go to bed. It'll be a while before I'm finished up here."

She went to bed and lay awake for a while, but soon tiredness overcame her. When Marcus came to join her she didn't wake, and when she woke in the morning the only evidence that he had shared their bed that night was the flung-back blankets and the indentation of his head on the pillow beside her.

He did spend more time at home after that night, yet paradoxically it seemed to Jenna that she and Marcus were growing further and further apart.

There was nothing she could put her finger on, no moment when things began to go wrong, no specific happening she could have cited. Sex was as sizzling as ever but it happened less often, and at other times Marcus appeared increasingly distant and almost abstracted.

Jenna told herself it was just that the honeymoon period of their marriage was over, but she sometimes thought wistfully that it had been awfully short.

She tried not to hope too much about the chances of having a baby, and when the calendar showed she was overdue she said nothing to Marcus. Better to wait until she could be sure.

Katie guessed first. She and Jenna were at her parents' house, putting the finishing touches to a family dinner celebrating Mrs. Crossan's birthday, when Jenna laid down the forcing bag she was using to pipe cream around a trifle and excused herself to rush to the bathroom.

When she came back Katie looked up from slicing

strawberries to add to the trifle, and said, "You're pregnant, aren't you?"

Jenna explained, "It's too early yet to be definite, and I haven't even said anything to Marcus. Don't tell anyone, will you?"

"I won't say a word," Katie promised. "You don't think Marcus suspects? It must be difficult keeping it a secret from him."

"I'm trying to for now." If she really was pregnant she wanted to surprise him, hoping the news would bring them closer again. She felt a faint shadow cross her face and banished it with an effort.

"He's bound to find out sooner or later."

"I'll tell him, of course, at the right time."

Thinking she heard a step in the hallway outside the kitchen, she turned her head, but there was no one there.

When it was time to drive home, Marcus handed Jenna the keys. "I've had a few glasses of wine," he said.

She had noticed him drinking more tonight than usual and had supposed that, as he was with his family and knew she wouldn't be overindulging, he'd thought it was safe to do so.

He leaned back in his seat and closed his eyes, and she wondered if he'd gone to sleep, but when she turned into their garage he was awake and alert, climbing out to open her door for her.

She brushed against him as she got out, the car key in her hand, and went toward the elevator.

When Marcus unlocked the door to their apartment the passageway inside was dark, and she groped for the light switch, encountering his hand doing the same.

His fingers curled around hers, and the light remained off. In the darkness he said her name and pulled her toward him. The car key dropped to the floor.

Startled, she put a hand to his chest, her palm against the body-warmed cotton of his shirt. She could smell his male scent, fresh and with an earthy hint of musk, and automatically she raised her face. Dimly she could just see his, a blacker outline against the blackness of the night.

Marcus found her mouth in a kiss that surprised her by its instant, primitive passion. With no preliminary at all he was kissing her deeply, thoroughly, almost aggressively.

She'd thought the unusual amount of wine had made him lethargic, but there was nothing lethargic about this. For several seconds she remained passive, trying to readjust to his mood after she had fully expected he would fall into bed and go straight to sleep.

His arms went about her waist, so tightly she could hardly breathe, her body a taut curving bow. She had to clutch his shoulders to keep her balance, then wound her arms about his neck.

She was tired, but her body was waking to the needs of his, her heart beginning a slow pounding while an answering passion stirred, sending a hot tremor through her.

He crowded her against the wall, and his hands shaped her breasts in an almost rough caress that brought them tinglingly to life. His hands tugged at the front of her dress and she was afraid he would tear it, but his mouth stifled her protest. Then he found the zip at the back and opened it with one decisive movement, hauled it off her shoulders and undid her bra.

Grabbing both garments, he finally released her mouth as he pulled them away from her.

"Marcus!" she gasped. "Be careful—"

He hoisted her into his arms and carried her the few steps to the bedroom, kicking the door shut before he lowered her to the bed.

She heard him strip off his clothes, and was still getting her breath when he lay beside her and quickly took off the rest of hers. "Marcus?" she said, nervous in the face of this silent, ruthless seduction.

"Shut up," he said, shocking her.

Suddenly she was afraid. Ridiculous, she assured herself. Drink had blunted his usual finesse, but Marcus would never hurt her, he would never force her. She trusted him utterly.

Nevertheless she was rigid when he took her in his arms. And he must have noticed. Although more than ready, he checked himself, held her while he took several deep breaths, and his touch gentled.

He didn't speak again, but his mouth brushed her temple, her cheek, the hollow of her throat, between her breasts, in soft, butterfly kisses. His hands shaped the contours of her body, lightly and knowingly, skimming over rib cage and hip and thigh, and his fingers teased the most sensitive erogenous spots.

Disturbingly, frustratingly, he kissed her everywhere except her mouth, until she felt as if a lambent fire was licking over her entire body, and she couldn't help begging at last, almost sobbing the words, "Marcus—please kiss me!"

He obliged with a soul-shattering, mind-obliterating kiss that was perfect in its blend of tenderness and passion, and she responded with her heart and soul. They were still kissing when he turned on his back and guided her onto his throbbing hardness.

She closed about him with a sigh of relief, moving ecstatically with him, until all too soon the marvelous release of tension took her over, and she was still whimpering with pleasure when Marcus turned again, thrusting deeply into her, bringing her to another pinnacle of passion, that became more intense when she knew he was there too. And just when she thought it was over she had to clutch at his shoulders again, heard his triumphant little laugh, and he watched her bite her lip as he helped her yet again over the brink.

She loved him. In every way, she loved him. The revelation blinded her.

Minutes later she opened her eyes to find him leaning on one elbow, still watching her. A high moon let white light into the room, but all she could see of his face was the sheen of his eyes.

"Marcus…"

He put his fingers over her mouth. "Don't talk. Not tonight."

Jenna didn't argue. She felt pleasantly exhausted—sated. She'd almost been going to mention the possible baby, but if she was wrong, she didn't want to disappoint him as well as herself.

In the morning she woke to find him watching her again, his expression brooding.

"You haven't been there like that all night, have you?" she asked him.

"No. Are you all right?"

"Of course."

"I'm sorry if I was a bit…insensitive last night."

"You weren't." She looked at him curiously. "You don't usually drink that much."

His eyes were suddenly bleak. "No I don't. And I won't again."

"I'm not complaining, Marcus," she said carefully. If anything, the episode had reassured her that no matter how importunate his own feelings, he would always take time and trouble to ensure that she enjoyed lovemaking too. He was never selfish.

"No," he said, and she was puzzled at the harshness of his voice. "You never complain, do you? A perfect wife."

Her brow knitted. "I'm not perfect… What have I done to annoy you?"

"What makes you think that?" he countered. "I just paid you a compliment."

Had he? It had sounded strangely like an accusation. But before she could challenge him on it, Marcus was out of the bed and shutting himself in the bathroom.

She must have imagined the rasping note in his voice, or perhaps the residue of sleep had produced it. Over the next few days he was, if anything, more loving—if that was the word for his slightly detached consideration and concern, and the watchfulness that sometimes unsettled her. She wondered if he had a suspicion she was pregnant.

Studying her while she cautiously nibbled on a

piece of toast one morning, he said abruptly, "Are you losing weight?"

"No!" She had no idea if she was, but the suggestion startled her. Today she'd woken feeling queasy, but most of the time she was fine. She hadn't had to dash to a bathroom after that one time at the Crossans'. Since then she'd kept away from rich foods and averted her eyes when she passed a bakery.

Hastily she took a bite of her toast and swallowed it.

"You should have a decent breakfast," Marcus said. "Toast and juice is hardly a meal." He had two poached eggs on his plate. "Have one of my eggs."

"No!" Jenna said. "I'm not used to a big breakfast. It would only make me feel...bloated." Actually she was sure it would make her feel sick. She could feel herself going pale already.

He made a little huffing sound of derision and looked over what he could see of her figure across the breakfast table. She saw a frown appear between his dark brows, and suddenly his eyes met hers.

"Do you have any plans for the weekend?" she asked quickly.

"I meant to tell you, Ted and Angela invited us to join them on their yacht. They're leaving on Friday night."

"Oh...um..." Sailing on possibly choppy waters didn't appeal right now. Her stomach churned just thinking about it. She had made a doctor's appointment for Friday after work. "The whole weekend?" she queried.

"Is it a problem?"

Jenna swallowed down disappointment. Supposing

the doctor confirmed the test she'd already secretly carried out, another couple of days before telling Marcus would make no difference. He loved sailing—he had plans to have a boat built of their own. "Why don't you go anyway? Katie wants me to go to the women's book fair over the weekend. I sort of promised." Not quite true, but she had told Katie it looked interesting.

"You didn't mention it."

"You didn't mention the Travers' invitation, either. I'll phone Angela and explain. We don't have to do everything together, do we?"

He pushed away his empty plate and stood up. "Are you feeling smothered, Jenna?"

"What makes you say that?"

"Except for a Friday-night get-together with your workmates, you spend most of your time with either me or my family. Do we give you enough space?"

"I have all the space I need." She wondered if *he* did. Marcus was accustomed to being alone a lot, or at least not having a wife to make emotional demands on him. Maybe that was the reason he was determined to preserve a sort of distance between them. She'd been married to him for six months and yet she sometimes felt she didn't know him any better than she had before their wedding.

Sunday she would tell him about the baby. When he was relaxed after a weekend sailing and they were alone for the evening, without any distractions or other commitments. If she was right.

She was, the doctor confirmed when she saw him on Friday, and the news made her feel giddy. Afraid to trust her own suspicion, or even the over-the-counter test despite its claims of accuracy, she had been holding in her emotions. Now she was dying to tell the world—but especially Marcus.

In the bathroom at home the atmosphere was slightly steamy, and a sleeve of Marcus's business shirt hung from the laundry basket, but he'd gone. She knew he'd planned on leaving the office early, and he must have taken a quick shower and changed before Ted and Angela picked him up to go to the marina. He'd left the car with her for the weekend so she and Katie could drive to the fair.

Stupid to be so disappointed. She'd had no intention of blurting out her secret right now. It would have been totally the wrong time. And Sunday was only forty-eight hours away.

At the book fair Jenna found her attention frequently wandering. While her face gave every appearance of absorption in the excellent presentations, her mind persisted in drawing pictures of a child with Marcus's dark hair and intent gray eyes—a solemn little boy or a winsome girl.

Katie had to nudge her when the panel discussion they'd attended was over. "Lunch," she said. "What do you fancy?"

"Nothing. Maybe a bread roll."

Katie eyed her suspiciously. "Have you seen a doctor yet?"

Jenna tried not to look smug. "I can't say anything until I've talked to Marcus."

Katie gave a squeak of excitement. "Haven't you *told* him?"

"I only found out for sure yesterday, and he's away for the weekend."

Katie hugged her. "Aren't you excited?"

Jenna allowed herself a smile. "I'm trying not to show it." She was saving it for the moment she told Marcus.

"I'm going to be an auntie to my best friend's baby!" Katie hugged her again. "Oh, this is great!"

She fussed over Jenna for the rest of the day, making sure she ate food that wouldn't upset a delicate-feeling stomach, and insisting that they arrive early for every event so that Jenna was assured of a comfortable seat.

On Sunday morning when Jenna got into the car and turned the key, nothing happened. After a few frustrating minutes she realized that the interior light was burning, although she didn't recall switching it on. The battery must have drained overnight.

Katie was waiting to be picked up. Jenna returned inside and phoned her.

"Dean's here," Katie informed her. "He can take us. We'll collect you on the way."

On their arrival at the venue, Dean looked interestedly at one of the posters outside. "I read that book," he said, indicating the cover of an account of a woman climber's expedition in the Himalayas.

"She's speaking this morning," Katie informed him. "Why don't you buy a ticket and come in?"

"With all those women?"

It took a bit more persuasion, but eventually he said, "Well, I don't have anything better to do, I guess."

As he was buying a ticket, Jenna said sadly to his sister, "He's still hurting, isn't he?"

Katie agreed. "Callie phoned him last week."

"She did? Why?"

Katie shrugged. "Just to see how he was, she said."

"She still cares."

"I guess. But if she's not coming back it might be better if she didn't get his hopes up."

Surprisingly, Dean stayed for the day and after a talk by a psychologist about male-female relationships, he even bought a copy of her book.

Afterward he dropped off his sister first. When they arrived at Jenna's apartment he took a jumper lead from his car and started the dead battery, accepting Jenna's offer of coffee when he'd finished. She had the feeling he didn't want to go home. He'd spent the previous night at Katie's after dropping in for a nightcap.

They chatted for a while, and watched the first part of the TV news before Dean got up to go. He looked at her keenly, his head cocked. "Are you expecting?"

"Did Katie give me away?"

"She was just sort of watching you and waiting on you. That's not like her."

"I still have to tell Marcus."

Dean grinned. "He'll be chuffed." The grin faded and became a little twisted. "I'm jealous."

"Oh, Dean!" She put her arms about him in a comforting hug. "Things will work out."

He hugged her back, burying his face against her hair. "She phoned me—Callie," he said in muffled tones.

"I know," Jenna said. "Have you thought about going to see her?"

Dean lifted his head. "I think about nothing else. It's tearing me in two. I want to get on a plane tomorrow—tonight—and grab her and make her marry me. I think she'd do it too. But in another three months, or six months or a year, maybe she'd find she couldn't hack it after all."

Jenna supposed that was a point. "You're sure you couldn't find a job over there?"

"Not legally, unless we're married."

"So…couldn't you do that?"

He frowned distractedly. "The trouble is, it feels like blackmail to persuade her to marry me so I can work in America."

"Even though it's because you love her and want to be with her?"

"See, I already put the heat on to persuade her to come home with me, but she wouldn't commit herself to marriage. Being engaged was a sort of compromise. I can't pressure her again." His voice shook. "But I love her so much."

The misery in his face wrung her heart, and she put one hand to his cheek. "I hate to see you hurting like this."

"Some mistakes you just have to live with, because trying to fix them will only make things worse."

"Could it be worse?" Jenna asked as his hold on her loosened. "Two people who love each other so much should be together! There must be a way…"

"It isn't that easy. How would *you* feel," Dean said, "if I asked you to choose between your family and the man you love?"

Jenna hadn't had the kind of family that Callie did, but she'd wanted one so badly it didn't take much imagination. She said, "I think I'd feel as though I'd lost a leg and an arm." But if the unthinkable happened, of course she would choose Marcus. There was no doubt in her mind.

A movement caught from the corner of her eye made her turn her head, and she was startled to see Marcus standing in the doorway.

Dean was taken by surprise too. He dropped his arms and ran a hand over his hair as though embarrassed. Jenna thought that surreptitiously he was also wiping at a wayward tear.

Understanding that he didn't want his brother to see him crying, she took a step toward Marcus in an instinctive shielding movement and put a smile on her mouth. "We didn't hear you come in," she said. The TV still murmuring in the background must have covered the sound of his entry. "I didn't expect you so early."

"Apparently not." He looked grim and cold.

"Hi, Marc," Dean said with false brightness just behind her. "How was the fishing?"

Marcus flicked him a glance. "What are you doing here?"

Quelling a stupidly alarmed flutter in her throat, Jenna explained, "Dean drove me home. The car was dead this morning—a flat battery."

"There was nothing wrong with the battery when I drove it on Friday."

"Somehow I left the interior light on. It's all right now. Dean fixed it and I invited him for coffee."

Silly. She had never found it necessary to give

Marcus chapter and verse when she invited anyone in, and Dean was family, for heaven's sake!

"I was just on my way." Dean sounded as nervous as she felt. He made toward the door that Marcus was still blocking, and hesitated in front of his brother.

Marcus seemed to be inspecting him. Then he stood aside, his attention concentrated on Jenna.

"Well…" Dean looked around rather helplessly. "See you. Thanks for the coffee, Jenna."

"Thank you," she said, "for the car and everything." One of them should see him out, but something kept her rooted where she stood, and Marcus certainly wasn't moving.

There was a tense silence as the outer door closed behind Dean.

"How long has he been here?" Marcus asked.

She blinked at him. "I don't know…about half an hour, I think, since fixing the car."

"Not the whole weekend?"

Her eyes widened in astonishment. "No. He came to the book fair today with Katie and me. Last night he was at her flat."

"And where were you last night?"

"Here, of course!" Incredulously she said, "Marcus—you're sounding like a suspicious husband!"

The idea was so ludicrous she couldn't help a small laugh.

"So I am," he said, and she thought he made a conscious effort to relax, his hands going into his pockets, although his eyes stayed watchful. "Are you telling me I don't have reason to be?"

Jenna gaped. "I told you, Dean gave Katie and me

a lift because the car wouldn't start. He came to the fair with us.''

"Doesn't sound like Dean's sort of thing," Marcus commented skeptically.

"Ask Katie if you don't believe me."

He was looking at her thoughtfully. Softly he said, "Katie would back up her twin in anything he said. You too. The three of you always stuck together."

"We're not kids now!"

"No," Marcus said, still in that soft tone of deadly mockery. "That's exactly my point."

Chapter Eleven

Jenna's head buzzed. "I don't believe this!" she gasped. The quarrel had blown up so unexpectedly, wrecking her plans for a quiet, loving evening, the revelation of a happy secret. "You're jealous!"

"Damn right I am," Marcus agreed calmly, the chill in his eyes, the rigid planes of his face, belying his tone.

"You've always been jealous!" she realized. This was about more than finding her exchanging an innocent hug with his brother.

It went right back to their childhood, when she and the twins had been nearly inseparable and Marcus, the big brother, was almost one of "them"—the adults. Outside the tight little circle of three.

Surprisingly, a line of color darkened his cheekbones. His jaw jutted. "I have a right now," he said.

A right to what? "To accuse me? Just what *are* you accusing me of, Marcus?" She glared at him, her own cheeks hot, her eyes ablaze.

He looked back at her, and she met his gaze un-
flinchingly. "What do you think I've done?" she
challenged him. "Spent the weekend in bed with
Dean? *Our* bed?" She took a shaky breath. "Do you
really believe that?"

The hint of color disappeared from his face, leaving
it drained and white. "No," he said, as if the word
was forced out between stiff lips. One hand rubbed
at his forehead, and he closed his eyes. For an instant
she thought he swayed where he stood. "No," he
repeated, dropping his hand.

There was a bleak weariness in his eyes. "I apologize, Jenna. Excuse me—I need a shower, and all
my clothes smell of fish. I've put some snapper fillets
in the fridge. Ted's taken a couple of kahawai home
to smoke for us."

The sudden descent to banality did nothing to dis-
sipate the tension in the air. He had left the room
before Jenna got her breath back, and shortly afterward she heard the shower running. It ran for a long
time, and then the washing machine began its swish-
ing cycle.

Meantime, on legs that felt rubbery, she got herself
into the kitchen. Looking at the fillets that Marcus
had brought home, she wondered if she should change
the menu and cook them but decided they would keep
for tomorrow. Listlessly she put the finishing touches
to the celebration dinner she'd planned.

She'd made the chicken and cashew salad yesterday. It would taste better after a day of being per-
meated by its special dressing, needing only a garnish
of asparagus tips and toasted almond slices. Mechan-

ically she shredded lettuce, sliced tomatoes and avo-
cado and drizzled them with vinaigrette.

The candles in their crystal holders no longer
seemed appropriate, so she left them on the kitchen
counter, took the bottle of champagne from the fridge
and hid it in the pantry. She'd thought she might be
having a token sip or two in celebration, but the bruis-
ing encounter just now had killed her mood of joyous
anticipation, leaving her sick and scared.

Instead she put a half-used bottle of still white wine
by Marcus's place and set a glass there before pouring
some mineral water for herself.

She was putting the salad on the table when Marcus
came in, his hair damp and his lean cheeks freshly
shaved. He wore a white shirt, open at the throat, and
dark trousers. His eyes met hers only fleetingly, seemingly without expression, and then he went to the table. "It looks good."

An olive branch, perhaps.

Jenna pushed her hair back over one ear as she took
her chair. A shower and a change into something soft
and pretty had been on her original agenda, but time
had run out before Marcus arrived. The cotton shirt
and jeans she was wearing would have to do. She'd
probably lost the makeup she had put on earlier in
the day, but it didn't seem to matter now.

She picked up the salad servers and transferred a
few greens to her plate, followed by a spoonful of
chicken.

Marcus helped himself, then glanced at her much
smaller meal. "Surely you can eat more than that,"
he said.

Jenna didn't feel like eating anything at all. "I'll

have more if I want it.'' She dug her fork into the chicken and had to clench her teeth to make the food go down her throat and stay there. Trying to distract herself, she said, ''It's nice of Ted to smoke your fish for us.''

''He and Angela sent their love.''

Jenna nodded and made herself eat some more. ''The fishing must have been good. I could make a raw fish salad tomorrow,'' she said. ''Or would you prefer it cooked?''

''Whatever suits you.''

They were being stiffly polite, and Jenna could have wept. She finished what was on her plate and waited for him. ''Do you want any more?'' she asked.

He shoved his plate away, shaking his head, then said perfunctorily, ''It was delicious.''

She had the feeling that he hadn't tasted it any more than she had. ''There's passion fruit mousse. I'll get it.''

''I don't want any! Jenna—sit down.''

She sat, waiting for him to speak again. He had half a glass of wine in front of him, his hand restlessly twirling the stem. His gaze was fixed on the glass, and when he raised his eyes they were dark and steady. Almost gently, he said, ''Do you have something to tell me?''

He knew? Her breath caught, and she fought an urge to laugh hysterically. Everyone seemed able to guess without being told. Was it that obvious?

She tried to smile. This moment shouldn't be spoiled by a foolish spat. ''Yes, I do,'' she said, and watched his hand curl about the wineglass, so tightly she thought the fragile stem would surely snap. "I'm pregnant."

She thought the silence would never end; it was as though the whole world stood still. Then Marcus slowly, stiffly, uncurled his fingers. She thought he was going to reach out to her, but instead the hand tightened into a fist on the table, and he stared down at it. "Pregnant," he repeated, as if he'd never heard the word before. And then, "Oh, God!"

He shoved back his chair and got up, taking a few swift strides away from her, then turned to look at her again.

She didn't understand his reaction at all. "Aren't you pleased?"

He didn't look pleased. He looked as though he didn't know how he felt. Something flared in his eyes and died. "Are *you?*" he queried abruptly.

"I *was.*" But everything had gone wrong somehow. "I thought you wanted a family!"

"What I *want*—" he started in a furious undertone, and cut himself off there. When he spoke again his voice was perfectly even. "The point is, what do *you* want, Jenna? What do you really want most in all the world?"

A strange question to ask her now. She couldn't comprehend what had triggered it. "To have this baby," she said, "and give it a loving home, security, a happy childhood. Everything that parents want for their children."

"Everything you missed out on."

The comment caught her unawares. She had never thought of herself as neglected or missing out on a normal family life. Other children had solo mothers too. "It wasn't easy for my mother after my father died, and no one, until your mother, realized she was suffering from depression and could be helped with proper medical advice. But she loved me and did her best for me." Even though at times she had seemed faraway, scarcely noticing that she had a daughter at all. "And your family gave me a lot of leftover love."

"Leftover love?" he queried. "Is that what it felt like?"

She hesitated. "Spilled over, maybe. There was so much of it in your home. Your mother was always there for me, filling in the gaps. And the twins."

Marcus too had been there for her—he'd picked up the pieces of the heart she had broken over Dean, and made it whole.

Showing again that he could follow her thoughts, Marcus said, "And Dean?"

"That's over," she said. "You were right, I should have grown out of it much sooner than I did. I don't know what on earth you thought when you walked in tonight, but it wasn't...anything that need worry you." Gaining confidence, she told him, "You're my husband, the father of my child..." She paused then, but his expression didn't alter. "The man I intend to spend my life with, to the end of my life. I love you."

The acknowledgment set free something inside her, like a light bursting into life. She loved Marcus in every way—as a friend, a lover, the one person she wanted to be with forever. He was everything she'd ever dreamed of in a man, and more.

"Very noble," he said, the words like a slap in the face. "I'm touched."

Jenna winced, her temples throbbing. "Marcus—please!"

He said harshly, "This whole sorry mess is my fault. I should never have asked you to marry me."

That took her breath away, sent her heart plunging horribly.

She had just said she loved him, and he was rejecting her. Had she left her declaration too late? Or had he found that marriage to her wasn't enough to make him happy?

He had never said he was in love with her—not in the way that he'd been with that mysterious woman who had broken his heart. Their marriage had been founded on mutual liking and understanding and their lifelong knowledge of each other, combined with the sexual spark that had ignited into unexpected, white-hot flame.

Hurt and stirring resentment turned to panic and broke through her bewilderment. "What the hell do you mean by that?" she demanded, her voice rising. "I'm having your baby!"

"And that's my fault too," he said. "I should never have let you—"

"If you're having second thoughts, it's too late. I won't have an abortion, Marcus!"

His face paled again. "I wouldn't suggest it!"

"Then what are you suggesting? I thought this was what we both wanted."

He seemed to be considering that. "I was wrong," he said finally. "I told myself it would work, that I could make it work for both of us. I respect your integrity, Jenna, your determination to do the right thing. You keep telling me I have no need for jealousy, you intend to stick to your vows. But...I'm greedy.''

''Greedy?''

His smile was twisted. ''I hustled you into marrying me even though I'd promised myself—and you— that I wouldn't. I should have known that leftover love is never enough.''

And that was all he could give her? ''But then...'' she said, thinking aloud, ''that was all you expected of *me,* wasn't it?''

It wasn't his fault that she had fallen into deep, irrevocable love that he was unable to return.

She got up and blindly collected the plates and cutlery, rattling them together as he said remotely, ''True. It was all I asked for.''

Humiliation made her cheeks burn. ''Well, I'm sorry,'' she said, turning to flounce out of the room before he saw the tears stinging her eyes. ''I can't help it if you got more than you bargained for.''

Her vision blurred as she entered the kitchen, and when she made to put the plates on the counter she missed. With a crash and a clatter everything landed on the floor, a plate breaking in half, knives and forks scattering.

She dashed a hand across her eyes and was on her knees picking up the pieces when Marcus appeared in the doorway. ''What happened?''

''What do you think?'' she countered viciously. ''I dropped them.''

He bent and helped her, dumping the knives and forks and the undamaged plate into the sink. He even took the broken pieces of china from her and wrapped them in newspaper ready to be disposed of.

Not wanting to face him, Jenna turned to the sink and began washing up. There was a dishwasher but she tended to use it only when they were entertaining.

As she squirted detergent and began scrubbing at the remaining plate, she sensed Marcus standing just behind her. Her shoulders stiffened.

"I didn't mean to upset you," he said. "Your news caught me off guard, after…"

"I thought you already knew. Suspected, anyway. Everyone else did."

"Everyone?"

"Katie guessed, and I'm sure your mother knows although she didn't say anything. Even Dean…" She put the plate on the drying rack and fished in the water for the cutlery.

"Oh, yes. Dean. Is that what the big renunciation scene was all about?"

Jenna dropped the forks she held back into the water. She swung to face him. "What big renunciation scene?"

"You and Dean," Marcus said impatiently. "Deciding to live with your mistake."

It took a couple of seconds for the penny to drop. "Dean's mistake! Not mine."

"Has he finally realized what he missed, what he could have had if he hadn't been so blind all those years?"

"Were you drinking before you came home?" It was the only logical reason she could think of for his wild accusations and illogical conclusions.

"I'm stone-cold sober."

"Then what's the matter with you?" How could he have thought…?

He put a hand on either side of her, trapping her against the counter. "Nothing that hasn't been the matter ever since I married you—no, before that. Because I was stupid enough to fall in love with a girl who was so besotted with my brother she hardly even knew I existed. And even more stupidly, I deluded myself that marriage might bring about a miracle and make her love me back."

Jenna found she couldn't breathe, though her mouth had fallen open. "Me? You were in love with *me?*"

"From when I came back from overseas and found that the gawky kid I remembered had turned into a gorgeous young woman, and without losing any of the qualities I'd loved about her all my life." Witheringly he said, "You had no idea, did you?"

No, she hadn't. "B-but you never said...you never...you never did *anything!*"

Marcus scowled. "It was glaringly obvious that the only man you had eyes for was Dean. I did wonder sometimes if he felt the same way. It's hard to tell with Dean because he hides his deeper emotions, when he has them, under that party-boy manner of his. And it's not true that I never said anything."

She looked blank. "I don't remember anything that could have..."

"I dropped heavy hints, but you didn't want to hear them. Since it was plainly useless and would only embarrass you, I gave up. At one stage I had thought, The hell with it, I wanted you so much I would risk everything—your scorn, hurting Dean, causing a disruption in the family. And when he went overseas..."

Feeling her way, Jenna said, "So then, why didn't you—"

"That would have been dirty play, wouldn't it? Wait until he's out of the country and then make my move?"

Dimly she saw that he would have felt that. Anything sneaky or unfair would have been anathema to him.

"I was hamstrung," Marcus said. "I told myself there were other women who weren't fixated on their childhood sweethearts, women who wouldn't stir up a hornets' nest in the family, maybe split it apart. But I couldn't get you out of my mind, out of my heart."

"I had no idea!"

"I know that!" He looked at her somberly. "I've messed up your life, Jenna—yours and my brother's. And I'm truly sorry."

She clutched the front of his shirt. "Marcus—I love you!"

"Oh, sure. Much the same way you love my parents and Katie—with the added fillip of sex thrown in."

"No, you don't understand!" She tried to shake him, only succeeding in tearing a button off his shirt. It dropped and rolled on the floor. "Marcus—" The adolescent yearning she'd had for Dean was a trickling, shallow stream compared with the wide, deep ocean of her love for Marcus. "It's not the same, it's—"

"I don't need a sop, Jenna," he said roughly.

And then the phone rang.

"Leave it," she said, but her fingers released the fabric of his shirt as he turned away.

He lifted the receiver with a curt, "Yes?"

She saw him frown. "How much?" he asked. "Why?"

Listening intently, he looked over at her, his expression strange. There was a long pause, then he said, "Yes, I'm still here. Of course you can have it. I told you, anytime. I know I'll get it back, not that it matters. Come to the office tomorrow and I'll have it ready."

He put the receiver down and stood looking at it. "That was Dean," he said, raising his eyes. He looked stunned, puzzled. "Asking for a loan to fly to America."

"He's going to see Callie?"

"Apparently."

"Oh, good!"

"Is it?" He seemed dazed.

"Of course!" Jenna said impatiently. "Now do you believe me?" she beseeched him. "It isn't Dean I want, Marcus. It's you."

He passed a hand over his forehead. "Then what the hell were the two of you talking about when I came in?"

"Callie, of course!"

"Callie?"

"Dean didn't want to force her to choose between him and her family. But she phoned him this week, and I guess that gave him some hope. He loves her a lot."

"And you don't mind?"

How was she going to get through to him? *"I'm not in love with Dean!* I know I thought so, but that was just what you said—a childish daydream. *You* made me see that! Why won't you accept it?''

He said slowly, ''What were you and Katie talking about at my mother's birthday party?'' When she looked blank, he said, ''In the kitchen, before dinner.''

''Oh, then! She guessed I was pregnant. I made her promise not to tell because I wanted you to be the first to know. I had it confirmed on Friday but you'd arranged to go sailing and I didn't want it rushed so I thought...tonight, and I made a special dinner and chilled some champagne, but...'' She stopped there because her voice was trembling and she didn't want to burst into tears.

Marcus said, ''And after weeks of soul-searching, I had made up my mind that the only decent thing to do was tell you to go to Dean if he was the one you wanted, to set you free. Because it wasn't fair for me to hold you when he was no longer committed. Then you threw me a curve ball about the baby. And made that brave little speech about spending your life with me.''

''It wasn't brave!'' she objected. ''It was true.''

As if he hadn't heard, he continued, ''I wondered if you were trying to convince me or yourself. I'd just decided to set things right, and it was too late. A baby complicated matters even further. The implications were horrendous. And yet...I couldn't help being glad that you were carrying my child. Couldn't help wanting it, and wanting you. Even though you'd be trapped in a marriage you'd realized was a mistake.''

''Oh, Marcus! It wasn't a mistake! It was the best thing I ever did. What do I have to do to convince you *I love you!* Not as a brother—as a lover and a wonderful, sexy, incredibly giving husband.''

Hot tears spilled over and she gulped back a sob. The stress of the last couple of hours was telling, and the room began to sway.

Marcus made a low exclamation, swooping forward to catch her up in his arms.

''I don't want to be free!'' She wound her arms about his neck as he carried her into the bedroom. ''I want to be your wife and have your babies and love you forever!'' she told him passionately.

''Shh,'' he soothed, and deposited her on the wide bed, saying, ''Don't move.''

She let her arms fall and lay there, tears dripping silently onto the pillow, while he went into the bathroom and came back with a cool wet cloth that he laid on her brow. He wiped the tears away with a tissue and after a while they stopped. His hand turned the cloth over. ''Better?'' he asked quietly.

''Yes.'' She saw his face was drawn, his eyes worried. ''Sorry about that. Pregnancy does funny things to a woman.''

He shook his head. ''I can't tell you how sorry *I* am! Jealousy does funny things to a man,'' he said wryly. ''I've been fighting it for so long, in the end I couldn't keep the beast in its cage.''

''Oh, please don't! You have no need to feel that way,'' she said. She took his hand and pressed it to her lips. ''Marcus, darling Marcus—I love you in every way there is. And if you don't believe me this time, I think I'll die.''

His hand tightened on hers. ''If that's true,'' he said

hoarsely, "then I'm the happiest man on earth. And the luckiest."

Jenna smiled up at him. "You're the happiest man on earth," she said. "And I'm the luckiest woman."

"Jenna…"

She stretched her arms up to him, and he fell into her embrace. He said her name again and kissed her, hard and hungry and long.

"I love you," she whispered, a little later, parting the rest of the buttons on his shirt and pressing kisses down his chest.

He unzipped her jeans and eased them off, splaying a hand over her belly. "I don't see any sign of our baby."

"It's too early yet. My breasts are changing already, though."

"Let me see?" His hand went to her bra, and she lifted her shoulders to let him take it off. "You're blushing," he teased, raising his eyes from his inspection. He touched her with great care and her heartbeat increased its rhythm, a delicious warmth invading her body. "They're beautiful," he said, stroking the newly tender skin. "You are beautiful."

"You might not say that in a few months' time."

"I'll always say that," he told her firmly. "I can't wait to see you all round and womanly with my child. I'm so sorry—"

She put her hand over his mouth. "Just make love to me, please."

Her fingers were pressed to his heart, and he said, "I want to make love to you night and day for the next fifty years or more."

"You haven't been, lately."

He looked up from feathering kisses across her shoulders. "I was so eaten up with rage over Dean splitting up with Callie and you spending all that time consoling him—and so sure you couldn't help but regret marrying me when you might have had him after all. I didn't dare bring all that anger and bitterness into our bed, souring our lovemaking."

And she'd had no idea of his feelings, his suffering. How could she have been so blind? But Marcus had a great deal of practice at concealing his emotions. All these years he'd been hiding them from her...from everyone.

She touched his hair, wanting to comfort him for the hurts of the past and assure him of their future. "Katie and I..." she said, starting to explain.

"I know, Dean needed support, comfort." He lifted his head briefly. "You and Katie rallied round as always." He kissed her quickly on the mouth.

"That's all it was, Marcus." She willed him to accept the truth. "Supporting a friend. Oh..." she added breathlessly as his mouth moved lower. "That's...do it again."

"With pleasure," he purred, and obliged. She clutched at his hair.

"I'm not hurting you?" he asked.

"No!" she gasped, and heard his brief, deep laugh.

"If only you'd told me how you felt," she said, trying to breathe normally while his lips and hands sent thrills from her toes to her breasts. "Even when you proposed."

She had left it almost disastrously late to confess her love, but equally, he had given her no inkling of his real feelings.

Marcus lifted her knee and caressed her thigh. "I thought it might frighten you off marrying me," he said. "Knowing you, I had a hunch you'd feel you were cheating if you knew how much I loved you and that you would turn me down out of some misguided sense of fairness."

His touch made her catch her breath with delight. He smiled and dropped another kiss on her mouth. "Besides," he admitted, his voice slurring a little as his mouth explored other places, "knowing you couldn't feel the way I did, I was damned if I was going to surrender the last shred of my male independence."

"Ch-chauvinist," she accused him. She was trying to keep her mind off the increasingly exciting things he was doing with his fingers.

"Witch," Marcus said lovingly, and smiled into her eyes before he kissed her again.

Their lovemaking had always been sensational, but this time an extra element entered it. No holding back, no reservations, no secrets. They gave to each other and received in equal measure, together as they had never been before, in the most intimate way possible.

Afterward they lay in each other's arms in perfect contentment, whispering words that had been uttered by lovers since time immemorial, but for them were new and wonderful, like the evening star that peeked at them through the window as they talked about the coming baby, the miracle of their new knowledge and the years that stretched ahead of them.

Chapter Twelve

The Crossans' garden was filled with people enjoying champagne and snack food.

Bees hummed in the brilliant open blooms of the orange and red hibiscus and over the extravagant little pink blooms of the manuka. A white-and-orange-spotted black butterfly dipped and swirled as Jenna sat on the old wooden seat around the puriri, looking down at the baby she had just discreetly fed.

Her son stared back at her, his eyes wide and solemn. Already they were like his father's, the same fathomless dark gray.

"How's my godson?" Dean stood before her, a glass in his hand, his other arm about a radiant Callie.

"He's fine," Jenna answered. Her eyes went past them, looking for Marcus in the throng on the lawn.

As if he'd felt her gaze, he turned from speaking to two of the guests and strolled over to join them. His hand went to his brother's shoulder even as he smiled at Jenna and the baby. "Isn't that young man asleep yet?"

"He's too interested in what's going on," Jenna said.

Callie bent to offer a finger, and the newly christened Simon Marcus Crossan obligingly curled his tiny hand about it, cooing.

Enchanted, Callie looked up at her husband. "I want one of these."

Dean grinned at her. "I'm sure it could be arranged. We'd better decide if it's going to be an American or a Kiwi."

Callie wrinkled her nose. "I guess a Kiwi would be okay." She and Dean had been married in the States, but agreed that he shouldn't quit his New Zealand job in less than a year. After that, he had promised, if Callie was still pining for her home he'd try for work in America.

Katie joined the group, the hand hooked into Jason's arm sporting a brand-new engagement ring. "How's my godson?" She unconsciously parroted her twin.

Jenna laughed. Simon opened his mouth in a yawn, and then let out a fretful squawk. "Ready for bed," Jenna said, rising. "I'll just put him down."

"I'll come too." Marcus put his arm about her and accompanied her into the house.

Upstairs, she tucked the baby into the portable crib and soothed his sleepy protest with hushed words and a gentle hand, until his eyes closed.

Marcus looped his arms around her from behind, and they both gazed down at the small miracle they'd created. He said, "I never thought I could love you more than I did on our wedding night, but when you gave birth to our baby, I realized I'd been wrong. I never imagined one man could be so lucky.''

''You were wonderful that night,'' she told him.

''Which?'' He turned her in his arms, looking down at her quizzically.

She laughed up at him. ''Both. Both times you were strong when you needed to be, tender when it mattered. Caring. I love the way you've always cared for me. And I want to care for you too. You and our children.''

''Children...plural?'' he teased. ''Isn't one enough of a handful for now?''

''For now. But we have plenty of love left over for more, don't we?''

''Of course we do. We have so much we can't contain it all. More than enough for a family.''

She slid her arms about his neck. ''I love you!'' She knew she couldn't say it too often for him. She liked saying it, watching the light that kindled in his eyes every time.

''And I love you,'' he replied, but she hardly heard the words because they were uttered against her mouth, just before he kissed her, putting his heart and soul into a wordless pledge, a promise for the future, while their son slept peacefully beside them, secure in his parents' spilled-over love.

*   *   *   *   *

FIRST TIME, FOREVER
by
Cara Colter

Cara Colter is the author of over thirty books. She shares ten acres in the wild Kootenay region of British Columbia with the man of her dreams, three children, two horses, a cat with no tail and a golden retriever who answers best to "bad dog."

Cara has two other great stories for you to enjoy! Visit www.millsandboon.co.uk for her brand-new Mills & Boon® Romance **THEIR CHRISTMAS WISH COME TRUE.** And in November 2007, catch up on her classic story, *Her Royal Husband*, part of the **FOR LOVE AND GLORY** collection from Mills & Boon Spotlight™.

Dear Reader,

One of the reasons I enjoyed writing *First Time, Forever* so much is because the hero is younger than the heroine. Evan is seven years younger than Kathleen, which coincidentally is the age difference between my real-life hero and me! What ten incredible years of togetherness has taught me is that when you say yes to the song of your heart – never mind all those rules – it keeps you young. Oh, the hair still has silver threads in it, and the wrinkles appear, but the feeling in your heart of being alive – on fire – gets stronger, rather than diminishing.

When I wrote *First Time, Forever,* I wanted it to be a book that honours the fire in each of us, while at the same time honouring our longing for the traditions that have carried us safely this far – marriage and family.

My greatest hope is that this book will bring you to a place of laughter and tenderness, tears and triumph.

With my sincerest best wishes,

Cara Colter

Chapter One

Evan Atkins had the book hidden behind a copy of *Sports Illustrated*. He drank his coffee and frowned at the words, trying to concentrate, but finding it difficult with all the commotion at the Hopkins Gulch Café this morning.

The café had six tables, two booths and a lunch counter. There were coffee cups half filled, and bacon and eggs half eaten at nearly all those tables, but the seats, save for the one Evan inhabited at a booth, were empty, abandoned.

The guys were three deep at the window, trying to get a look at the Outpost, the town's general store, across the street. A strange car was parked out front, a U-haul trailer behind it. The car had caused this great stirring of interest when a pair of strangers had emerged from it. Both of them had looked around briefly, and then disappeared into the Outpost.

''If they were just askin' for directions,'' Sookie Peters said wisely, "they would have left the engine running."

"Did you see her?" Jack Marty asked for about the sixtieth annoying time. "She looked just like Julia Roberts. I swear. Well, maybe a little older. And not scrawny like Julia." He said this with easy familiarity, as if Julia were his second cousin.

"Nah, she dint," Sookie said. "More like the other one. The one from the movie about the bus. That's who she looked like."

"Sandra Bullock?" Cal, Sookie's brother, hooted. "She did not!"

"Oh, what do you know?"

The banter went back and forth, Evan furrowing his brow and trying to ignore the nonsense as best he could. All those guys at the window should take a lesson from him. Good things did not necessarily come in pretty packages.

Millie came and refilled his coffee cup. He didn't quite get the *Sports Illustrated* up fast enough or high enough, and she caught sight of the book hidden behind it, crooked her head, read the title, and smiled.

If she told the guys he was never going to live it down.

Potty-Training for the Hopelessly Confused.

But she just smiled, in that way he was never going to get used to, as if being a single dad made him adorable to the female populace, like a teddy bear.

"Where is Jesse this morning?" she asked.

"I dropped him off at Beth's Day Care for a while."

"That's good. He needs to be with other kids sometimes."

"So I've been told." Evan scowled at the book. Step Five: Pray.

He thought that was a mighty strange step to include in a book on potty-training, not scientific at all. On the other hand, when his son had gone missing and he had done everything he knew how to do, applied all his intellect and strength and devotion, *everything,* to getting Jesse back, and nothing had worked, isn't that what his days had become?

Please God, please God, please God. If You can't bring my baby home, look after him. It would shock those guys at the window to know he had done that, prayed every day, but he'd been shocked himself the first time those words had gone through his head. Shocked, and then surprised, the words bringing him the only measure of peace he'd had in those desperate years.

Jesse was home now. Okay, it had taken two years, but then Evan would admit to being somewhat rusty in the prayer department, since he'd spent most of his youth moving in the other direction, hell bound.

Still, a two-year wait was a might scary thought in terms of potty-training.

It was very hard to formulate a proper potty-training prayer with all the commotion at the window.

"What do you suppose she's doing over there?"

Millie, known for her foghorn voice, called out, "You know Pa hasn't been feeling so hot. They tried to sell the place, but now they're just hoping to get someone to run it for them."

"That would mean she'd have to live here," Mike Best pointed out sagely.

The crowd at the window contemplated that for a few minutes of blessed silence that allowed Evan to review his prayer. He decided to keep it simple. *God, help.* Satisfied, he looked back at the book.

And realized he had read it incorrectly.

It didn't say *pray*. Step Five said *play*.

He read carefully: *Be sure and make potty-training fun. A game.*

The guys at the window started up again, sounding like a gaggle of old hens excited about an unexpected windfall of worms.

"Hey, there's the kid. He's coming out by hisself, though."

"Don't he look like trouble?"

"Aw, you don't suppose she's married, do you? She must be. That kid is hers. Is the spitting image of her."

This observation seemed to put a momentary damper on the ardent bachelors at the window.

"He does have the look of her."

"Guys," Evan finally called, beyond impatience, "would you give it a rest?"

A few of them turned and acknowledged him with grins that were not in the least contrite, but basically they ignored him.

He did his best to shut them out.

But it penetrated his gloom about potty-training when one of them said, "I guess Mr. High and Mighty over there wouldn't care that the kid is looking at his truck."

Evan rattled the magazine. So what if someone was looking at his truck? It was a damned attractive truck, far worthier of a fuss than a strange woman passing through town.

"Guess old Mr. Lonesome over there wouldn't care, either, that the boy's looking over his shoulder right now. I don't like the look on his face, either, not one little bit."

Evan pretended he wasn't listening, but the truth was

they had his attention now. He was pretty protective of that truck. A fact they all knew. They were probably ribbing him a bit, trying to get him over there at the window to moan and groan over a complete stranger, just like them.

"It looks like he's writing something on it."

Well, okay, he hadn't been through the car wash for a while. Maybe the kid was writing a message in the dust. Big deal. Hardly headlines. Not even for Hopkins Gulch.

"Is that a nail he's using?" Sookie asked, amazed.

"I do believe it might be. Oh, that's an *S* for sure," Jack said.

Evan was up out of his booth now.

"Yup. And that's an *H*."

Evan crossed the café in one long stride and shoved his way through the guys to the front of the window. Just in time to see the little creep putting the finishing touches on an *I*. On his brand-new midnight-blue Dodge Ram Diesel extended cab pickup truck.

The guys were all staring at him, silent, horrified, knowing that that unsuspecting child's life as he knew it was about to end.

He pushed back through them and went out the door and across the dusty street in about one-tenth of a second.

The kid didn't even have time to put a dot on that *I*. Evan spun him around, and shoved him hard against his truck.

He was only about twelve. A good-looking boy, even though his features were contorted with fear and anger.

"What the hell do you think you're doing to my truck?" Evan demanded.

The boy sputtered and squirmed and began to turn red, but he didn't give anything that could qualify as an answer, so Evan twisted his shirt just a little tighter.

"Unhand that boy at once."

The voice was soft, sultry as silk, and with just a hint of pure steel in it.

Evan kept his grip on the boy's shoulder but spun on the heel of his cowboy boot to find himself staring into the most gorgeous set of brown eyes he had ever seen.

His first thought, foolishly, was they'd been wrong. All the guys had been wrong. There wasn't anything he'd ever seen in a Saturday night movie that even came close to this.

She was beautiful, her hair long and dark brown like melted chocolate, pulled back into a stern ponytail that ended between her shoulder blades. Her skin was the color of a peach, and had blushes in all the right places. Her eyes were so dark they were almost black, some flicker of anger in them hinting at a nature more hot and passionate than the primly buttoned lace-collared blouse was saying. Her cheekbones were high and proud, but her nose was a dainty, tiny thing, with a funny little smattering of freckles across it, and her lips were full and luscious and practically begged for kisses.

Begged.

But he was a man who had paid an enormous price for not saying no the last time lips had begged for kisses, and so his voice was frosty when he answered her.

"Ma'am?" he said.

"I said take your hands off my boy. What do you think you're doing?"

He shook his head, trying to think what he was doing, trying to shake the vision of her away so he could think clearly.

Her boy.

Vandalizing his truck. That was it.

"Yeah, take your hands off of me," the boy said, sneering.

Reluctantly he did.

The boy smirked, brushed at his sleeves deliberately, and then, like something unfolding in slow motion, reached over and wrapped his fist around the truck antenna. Before Evan could even think, he'd snapped it off.

Fury, hot and red, rose in Evan, not just because of the boy's flagrant lack of respect for his property but because of the soft gasp of shock and horror he heard from the woman. He shot her a quick glance and was dismayed by the transformation in her.

Cold, angry beauty he could handle with one hand tied behind his back. But now she was fundamentally altered as she stared at her child as if he had turned into a monster before her eyes. There was the faintest glitter of tears, of embarrassment and dismay, in eyes that he suddenly saw were not all brown, but partly gold. Her full bottom lip was trembling. And then she caught a glimpse of the nice letters scratched out with a nail in his brand-new paint, and he watched the color drain from her face.

"How could you?" she whispered to her boy.

"It wasn't hard at all, Auntie Kathy," the boy snapped at her, with disrespect that made Evan angrier, if that was even possible, than the damage that had been done to his truck. Even so he registered the "Auntie." She was not the young hellion's mother.

By now most of the guys from the café had gathered around and were watching with unabashed interest, nudging each other with satisfaction now that the kid had pushed Evan a little further.

Evan knew he had a well-deserved name as Hopkins Gulch's bad boy. He was a man with a reputation. Tough as nails. Cold as steel. Wild as the winter wind. A man who wasn't pushed. Quick to anger. Quick to take a dare. Quick to settle things with his fists. Quick to just about anything, if it came to that.

And he knew he looked the same as he always had, so these men he had grown up with assumed he was the same.

But he was not.

The wildest boy in town had wound up with the wildest girl in the world. Nothing less than he deserved. But the child had deserved something else. The change in Evan had begun the day his son had been born.

And deepened with every day that his boy had been missing.

Evan moved toward the kid. He had no intention of hurting him, would be satisfied to throw a scare into him good enough that he'd be an old man in a rocking chair before he ever messed with another man's truck.

But for a moment, his eyes locked on the boy's and he saw something. Something he didn't want to see. He skidded to a halt, and stared at those large gray eyes.

There was defiance in them, for sure. And a little deeper than that, fear.

And a little deeper than that…there was need. Need so raw and naked it killed the anger dead within Evan.

He ran a hand through his hair, and looked at the woman, a mistake, since it only confused him more.

"You just passing through?" he asked her, hopefully. She couldn't possibly be planning to stay here—a tiny spec on the map, an equally long distance from either Medicine Hat, Alberta, or Swift Current, Saskatchewan.

She dragged her gaze away from the boy who was sullenly inspecting the toe of his sneakers. "Actually, no. I've been hired at the Outpost. Of course, I'll pay for the damage to your truck. Right now. I'll—" She started fumbling with her pocketbook. "I'll write you a check. If you'll accept one from an out-of-town bank, for now. I—"

"No." Evan almost had to look over his shoulder, so dumbfounded was he that the emphatic no had issued forth from his mouth.

Because he *knew,* absolutely, that the thing to do was take her check.

Or let the cops handle it.

He *needed* to be in his nice new truck, driving away from her. Fast.

"No?" she repeated, the pocketbook hanging open, her hand frozen in its desperate search for a checkbook.

"No," he repeated, knowing he was going to do it. The good thing, the decent thing. Damn, sometimes it was hard. The easiest thing in the world was to be a self-centered SOB. He knew; he'd had lots of practice.

But if Dee had run forever with Jesse, if she hadn't died in an accident, this could be his boy standing here, nine or ten years in the future. If Evan was going to be the father his son deserved, he had to learn to do the right thing. Every time.

He suddenly felt calm and detached and like a voice deep within him, a voice he had learned to respect long ago, when the bull charged, when the brakes failed, when the thermometer registered thirty below and the cows still had to eat, when his son was gone and he just needed to get through one more day without losing his mind, that voice was telling him what to do.

He addressed the boy, low and firm, like he talked to a green colt, who was rebellious and scared, but wanted, in his heart, to know nothing more than he could trust you and you would never hurt him. "That five seconds of fun you just had is going to cost you about two weeks of moving manure. School's out for the year, right?"

"What?" the boy sputtered. "Why would I move manure for you?"

"Because you owe me, and that particular subject apparently holds some fascination for you since you feel inclined to write about it on the sides of people's trucks."

There was a murmur of surprise from the assembled crowd. Evan knew he was considered a man of few words, and most of those unprintable. But he heard the approval there, too, in the way he'd handled it.

"I'm not moving no manure." Only the boy didn't say manure.

Evan knew he had enough on his plate. His own son was just about to turn three, a stranger to his daddy, still in diapers, still sucking a soother, still crying himself silly if he got separated from his toy purple truck. Add to that a farm to run, doing his best to cook nutritious meals, laundry to do…how could he even be thinking of taking on anything else?

"Yes, you are." That was his voice, all right. His horse breakin' voice. Calm. Steady. Sure. A voice that did not brook defiance, from animal, nor man. Nor child.

"Make me."

"All right."

The boy's aunt finally spoke. Evan hazarded a look at her and saw, to his relief, her bottom lip had stopped quivering. Hopefully she wasn't going to cry. Her voice was soft, like velvet, the kind of voice that could bring a weak man to his knees.

Something he had learned his lesson from already, thank God, being weakened by feminine wiles.

"Moving manure?" she said uncertainly. "But we don't even know you."

He stuck out his hand. "Evan Atkins," he said.

"Kathleen Miles," she returned, accepting his hand with some reluctance.

Her hand in his was about the softest thing he'd ever felt, and he snatched his out of her grasp after one brief pump.

"Now we know each other," he said. He heard the cold note in his voice, turning it to ice, and recognized it was a defense against the sudden racing of his heart. Wouldn't do for her to know about that, no sir. She looked as if she was going to protest, but he cut her off. "Where's the boy's folks?"

"I'm his folks," she said stiffly.

"And you'll be working at the Outpost, for the Watsons?"

"Yes."

"You can ask them if it's safe for your boy to come work for me. They'll tell you."

"Oh."

He turned again to the boy. "And your name?"

"None of your business!"

"Okay, none-of-your-business, I'll pick you up right

here at five-thirty tomorrow morning. If you make me come looking, you'll be sorry, you hear?''

He noted the boy's aunt looked astounded when he offered a sullen ''I hear.'' Apparently thinking he'd given in too easily, the boy then added the word he had nearly succeeded in printing on the side of the truck.

She gasped again, but Evan just smiled and leaned close to the little delinquent. ''If I ever hear you say that word again, I'll wash out your mouth with Ma Watson's homemade lye soap. You can't believe how bad it tastes.''

Ma Watson, five foot one, in a man's shirt, with her gray hair neatly braided down her back, had appeared on the sidewalk. She chortled now, and said, ''And if anyone would know it would be you, Evan Atkins. Seems to me we went through a little stage where I felt it was my personal obligation to this town to have you spitting suds every ten minutes or so.''

Her comment broke the tension, and a ripple of laughter went through the assembled crowd, or as close as Hopkins Gulch ever came to a ''crowd.'' They began to disperse.

''Evan,'' Ma said, sweetly, ''can you show Kathleen over to her house? I just had a customer come in.''

Evan glanced at the store, pretty sure the door had not swung inward in the last ten minutes or so. Still, he couldn't very well call Ma a liar in front of her new employee, and besides, for all she sounded sweet, she had just given an order, drill sergeant to buck private.

The old gal had really done more than anyone else in this town to try to show a boy going wild the difference between right and wrong, and enough of her tough caring had penetrated his thick skull to keep him out of jail over the years.

Once, when he was sixteen, she had said to him, "Evan, each man has two knights within him, a knight of lightness and a knight of darkness. The one you feed the most will become the strongest."

At sixteen, he had found the words laughable, thought they had gone in one ear and out the other. But in actual fact, those words had stopped somewhere between those two ears, and for some reason now, ten years later, he found himself contemplating them, embarrassed almost by his longing to choose the right one.

"Evan?" Ma said.

Besides, Medicine Hat was a long haul for groceries. "Yes, ma'am," he said, "I'll show her the house." He assumed that meant have a quick look around inside and make sure a rattlesnake hadn't cozied up in some dark corner for the winter. He also assumed Ma wouldn't want him to share that little fact of life in Hopkins Gulch with her new employee just yet.

"Kathleen, dear, you take your time getting settled. Let Evan and the boy bring the heavy stuff in. I'll see you here at the store tomorrow."

Evan took a deep breath, intending to point out that showing Miss Miles the little empty house Ma owned, three blocks from here, and moving her into it were really two separate tasks. One look at Ma and he bit his tongue.

Why was it that woman could turn him into a twelve-year-old with his hand caught in her candy jar in a single glance? Why was it she made him want to be the white knight? A joke, really. He was just a farmer, and part-time cowboy, in muddy boots and torn jeans. He turned on the heel of one of those boots, got in his truck and watched in the rearview mirror as the beautiful Miss Miles herded the boy into her car and pulled in behind him.

She had a beautiful figure, full and lush, a figure that could make a man like himself, sworn off women, reconsider, start to think thoughts of soft curves and warm places.

Evan, he told himself, it only leads one place. It starts with an innocent thought: I wonder what it would be like to kiss her. The next thing you know, *Potty-Training for the Hopelessly Confused.* He realized he left his damned book in the café, and hoped that Millie possessed enough mercy to hide it for him until he had a chance to get back in there and pick it up.

He was angry, Kathleen thought, as she pulled to a stop behind him, and watched him hop out of his truck.

Well, who could blame him? The most noticeable thing about his vehicle now was the two-foot high *S H I* printed on the side of it.

Still, she didn't have much experience dealing with angry men. And certainly not ones who looked like this. Even with that menacing scowl on his face as he waited on the sidewalk outside the gate of a yard, Evan Atkins was gorgeous.

He looked like a young Redford, with his corn silk and wheat colored hair, though his grayish-blue eyes held none of Redford's boyish charm, only a hard and intimidating hint of ice and iron. His features were chiseled masculine perfection—high cheekbones, straight nose, wide mouth, firm lips, a strong chin.

He was average height, maybe five-eleven, but the breadth of his chest and shoulders had left her with the impression of strength and leashed power. He was narrow at his stomach and hip, and his long, blue jean-encased legs looked as if they'd wrapped themselves around a lot of horses. And probably quite a few other things, too.

Kathleen decided Evan Atkins was not a safe man for her to be around. Lately she had noticed that her mind wandered off in distinctly naughty directions with barely the slightest provocation. Part of being old, she was sure. Not just old, but an old spinster.

She was kidding herself. It was because of Howard announcing his intention to marry someone else. Hope quashed.

"Thank you," she called to him, half in and half out of her car. "Is that the house? I can manage now."

He didn't budge.

The house was hidden behind a tall hedge. Throughout the long drive here she had been so eager to see the accommodations that came with her new job. Now she had to get past the guard at the gate. Now she wasn't nearly as interested in that house as she had been a thousand miles ago. He had a kind of energy about him that made everything else seem to fade into the distance, uninteresting and unimportant.

"Three days is too long to drive," she muttered to herself.

"Auntie Kathy, you're getting old," Mac informed her, an unfortunate confirmation of her own thoughts. "You're talking to yourself." He glanced at the man standing at the gate, wriggled deeper into his seat in the car and turned a page of his comic book.

She made herself get all the way out of the car, and walk toward Evan.

"Really," she said, "Thank you. You don't have to—"

He held open the gate for her. The opening was far too narrow to get by him. She practically touched him. She caught a whiff of something headier than the lilacs blooming in wild profusion around the yard.

"I'm sorry about your truck," she said, nervously. "Mac decided he was going to hate it here the minute I told him we were moving. I think he can get himself run out of town on a rail."

"I guess if this town could survive me as a twelve-year-old, it'll survive him."

She realized she liked his voice, deep and faintly drawling, and something else.

"How did you know? Twelve?"

"Just a guess. Where are you coming from, ma'am?"

She realized what the "something else" was in his voice. It was just plain sexy. The way he said ma'am, soft and dragged out at the end, made her tingle down to her toes. She snuck a glance at him. It occurred to her he was younger than she. That should have made his raw masculine potency less threatening, somehow, but it didn't.

"Vancouver," she said. "We're relocating from Vancouver."

"That's one hell of a relocate."

"Yes, I know." Though he didn't ask, she felt, absurdly, that she had to defend herself. "The ad for the position at the Outpost said this was a great place to raise a family."

He snorted at that.

"Isn't it?" she asked, desperately.

"Ma'am, I'm the wrong person to ask about families."

"Oh." She snuck a glance over his broad shoulder

at the house, and tried not to feel disappointed. It was very old, the whole thing covered in dreadful gray asphalt shingles. The porch looked droopy.

Feeling as if she was trying to convince herself she had not made a horrible mistake, she said, "Vancouver is starting to have incidents with gangs. There are problems in the schools. Children as young as Mac are becoming involved in alcohol and drugs."

Of course she was not going to tell him the whole truth, her life story. That her boss, Howard, whom she'd once been engaged to, was going to marry someone else.

A little smile twisted his lips. "You don't say?"

She bristled. "You're not suggesting my nephew might be involved in such things just because of that incident with your truck, are you?"

"No, ma'am. I don't know the first thing about your nephew, except he seems to have a talent for spelling. But I know I wasn't much older than that when I first sampled a little home brew, right here in Hopkins Gulch."

She stared at him, aghast.

"Kids as wild as I was find trouble no matter where they are," he said, apparently by way of reassurance.

"And are you still wild, Mr. Atkins?" she asked. Too late, she realized she sounded as prissy as an old maid librarian.

He seemed to contemplate that for a moment, his eyes intent on her. "Life has tamed me some."

There was something vaguely haunted in the way he said that, something that made him seem altogether too intriguing, as if the steel and ice in his eyes had been earned the hard way.

She reminded herself, sternly, that she was completely unavailable to solve the puzzle of mysterious men, no matter how compelling they might be. She had a boy to raise. When her sister had died, Kathleen had vowed she would give that job her whole heart and soul. Howard had broken their engagement over her decision, and after that she had decided that Mac didn't need the emotional upheaval that seemed to be part and parcel of relationships.

It really wasn't until Howard had announced his engagement a month ago at the office that she had realized she had held the hope that he would change his mind, or maybe even that he was waiting for Mac to grow up, that later would be *their* turn.

What had she thought? That he would wait until she was really old? And probably saggy, too?

Like this old house. She forced herself to look away from Atkins, to take note of the yard that was now hers. Behind it, through a hedge of more lilac, Kathleen could see the prairie, huge, undulating, without a tree or a shrub or a flower for as far as the eye could see. The yard itself was ringed with blooming lilac bushes. The flower beds had been long neglected and the grass was too high, but the yard was large and private and she could tell just a little bit of tender loving care could make it lovely. There was the garden space, at the side of the house. She took a deep breath of the lilac-scented air.

"What is that smell?" Mac asked, catapulting through the gate.

"Lilacs," Kathleen told him.

"I think I'm allergic."

"Mrs. Watkins told me there's a pasture right on the other side of the hedge if you happen to decide you want a pony,'' Kathleen said, hoping to find one thing he could like and look forward to.

"A pony?'' he said, giving her a slightly distressed look, as if she had landed on earth after being hatched on a distant planet. "Is that, like, a brand of skateboard?''

She saw Evan duck his head, but not before she saw the quick grin. It changed his face, completely. Completely. He had beautiful teeth and deep dimples. He could look very boyishly attractive, after all.

"A pony,'' she snapped. "Like a horse.''

"I'm allergic to horses, too,'' Mac decided, and then added, sending Evan a sidelong look, "And also manure.''

Evan ignored him. "I'll just take a quick look inside the house for you.''

"Why?''

"It's been empty a spell, I think. You never know what might have taken up residence.''

She stared at him in horror. "Such as?''

"You never know,'' he repeated, deliberately unforthcoming.

"Like a homeless tramp?'' she asked unsteadily.

"No,'' he said, his mouth quirking reluctantly upward at one corner. "Hopkins Gulch doesn't have any homeless tramp problems.''

"Mice?'' she pressed.

"Well, I was thinking of, uh, skunks, but sure, mice.''

She scanned his face, suspecting he wasn't telling her the full truth.

"I'll bet that place is full of mice,'' Mac said, sensing a weakness. "I'll bet they'll be running over our faces at night when we try to sleep. I'll bet we'll find little paw prints in the butter. I'll bet there are dinky round holes in the baseboards, just like in the cartoons. I'll bet the only thing that keeps the mice under control are the skunks. I'll bet—''

"I'd say that's enough bets," Evan said quietly, glancing at her face.

Mac looked mutinous. "It's a very old house. Probably even older than you, Auntie Kathy."

She felt Evan's gaze on her face, again, but he made no comment on her age in relation to the house.

Mac flopped down on the grass, rolled his eyes, grabbed his throat and began gagging. Whether it was in reaction to the lilacs or the house she decided it would be wise not to ask. Following Evan's lead, she ignored Mac who was now writhing dramatically, and went up the creaking steps.

The door swung open, and her first impression was one of gloom. Fighting not to show her disappointment, she followed Evan through the empty house. He was wearing a chambray shirt and faded jeans. This back view showed off the broadness of his shoulders to breathtaking advantage. The jeans were soft with wear and hugged the taut line of his backside and the firm muscle of his leg. He made all the rooms seem too small. He'd brought that smell right in with him—clean skin, faint aftershave, man-smell.

He opened the closets and looked through the cupboards. She didn't follow him into the basement, but he came back up the stairs, and proclaimed her new home varmint free.

Mac, obviously disappointed that his lilac-induced collapse on the front lawn had failed to convince anyone of his distress, came through the door, a sour expression on his face.

''What a dump,'' he proclaimed. ''This whole town is like the dumpiest dump that I've ever seen and I hate it here.''

Evan ignored him. ''Ma'am, do you need a hand with your things?''

This was offered only politely.

''No, thanks,'' she said proudly.

She wanted the man out of her house. So she could concentrate. So that she could deal with Mac, figure out what had to be done to make the place livable, and then shut herself in the bathroom and cry.

Chapter Two

"Thank you for giving it a fair chance," she said icily to Mac, after Evan had left. "I cannot believe you behaved like that. Broke Mr. Atkins's antenna off his truck, wrote that word. What on earth has gotten into you?"

Mac looked at his toe, clad in expensive sneakers that he *had* to have, and that seemed to have brought him joy and contentment for exactly ten seconds, and then shoved his hands deep into his pockets before he shot her a look loaded with defiance. "I hate it here, that's why. I want to go home."

"This is going to be home," Kathleen said with determination. Her eyes were adjusting to the gloom in the room, and she noticed the floors were old gray linoleum, peeling back in places, the walls needed paint desperately, there were spiderwebs in the corners. She went over and tugged at a blind. It rolled up with a snap, and the sunlight poured into the empty room, but did nothing to improve it. *This* was going to be home?

She thought of her and Mac's cozy little apartment in Vancouver and felt heartsick.

"You won't believe how rotten I can be," Mac warned her.

She let none of her own doubts show. She said calmly, "Then you will just have to get very good at shoveling manure. I'll bet there is no shortage of that around here."

"Well, you got that right," Mac said heatedly. "How could you do this to me? You've ruined my whole life. Me. Mac Miles in Poop Gulch, Saskatchewan." Only he didn't say poop.

"The first thing I'm going to do at work tomorrow is find out about that soap," Kathleen said.

"And what am I supposed to do while you're at work?"

"You already sorted that out, Mac. You'll be shoveling manure." Only she didn't say manure, either.

He stared at her, obviously stunned that his aunt would use that word. He changed directions swiftly. "I suppose you thought that guy was good-looking."

And for the briefest moment, she saw the little boy in him, and saw how scared he was. He was sad and scared and he was too anxious to be a man to say so.

"Oh, Mac, come here."

He came, and even allowed her to put her arms around him and she found herself saying, "Everything will be fine." With him snuggled against her, those words felt true, and it actually did feel as if it could be home here.

Mac tolerated her embrace for three seconds or so, then pulled away and walked down the narrow hall. "I guess I'll have this room," he said after a minute.

"Auntie Kathy, you never answered me. Did you think that dust hopper was good-looking?"

"Dust hopper?"

"The goof with the truck."

She didn't answer, appalled by this creature who was her nephew.

"I thought he was real ugly," Mac said. "Real. And way too young for you. *Way.*" He slammed his bedroom door.

She thought of him sitting in that empty room, nursing his own bad humor, and sighed. She looked around again at her homely house, and went into the bathroom. More aging linoleum. She thought of Evan Atkins being *way* too young for her, and him not even commenting, when he'd been given the opportunity, that the house was obviously years older than she was.

Howard's new fiancée was young, blond, perky.

You broke up with him five years ago, Kathleen reminded herself savagely. You're over it. She barely locked the door before the tears started to fall.

It had been a stupid thing to do, to take a job in a place she had never heard of. Stupid, stupid. Stupid. When she'd been hired sight unseen, when that letter had arrived, she'd actually thought, naively, whimsically, that it had been heaven sent. She had told herself this was her chance to start anew. To be somebody new. Somebody who worried less and laughed more. Who did daring and bold things—like moved to a town they had never heard of.

Kathleen allowed herself to snivel for ten minutes, and then came out, knocked firmly on Mac's bedroom door and told him they had a great deal of work to do to make this house into their home.

Stupid or not, they were here, and she had to make the best of it.

She unlocked the U-haul and after some rummaging handed Mac a broom. When he rolled his eyes, she said, "Be thankful it's not a shovel."

"I don't like this house," Mac said.

"It didn't live up to my expectations, either," she admitted, "but I can make it clean, and in time it'll be cute, too."

"Oh, *cute*." He shot her a sideways glance. "Did you think *he* was? Cute?"

"No," she said, "not at all."

Her response was completely honest. Evan Atkins *cute?* It would be like calling a grizzly bear adorable. Howard had been cute with his big brown eyes, his curly hair, his little potbelly.

Mac was clearly relieved with her answer.

She spent the rest of the day feverishly cleaning the little house from top to bottom, scrubbing walls and floors and appliances. Mac was surprisingly helpful, but only until his boom box came out of the trailer. By nightfall, Kathleen had only the energy left to move in two mattresses and a box of bedding.

"You don't have to get up with me in the morning," Mac told her. "You look really tired." When she got up in the morning, he was gone, but he had found the coffeepot and made coffee for her. Just when she was about to lose hope in him, he would win her back by doing something sweet and thoughtful like that.

She walked the three blocks to work, noting they comprised most of the town. She spent the day at the Outpost, learning the inventory, which was extensive, and prices, and how to use the archaic cash register.

She was amazed by the number of people who came

through the store, until Ma told her they were coming from miles around to check her out. She was asked on six dates before noon! It did wonders for her flagging spirits, even if she did say no to all of them.

At four she headed home, exhausted, knowing she had that U-haul to unload. Still, she had all the ingredients for Mac's favorite spaghetti supper, and couldn't wait to fill up that little house with the good smells of garlic and tomatoes and pasta.

But by five o'clock Mac still wasn't home.

She scanned the road yet again. She thought she had heard a truck, but it proved to be a large farm vehicle.

Mac had left at five this morning. Twelve hours? Didn't that seem a little long to work a twelve-year-old?

It occurred to her he might have been in an accident.

She laughed nervously at that. It would be the worst of ironies if she moved from busy Vancouver to sleepy Saskatchewan, mostly for Mac's sake, only to have him maimed or killed in an accident.

Of course, she had never actually seen Evan pick him up. What if he had gone to the highway and hitch-hiked away? What if even now—

Stop, she ordered herself. This was what her book on positive thinking said she must not do, think in negatives, create whole scenes and scenarios. The book, she recalled, instructed her to try to turn her negative thoughts around, to think now, of something positive.

She tried to picture Mac having a wonderful day. She pictured him on a farm. She pictured him chasing through tall grass after a butterfly, having just the kind of day she had pictured when she'd applied for this job.

She went back and stirred the spaghetti sauce. Why had she made so much?

Kathleen Miles, you are not inviting that man in for dinner.

Just then she heard a truck pull up. She set down the spoon in such a hurry it splattered sauce on her white blouse. She ran to the front window.

The right truck. She went out of the house and onto the porch.

Mac got out of it and slammed the door. He marched up the walk, his back straight, his clothes absolutely filthy, a pungent aroma following him.

She glanced anxiously at his running shoes.

Clean.

"How was it?" she asked him.

"How do you think?" he snapped.

"Oh."

"Hey, none-of-your-business." Evan Atkins had gotten out of his truck and was coming down the walk toward them.

Mac turned and glared at him.

"Same time, same place," Evan said.

Mac gave him a dirty look and when it didn't phase Evan, he gave it to her instead. Then he muttered a word she couldn't quite make out and the porch door slammed shut behind him.

Evan Atkins continued down the walk toward her.

She tucked a strand of hair behind her ear, and suddenly felt very aware of the little splotch of spaghetti sauce on the front of her. She wasn't going to let him see that she felt vulnerable!

He walked with the easy assurance of a man completely comfortable within his own body, a man sure of himself. His self-certainty annoyed her even more in the face of her own lack of it.

"I wish you wouldn't call him none-of-your-business," she said, far more sharply than she intended, sounding exactly like the aging spinster she was. "His name is Mac."

"Actually, I know that. I'm just waiting for the invitation to come from him."

His voice was low and calm, a faint thread of amusement running through it, though he wasn't smiling. Did he find her amusing? Probably that spaghetti splotch. He stopped, rested one foot on her bottom step and looked up at her.

"Where on earth have you been?" Her voice was still sharper than she intended, but definitely the tone of a woman who planned to be taken seriously.

His eyes widened. "Ma'am?"

His eyes were dark ocean-blue, with flecks of the most intriguing gray.

"He left at five-thirty this morning!"

"My place is a good half hour drive from here, ma'am. That's an hour round trip. I had a lot of work to do today. I couldn't just stop everything to drive him back into town when he thought he'd had enough. Which was about five minutes after he started."

"Twelve hours is a long time for a little boy to work."

"He's not that little. Besides, we stopped for lunch."

"I don't even think it's legal to work a man that long!"

"Well, ma'am," he said, a bit of a fire lighting in those cool ocean eyes, "if it makes you feel any better, we didn't even make a dent in that anger he's carrying around."

"Mac is not angry!" She had no idea why she said that, when it was so pathetically obvious he was.

"Scratching that particular word in the side of a person's truck can't exactly be interpreted as 'I come in peace.'"

"I don't think he better work for you tomorrow."

"Now, ma'am, it's really none of my business, but I think that would be a mistake."

"Really?" she said haughtily.

"I don't think you want to be teaching that boy that he can behave any old way he likes, and that there won't be any consequences for it. Mama Bear will bail him out."

He was right, and they both knew it.

Still, she couldn't seem to stop herself from saying, "And you're an expert on raising children, are you?"

She was sorry the minute she said it, knowing she was taking out all her anxiety about her move and Mac on him, and that he didn't deserve it. Besides, as soon as she said it, in his eyes she caught a glimpse of a pain that was as raw as an open wound.

But his voice was steady, and completely unflappable. He answered slowly, measuring his words. "No, I'm sure not that. It just seems to me if you bail him out now, you'll be bailing him out in quite a different way in the future."

She took a deep breath, realized she was being both cranky and unfair and that he was right and she was wrong. She was completely unable to admit that. "I was worried about him. I was worried when he was gone so long."

It was Evan's look of genuine distress that soothed some of the irritation she had been feeling.

"I didn't mean to cause you worry. I guess I should

have called." He smiled, shook his head and said, "I feel like I've said those words a few times before in my life."

She just bet he had. Those charming dimples had probably won the hearts of hundreds of women who had waited by their phones with bated breath for his call. That never came. She planned never to be one of them. Never. That was one very good reason she couldn't invite him to share spaghetti with them.

"I guess I thought I'd keep him out of your hair while you were at work," he said.

He'd been doing her a favor, or thought he was, and she was giving him a hard time about it?

"He's not such a bad kid," she said defensively, and then realized, suddenly, how ridiculous she must seem—a mother bear protecting her cub, just as he had said.

"Ma'am, I can see that."

"You can?"

His smile deepened and she was now certain she did not like his smile. It made him, in an instant, in to one of those men who can have anything. Anything. Had she really cooked that dinner just for Mac? Was she feeling prickly as a pear because her nerves were leaping with awareness of this attractive stranger resting his boot-clad foot on her front step?

"In the odd moment. I had him bring the mix out to my calves. I wish you could have seen the look on his face."

"I wish I could have seen that, too."

"Well, maybe you will one time."

"Thanks. Maybe I will." But since that would mean tangling her life a little more with Evan Atkins she decided she wouldn't. She had pinned her hopes on

Howard, and he had let her down, and the hurt was terrible.

And Howard wasn't nearly as...compelling as the young, and gorgeous Mr. Atkins. In fact, Howard suddenly seemed very blah, boring. If a blah and boring man could hurt her so much she really didn't want to think what an exciting and passionate one could do.

"How did things go your first day on the job?"

"Oh. Fine." What made her think he was passionate? The smoky look in his eyes? The uncomplicated sensuality of his lips?

"Everybody within a hundred miles dropped by to say howdy?"

She felt some of the stiffness leave her and she laughed. "A thousand, I think."

"Ma'am, I wouldn't be surprised."

"Quit calling me ma'am!" Why did her tone have to be so querulous with him? "Please."

"All right." He waited.

She blushed, as if she had just turned sixteen and not thirty-four. "Kathleen."

"Well, Kathleen, I'll bet your dance card is full right up for the next year or so."

"Pardon?"

"They all ask you out? The bachelors of Hopkins Gulch?"

"Oh. A few of them. I don't do that. Go out."

"You don't? Why not?"

Why not? There was no Howard to be loyal to anymore. What kind of woman was loyal to a man for five years after he'd broken up with her? A dolt, that's what kind.

"I don't think it would be good for Mac."

"How's that?"

"In my experience—" admittedly limited, though she didn't say that "—romance seems to be distinctly upsetting."

"Distinctly upsetting," he repeated thoughtfully. "I'd have to go along with you on that one. By the way, does Mac really have allergies? To horses?"

"No. Did he tell you that?"

"Deathly, according to him. One whiff of horse and immediate anaphylactic reaction. Said he forgot his kit at home. Like a beesting kit, only a horse whiff kit."

She was staring at Evan trying to hide her horror. When had her nephew become such an accomplished liar? She didn't even know Mac knew the word anaphylactic.

"I take it," Evan said at her silence, "it would be quite safe to have him feed the horses tomorrow?"

"Quite safe," she murmured.

"If he comes."

"He'll come."

"I'll be here at five-thirty, then."

"All right."

He turned and walked away. She was fascinated by the way he walked, loose-limbed and confident, like a man who owned the earth.

"So, what should I call you?" she called after him.

He stopped and looked back at her. "This is a pretty casual kind of place. Evan would do fine."

"Thanks, Evan, for looking after his shoes." Was she actually trying to keep him here? If she didn't watch herself, she'd be inviting him in for supper in a minute.

He gave her a lopsided grin that chased the shadows from his face and made him look charming and boyish and about a hundred years younger than she.

"Did you really pay two hundred dollars for those shoes?"

"Not quite," she said, "but close."

He shook his head incredulously. "Why?"

"They're magic shoes," she said with a sigh. "They were supposed to make him happy."

"If you got that in writing, I'd take them back." He turned then, went down the walk and got into his truck.

She had to bite her tongue to keep herself from stopping him one more time, asking him if he'd like to join them for spaghetti.

It wouldn't be a date. Not even close. Just a neighborly kind of thing.

Not wanting to look pathetic, she did not watch while he drove away.

She went into the house just as Mac came out of the shower, toweling his head. The freckles had darkened across his nose, and his cheeks were full of color from the sun.

"I really hate that dust hopper," he told her. "I worked hard enough today that I shouldn't have to go back."

"Well, you do," Kathleen said, glad that her resolve had been strengthened by her talk with Evan.

"He worked me really hard, and didn't give me enough to eat or drink. I think there are laws against treating kids like that."

"There are laws about damaging people's property," she said sternly. She tried to get him to think positive, just as the book said. "Tell me one good thing that happened to you today."

He scowled at her. "There wasn't one."

"Oh, come on. Tell me about the calves."

"They're really stupid and they stink. Just like his kid."

"His kid?" Kathleen asked, stunned.

"Yeah. He has a little boy named Jesse. He's nearly three and he wears diapers. Is that normal?"

"I'm not sure."

"He doesn't talk much, especially when the Gestapo is around."

"Who doesn't talk much? And what Gestapo?"

"The baby doesn't talk much. And the Gestapo is the dust hopper you think is so cute."

"I never said I thought he was cute." She was sure she was going to blush and give herself away, so she turned quickly. Over her shoulder she said, "Don't call him that again. Gestapo. That's dreadful."

"Well, so is shoveling for no pay. That kid can't say *r*. Is that normal?"

"I don't know." Why was it making her feel so inadequate that she couldn't answer his questions? Making her feel as if she had missed something. A baby of her own. Another dream Howard had stolen from her. If she waited until Mac was grown up, another six years at least, wouldn't it be too late then? She'd be forty!

"It doesn't seem normal. He says wabbit for rabbit. Could I say *r?*"

"I don't ever remember you not saying *r*."

"That's good because it sounds really stupid."

"Where's Jesse's mom?"

"She died in a *caw*."

"Oh, Mac."

"It really stinks, doesn't it, when mom's die and leave their kids? At least he has a dad who cares about him, even if he is the Gestapo."

Spoken carelessly, it failed to hide his pain. He was still grieving the loss of his mother, even though it had been nearly five years now. And his father. Kathleen felt a nameless fury. He'd never even seen his son. Abandoned her sister and his unborn child as soon as he'd learned she was pregnant.

And of course, then there had been Howard, who had told her, shortly after her sister's death, "It's Mac or me." Not quite in those words, of course. Howard was always so good with words. Educated. Sophisticated. Things that had impressed her once.

"I care about you, Mac," she said firmly. "I love you more than a leopard loves its spots."

Mac couldn't resist the game. "I love you more than a toad loves its warts."

And suddenly the anger melted from his face, and he was just her sweet little boy again. And he said, "Did you make me spaghetti for supper?"

"Just for you." Why did that sound like a lie?

He smiled. "I love you more than a pizza loves pepperoni."

It seemed to Evan that all of life really turned on a hair. He glanced in the back seat, where Jesse was fast asleep in his car seat. A little puddle of drool was forming on the tiny Western shirt Jesse had spotted at the Outpost several days ago. It had been on a mannequin, and Jesse had stood in front of it, silent, his eyes large with wanting. It had broken Evan's heart that he didn't ask. He'd bought it for him anyway. Now he was having trouble getting the shirt off his son long enough to put it in the washer.

He looked back at the long ribbon of road and

thought, a choice made here, a split second there, and everything changes.

He'd met Dee at a rodeo, she a top-rated barrel racer in sequins and tight jeans, he a not so highly rated bull rider with quite a bit more nerve than talent. She had short blond curly hair and huge brown eyes, and a tiny china doll figure that belied the power she showed on a horse. She was without a doubt the most beautiful woman he had ever laid eyes on. She was also the only woman he'd ever met who could match him drink for drink, who could party all night and go all day. Maybe he should have taken that as a danger sign, but he hadn't.

Now, he wondered sometimes, if he'd gone to a different rodeo that day, or stayed at home, or had a flat tire, or taken a wrong turn, maybe he would have never met Dee. Maybe that little life in the back seat would have never happened.

All of life turned on these split-second decisions that a man had no hope of recognizing at the time he made them.

And here he was again.

His life turning on a hair.

If he hadn't been in town yesterday, his life wouldn't be intertwining with hers, with Kathleen Miles. If Mac had snapped off a different antenna, everything would be, well, different.

He wouldn't be driving home to his empty house, thinking about the smell that had been wafting out her open porch door. Something mouthwatering. Italian. And thinking about that U-haul out front, still as full as it had been yesterday.

"Evan, don't even think about turning this truck around," he ordered himself.

Just as firmly he told himself he was not thinking of Kathleen Miles romantically. Not at all. He was a man who had learned his lessons about romance. What had she said?

Oh, yeah. *Romance was distinctly upsetting.* Apparently she had learned her lessons, too.

So, why, if he had learned his lessons, had he been absolutely compelled to ask her if she'd been asked out? He knew she would have been. Those guys that had lined up three-deep at the café window yesterday would have lost no time in getting over to the Outpost to check her out today.

Her response to them was none of his business. None. Still, there was no denying he felt happy that they had all struck out with her.

Not, he thought darkly, that Sookie Peters was going to take no for an answer. Kathleen was too beautiful. Sookie would be back over at the Outpost tomorrow, probably with a little bouquet of flowers, and lots of sweet talk. Kathleen didn't date? That wouldn't be a problem for Sookie. He'd think of a way for it not to be a date.

In fact, Sookie probably wouldn't wait until tomorrow. He was probably at her place right now, unloading that U-haul, and getting himself invited in for a homemade dinner. That wouldn't be a date, would it? No, sir, that would just be being neighborly.

Dinner. Evan tried to think what he had at home that would qualify and hit all four food groups at the same time. Frozen pizza. Canned stew. Before Jesse he would have thought a food group was the fries next to the burger on his plate. But that lady lawyer in Swift Current had told him, when Dee's parents had been acting as if they were going to challenge him over guardianship, that he would have to be really aware of things like that. Nutrition. Child psychology.

He suddenly felt achingly lonely and overwhelmed.

"Don't you dare turn the truck around," he said to himself. "You can't just show up at a woman's house at dinnertime, hoping she'll feed you."

In exchange for unloading her U-haul, the other voice said indignantly.

The kind of thing a white knight might do, except a real knight wouldn't expect dinner.

Sighing, recognizing all life turned on a hair, and there was not a damn thing he could do about it, Evan Atkins slowed, stopped and turned his truck around.

He told himself that she looked like the kind of woman who might know a thing or two about potty-training.

Chapter Three

"Oh," Mac said, through the screen. "It's you. Auntie Kathy, Colonel Klink is here. And he brought Mr. Stinky Pants with him. Is Mr. Stinky Pants alive?"

"Yeah, he's just sleeping." Evan could feel his son's warm breath against his shoulder.

"Hi," Evan said, when she appeared at the door. Did she look pleased to see him? Even after that introduction?

"I'm sorry," she said, tossing an annoyed look back at Mac. She had a tea towel over her shoulder, and her hair was falling out of her ponytail and curling around her face. "Where does he come up with this stuff?"

The smells coming out that door were even more heavenly than before.

"Hogan's Heroes," Evan guessed. "Late night." He knew all about late nights.

"Is this your son?" A good sign. Not, *What are you doing back here?*

"Jesse," he said, "otherwise known as Mr. Stinky Pants."

She smiled and came out the door and looked at Jesse's sleeping face. She reached out and touched a blond curl.

"He's gorgeous," she said, her voice rich with tenderness, "He's just like a little angel."

A man could not be jealous of his three-year-old son. It was not permissible. Especially when he was not here about romance, heaven forbid. Simply being neighborly. Or a knight, however one wanted to look at it. Still, a man would probably go a long way to have a woman look at him with that kind of bone-melting sweetness.

"I was thinking if you had a place I could lay him down, I'd haul that stuff in from the trailer for you."

"Oh," she said, and blushed.

Who would think a woman that age could blush? He tried to figure out her age. Older than him. Mid-thirties, maybe. One of those women who aged with uncommon grace, her body full and ripe, her face kind, her dark eyes steady and serene. Why was it women thought they needed to be forever young when he found this so appealing?

Women liked him. That had been a fact of his life for as long as he could remember. But it always seemed to be a certain kind that was attracted to him—young, full of breathless giggles and chatter, dyed blond hair and shirts that showed off their belly buttons. Women who didn't blush, and who seemed to like the word *cool* best out of the entire English language, who wore red, red lipstick and chewed gum. An evening with a woman like that left him feeling so empty and exhausted he'd pretty much given up on it. Especially now that Jesse was home.

But he could tell just by looking at her, just by looking at her eyes, that Kathleen Miles was a different sort of woman—one of those women who would truly keep getting better as she got older.

"That's very kind of you," she said. "Come in."

She held open the door for him. Underlying the smell of garlic and butter and onions, he could smell lemon-scented cleaner and window shine. And her.

No Poison or White Shoulders or Shalimar, just her, clean and fresh and real.

Her house was still practically empty, but spotless now, the walls dirt free, the floor sparkling, no dust motes or spiderwebs anywhere, not even in the corners. Evan thought of how the floors in his house had become a little bit sticky, handprints multiplying on his walls.

Mac had disappeared, but Evan could hear loud music from behind a closed door. "Don't go messin' with a son-of-a..." A song he'd practically considered his theme song ten years ago. Kids were still listening to it? And watching *Hogan's Heroes?* Maybe he and Mac had more in common than a two-story high pile of manure that had to be moved.

"In here," she said.

He followed her into a bedroom that only yesterday had seemed cold and empty and a bit ugly. Today it had her mattress in the middle of the floor, all neatly made up in white eyelet, so feminine and pretty it made his mouth go dry.

"I don't think I better put him on that." He thought of the rumple of sheets and blankets on his bed at home. When was the last time he'd made a bed?

"It washes," she said with a shrug.

In his house, "it washes" didn't necessarily mean it got washed. It got put in one of those piles that he did his best to ignore until he or Jesse started running out of stuff to wear.

He laid his son down on her bed, hoping the shirt that Jesse had had on for three days wouldn't leave any smudges on the pristine white of her bedspread. He noticed she had hung a white sheet over the window, and tied it back with a bow. It lifted with the breeze, and fluttered and made him think, irrationally, of things exotic and mysterious and feminine. How could those two small changes to the room make it feel so different than it had felt yesterday?

"I'll get your bed frame set up," he said. "You shouldn't be sleeping on the floor."

"I know," she said. "The mice will be running over my face."

He decided not to tell her the plus side of living in rattlesnake country. They did keep the rodent population under control.

"Would you like something to eat first? It's almost ready."

"Well," he hesitated, "if you insist."

She didn't even look suspicious! He followed her into the kitchen. It, too, hadn't had much done to it, though it sparkled with cleanliness. He thought if he moved every stick of furniture in his kitchen outside onto the lawn he could do this, too. Just bring in a garden hose and spray down the whole kitchen—blast the jam off the floor, the spots off the countertops, the grime off the stove, the fingerprints off the fridge. A good project for summertime, when the cattle were less work.

He looked out the window. Sookie Peters drove by, spotted his truck and kept going. He and Sookie had duked it out in Grade Eleven. Over Betty Sue Mc-Donald. He hadn't had to reestablish dominance since then.

Betty Sue had been real pretty. Smith, now. She and her husband lived in Swift Current. The last time he'd seen her he'd noticed how her prettiness was fading, petals falling off a rose.

No doubt about it. Kathleen Miles had a hardier kind of beauty, growing more lustrous, rather than fading, like those flowers that look their best in the autumn. Probably not one single person in her high school would have recognized that for what it was.

"Was that an old red truck driving by?" she asked from the stove.

"Hmm." Was she *expecting* Sookie?

"It's driven by here about half a dozen times. Do you think I should call the police?"

"Call the police?" he asked. "On Sookie?" Come to think of it, it might be kind of fun.

"On who?"

"Sookie Peters. He was probably one of the guys in the Outpost today trying to get your phone number."

"Oh! I thought it was some sort of weirdo. Maybe watching Mac."

It was tempting to brand Sookie as a weirdo, but the white knight, stronger now because he was going to do a good deed and move her furniture for her, gave him a little prod. "Kathleen, I know those kind of weirdos don't generally hang out signs, but I'm pretty sure we don't have any in Hopkins Gulch. You are one big city woman, aren't you?"

"I am. I grew up in Vancouver. Can you imagine? This is the first time I've been away."

She tested her spaghetti sauce, then held out the spoon to him.

It was a ridiculous thing to find sexy. Ridiculous. But when he put his lips on the spoon where hers had been he felt weak with pleasure.

Because of the spaghetti sauce, he told himself. "That's pretty good," he told her, an understatement. But if he said what he felt, *orgasmic,* she'd for sure think he was weirder than Sookie.

"More garlic?" she asked him.

"You can never have too much garlic." She had a little speck of sauce on the corner of her lip. He couldn't take his eyes off of it.

"Could you look through those boxes and see if you can find me a colander?" she asked, turning back to her sauce.

"Like with months on it?"

She laughed. "Handy in the kitchen, Mr. Atkins?"

"Pathetic, Miss Miles."

"A colander. Mine's red plastic. With holes in it. For draining spaghetti."

"Oh, that kind of calendar." He opened a box and looked through it, keeping one eye on her. He shouldn't have come back here. Really. What did he have for a spine, anyway? One of those noodles?

A woman like that could make life complicated without half trying.

But only, he reminded himself, if the romance part developed, the distinctly upsetting stuff. And that didn't have to happen. No, sir. He was going to eat spaghetti, and unload boxes, and then get the hell out of here and never come back. Except to pick up Mac in the morning. And again the morning after that. And again the morning after that.

Life had already turned. You couldn't make it turn back.

He found the colander. "Defective," he told her. "It's missing November."

A stupid thing to say, but she rewarded him by laughing. She laughed again when they heard old Sookie's truck grind by.

"Maybe you should call the police," he said, taking the little sample of garlic bread she handed him. "Of course, he'll most likely have given up and gone home by the time they get here."

"Why? How long does it take them to get here?"

"Depends where they are, but they don't have a station around here, anywhere. I guess it could take an hour or two."

"An hour or two? What about emergencies?"

"What kind of emergency?" he asked. The garlic bread was perfect—crunchy on the edges, soggy with butter in the middle.

"Like a home invasion."

He laughed out right. "I think we did have one of those...1995. Cal Peters got drunk and Mrs. Maude Butterfield found him on her chesterfield in the morning."

"Cal Peters? Any relation to the Peters driving around and around my block?"

"Brothers."

"Does Suckie drink? And wind up in strange houses?"

He decided not to correct her pronunciation. "He drinks some. I think he usually manages to make it to his own house, though."

"I'm reassured," she said, casting him a glance. "I'm serious. What do you do in case of an emergency. Like a house break-in?"

"A house break-in? Robbers?"

She nodded, serious.

He tried not to laugh again. "Half the houses in this town don't have locks. The other half have a loaded shotgun behind the back door."

"Loaded?"

Her eyes were huge, as if she thought she'd moved to a place where she was going to be in mortal danger all the time.

"Coyotes," he said. "Skunks. Rattlesnakes. But no robbers. No robber in his right—"

"Rattlesnakes?" she breathed. "Are you serious?"

He was sorry he'd let that slip.

"What about that kind of emergency?" she demanded, her voice shaky. "When someone gets bitten by a snake kind of emergency?"

"That's a pretty rare occurrence. Rattlesnakes are basically shy creatures that don't like to be bothered."

"But when somebody does bother one of them?" she persisted. "And it bites them? Then what?"

"I guess folks around here grow up knowing they've got to rely on themselves and their neighbors if things go wrong. And they get pretty good at it."

"What about me? I grew up with 9-1-1! I'd be terrible in an emergency. Especially an emergency that involved a snake!"

"Kathleen, are you one of those people who has a tendency to worry? About things that never happen?"

She began to breathe again, smiled faintly. "How could you tell?"

"You got this little wrinkle, right here, between your eyes." He put his forefinger to his own forehead.

She rubbed at her worry wrinkle self-consciously.

"In the unlikely event you have to deal with an emergency, your neighbors will help you out," he told her.

"My neighbors? Like the Peters brothers?" She quit rubbing the worry spot and frowned at him.

What he wanted to say was, *You can call me. Anytime. What are knights for, anyway?* But he was half an hour away, a long, long way if there was a snake in the basement. "You got a nice old couple on your west side here. Retired farmers. Sandersons. And the Watsons."

"Oh."

"If it's a medical emergency, like a snakebite, they bring in the helicopter. Med evac just like *M.A.S.H.*" More late-night programming. "Meanwhile, a little snake sense goes a long way."

"Snake sense," she repeated. She gave the worry wrinkle another little rub.

"Don't be reaching into any dark corners in your basement, especially behind that old furnace."

"My basement? *My* basement? The basement through that door right over there?"

"The noodles are boiling over," he said gently.

She turned to them with a little cry of dismay, and he realized unless he wanted dinner ruined he better wrap up the snake talk.

"Nobody's seen a rattler in town for a while." He didn't add that the last time one had been seen it *was* cuddled up right behind Maude's furnace in her basement. Maybe Maude attracted varmints of various varieties.

* * *

Spaghetti was the world's hardest food to eat with
dignity, but it made it easier that she didn't have a table
set up yet. The weather was unusually hot, so they took
their plates out on the porch and sat on the steps. He
noticed she rolled her noodles up neatly against her
spoon and popped them in her mouth.

Mac was on the other end of the scale, relishing
slurping back long tendrils, in between treating him to
dark looks of savage dislike.

He tried to be somewhere in the middle. He thought
it was probably the best spaghetti he had ever eaten.
Orgasmic. "This is pretty good," he said.

He offered to help with dishes, but she shooed him
away, and he commandeered Mac to help him get the
furniture in.

"Amazing how much stuff you can put in one of
these," Evan commented on the U-haul, to nobody in
particular, since Mac answered him only in grunts. He
took off his shirt, ready to work, and tossed it on the
hood of his truck.

Sookie drove by again. He nodded at him. Sookie
ignored him, as if he had ended up on this block by
accident. As if that were possible in Hopkins Gulch.

"Who is that?" Mac said.

"Sookie Peters."

"Is he a weirdo, or something? He keeps driving by
here."

"Nah, he's waiting for me to leave so he can move
in on your aunt."

"Hah. He might as well not waste his time. Auntie
Kathy doesn't go out with people. Not anyone. Not
since Howard, the bowwow."

Don't ask, he commanded himself. "Who?"

"Some guy she was going to marry. A long time ago. He's going to marry someone else now."

So, there was a little more to her winding up in Hopkins Gulch than her nephew's welfare. He told himself to leave it. "How long ago?"

"They broke up five years ago. I guess 'cause of me." There was more pain there despite Mac's practiced indifference. "I mean they still went for lunch and stuff 'cause they worked in the same office."

It seemed to Evan five years was a long time to nurse something like that. It did not, he told himself sternly, qualify her as a damsel in distress.

He knew he should leave it there, but who knew if the kid would ever talk to him in full sentences again? He tugged a metal bed frame out of the tangle of boxes and furniture. "Don't you think she gets lonely sometimes?"

"No," Mac said, vehemently. "She doesn't. Old people don't get lonely."

Evan handed him the bed frame, watched to make sure he could handle it and then took a dresser out and started up the walk.

"How old is she?" He didn't think she'd appreciate him asking, but he did anyway.

"She's thirty-four." The boy was panting a bit.

Good. Wear him right out and he'd be less apt to be looking for trouble.

"That's not exactly ready for knitting sweaters on August afternoons," Evan said dryly.

"She does so knit! Well, hooks rugs, same thing. And I'll bet she's a lot older than you!"

"A little older than me." For some reason he liked that picture of her, making rugs.

"Ha. How old are you?"

"Twenty-six." He held open the door for Mac.

"That means when you were in Grade Two she was in Grade Ten. That's a lot older than you."

Evan shot him a look. Mac was getting riled. One more good reason to keep everything neighborly. Which was going to be really, really simple. As long as he never again thought of her lips and his on the same spoon.

"Is this your stuff or hers?" he asked, pausing in the hallway.

"Hers. You were eight when she was sixteen. She could have been your baby-sitter."

"I think I got the point the first time." He hoped she wasn't listening. Next trip, he was going to load the kid down a little heavier. Now that he'd got him talking, he was sorry.

"When she was having her first kiss, you were playing with Tonka trucks."

That big old armchair looked heavy enough to shut him up next trip. Meanwhile they were in her bedroom, and he was thinking of her first kiss, his mind going there despite Jesse, his reminder of kiss consequences, snoring away on her bed. He wondered what it had been like for her, that first kiss. Had it been as sweet and as innocent as pure white lilies coming up at Easter? Had it made her heart pound wildly, and stirred in her longings for things she had never known? He wondered what she kissed like now, now that she had known some of those things?

Was it crazy to be disappointed that he would not be the one to experience firsts with her? Was it crazy to wonder what she would be like in his bed?

Yes.

She was probably mature enough not to even think

such things, he thought, retreating from her bedroom as fast as he could. Those were exactly the kinds of things and the kinds of thoughts that made romance so distinctly upsetting.

When it wasn't being distinctly tantalizing, distinctly world-shaking, distinctly, well, exhilarating.

Sookie was coming around the block again.

Bad timing. Evan stepped out on the road, stopped Sookie, went around to the driver's side of his truck.

"They're starting to think you're a weirdo, Sookie."

"You're just saying that."

"Okay. *I'm* starting to think you're a weirdo. If you drive by here again, I'm going to haul you out of that truck and finish what I started in Grade Eleven."

Sookie took off in a shower of dust and gravel.

"What did you say to him?" Mac asked with reluctant admiration.

"Let's just say I acted my age." He didn't say out loud, young. And stupid. Not in the least like a white knight. He was somebody's dad now. He really needed to try resolving situations with maturity—not by threatening to pound on people. He somehow doubted Kathleen would be impressed with how he had gotten rid of Sookie.

Which was good. The last thing he needed was to be thinking of impressing Kathleen Miles.

His immature mind insisted on adding, *in bed or out*.

Mac grunted under the weight of the armchair. Evan took on the big old sideboard for himself. Maybe Mac wasn't the only one who needed to be worked until he couldn't even think about getting into trouble.

Kathleen looked out the window. Evan had taken off his shirt! Well, why not? He was working hard, and it was unusually hot out, even now with the sun beginning to wallow over that endless prairie horizon.

Why not? Because it could make a woman lose her head. It could make her forget all about her responsibility to a young boy struggling to become a man.

Still, there was no harm in looking. Being on a diet didn't mean you couldn't look at double chocolate brownies with hot fudge icing.

He had her sideboard up on his shoulder, and every muscle he had, and that seemed to be a considerable number, was standing out, hard-edged and rippling.

For all that his muscles were straining, he didn't look as if he was even breathing hard. Not like Mac who was struggling under the weight of her huge old armchair. She thought to protest that Mac had probably done enough today, but the prospect of him just tumbling into bed exhausted instead of wandering around town looking for trouble was too appealing.

Her eyes went back to Evan, the young, raw beauty of his body exerting a magnetic force over her. He adjusted the sideboard, and the muscles in his arms coiled and leaped under flawless skin and fine arm hairs bleached to golden threads by the sun.

His pectoral muscles were deep, and mounded, even his stomach looked hard and muscular. On her way to work, in Vancouver, Kathleen sometimes passed by the glass picture window of a gym, but somehow it was more impressive that Evan looked like this without the benefit of a gym. He undoubtedly possessed this hard, uncompromising man's body because he did hard and uncompromising man's work.

Kathleen, she told herself, how do you know he doesn't go to a gym?

She forced herself out of her trance, and held open

the door for them. He brushed by her. If she reached out, half an inch, she could touch him.

"Do you work out?" she asked him.

He set down the sideboard, turned and gave her a quick, incredulous look. "Yeah," he said. "Every day. From sunup to sundown."

She wanted to touch him. Never once, in all those years of working side by side with Howard had she wanted to touch him. Not even when the engagement was on.

"Where do you want this?"

"Could we try it under the window?" A complete coincidence it was the spot furthest away from them and would give her perhaps a whole additional second or two to admire him while he was unaware.

He lifted the sideboard with seeming ease, moved across the room.

Be still my foolish heart, she ordered herself. He looked like one of those guys on calendars that the women in her office had drooled over. Howard's office. Howard's company.

That ad in the *Vancouver Sun* that had jumped out at her just hours after Howard had announced his engagement and introduced his fiancée around had not said one single word about rattlesnakes. Or the Peters brothers. Or men who looked like calendar boys.

Make that colander boy, she said to herself, watching him wrestle the sideboard into the window well. Mr. November.

Still, his body being at its peak like that reminded her that hers was not. She was a lot closer to forty than twenty. And when men looked at calendars, it wasn't forty-year-olds, they drooled over. Howard's fiancée was twenty-two.

Evan Atkins would probably never see her the way she saw him—as young, earthy, sexy, desirable. A man had not triggered these strange longings in her since, when? Ever?

Even her first kiss had been a disappointment. A sloppy, awkward incident that had left her wiping frantically at her lips.

She had never attracted men like Evan. During high school, she most likely would have qualified as a wallflower—very shy, very unsure of herself. On those rare occasions that she had been asked out, it was always by the kind of boys with wire-rim glasses who wore V-necked sweater vests and belonged to the science club. Once she had started work it had been different. Men seemed to find her attractive, and she had gone through a stage where she had dated a fair bit—but not men like Evan.

Men with business suits, and thinning hair, and little paunchy stomachs. Men who worked on computers or sold insurance or worked with numbers. Men who talked about the stock market, prime and their mission statement. Men who liked improbable movies about men who were not like them saving the world from terrorists. Men who wore highly polished black shoes, golfed on weekends and hired it out if they wanted something heavy moved. Not unattractive men, but not *exciting*. Men exactly like Howard.

That probably, she thought wryly, would explain why she was still a virgin, even after the world's longest engagement, prolonged by her sister's illness.

"Hey, Auntie Kathy, where do you want this chair?"

"I can't believe how strong you are," she said to

Mac, and watched him beam. "Right over there would be great."

The sideboard positioned, Evan stepped back and regarded it thoughtfully. She noticed his skin was now coated in a fine sheen of sweat.

It made her want to touch him more than ever.

The truth was, she had never in her life felt so physically aware of a person as she felt of Evan Atkins. She had never been so aware of how beautifully men were put together, never wanted so badly to run her fingers over silken skin, to feel her softness being gathered in that hardness.

She had the awful, naughty thought that if her first kiss had been with Evan instead of Malcolm Riley, she wouldn't be the world's oldest virgin today!

Of course, at the time she was fending off Malcolm's saliva-filled kisses, Evan would have been what? Ten or eleven?

He's not ten or eleven now, a voice inside her head told her with wicked smugness.

That was the problem with a person on a diet looking at sweet things. First it was a harmless look. And then a little sniff. And then just a wee taste. And then the whole pan gone.

She wasn't sure what that meant in terms of liking to look at Evan Atkins.

He glanced up and saw her. He folded his arms across his naked chest and narrowed his eyes at her.

On second thought, she knew exactly what it meant. And from the look in his eyes, so did he.

From the look in his eyes he didn't mind looking at her, either. He wasn't seeing her as old, at all. He seemed to be seeing her as something she wasn't.

Daring. Passionate. *Experienced.*

He couldn't really be much further off the mark. He, thankfully, stopped looking at her, and he was giving Mac a hand shoving that armchair up against the wall. Had she imagined that flash in his eyes, a look so smoldering it turned their color to gray smoke?

He glanced, quickly, over his shoulder at her. His muscles rippled through his shoulders and his back as he gave the chair one final push.

She hadn't imagined it.

She felt more prepared to deal with a rattlesnake than this kind of emergency: suddenly realizing she didn't know the first thing about herself.

She longed to touch him. His skin, his muscles, his lips. She hungered to touch him. And her hunger shocked and appalled her.

She practically ran back into the kitchen.

"Auntie Kathy, where do you want the TV?"

"Anywhere," she called. "I don't care."

And it was true. Suddenly she didn't care one whit where the furniture went. Her mind had been commandeered by these strange and powerful longings inside of herself.

She heard Evan say something to Mac; from here his voice a deep and reassuring rumble. The kind of voice a woman could turn to when she was afraid of a snake in her basement or a stranger at her door. A voice that promised sheer and uncompromising strength.

When had she gotten so tired of doing it all on her own, carrying it all by herself?

She heard Mac laugh, reluctantly, at something Evan had said, and felt yet another new doubt crowd her mind.

All these years she had thought and never doubted that she was doing Mac a favor, keeping his world safe from the ups and downs of her having romantic entanglements. Secretly she had thought Howard would come around. He still had taken her for lunch once a week, seemed to enjoy her company.

But now Mac was twelve. On the verge of becoming a young man.

Who was going to teach him how to do that? Who was going to teach him not to be afraid of snakes? Who was going to teach him he couldn't get what he wanted by sulking or behaving terribly until the other person gave in?

Who was going to show him how to shave, and how to talk to a girl, and how to be strong in the way men were strong? Who was going to teach him how to be capable—the kind of man who could fix a truck, or mend a broken window, or nail the back step down?

Who was going to teach him to be a man of honor? Look at how Howard had behaved! He could never have taught him that. For the very first time, she felt a small niggle of gratitude that he had not come back, changed his mind, begged her to marry him.

Who was going to teach him that the love between a man and a woman was sacred and beautiful and worth any risk and any heartbreak, when she had acted scared to death of it ever since Howard had called off their engagement? When she had played everything in her life so safe?

"We need something to drink, Auntie—" Mac came through the kitchen door, skidded to a halt. "Are you okay?"

"Oh, sure," she said, busying herself at a sink that had already been cleaned.

"You look like you're crying," he said suspiciously.

"No, no. I just got something in my eye."

Chapter Four

Jesse still hadn't woken up when Evan went and carefully picked him up from her bed, tucked him into his shoulder.

"Is he going to sleep tonight?" Kathleen asked, taking his hand, Evan's, and folding his fingers around a container of leftover spaghetti. Did her hand linger on his just a bit longer than was absolutely necessary?

"Are you kidding? It's part of his torture Daddy routine. He falls asleep around four every day, wakes up at eight or nine, raring to go."

"And how long does he go for?" Kathleen asked.

"Until one or two in the morning."

"You get up at five-thirty!"

"If I'm here at five-thirty, I've been up since four-thirty. Don't you see the bags under my eyes?"

"No."

He liked the way she was looking at him. If he was not mistaken, she liked looking at him just fine. And that "no" had come quick enough to make him think she might have been sneaking the odd peek while he was moving her furniture.

"Has he always been a little night owl?" she asked.

"I've only had him since my wife died a couple of months ago. Dee and I had been separated since Jesse was a baby. I didn't see him." He took a deep breath. "Most of the time I didn't even know where he was."

"Why?" she breathed.

"It's a long story. Believe me, you don't have time for it." But it scared him how much he wanted to tell her, to pour out his heart to her. It scared him how much he felt like he could trust her, on the basis of a very short acquaintance.

And one superb spaghetti dinner.

He was supposed to be the knight here, saving her, not looking to be saved.

"Look, would it help if I drove Mac out in the mornings?"

"No. I'll manage." Recognizing he felt vulnerable made him want to push her away, hard.

"How about if I pick him up after work? It's the least I can do. I can't believe the two of you got all this stuff in the house. I can't believe you wore Mac out."

They went into the living room. Mac was fast asleep on the couch.

"You get your boxes unpacked," he told her. "Then if you want to pick him up some afternoons, we'll talk about it."

Jesse muttered something in his sleep, his fist tangled in his daddy's shirt, and then relaxed.

"You're going to have to bite the bullet and get his schedule turned around."

"I think he keeps the same hours his mama kept,"

he said quietly. "Everything takes time. He'll love the spaghetti. Thanks."

It wasn't until he was halfway home, when Mr. Stinky Pants lived up to his name, that he remembered he'd completely forgotten to ask her the most important question.

But it remained unasked for several more days, because Evan was running flat out, torn between the demands of farming and single parenting. He was actually relieved she didn't invite him in again, and not just because he was worried he'd be the most boring of company and go to sleep in his supper.

It was because she made him yearn for all the things he thought he was going to have when he and Dee had said "I do." Made him want to believe again in those very things that had taken his heart and pressed it through a meat grinder.

He'd never had a family to speak of. His ma had died when he was young. His pa was tough as nails and about as tender. Evan had grown up farming this hard country. His childhood memories were of hard work, lousy food, his father silent and unbelievably stern. There were times when he had thought prison might be a step up. Prisoners had a few rights.

He'd mistaken what he found at rodeos and in bars, in fast cars and faster women, for freedom. He'd mistaken excitement for fulfillment.

And somehow when Dee had announced her pregnancy he had thought he was going to have all those things he'd never had: a houseful of warmth and laughter, kids chasing around, home-cooked meals, most of all, someone to love and to love him back. Those were the empty spaces that he had tried to fill in all the wrong places.

He should be older now, and wiser. And way more cynical.

Trying to become a better person—decent, good— didn't mean he had to be stupid. He was smart enough to be wary of anyone who made him want to believe in dreams. And that was Kathleen Miles.

He was dropping Mac off after work, and practically burning out of there. A man could drown in the light that glowed in her dark eyes. Besides, Mac was keeping him filled in on the progress of her other admirers. Sookie had not driven around the block again. Jack Marty had come to call and had been politely turned away.

"Not even lemonade," Mac said with satisfaction.

Mac was turning out to be a good kid. A hard worker, somebody he could trust Jesse with when he had to see to cattle or go out in the field. It occurred to Evan he was really going to miss him when the two weeks were over.

And probably miss catching the odd glimpse of her, too.

"See you tomorrow, Mac," Evan called as the boy got out of his truck.

"Bye, Mac," Jesse called frantically from his car seat in the back. "Bye."

Mac turned around, hesitated. "Do you guys want to come in for a minute? Jesse might like some lemonade. Auntie Kathy makes it from scratch. Not like that powdered stuff you have."

Evan saw Jesse trying frantically to get his own car seat buckle undone. And he saw Mac offering him something fragile.

Regardless of his feelings of wanting to stay away from all the sweet temptations of Kathleen Miles, he'd known from the beginning the boy needed something from him.

"Sure," the white knight said. "Lemonade sounds great."

Kathleen heard the truck turn off, and came around from the side of the house where she was cautiously digging up the garden, one eye ever watchful for lurking snakes.

Mac was jogging up the walk. "Evan and the kid are going to have lemonade with us, okay?" He looked so pleased, took the steps two at a time and moved by Kathleen in a pungent cloud.

Evan was bent over the back seat of his truck, extricating Jesse. He finally did, and set Jesse on the walk, took his hand and they came toward her together.

"Hi, Jesse," she said, gently. "We've met before, but you were asleep. I'm Kathleen."

The little boy tucked his head behind his father's long leg, and peeked out at her warily. His eyes were not his father's, but huge and brown.

"Jeez, is that stinky kid out there?" Mac growled from in the house.

She watched, amazed, as Jesse's face dissolved into a smile. "Mac!" he cried, and squirmed out of his father's grasp. Evan released him and Jesse ran on pudgy legs over to the screen door and pressed his face against it. "Mac?" he called. "Mac?"

Mac came to the door. "Oh, gee," he said. "My first friend come to call on me. The only problem is he's only two feet high."

"Mac play me. Plea?"

Mac opened the door. "All right. You can come see my room only because I don't happen to have anything better to do in this dumpy town."

"Mac, you could always pull another shift at my place if life is too unbearably boring," Evan said. His voice was calm, but there was just a hint of steel in it.

"No, thanks," Mac said. "Come on, Jesse, but listen up. If you make stinky pants, that's it for you. Out. Got it?"

Jesse nodded solemnly and marched in the door. It slapped shut behind him.

"Jesse adores Mac," Evan said.

"I can't imagine why," Kathleen said.

"Sorry. I can't, either."

They both laughed softly.

"I noticed you've progressed from none-of-your-business," she said. "That's great."

"Oh, that's not the half of it. He invited me in for lemonade."

"Seriously?"

"He promised homemade." He smiled, and it was slow and sensuous, a smile that must have turned dozens of women to butter. Dozens. Her own mouth felt a little dry, though, of course, she had no intention of giving in to Evan Atkins's considerable charm. After that night, nearly a week ago now, she knew she had to build a fortress around her own vulnerability when it came to him.

He had a ball cap in his hands and was turning it in circles. Was that an indication he was about to exercise that charm on her?

Maybe he was going to ask her out! A blush crept through her cheeks as if he actually had.

"How was work today, Kathleen?"

She felt disappointed. Really and truly disappointed, as if she had thought he was going to say, "Kathleen, let's go grab a bite to eat together."

Which she should say no to. After the other night when Evan had been here she had just felt so hopelessly confused, as if she didn't know what was right or wrong for herself, let alone Mac. She had spent the whole week reviewing her choices in the past five years.

She had chosen Mac as her life. Without hesitating, with never a glance back. What she couldn't believe was that she had spent five years waiting for Howard— a man who had resented every day of her sister's illness, and who had been too self-centered to see Mac for the blessing that he was. Now, she was even beginning to be thankful that Howard's Catholic upbringing had prevented them from ever being intimate together, even if that did make her just about the world's oldest virgin.

Had it been a mistake to reject romance totally?

It *did* cause too much tumult; it *took* too much. Time and energy and devotion. Mac needed all she had to give. When he had first come to live with her he'd been afraid every time she went out the door, afraid she was never coming back.

What had been her options in the face of his fear? Hire a baby-sitter and go on a date? Or rent *Star Wars* one more time, make popcorn and cuddle on the couch with the one who needed her most?

Of course, Mac had changed a great deal since he was seven. He was a confident and independent boy who would survive if his aunt went for a bite to eat with her employer. She decided, right then and there, eating with Evan wouldn't qualify as a date. They'd already done it once, after all.

But would it be opening the door to romance? And

didn't she need to make a conscious decision about that, not just fall into something?

She reminded herself, sternly, Evan had not asked her for dinner. What had he asked her?

"Work?" he reminded her, amused.

Work. How had he managed to pick the one thing she didn't want to talk about? She sighed and picked a dead marigold stem from her flower box.

"I like the job, but..." She took a deep breath, and said it, "I don't think Ma's happy with me."

"What? That's impossible."

She liked the way he said that. As if he knew she would always do her best, even though he hardly knew her. Still the facts were the facts. "No, it isn't. There's a man poking around. Ma keeps giving me these looks like she's going to burst into tears."

"I'm sure you're misinterpreting it," he said, and came slowly up the stairs. "Pa hasn't been well. She's probably worried about him."

"I hope you're right."

He startled them both by reaching out and putting a gentle finger on the bridge of her nose between her eyes.

"There it goes again."

She laughed. "Did your mom ever tell you your face would freeze like that? When you made faces growing up?"

He took his hand away, and she rubbed furiously at the furrow, until she noticed him looking away in the distance.

"Did I say something?"

He looked back at her. "I didn't have a mom, Kathleen."

"I'm sorry."

"She died when I was just a tyke, not much older than Jesse. I would have liked to have heard that, though. I guess I would have liked to have had a mom."

He actually looked shy, and just a little embarrassed that he'd said it.

"I never used to worry so much," she said, fighting the sudden impulse to touch his cheek tenderly, "but when Mac came along, I felt so responsible."

"I know that one."

"You would. How's Jesse sleeping?"

"I tried to keep him up one day. He won." Evan looked away again, and she got the distinct impression he wanted to ask her something, but he didn't.

"You want to sit out here and have that lemonade?"

"Sure," he said. "You've got a porch swing. I always wanted to sit on one."

"You?"

"Why not me?"

"I don't know. You don't look like the porch-swing type." Which should really be telling her something. Or maybe not. Howard had been the porch-swing type, *exactly.*

"What type do I look like?"

He looked like a man who wouldn't be happy sitting still for long. A man who was strong, and physical and who moved. If you put him behind a desk for a day, he would probably go crazy.

"I don't know," she lied. She went and got the lemonade, and sat down beside him on the swing. It was very close. Her shoulder touched his.

It felt just the way she had known it would when she saw him without his shirt on. Hard. Warm. A shoulder a woman could lean against for a long, long time.

"How did Mac do today?" she asked. Okay. Here was the pathetic truth—she was a tragic spinster, and she liked the feel of his shoulder against hers. And she liked looking at him out the corner of her eye. Just looking. At the little crinkles around his eyes, and the way his muscles in his arms looked when he moved them even a little bit.

"He groused and bellyached, but a little less than yesterday. He's actually a good worker. The funniest thing is how Jesse's taken to him. He seems reluctantly touched by that."

"They're both boys without mothers."

"Mac's got you."

"And Jesse has you."

"He'd trade."

"He would not."

"For lemonade and spaghetti? In a second."

Kathleen and Evan both laughed, but she felt acutely aware of something. Jesse had him. Mac had her. If they ever got together, those boys would have it all.

Got together. Ridiculous to even entertain such a notion. He was the type of man who would date the kinds of women she saw on the covers of magazines—beautiful, not in the least afraid to show off their belly buttons.

And she was the type of woman who didn't date. Shouldn't. Was allergic to romance.

But if she did, wouldn't it be someone like Howard again, a basically boring guy, bald, computer literate, could recite his company's mission statement by heart? She decided she'd rather remain a virgin forever.

"Do you know what a mission statement is?" she asked, by way of a test.

"Say again?"

"A mission statement?"

"No. I mean I could guess, but you'd probably slap me."

She laughed softly. He passed. And what did that mean? That she wasn't going to remain a virgin forever, and that Evan Atkins figured into that equation? Dream on, girl.

"So, you going to tell me? All about mission statements? I hope it's wicked."

"It's not, and no, I'm not going to tell you."

"Kathleen, there's something I've been meaning to ask you."

She could feel her heart beating inside her throat. He was going to ask her out. And she was going to have to decide whether to say yes or no. Two very small words. Why did it feel as if she was standing on a springboard, deciding whether to jump into deep, mysterious and unknown waters, possibly dangerous and shark-infested, or whether to back up to where she had always been safe and comfortable?

She hadn't felt this ridiculously giddy since Mark Morrison had approached her the day before the senior prom.

"Uh, I was wondering—"

"Yes?" she asked breathlessly.

"I was wondering if you happen to know anything about potty-training?"

She stared at him. All right. So this was a pattern in her life. Because Mark Morrison hadn't asked her to the prom, either. He'd asked for her science notes.

"Potty-training?" she sputtered.

"I can't seem to get Jesse to get it. It's the stinky pants issue."

Despite her disappointment that this was about the farthest thing from her fantasy, she laughed. "Evan, you're on your own. Mac came to live with me when he was seven. I'm afraid the hard stuff was already done."

"How did he come to live with you?"

"My sister died. She had a rare form of cancer."

"I'm terribly sorry."

"Me, too. But at least I have Mac. He's very like his mother in many ways. He looks like her. He laughs like her. She goes on."

"Jesse takes after his Mom, too."

"She must have been very beautiful."

A pained look crossed his face. "She was. She was incredibly beautiful."

"Mac said she was in a car accident?"

"Yeah." He scuffed his toe. There was a great deal of pain here, and she had the sense not to probe it. She moved back to the other issue.

"Sorry, I can't help with the toilet training. Is there a library nearby? I'm sure they would have a book—"

"I've got a book. Had a book. I left it somewhere. It wasn't helping anyway. Make potty-training fun. Right."

She laughed again. Why did he make her feel like this? So happy? So alive. In what possible way was potty-training more interesting than mission statements?

It just was. "Maybe that's not such a bad idea, though. You know, I do remember when Violet took Mac off the bottle, she had a little party for him, with balloons and cake and ice cream. She told him they were celebrating that he wasn't a baby anymore. And after, she put away the bottles and the crib, and that was it.''

"That was it?" Evan said hopefully.

"That was it. We had a great time."

"I could do that."

"Yes, you could."

"Would you come? If I did it?"

"Pardon?"

"If I have a potty party for Jesse. Would you come? You and Mac?"

It wasn't exactly the date she'd been hoping for, and yet somehow it appealed to her even more.

"Of course we'd come."

"Come where?" Mac asked, slipping out the door. She noticed Jesse had a tight grip on his hand. In Jesse's other fist was one of the *Star Wars* figurines Mac coveted. "I'm not giving it to him," he said defensively, when he saw her looking at it. "I'm just lending it to him."

"Mac lend Yoda," Jesse confirmed solemnly, "to his fwend, Jess."

"Thanks, Mac," Evan said.

"You could show your gratitude by calling it even on the antenna," Mac said hopefully.

"Dream on."

Mac actually grinned.

"I'll invite you to a party, though."

"A party? What kind of party?" Mac asked suspiciously.

"A farewell party."

"Really? For us, I hope."

"Nope, for Jesse. He's going to say farewell to his diapers and his soother."

"A pawty for Jesse," Jesse said, wide-eyed. "Pwesents?"

"Oh, sure," Evan said. "Presents. Cake. Ice cream. The works. To celebrate you not being a baby anymore."

"Yeah. I can't be *fwends* with no baby," Mac said.

"Awight," Jesse said.

Kathleen laughed. "When and where?"

"Oh, God. My place. But I have to do something about it first."

"You're not kidding," Mac said under his breath.

"Give me a couple of days."

"That's optimistic," Mac said.

"So, Friday. I'll give you instructions to my place. Maybe you could put away a few party things on my account at the Outpost. And a present. Mac, you want a break from shoveling?"

"Let me guess. I get to clean your house?"

"Easy work. You get to keep your shoes clean."

"Whatever. You're the boss."

Kathleen heard the respect in Mac's tone and marveled at it.

Evan glanced at his watch. "I have to go. Thanks for the lemonade, Kathleen." He picked up Jesse and settled him on his shoulders and went down the walk.

"This idea is stupid, stupider, stupidest," Mac told her, but tolerantly.

"How bad is his house?" Kathleen asked.

"You know, Auntie Kathy, it's a *guy* house."

"I'm not sure that I do know."

"It means you don't wash the dishes until you run out. And everything you eat comes out of the freezer or a can. It means the towels in the bathroom have hand prints on them. And when you drop something on the floor, you don't wipe the spot off. It's great.''

''Oh.''

''That little Jesse is so dumb he didn't know who Yoda was.''

''It's a good thing he had you to show him,'' Kathleen said, deadpan.

''You got that right. Do we have wrapping paper?''

''Wrapping paper?''

''I found those posters I used to have in my room. The dumb Dumbo ones. I might wrap one of them up for the kid. He likes Dumbo things.''

Kathleen found she had the funniest little smile in her heart as she helped Mac wrap up all his old posters for Jesse.

In her spare moments at the store, she sorted through a small collection of toys and picked out a tiny dump truck to give Jesse from herself and a matching cement truck to give him from his dad. She put together a bag of hot dogs and buns and potato chips, and tucked them into the store fridge.

''Where are the balloons?'' she asked a preoccupied Ma Watson.

''Balloons? Right on the top peg above the birthday candles. I used to have them lower, but I don't like putting things in the eye range of children. They bug their parents for them.''

''I think that's actually the strategy of bigger stores,'' Kathleen told her.

For some reason, that seemed to distress Ma even more. ''Oh,'' she said. ''That's terrible. If they ever do that in my store, I'll—'' She stopped and looked at Kathleen. ''Oh, dear,'' she said. ''Oh, my dear.''

''Ma, what is the matter? I feel like I'm not working

out for you. If there's something I need to change,
please tell me.''

Ma looked as if she was going to say something, and
then changed her mind. "Tell me what you need balloons for," she said. "A party? Is Mac having a birthday?''

"No, not for a while. Evan's going to have a party
for his little boy. He invited Mac and me out to his
place.''

"Oh, that is wonderful. You and Evan. And Mac, of
course. And Jesse. But Jesse's birthday isn't until, let's
see, July. No, that's the other Jesse. Jesse Atkins is
August.''

"You know everyone's birthdays?" Kathleen asked,
astounded.

"Of course," she said proudly. "You know, people
can shop for groceries cheaper in Swift Current or
Medicine Hat. They come in here because we know
them.''

Kathleen smiled. "That's exactly why I wanted to
move to a small town.''

Ma Watson stared at her, looked down at her feet
and then burst into tears. Kathleen looked after her in
distress as Ma hurried from the room and firmly closed
the door that joined the store to her private apartment.

Ma still hadn't reappeared at closing time, but she
had shown Kathleen how to close up and had given
her a key, so she did.

She loved the drive to Evan's farm, the landscape so
different from the sea and mountainscape of Vancouver. But her uneasiness about the incident with Ma
wouldn't leave her.

Evan came out to meet her. "What's wrong?" he
asked, taking the packages from her.

"What makes you think anything's wrong?"

"That wrinkle is the Grand Canyon at the moment."

Uneasily she related the story to Evan.

She noted that as unhappy as she was feeling about the situation, she still managed to notice how his muscles rippled when he picked up those bags of groceries.

"Jeez, and I thought you hated my farm."

She looked around. White buildings with green trim, miles of rolling country around them.

"I love your farm," she said.

"Okay. So Ma was talking about birthdays, and then she started to cry?"

"Yes. I feel terrible, Evan. I know she's sorry she hired me."

"Kathleen, you are reading this wrong. I think Pa Watson must have taken a turn for the worse. Ma isn't from a generation that talked about how they felt. She's from the stiff upper lip school of thought. It's probably just all too much for her. I bet the doctor told them not to expect another birthday, or something like that."

"I don't think so."

"All right. If it makes you feel better, I'll stop and talk to her when I drop Mac off tomorrow. She's known me all my life. She might tell me what's wrong, but not want to burden a stranger."

"Thanks, Evan."

"No problem. Now lighten up. You'll be like having Eeyore at a birthday party."

"Oh, darn," she said in a slow, deep voice. "My balloons always pop."

They started laughing. Lordy, this man made her laugh, made her feel as if champagne ran through her veins instead of blood.

She looked again at the landscape. It was almost a

moonscape. Gently rolling land, with scrubby grass beginning to grow, but not a tree in sight.

"Do you find it depressing?" he asked.

"The landscape?" she said surprised. "Not at all. I find it quite beautiful in its own way."

"And what way is that?"

"It's like no one has messed with it. It's probably looked pretty much like this since the beginning of time. I bet the Indians rode ponies after buffalo through here."

He told her then, about the centuries old grasslands they were on. "Most of this land has never known a plow. It's grazing land, and not great grazing land at that. A man has to have a lot of acres to feed a few cattle. But I like it. It's big and untamed and I like it."

Inside his house, she understood immediately what Mac meant when he said it was a "guy" house. Though it was obvious that some quick surface cleaning had been done recently, she could tell the state of Evan's house was not high on his priority list. It made her feel the funniest little pang for him and for his little boy. It was as if this house craved softness—someone to care about it, the smells of bread or cookies baking. And that's how Evan seemed, too, as if under all that strength, under all that hard masculinity, he needed something soft.

Mac and Jesse were playing fort in the living room. They had used sofa cushions and bedroom blankets and chairs from the kitchen and had built themselves a tent and a system of tunnels.

It reminded her, poignantly, that Mac was in that funny place somewhere between being a little boy and a big one.

"I wasn't having fun," he told her, crawling out

from under a blanket. "Evan told me I could knock off work a little early if I looked after Mr. Stinky. He likes forts, don't you, Mr. Stinky?"

"Mac, don't call him that!"

"Auntie Kathy, he likes it!"

"I like fowts," Jesse announced. Unfortunately, because he couldn't pronounce his *r*'s very well it came out sounding more like farts than forts, which just cracked Mac up.

Mac made a horrible noise, with his lips against his arm.

"Mac!" Kathleen said.

But Evan touched her arm, and shook his head. She followed his gaze, and saw Jesse was howling with laughter, rolling on the floor holding his sides. She took in the look on Evan's face, and there was such wonder there.

She realized, a little sadly, that for some reason, little Jesse did not laugh often.

"How do you like your hot dog," Evan asked her, "Rare, medium or burned?"

"Medium."

"Damn. That's the hard one." He went outside and she could see him lighting an outdoor fire pit.

Kathleen surreptitiously looked around with interest. She felt puzzled. Was this not where Evan had lived with his wife? If it was, all signs of her were gone.

There was not a picture on the wall, or a feminine touch anywhere.

"Decorations by Zen," Mac said to her in a whisper.

"Mind reader," she said.

He laughed, and ducked back under the tent with Jesse. Their shouts and laughter came out only slightly muffled, and she realized she had not heard Mac laugh

that much lately, either. And that she had missed it
very, very much. She took a chair and just listened to
them laugh and let it wash away the part of her that
was worried about Ma Watson.

After a while, she realized Jesse was peeking out at
her. After studying her for a long time he came out
from under the blanket. He went down the hall and
came back a few minutes later. Shyly he handed her a
little toy truck, purple where it had paint left on it, two
wheels missing.

"This is my twuck," he said. He watched anxiously
while she looked at it.

"Pretend to put it in your pocket, Auntie Kathy.
He'll really yell about that."

"I don't want him to yell," she said smiling, and
handing Jesse back his truck. He accepted it with obvious relief, inspected it and smiled at her. "What a
nice truck."

Evan came in, called them to the table.

They ate hot dogs that were only slightly burned.
Jesse had to have his mustard squeezed in a squiggle
just like Mac's. Mac told horrible jokes, and Jesse
squealed with laughter. She laughed just because of
Jesse's reaction and because it felt so good to be here,
with the boys laughing and Evan smiling indulgently,
obviously enjoying his son and her nephew very much.

At the end they had cake and ice cream and Evan
put a single candle on the cake.

"Blow it out, Jesse," he called. "Goodbye to diapers."

They all clapped and cheered as Jesse blew out the
candle.

Evan relit it. "Goodbye to your pipe!"

Jesse looked a little more uncertain about that one,

but he blew out the candle. He opened his presents, inspecting the new trucks solemnly. But the posters from Mac were what won his heart and made him smile.

"I'll help you put them up tomorrow," Mac told him gruffly.

They all went outside afterward and Jesse threw his soother and a token diaper into the fire pit. Then Mac showed her the calves that had been recently weaned from their mothers and told her that it was one of his jobs to feed them. The calves obviously associated him with food because they came running when he appeared at the fence.

He looked very pleased by that.

It began to get cooler as the sun went down, and Evan suggested Kathleen go back to the house with Jesse. Mac and he would do a few chores. "It'll only take a few minutes."

She did, and was busy doing the dishes, Jesse standing on a chair beside her playing in the suds, when the phone rang. She hesitated and picked it up.

"He's out doing chores—oh, wait, I think I hear him coming. Just a sec. Evan, phone."

He came in through the door, and picked up the phone. She could tell right away something was wrong. He turned his back to her, and his conversation was curt and monosyllabic.

She could hear a growing edge of impatience in his voice.

Finally he said, "Look, I have company right now. Could we have this discussion another time? I beg your pardon? Is it a woman? I think you know it's a woman. She answered the damn phone."

He listened for a minute and then said in a quiet tone

that did not disguise his fury, "You want to know what? She's a hooker all the way from Vancouver. We're having a wild party. I let the dogs clean the plates, and Jesse plays with barbed wire because I'm too mean to buy him toys. Got it?"

He slammed down the phone, kept his back to her for a moment and then turned to her slowly.

"I'm sorry. I lost my temper. I should have never said that."

She stared at him, her mouth open. "A hooker?" she finally whispered. "Me?"

"I just said that because Mac told me you hook rugs. Sorry. It was a lousy thing to say. Sometimes I just start spouting. A fault. One that probably won't make me look very good in court."

"In court? Who was that?"

"Jesse's grandparents, Dee's folks. They phone now and then and accuse me of being a lousy parent. They suspect I don't feed him, or keep him clean because my house is overrun with women and I have wild pot parties."

"Well," she said. "Close. It was a potty party."

He tried to smile, but didn't quite pull it off. "They've requested a home study on me, a preliminary to starting legal action for guardianship of Jesse."

She gasped. "Evan! They can't have a hope."

He shrugged, rolling his shoulders, as if trying to lift a burden off them. She wanted to rub the anxiety away.

"They've talked about this before. I'm not completely blameless. When I first met Dee, I was hardly a parent's vision for their daughter's future. But they don't want to believe I've changed, and I don't have the time nor energy to convince them. Besides, I think if I was okay, they might have to start looking at Dee, and ultimately at themselves. Who wants to do that?"

"Do you have a lawyer?"

"Yeah. She says as long as I keep my nose clean, I should be okay."

"Should?" she whispered, wanting to erase the worry line that had appeared on his forehead.

"I'd have a better chance if I were married."

"That's unfair."

He smiled, but it was deeply cynical. "So, who expects life to be fair?"

The phone rang again.

He closed his eyes, and took a deep breath. "They forgot to tell me they wished it was me instead of their daughter," he guessed, and picked up the phone. "Yeah?"

His tone changed instantly. "Ma? What?" He listened, turned his back to her again. "Yeah, okay," he finally said, hanging up the phone. He stood very still for a long time before he turned back to her.

"This has turned into a really lousy party," he said. "That was Ma Watson."

Kathleen felt dread spreading over her. "And?"

"She knew you were here. She didn't want you to be alone when you heard."

"Heard?"

"They sold the store. The deal was finalized a few minutes ago. It wasn't listed or anything. It was a buyer who was interested last year and came back."

Mac came in, holding Jesse's hand. Jesse's little blue jeans had a dark, wet stain down the front of them. "I tried to tell you this idea was stupider than stupid," Mac said, then looked from her face to Evan's and back again. "What's the matter?"

"Somebody bought the store," Kathleen told him.

"The store where you work?" Mac asked.

"Yes."

"Does that mean you don't have a job?"

She looked to Evan.

"They want to give you a month's notice. She said you could stay in the house as long as you need to. They'll pay for you to go back to Vancouver."

"Yippee!" Mac howled.

Kathleen turned away. She felt Evan's hand on her shoulder, and looked up at him. She could see the concern in his face.

She tried to smile. He had enough on his plate right now. She said bravely, in her very best Eeyore voice, "I told you my balloons always pop."

Chapter Five

Kathleen swam out of a deep sleep and groped for the phone.

"Hello?" she asked groggily.

"Hi."

"Evan?" She came slowly awake, looked at her clock. It was after two in the morning.

"I'm sorry to wake you. I'm having a little problem."

So was she. That it felt so much like a dream to wake up to the deep timbre of his voice, that she couldn't really be sure if she was awake or sleeping. "What?"

He held the phone away and she could hear Jesse shrieking in the background.

"Oh, my God," she said, coming awake in a flash. "What on earth—"

"Remember the ceremonial torching of the soother? Not such a hot idea, no pun intended."

"He's making that noise about a soother? It sounds like—"

"I know. It sounds like I'm killing him. If I had neighbors the police would be here. I'd be getting hauled out in cuffs. That wouldn't look so good on the court report."

"It takes them two hours to come," she reminded him, marveling at the thread of good humor in his voice, despite the noise in the background.

"That means they would have been here half an hour ago."

"Oh, Evan."

"I'm going to ask you the biggest favor of my life. I'll never ask you for anything else."

"What?"

"Have you got a key to the Outpost? Can I get in there and buy a soother? I didn't want to bother Ma. Pa's sick again, and she sounded about done in herself when I talked to her earlier."

"How could I say no to that? Should I meet you there? Half an hour."

"I bet I can make it in twenty minutes."

"Evan, I have to tell you something."

"That I owe you my life?"

"Besides that."

"You want my firstborn son? Take him."

She liked his voice on the other end of the phone, snuggled deeper under her blanket, let herself savor it. It felt sensual somehow to be talking on the phone in the middle of the night to the best-looking man in Hopkins Gulch. And not at all dangerous, since she would be leaving soon.

"I want you to know," she said firmly, "that you

are going to do just fine if it comes to a court case. I think you're about the world's best daddy."

She wouldn't have been able to say that to his face, or if she were staying, either, but the phone gave her a strange sense of intimacy that she never wanted to let go of.

Pathetic old maid that she was.

She reminded herself he wouldn't be enjoying this moment quite as much as she was, since he wasn't in bed and since she was competing with a child screaming in his other ear.

There was a long pause on the other end of the line, and then his voice hoarse, he said, "That's about the nicest thing anyone ever said to me, Kathleen. I'll pick you up. Twenty minutes."

Twenty minutes was not a fair amount of time to give a woman approaching thirty-five to get ready for anything. She had to be content with running a brush through her hair, scrubbing her face, brushing her teeth. She pulled a button-up sweater shirt and a baggy pair of slacks over the baby doll pajamas she wore to bed and went out into the night.

She was not sure she had ever seen a night so magical—stars in Vancouver competed with all the other lights, got lost somewhere. But here the universe looked enormous, the stars glittering in shining abundance. It made her think thoughts of larger things.

"Is there a plan for me?" she whispered to the night sky. "Everything seems to be such a mess."

She could have sworn a star winked at her, reassuringly. It made her want to memorize the Saskatchewan sky, to hold it in her heart forever, that moment when she felt so sure that, despite all the evidence stacking up to the contrary, everything was going to be all right.

The truck pulled up with a throaty rumble, and she ran lightly down the walk. She could hear Jesse before she had covered half the distance between her house and the truck.

Evan reached over and popped open the door for her, the sound intensifying almost unbearably when he did so.

She climbed in. "I don't know how you stand it. How did you not have an accident on the way here?"

Evan was wearing a jean jacket that fit snugly over the broadness of his shoulders and made him look like a cowboy—compelling, tough, mysterious. Then she noticed his hair was standing up in the front, as if he had run his hand through it once too often, and the cowboy image faded, replaced by one of a young dad, exhausted and frustrated.

No answer. She looked back at Jesse. His face was purple, his arms and legs flailing wildly. She knelt on her seat and reached into the back. She found herself undoing his car seat buckles and gathering him in her arms. "It's going to be okay," she said. "Jesse, we're on our way to the store to get you a soother."

She turned back around, held him tight against her and rocked, talking soothingly, even though there was not a chance he could hear her. At least the flailing stopped. He wrapped a hand in her shirt, and yelled against her breast.

She looked out the truck window at the stars. They were so beautiful. Somehow if felt just right to be sitting next to this gorgeous man in his pickup in the middle of the night. She didn't even mind Jesse's noise, the damp spot growing on her sweater where his tears were falling. Jesse had brought her to this moment, where she could admire the stars. She had not been up at this time of night since she was a teenager.

She felt a boldness she would not have felt in the light of day—as if each of those stars beckoned for her to say what was in her heart. Or maybe it was a bold- ness brought on by knowing her time her was already ticking away.

And so she said, "Isn't it a gorgeous night?"

Evan didn't say anything.

"The kind of night," she said as softly as Jesse's yelling would allow, "when a person could believe in all kinds of things they never ever believed in before?"

No answer. Evan put the truck in gear and pulled out.

"The kind of night," she continued, "that could make a person believe in a prince and a glass slipper and a midnight kiss."

She ducked her head, hardly believing she had said that, mortified. A child was screaming, practically bursting blood veins, and she was trying out as the queen of romance? Romance, something she had sworn off!

When Evan remained coolly silent, she looked at her toes, debated opening the truck door and leaping out to save her dignity. Jesse in her arms stopped her.

Evan nudged her shoulder.

He had his hand outstretched to her. In it were two small cylinders. She took them. Foam. She rolled them around in her free hand, then looked askance at him. He pointed to his ears.

"Can't hear a damn thing," he bellowed.

She put the earplugs in, not sure if she was happy to have been saved from herself or not.

Evan got them to the Outpost in five seconds flat.

"Give me the key," he said.

"I'll go in."

"After what I told you about loaded shotguns behind doors in this town? I'll go."

She handed him the key. "The baby things are—"

"I've practically lived in the baby aisle for the last three months. I'll leave a couple of bucks on the counter."

"I'm sure you can be trusted for it." She ran her hand through the sweat-dampened curls on Jesse's head. He was making less noise, sneaking little looks at her.

Evan hopped out of the truck, put the key in the door and was back out within minutes. He couldn't get the soother out of the package fast enough. He turned and plopped it into Jesse's mouth.

The silence was so sudden and blessed that she could hear herself breathing.

Evan leaned his head against the steering wheel. "I knocked something over in there. I hope I didn't wake up Ma."

"You probably would have had a backside full of lead if you had."

Jesse watched her with big eyes, sucking frantically, as if to make up for lost time. Then his eyes closed, opened, and closed again.

"He's going to sleep," Evan said. He tugged the earplugs out of his ears.

She took hers out, too, gazing down at Jesse. He was still sucking frantically, but his eyes were closed and his head nodding against her.

"Look at those stars tonight," Evan said, as if he was seeing them for the first time.

She said nothing.

"It's enough to make a man believe in things bigger than himself."

The silence stretched between them. He made no move to turn on the truck.

"You know how I said I'd never ask you for anything else?" Evan said.

"Yes?"

"I lied."

"And?" she said, amused. "What else are you going to ask me for? If it's disposable diapers, let's do it now, before I go back to sleep."

"It's not that."

"Well?"

He shook his head. "I should go home and get to sleep. I've been up nearly twenty-four hours. I should feel like I'm about to die."

"But you don't?"

"No, ma'am."

"If you call me ma'am again, I'm going to call you—" she thought for a second "—Buster!"

He laughed. "I've been called a little worse than that on the odd occasion. Is that the best you can do in the name-calling department?"

"At this time of night!"

He took a deep breath. Go home, he told himself, think about this. Don't just go blurting it out, and then regret it later.

As if that wasn't the story of his life.

But it felt so magical right now. The stars. The silence. Her beside him, her hair down, a little pajama bow showing at the V of her sweater. His son in her arms, looking so relaxed now and at peace, and the look of unguarded tenderness as she looked at his son made her look like a Madonna.

She smelled good.

He bet he didn't. Which was a good thing. It would keep him on his side of the truck, where he damn well belonged.

"You should wear your hair like that more often," he said. *Back off, Evan.* But it was easy to override that voice when he was so tired. His guard wasn't just down. It was dead.

"Is that what you're going to ask me? To wear my hair like this?"

Say yes. "No." He started the truck. His heart was beating fast. He'd never ever felt like this about this particular task. He'd never cared, particularly, if someone said no before. There were lots of fish, after all.

He contemplated caring so much. Another good reason to make up a question, then drop her off and drive away.

"I want to see you. Just you. No Mac and no Jesse." Maybe it wasn't a question, after all. A statement. His guard dead, and the feelings running free. "I want to see you. Not as Mac's aunt, and not as Jesse's daddy. Am I making any sense?"

"I think so."

"As a man," he said gruffly, "and a woman."

She looked terrified, liked he proposed they jump out of an airplane together with no parachutes.

"I'm way older than you," she said, after a while, looking deliberately away.

"I know you're a bit older than me."

"And I don't date."

"I know that, too."

"Then why are you asking me this?"

"Because I'm dead tired, and the stars are out, and you just saved my life."

"Oh," she said relieved, "because you owe me one."

Say yes. "No," he said.

She turned her eyes to him wide and filled with starlight, her hair hanging in a curtain of silk over her shoulder, her face filled with tenderness and uncertainty.

"Because you're the most beautiful woman I've ever seen."

He couldn't believe that had popped out. She turned rapidly from him. He thought she might be blinking back tears. He leaned over, touched her chin with his finger, forced her to look back at him.

"You are," he said. Sure enough, little diamond tears sparkled at the corners of her eyes.

"You know I'm not. And I don't. Can't. Date."

"Make an exception. I know you won't be here much longer."

"And what will we do with the boys?"

He noted that looking for an excuse was a bit different than an out-and-out no. "Tie them up and feed them to rattlers?" he said hopefully.

"Have you got a Plan B?"

"For the date, or the boys?"

"The boys."

This was looking very hopeful. "Ma Watson?"

She took a deep, shuddering breath, as if she was standing on a high diving board, looking down. "I'll ask her tomorrow."

"Play on her guilt."

"Evan, this isn't the distinctly upsetting part starting is it?"

"I don't think so. I sure as hell hope not. Just two

people who need a break from their kids. When's the last time you had a break from your kid?''

"Not for a while."

"Ask her about tomorrow night."

"All right. You know," she said, "for a woman who doesn't date, I've capitulated with a disgraceful lack of fight."

"Thank God. I'm too tired to arm wrestle you for it tonight. I mean, if I had to I would, but I'm feeling fairly thankful I don't have to."

"You'd arm wrestle me for a date?"

"Best out of three."

"I wouldn't have a chance."

"That's the basic idea."

"Evan." She was suddenly serious, her eyes huge and frightened. "No. I can't. I've changed my mind. I mean I'm too old to be lying awake tonight wondering if I'll have to kiss you good-night after."

"If you kiss me good-night after, it won't be because you have to."

Her mouth fell open. She plunked Jesse in his arms, and wrestled with the door, practically falling out backwards. She hesitated for a moment.

He gave her a slow salute. "See you tomorrow night." She slammed the door and bolted. He put the truck in gear and drove into the night.

There. He'd gone and done it. Weakened by Jesse screaming for three solid hours, nearly out of his mind with it.

But really, he'd thought of nothing else since the moment Ma had called him and told him Kathleen's job was over.

That she was leaving. What would the harm be in

trying to alleviate her anxiety a bit? Get her mind off her troubles, which seemed to be multiplying?

That was all. He was trying on a new role, late in life. Altruism. He'd take her for a nice dinner, out to a movie. Something like that. He was a man aiming for knighthood, after all.

What was this singing inside of him? What was it?

Kathleen looked in the mirror yet again. She had heard his truck pull up, but she was afraid to go out. She was wearing a beautiful white silk tailored shirt and gray slacks, the tenth outfit she had put on.

It made her look old and boring and ready for the office.

She wanted to be able to carry off one of those cute tops that showed the belly button, but those days were over for her. And she'd never even had a baby to blame it on.

There was a loud knock on the door. She made no move to answer it. She had left her hair down, but now, studying herself, she thought it looked awful. As if she was trying to look younger than she was.

Hastily she hung her head upside down, gathered up her hair and straightened. She began shoving pins in.

He knocked again.

With any luck he would go away.

She was just too old for this. The excitement felt as if it was too much. No wonder she had hidden behind her responsibility to Mac all these years.

Mac who had gone to Ma Watson's half an hour ago in a fit of disgust.

Bang. Bang. Bang.

She hastily wiped the bright red lipstick off, then sat on the edge of her bed. She closed her eyes and willed him to go away. When that didn't work, she tried desperately to remember her positive-thinking book. She tried to visualize something positive.

She could picture his beautiful smile, directed at her, full of the most heady tenderness.

"Kathleen?"

She started, opened her eyes and let out a little squeak of shock and dismay. He was standing in her bedroom door, looking at her.

"How did you get in?"

"I opened the door and walked. I thought maybe you didn't hear me knocking. Or were in the basement, dying of snakebite."

She glared at him.

He came and sat down beside her on the bed, too close, his rock-hard thigh touching hers. She scooted away.

"You're sorry you said yes, aren't you?" he asked quietly.

"How did you know?"

He reached up and touched her forehead. "It's running across here in big black letters."

"Are you sorry you asked?"

"No."

"Evan, I just don't know what to do. I don't know what to wear or what to say. I can't even put my lipstick on. I hate this. It's like I don't know who I am, I'm so nervous."

"I'm not so scary."

"Yes, you are!"

"In what way?"

She was stubbornly silent.

"In what way?" he asked again.

"You're very good-looking," she finally said.

He hooted. "And you aren't?"

"Not in the same league. At all."

"That's completely untrue."

"Well, you are very good-looking," she said, stubbornly, as if that was a legitimate thing to hold against him.

"It's not as if I can help it. An accident of birth."

"And you're too young for me."

"Didn't we cover this territory once before?"

She said nothing.

"Can I tell you something?" he said quietly, that stern note running through his voice that she'd heard him use on Mac.

"If you must."

"You aren't exactly acting your age at the moment."

"And what age am I acting? If you say thirteen, I'm going to lock myself in the bathroom."

"How about sixteen?"

"Do you see why this can't work?" she demanded. "You're younger, but you're not acting sixteen."

"You don't know what I'm feeling."

"You are not feeling sixteen."

"Seventeen, then. All scared inside. I don't know what to say, either. I'm worried you'll think I'm a dumb country boy who thinks a bull market is about bulls and stock is about those things that go moo in my backyard."

She smiled, despite herself.

"I'm worried I'll slip up and use the wrong fork at dinner," he said, his hand finding hers, and taking it. "And that you'll think I'm not dressed right."

She let him keep her hand and slid a look at his

pressed jeans, and the nice Western shirt, buttoned high, the shining boots, the neatly combed hair.

"Oh, Evan, you look wonderful, as if you couldn't."

"I'm worried," he said, his voice low, "that I'll order something with garlic in it, and you won't, and then I'll be scared to death to kiss you good-night, even if I can tell you want to."

She laughed a little. She liked him. Maybe that was why she was so scared.

"So can we go now? Now that we've established that we're both scared witless?"

She took a deep breath. "All right. Where are we going?"

"A little place in Medicine Hat. Medium fancy. Can you coach me which fork to use?"

"What makes you think I know?"

He slid her a look. "You know."

"What are we going to talk about?"

"You're going to tell me all about Vancouver. You can tell me about your favorite season and your favorite holiday and your favorite flavor of ice cream."

"That should take five or ten seconds."

"Then you can tell me about what you think you're going to do in a month."

"Another ten seconds. What are you going to talk about?"

"I'll dispel the romantic myth surrounding the rodeo cowboy by sharing the highlights of my brief bull riding career with you. That will be good for another ten seconds."

"You were a rodeo cowboy? A bull rider? Really?"

"Really. Maybe I'll take my ten seconds now." Without releasing her hand, he stood and tugged her up behind him. Talking gently the whole time, describing a big, wicked Brahma bull with mean red eyes, he led her to the door, fished her sweater out of her closet, tucked it around her shoulders and opened the door for her.

"I do not believe the bull's name was Mr. Stinky Pants. What do you take me for? A city girl?"

"It was. Well, maybe Mr. Stinky. And he deserved it, too. Killed maybe three or four cowboys before I rode him."

"He did not." He held open the truck door for her, and she climbed in, noting Jesse, too had already been delivered to Ma.

He went around his side, got in, started the truck and then patted the seat next to him. Slowly she slid over, until her shoulder was just about touching his, and her hip was, too.

"He did. Gored one. Danced on the other. Fell on one. Other one died of plain fear."

The truck moved forward.

"Thank you," she whispered.

"For what?"

"For making me be more than I am."

"Kathleen Miles, a simple cowboy like me couldn't do that."

"You're not a simple cowboy, Evan."

"No?"

"I think you're more like a knight."

"Have you been talking to Ma Watson?" he asked sharply.

"About knights?" she said incredulously. "No."

"I think a knight would know which fork to use," he said, recovering, flashing a grin at her.

"Really? I wouldn't have even thought they had forks back then."

"Good point. Now the rules for this evening."

"Rules?"

"Yup. Absolutely no talk of the boys—not one word."

"All right."

"And no worries. Not a single one."

"All right."

"Now, where was I? Oh, yeah, he had a look of fire in his eye, that bull."

They were nearly halfway to Medicine Hat when he finished the story, a story that managed to tell her quite a lot about the life of a bull rider, for all its tall qualities. It finished with the conclusion that with any luck they'd be eating that old Mr. Stinky for supper tonight.

"Your turn," he said.

"After that? You don't seem to get it, Evan. I'm boring."

"No, you don't seem to get it, Kathleen. You aren't."

"Well, I can't think of one interesting thing to say."

"Start here then—when I was a little girl my favorite thing was…"

"When I was a little girl my favorite thing was going to the Vancouver Aquarium."

"Really? Now there's something I've always wanted to do. Tell me about it."

And it was that easy.

Dinner was wonderful. He was charming and funny and endearingly humble about the very lack of finesse that made him so appealing, so real.

She ordered Caesar salad with prawns on it, and he teased her about the garlic.

"Hello, Evan."

Kathleen looked up. The woman was icily beautiful

in an electric-blue silk suit, the skirt four inches above the knee. Her dark hair extremely and stylishly short, her makeup perfect. Red, red lipstick looked fine on her.

"Mary Anne! Hi. You're not licensed to practice in this province are you?"

"Depends what I'm practicing," she said, sending a look back to her table, where a distinguished-looking man in a suit was sitting. "Law, no."

"Kathleen, this is my lawyer, Mary Anne Grey."

"Hello, Kathleen. Nice to meet you. Look, Evan, I hate to do business when I can't send you a bill, but I got a fax from your in-laws' attorney this afternoon." She shot Kathleen a look, hesitated and looked back at him. Evan nodded that it was okay for her to continue. "They plan to make your life difficult."

"My life has always been moderately difficult," he said.

"They want the court to order a home study."

"I heard."

"You're supposed to tell me when you hear these things!"

"But then it's billable," he said, his tone teasing.

Kathleen watched the lawyer's icy composure give way to her obvious affection for Evan.

"I guess," Evan continued, "I hope if I ignore them, they'll just go away. Look, Kathleen and I made this pact not to talk about anything that was troubling us tonight. Can I call you later in the week?"

The lawyer turned and regarded Kathleen thoughtfully. "Want some advice, cowboy? Absolutely free?"

"Is this a first in the Western world?"

"Probably." She turned back to him.

"All right. Advise away."

"Marry her." She winked at him, and walked away.

Evan studied his plate. Kathleen studied hers. She dared to look up at him. He looked at her.

"As if a lady like you would ever marry a guy like me," he said.

"You mean a knight?" she asked. And then it came out, simply and from her very soul. "I would."

And then she blushed so hard she thought the waiter was going to have to put out the fire on her face. "If I was asked properly," she said, trying for lightness. "Did I tell you about Whistler?"

He shook his head, looking shell-shocked.

"My second favorite place. I love to downhill ski. Do you ski?"

"In Saskatchewan?" he asked, but it was obvious he was thinking of something else, and she knew she had managed to spoil everything.

Chapter Six

Mary Anne and her beau invited them for a drink after dinner. Mary Anne was becoming less inhibited by the second. Evan drank Pepsi and thought Mary Anne's man looked like the kind of guy Kathleen deserved.

White collar. Classy. Rich. He owned some sort of computer company.

He'd probably know how to ask *properly,* a phrase Evan had been mulling over ever since it came off Kathleen's lips.

She had spoken it casually, he reminded himself. For Pete's sake, she had been kidding.

"So, were you affected by Y2K, Evan?" Roger asked, when the conversation slowed to a trickle. "The Big Crash?" It made Evan very sorry they'd agreed to join them.

"I rode a bull named that once," Evan said, drawling deliberately, "and it was a pretty good crash. Busted three ribs."

Mary Anne sighed, took a long pull on her second Irish coffee and said, "Cowboys are so sexy."

"Well, not with busted ribs, they're not," Evan said. He glanced over at Kathleen, who had ducked her head and was stirring her drink. Had he embarrassed her? Maybe sometimes he was a little too earthy. A flaw.

One of many.

Mary Anne laughed. Roger looked put out.

But Kathleen looked up at him, and the look in her eyes nearly stole his breath away. Whatever she was, it wasn't embarrassed. He thought, again, that she was better looking than Mary Anne—warmer, fuller, richer. He liked the blouse—soft, prim and yet just a little bit clingy.

Roger gulped down his drink. "Mary Anne and I want to catch the movie, so I guess we'd better move on."

"Do you want to come?" Mary Anne asked. "Evan, you'd love it. Roger's been dying to see it forever."

"I don't think he'd like it," Roger said. "It's not *The Cowboy Way*."

"Or *Eight Seconds*," Mary Anne said wistfully.

"Uh, Kathleen?" Evan did not want to go see a movie. At all.

Kathleen was looking at Roger. "Is it a movie that takes place on an airplane? With terrorists? And then Arnold saves the plane, the president and North America?"

"The space shuttle, actually," Roger said with pleasure. "Sylvester."

"Maybe another time," Kathleen said. "Thanks."

Maybe another time, Evan repeated in his head. So much nicer than, hell, no, I don't want to go. These people all spoke the same language.

They finished their drinks after Mary Anne and Roger had left. She'd had hot chocolate and there was a little fleck of whipped cream on her lip.

"I think your lawyer friend liked cowboys," Kathleen said.

"Nah, she didn't. She likes what she thinks cowboys are."

"And what's that?"

"Well, you see a guy for a few seconds riding a few tons of raging beef, and the guy probably looks heroic, instead of just plain stupid. There's something larger than life about riding bulls. It makes the men who do it seem romantic, I guess, brave."

"A bit like a knight from days gone by?"

Evan snorted. "Not hardly."

"Then what is he really?"

"Usually a guy like me. Part-time cowboy, full-time dirt farmer, trying to make payments on a truck, up to the top of his boots in poop of various varieties most of the time. Real cowboys aren't romantic. They're just real."

"Maybe some people would find that romantic."

"Compared to what? A skunk?"

"Compared to, say, Roger."

"Really?" He found this information astounding.

"Yes."

"What was wrong with Roger?"

"Nothing was wrong with him. But I'll bet if he wants his piano moved, he hires someone to do it."

"He looked pretty good to me. Nice suit. His own business. Six-figure income. No wonder he hires someone to move his piano!"

"Evan," she said quietly, "are you trying to match me up with Roger?"

"No! I could just see what the attraction was for Mary Anne."

"Men have no idea what women like, do they?"

"I'll pay you to tell me."

"How much?"

"Ten bucks." He fished it out of his pocket, held it between his fingers.

"Sold."

"So, what do women like? I'm going to write it down and make it into a book."

"Muscles." She plucked the ten out from between his fingers.

He stared at her. "One word is a pretty short book."

She shrugged, flattened the ten on the table and looked at it with pleasure.

"Muscles? You're joking right?"

"Nope."

"It's pretty hard to build a relationship around that."

"Who said anything about a relationship?" she said.

"Ten bucks, and it's not even a relationship. What is it? They like to peek?"

"Yup."

"I've been robbed."

"I'll buy you a drink, cowboy."

"Great. Make it a double. Pepsi. I'm not even going to tell you what men like about women."

"You don't have to. I already know. And it's not their brains."

"Cynic. What made you so cynical? That guy you were going to marry?"

"How do you know about him?"

"Mac mentioned him on one of those rare occasions when he spoke to me."

"And what did he say?"

"That he left you. Because of Mac."

"Oh."

"Is that true?"

She nodded, unable to look at him.

"I don't think you should be ashamed about it. He wasn't worthy of you."

She did look at him, then smiled. "You know something? I must be a slow learner, because I'm just starting to figure that out."

"Did you want to do something else?" he asked. "There might be another movie on."

"Evan, I want to do something that I can't do in Vancouver, that I won't be able to do when I get back there."

"So that's where you'll go?" He felt the disappointment. What did he think? That she would really consider staying here? He doubted that. Even if he asked *properly*. No sense even embarrassing himself by asking. There were limits to chivalry, and marrying the maiden was likely going beyond the boundary.

"I think so. My work experience has all been in big offices. I kind of applied for the job at the Outpost in a moment of whimsy, thinking for once in my life I should be bold and daring and adventurous. It doesn't seem to be panning out. I should go back to what I know, take Mac back to what he knows."

He heard the regret in her voice. "I think being adventurous looks mighty good on you, Kathleen Miles," he told her, and then ducked his head, embarrassed after all. "So, what can we do here that you couldn't do in Vancouver?"

"You know what I want to do? I want to lie in the middle of the prairie and look up at those stars."

He was positive there was nothing in that hot chocolate but chocolate.

"You're not worried about snakes?"

"Of course I am. That's why I'm bringing you."

"I don't think that blouse was made for lying on the prairie, Kathleen. Luckily for you, I keep a blanket in the back of my truck. For emergencies such as this one."

They stopped a few miles outside of Hopkins Gulch and under a star-studded night sky. She put on her sweater and they hiked up to a knoll. He spread out the blanket, and they lay down on it, flat on their backs, but close.

"Do you know the constellations?" she asked him.

"Some. That's Orion."

"Where?"

"See the three stars in his belt?"

"Oh, I do see it."

"And the Big Dipper, and the Little Dipper. The Morning Star. The Milky Way."

He looked over at her. Her eyes were huge and full of wonder. He knew now was the time. He moved his arm over slowly, curled it under her shoulder.

"Is that a snake?" she asked, holding her breath, but her eyes full of laughter.

"Uh-huh. Of the human variety."

He rolled over, and looked at her.

"What are you doing?"

"I like this view better."

"You're looking at me!"

"Exactly."

"Evan, stop it."

"Okay." But he didn't. He leaned toward her. Her

eyes got larger. Her hand moved up and covered her heart.

He brushed his lips against hers, and could feel the tentativeness in her response.

Her lips were sweet, unbearably soft. He closed his eyes, and tasted her, felt her response, and was jolted by the innocence in it.

He opened his eyes, rested on his elbows, and looked at her.

"What?" she whispered.

"You haven't done much of this, have you?"

She looked mortally embarrassed. "I'm thirty-four years old, Evan."

"That's not what I asked you."

It seemed the strangest of ironies. He'd been with women ten years younger who knew ten times more. About what brought pleasure, how to use their bodies and lips and hands.

But nothing had ever made him feel like this.

He wanted her more than he had ever wanted any one of them. And his body was not about to hide that fact.

Probably scare her to death if she knew what was happening to him. He rolled away from her, stared up at the stars.

"Evan, I'm sorry."

"There's nothing for you to be sorry about."

"Could we do that again?" she whispered.

"No," he said, his voice raspy with thwarted need. "No, we can't. I think we'd better go."

He could tell he'd hurt her. That's why she needed a man like Roger, with more finesse, more grace. She needed someone who would know how to kiss her hand, be familiar with knightly protocol.

He dropped her off at her house, but they picked up the boys first, so even though he wanted to kiss her again, felt compelled to taste that sweetness again, he couldn't very well with Mac scowling at him.

"Mac, I'll see you Monday," he said. That should give him a whole day to set things right in his head. To figure out what it was he wanted from Kathleen Miles and what it was she wanted from him.

But by four in the morning when he still hadn't slept a wink, he knew it wasn't going to be that easy to figure out.

Because he was still pondering that *I would. If I was asked properly.*

Asked properly? He couldn't even kiss her properly, a department he had never failed at before. Of course, before, he knew it was going one place, and he couldn't wait to get there. With Kathleen, there was an element of respect there he was not sure he'd ever felt before.

She wasn't a quick tumble.

She was the kind of woman you took to a church, with all your friends and neighbors watching, and said "This is it. Forever. She's the one."

He'd said those words to Dee, of course. In a tacky chapel in Las Vegas, knowing somewhere in his heart it couldn't work, and wanting to desperately for that to be different because of the life she had inside of her. His baby.

Really, it wouldn't make any more sense this time. He'd known Kathleen even less time than he knew Dee.

So why did it feel like he knew her? Really knew her?

He supposed it was because she was more honest than Dee; there was nothing hidden about Kathleen.

From the minute he had first looked into her eyes, he had simply felt he'd known her forever, that his heart could find rest with her.

What had prompted Mary Ann to plant that impossible idea in his head? That he should marry Kathleen?

Well, that's what lawyers did. That's what you paid them for. To make sense of a world you didn't understand.

It would make sense for him and Kathleen to hitch their wagons together. She needed a place to go. There was nothing left for her back in Vancouver. That boy of hers needed a man's influence at this point in his life.

And this boy of his needed a woman's softness. He had seen how Jesse reacted when she gathered him in her arms in the truck yesterday, relaxed against her, trusted her in a way it seemed like he might never trust him.

Damn Dee.

And that was the other thing. You couldn't get any further from Dee Mortimer. Dee had been wild, Kathleen was calm; Dee had been hyper; and Kathleen was steady; Dee had been giddy, Kathleen's good humor ran deep and clear; Dee had appeared strong but had been weak, and Kathleen was exactly the opposite.

It seemed to him that if a man was going to marry, it would make all the sense in the world to pick someone like Kathleen.

If.

Of course, he wasn't going to. Besides, it wasn't as if he needed to get married. He was doing a pretty fair job of raising his son, if you didn't count potty-training.

He realized, suddenly, aghast with himself, he

wanted to marry her, and that desire had very little to do with the well-being of Jesse and Mac.

She was the only woman he'd ever met who would choose the cold, hard ground and looking at the stars over Arnold. Or Sylvester.

She was the only woman he'd ever met who'd been so shy and sweet and uncertain of herself—and yet underneath there flowed a spring of strength and goodness and light and laughter. He could see it in her eyes.

It would be a solution for both of them.

She was only kidding, he reminded himself.

But he made himself think back to her eyes, when she'd said it. They'd skittered away from his—not the look of a woman telling a joke, but the look of a woman terrified, vulnerable. Suddenly he wasn't so sure that she had been kidding.

Which left him right back at square one. How did a man go about asking *properly?*

He groaned, smacked his pillow, threw his covers on the floor.

He wondered if he was ever going to sleep again.

"So what did you guys do?" Mac asked.

"Pardon? What time is it?" Kathleen took her head out from under the pillow. Mac sat on the edge of her bed, glowering at her. She closed her eyes, thinking not of Mac, but of a star-filled night and a kiss that had changed her whole world.

An ember of desire had been glowing within her. That kiss had fanned it.

Wildfire.

And she had asked for more. Her eminent departure from this town had made her into a woman she didn't know. Bold. Brazen.

"It's nine o'clock, Sunday morning. You never sleep in." This was said accusingly.

"I had trouble falling asleep last night. I think it was after four before I finally dozed off."

"Why?"

This also had traces of accusation in it. She wasn't about to tell Mac why. Because the kiss had turned her world on end, and then Evan's baffling rejection had left her feeling wounded and vulnerable. Despite her best efforts it seemed the distinctly upsetting part was going to happen anyway.

How could it? She was leaving. She made herself repeat it three times. Leaving, leaving, leaving.

"I drank hot chocolate. It has caffeine in it. That probably kept me awake."

She had never lied to this boy, ever. Well, maybe once. When she had told him she had made that spaghetti just for him, and been nursing a hope, in the back of her heart, that company was coming. Company in cowboy boots and jeans.

Ridiculous. A woman her age nursing hopes.

Especially about Evan Atkins.

Sexy. Young. Sexy. Strong. Sexy. Gorgeous. Sexy. Even the lawyer had seen how sexy he was.

"Auntie Kathy, what did you do?"

"We went out for dinner in Medicine Hat."

"What did you eat?"

"I had Caesar salad with prawns."

"You went out for dinner and had *salad?*"

"I'm afraid so."

"What did he have?

"A slab of Mr. Stinky. A bull he rode once."

"Didn't they have hamburgers on that menu?"

"It was a step up from McDonald's."

"Ha. There is no step up from McDonald's. Do you think Evan would show me how to ride bulls?"

"I hope not!" She pulled her pillow back over her face, a hint that she wanted to be left alone.

"Did you kiss him?"

"Mac!" She peeked out from under the pillow, and said sternly, "I don't see how that could be any of your business."

"I'll bet that means you did. Yuck. Did you go to the movie? I just noticed it's playing in Medicine Hat. It's called *Six Minutes to Blast Off*. Sylvester."

"We didn't make it."

"Good. Maybe he'll take Jesse and me."

"Maybe he will, sometime. You know, Mac, I think I'm just going to laze around today. Stay in bed and read a book."

"This book on your end table?" Mac picked it up and squinted at the title. *"A Bride Worth Waiting For?"*

"As a matter of fact, yes."

"Ugh. My teacher says these kinds of books are trash."

"That means your teacher has no respect for women. I'm glad we moved."

"She was a woman!"

"That makes it even worse."

"Is this book about kisses?"

"It's about love and hope. It's uplifting."

"That's all? It sounds kind of boring."

"It's true that not one person will be maimed or killed, and no one will save the world from terrorist threats, but when I'm done reading it, I'll feel happy, and think the world is a nice place to be."

"Oh." Mac set the book down as if he had developed a new allergy. "I think I'll go see if I can catch a snake."

"What?"

"Just a garter snake, Auntie Kathy. They don't bite or anything. Can I keep him in my room?"

"No."

"I think that shows you have no respect for twelve-year-old males."

"My apologies."

"I'll bet kissing is better in that book than it was for real," Mac said, his parting shot.

She waited for the door to close behind him before she muttered, "I'll bet it's not."

She closed her eyes and thought of muscles and all the other things women liked about men. Crooked smiles, smoldering eyes, lips that tasted like raindrops, low, deep voices, an ability to laugh. Sincerity. Humility. Honesty.

It seemed to her she knew quite a bit more about what women liked about men than she had a week ago, or a month ago, or a year ago, or a lifetime ago.

And she knew something else, but did not know how she knew.

She knew Evan Atkins was going to spend the whole day wondering if she'd meant it, when she said, *I would. If I was asked properly.* He was going to wonder that even though he had backed away from her kisses.

She wondered why.

She had seen the look in his eyes, after all.

She decided it might have been the garlic.

She was up, stumbling around in her housecoat, when a knock came on the back door. Evan looking fresh and young and like he'd slept beautifully.

"Come in," she called through the screen.

He did. "Hi."

"Hi."

"Mac called me this morning."

"Mac called you?"

"He asked me if I'd teach him to ride a bull."

"And what did you say?"

"I said I was pretty sure you'd kill me if I said yes."

"That's correct."

"Then he asked me if I'd take him and Jesse to that movie. The one you nixed last night."

"That's a long way to drive to take some kids to a movie."

"You get used to driving."

"Why are you looking at me like that?"

"Like what?" he asked innocently.

"Like you've never seen me before."

"Well, ma'am, I've never seen you in your housecoat before."

"A treat, I'm sure. Don't call me ma'am."

"Kathleen, are you grumpy in the morning, generally?"

"As a matter of fact, yes. How many cowboys does it take to make breakfast?"

"I don't know."

"One, if you slice him thin enough."

"On that friendly note, I'm going to collect those boys and go."

"Evan?"

He turned and looked at her.

"Thanks for last night. I'll have dinner ready when you get back. Roast Stinky. No garlic." Let him contemplate what that meant all day.

"No cowboys, either, I hope."

"I promise."

She spent a wonderful afternoon puttering in the garden and making dinner, not giving one thought to the fact she would never harvest that garden. Evan came in with the boys, who had liked the movie very much.

"How did you like it?"

Evan rolled his eyes.

They ate dinner together, laughing and talking, and then Mac unearthed an old foam football in his room and they headed out to play.

She was coerced into being on Mac's team, and she ran and tackled and ran some more until she was nearly sobbing from exerting herself so much.

She lay down on the grass, and Jesse came and lay beside her, going to sleep.

Evan and Mac continued to run around, until the light faded. Mac declared he was going to have a shower, and Evan joined her on the grass.

"So what's the proper way?" he asked, not looking at her, touching Jesse's curls.

She knew instantly what he meant, and her mouth opened, but not a single sound came out.

"Like would it be with roses, and a ring, and down on one knee?"

"No," she squeaked.

"No?"

"No."

"It doesn't make any sense, in some ways. You know that, don't you?"

"Yes."

"But in others. In terms of the boys it makes sense."

"Very practical," she agreed hollowly.

"And, of course, it would save you a long move."

"Great."

"I'm sure you'd find my place a full-time job."

"Just what every girl dreams of. A full-time job."

"I guess I'm not doing this very good."

The silence stretched between them.

"Kathleen?"

"Yes, Evan?"

"Sometimes I'm so lonely I hurt. I don't think I'm any kind of a prize, but I'm better than I used to be, and I hope to keep improving. I know in Vancouver you're probably used to suave guys like Roger who make about a million bucks a year and could buy you fur coats and diamonds. Do you like fur coats?"

"Not particularly. I don't need diamonds, either."

"What I'm trying to say is that if you want to try this, I promise you I'll care about you and respect you and look after you. I'll treat Mac as if he was my own, and I'll do my best to help you make him into a strong independent man you can be proud of."

Silence.

"Kathleen?"

Silence.

"Are you crying?"

"Yes."

"Yes, you're crying, or yes, you'll marry me?"

Don't say yes, she warned herself. She'd had her brief fling with adventure; she'd thrown her hat in with fate when she'd answered that ad.

And it occurred to her it had brought her right here. To this gorgeous man, who had no idea how good his own heart was, asking her to marry him.

How was that for an unexpected twist on life's highway?

"Well? Yes, you're crying or yes—"

Once you had been bold, it was nearly impossible to go backward. "Both."

And he kissed the tears off her cheeks.

Chapter Seven

"**A**nyone could have seen Dee was all wrong for him," Ma said, through a mouthful of pins. "Not the kind of girl a boy would take home to his mama. Of course, he didn't have a mama. That was always the problem."

Kathleen stared at herself in the mirror as Ma put another pin in the long white gown. For some reason it was in the store's rather eclectic inventory, and for some reason, it fit Kathleen nearly perfectly. It seemed when there was a plan for you, *everything* fell into place.

Even so, she had tried to reject the dress when she had first seen it, even though her heart cried for it, even though she could not remember when anything had made her as wistful as the idea of wearing that dress.

"Oh," Kathleen had said when Ma had hauled it out. "I don't think that's what we have in mind. We'll probably just go to a justice of the peace somewhere and do it quickly and quietly."

Still, she had reached out and touched the fabric.

"No, you won't," Ma had said sternly. "He run off last time. It don't sit well with folks around here. They'll be wanting to welcome you to the community."

"You mean gawk at me. I feel like a mail-order bride. And Ma, I'm far too old for this dress."

"I think you were a mail-order bride of sorts. I sent you the letter, thinking I knew why, but God knew the real reason. The dress is beautiful on you. Stop this nonsense about your age. Some women age with uncommon grace. I wasn't one of them. Plump all my life, got worse as I got older. But not you."

"Evan has that kind of pull with God?" Kathleen said, trying to joke about it. "I just arrived in Hopkins Gulch, Saskatchewan, because a young cowboy needed to get married?"

"Evan? Evan doesn't *need* to get married. I think it's time for *you* to have some happiness of your own."

"Happiness," Kathleen said, and felt that funny, sick twist to her stomach. "I haven't thought anything through. We don't know each other."

"Kathleen, you are one of those rare people who thinks far too much. You could worry a banana out of its peel. Not even have to touch it, just worry on it. For once, you just acted. Maybe it's a miracle, for Pete's sake."

"But—"

"I don't want any 'buts' out of you. From the minute I saw that boy first look at you, I knew why you'd come here. To love him, plain and simple, and to allow someone to love you."

"Mac loves me," she wailed, "and he's terribly upset."

"Well, that's your own fault for letting him run your life for so long. You're not doing him any favors. That lad needs Evan nearly as much as Evan needs you. But Mac's twelve. Do you expect him to know what's good for him? He'd eat chocolate bars for breakfast if you let him. He's not ready to make some decisions—especially your decisions."

"Ma," she whispered, looking at the beautiful stranger in the mirror, "I'm scared."

The dress made everything seem even more like a fairy tale than it already did. The dress was high-collared, the collar and the entire fitted bodice beaded with tiny mock pearls. There were thirty-eight buttons up the back, making it hug her breasts, her tummy, her hips. Then it dipped in a V at the waist and the small of her back, and flared out in a decadent, ridiculous, wonderful waste of fabric.

Pure white...it was something a young woman full of romantic notions and innocence would wear. It was a dress made for a dream. A dress made for a princess.

Innocence, she had in embarrassing abundance, but romantic notions?

She thought of her husband-to-be, and she could feel her face heat up. All right. Maybe she had just a few romantic notions, too.

No wonder she was frightened. She repeated the sentiment, since Ma was busy tucking and pinning and didn't seem to have heard her the first time.

"I'm scared."

"Good! If you're never scared you're way too comfortable. Real life has some unpredictable moments. It's waiting to give you some gifts. But every now and then you gotta do something that scares you right off your sofa."

"I'm marrying Evan Atkins tomorrow," Kathleen whispered. "Me. He's too young for me, isn't he?"

"Kathleen, you get that knot out of your forehead. It spoils the look of the dress entirely. Entirely. He's not too young for you. That boy was born old. You'll probably lighten him up some."

"What do you mean, he was born old?"

"Darling, his mama died when he was just a tyke, and his papa asked him to be a man long before he was ready. He went through a wild stage—you probably would not believe how wild—but I knew he was just looking for what he never had. What he knew in his heart every person is supposed to have."

"Love," Kathleen guessed, tears in her eyes.

"You love that man, Kathleen, and you will see miracles happen. And if you let him love you back, your life will take on a richness and a hue you never believed possible. You let him be the man he needs to be. He's an old-fashioned man. Lots of guys from around these parts are. He'll want to protect and provide for you. It will be up to you to show him that love, these days, has progressed beyond that. It's about you helping him to be who he was always meant to be, who he really is in his heart and his soul. Personally I've always thought that was a knight of lightness."

Kathleen gazed down at the little woman at her feet and felt as if she was in the presence of great wisdom. It did feel, for an insane moment, as if reality tilted, and that maybe fate or God had brought her here.

She remembered looking at those stars, awestruck, and feeling them answer her humble question.

Is there a plan for me?

But what if this wasn't it?

"I don't know," she admitted, "how much love has to do with any of this, Ma."

"Worry line!" Ma reprimanded her. "Stand still. Two more pins. What do you mean by that?"

"He hasn't. I haven't. Said it. You know."

"Good grief. A word is just a word. It represents the thing, it isn't the thing. I've seen young couples that say 'I love you' every time they draw a breath. I'm not always convinced."

Kathleen forced herself to relax, watched the worry line fade from her forehead and practiced a tentative smile.

She stared at herself, astounded. She looked radiant.

Ma looked at her and smiled. "Now *that* convinces me."

"Are you going to faint?" Sookie Peters asked him.

Evan glared at him, but it was true, he could feel the blood leaving his face, pooling somewhere in the vicinity of his feet. "It's too hot out here," he said, tugging at the stiff white collar that was too tight around his neck.

It was a lie, of course. They were in the shade of the biggest tree in the churchyard. The truth was he was scared out of his mind.

Him, Evan Atkins, who had ridden a bull called Mr. Stinky without his pulse even changing, was so scared he could hardly breathe. Him, Evan Atkins, who had driven cars faster than they were meant to be driven, who had jumped from the peak of a barn roof on a dare, who had challenged his nerves at every available opportunity and walked away laughing, was terrified.

Not that he was about to make a mistake, but that he was unworthy of this woman who had said yes to him. That he didn't have any of the tools to make this thing work. Other people grew up in families. They had some idea how to do it, what the rules were. But for him this was strange country he was venturing into. Like a pioneer setting out in a covered wagon, having no idea what challenges and terrors lay ahead.

He hadn't even told her he loved her.

He felt as if he hadn't known her long enough to say that.

A very good reason not to be making that long walk to the altar in—he consulted his watch—three minutes.

"Sit down," Sookie suggested.

He did, on the grass, heedless of the suit. The suit was not his idea. Black, short jacket, string tie. At least they'd let him have a cowboy hat.

Word had gone through this town like wildfire that he and Kathleen were getting married. She'd told Ma Watson.

Evan, in his need to be a man worthy of her, had dropped by Sookie's and apologized for that day he'd threatened him for driving by Kathleen's house. Somehow, he'd had trouble keeping all his good feelings to himself, and ended up confiding in Sookie he was going to marry her. A mistake.

Sookie Peters and Ma Watson in charge of a wedding. It was like the pair of them had found a bear cub—thought it was real cute at first, but as they kept feeding it, it kept getting bigger and harder to control.

Before Evan had known what was happening, the whole town was getting involved. Preacher booked, church dusted out, hall ready, a decorating committee, for Pete's sake. Presents had been arriving at his house all week. Jesse opened them as they came, looking more and more disgusted at blenders and knife sets, matching bath towels and sheet sets.

Disgusted, Jesse told Evan that wrapped things were supposed to hold toys. Evan had told him what was happening. That Kathleen would be coming to live with them, and in time Jesse might come to think of her as his mother.

Jesse had looked at him blankly. "Mac coming live hew?"

"Yeah."

He'd looked inordinately pleased about that.

"You'll be like brothers," Evan said before he'd thought it through properly. Mac was Kathleen's nephew; that wouldn't make the boys brothers.

But Jesse latched onto the idea with great enthusiasm. He even let Mac, who was still coming to work, in spite of the pre-wedding excitement that held Hopkins Gulch in its grip, or maybe because of it, open some of the presents. Mac was as disgusted as Jesse with the items.

"Initials," Mac said, staring at the white towels. "*EA* on this one *KA* on this one. Yuck."

Evan tried to hide his own horror. White towels? His personal feeling had always been the darker the color of the towel the less handprints showed. Monogrammed to boot. People seemed to have figured out Kathleen was a different class of person than he was.

Jesse and Mac's disgust had intensified this morning when Sookie had showed up with matching suits, and a little pillow for the ring.

Mac was supposed to be an usher; Ma and Sookie were in charge of getting him ready. Evan had been returning his dark gaze steadily all week, letting him know he wasn't going to back down from him, trying to let him know everything would be okay.

He suspected he wasn't very convincing, because he had doubts himself about whether it was going to be okay.

He'd found the two boys hiding in the barn an hour before the wedding and herded them to the house to clean up and sullenly don their suits.

Now the music started to play. Fresh sweat broke out on Evan's brow. The side door of the church opened.

"Evan, get up off that grass," Ma said. "Lord, boy, haven't you ever worn a suit before?"

"No, ma'am." And he never had. In Las Vegas they couldn't care less if you got married in your underwear. He'd been wearing jeans with a rip in the knee if he remembered correctly. He stood up, brushed some dry grass off the seat of his suit.

Ma looked him over and smiled. "It looks real good on you. You cut a rather romantic figure, like an old riverboat gambler. Come on."

Why not look like a gambler, he thought darkly. He was gambling. With his life and hers and two kids thrown in for good measure. He looked wistfully at the open prairie and thought briefly about bolting.

But it would break her heart if he did that, after she'd taken a chance on him, and if there was one thing he was determined not to do, it was hurt Kathleen. Ever.

Meekly he followed Ma into the church. She showed him where to stand at the altar, positioned Sookie at his elbow. He looked down the long aisle at the main door of the church. The church was filled to the rafters, a blur of faces. If he thought it had been hot outside, it was unbearable in here. He found he couldn't even focus on who was there, could not answer the smiles directed at him.

The music seemed to go on forever, and for a sick moment he thought, She's come to her senses. She won't come.

And then the back door opened and Jesse came toddling up the aisle, holding a mutinous Mac's hand with one hand, and the little pillow with the other.

She had said she didn't want a ring, but Evan had bought her one anyway. Not a showy one, because that wouldn't have been right for her. A band of pure solid gold. Now that was Kathleen.

Mac arrived at the altar singing, "Here comes the bride, big fat and wide," under his breath. Evan nudged him and gave him a look. He shut up.

The door opened again, and she came in.

Evan's jaw dropped.

He could not believe that this woman had said yes to him.

She was a princess in her yards and yards of white, the collar high around her beautiful throat, her hair laced with flowers and piled up on top of her head. She looked like she was floating down the aisle toward him, and she looked like all the things he was not—calm and composed to begin with, and sophisticated and worldly to end with.

Her eyes never left him, shining.

Radiant.

No worry line, he was pleased to see.

Maybe she wasn't worried.

She glided to his side, smiled, and her smile stilled the wild beating of his heart. He looked into the calm in her eyes and felt it wash over him. He took a deep breath, and could feel himself fill with confidence.

This was the right thing to do.

Maybe not orthodox, maybe not how the rest of the world did it, but right for him and for her.

His voice suddenly strong and sure, hers like music, they said their vows.

And kissed until Mac, making gagging noises, brought them out of it.

The minister pronounced them man and wife.

"Me got Mommy," Jesse announced, running down the aisle in front of them, apparently having understood more of that conversation a week ago than Evan had guessed.

"Don't expect me to start calling you Daddy," Mac said in a sullen tone to him.

Evan eyed him. "I don't have that expectation, Mac."

Then a flash of disappointment went through Mac's eyes, and Evan had a premonition that this one was going to be hard to win.

Side by side, Evan and Kathleen greeted friends and neighbors. They walked out of the church to thousands of soap bubbles, their guests each having been given a little bottle and a blower.

Somehow he got through it all, the speeches and the food and the dancing that went well into evening, without making a complete ass of himself.

Because all he wanted to do was be with her.

Alone. Away from all these people who meant so well.

Mac and Jesse were going with Ma for a few days, and finally he and his bride were on their way home. Alone.

"Let's stop," she said, "and look at the stars."

So he stopped the truck and they got out, she gathering up her dress, and hiking across the prairie. She tilted her head back, and looked and looked and then looked at him, and smiled.

"Evan, I have something I have to tell you. Maybe I should have told you before. The time just never seemed right."

Oh, God. She was already married to someone else. She was an illegal immigrant and would have to leave the country. She had a deadly illness.

"Hey," she said, pressing her hand against the worry lines on his forehead, "that's my department."

"What do you need to tell me?" His voice sounded grim in his own ears.

The color rose in her cheeks. "I've never done before what you and I are going to do tonight."

For a minute he didn't comprehend what she was saying. "Uh, pardon?"

It was her blush, darkening over the high arc of her cheekbones, that made him get it.

"You've never been with a man before?" he asked quietly.

"It's awful, isn't it? I mean at my age, can you believe—"

"Hush," he said, moving to her swiftly. He looked into the luminous darkness of her eyes, and saw fear and anticipation there. "No one's ever given me a gift like this before. Never. It's the most beautiful thing I could imagine."

He lifted her into his arms, and felt her arms twine around his neck, her head lean against the column of his throat.

He tilted his head up at the stars.

There were never instruction books when a man really needed them, or at least not ones that worked. Not for potty-training, not for this wondrous surprise that had been dropped in his lap.

Step five out of *Potty-Training for the Hopelessly Confused* came to him for some reason. *Pray.*

And then he remembered he had read it incorrectly. It had really said *play.*

And probably both were applicable to the night ahead of them. He kissed the tip of her nose, prayed to be the sensitive guy she needed to get her through this and then felt his heart grow inside his chest, until it felt as if it was two sizes too large, just like a cartoon he'd seen once.

It was like a dream, being in his arms as he carried her across the threshold. He did not set her down, but went quickly through the darkened house, down the hall and into his bedroom, closing the door behind him with a kick of his heel. He set her on her feet gently.

A lamp had been left burning. And the bedroom, too, looked like a dream.

"The bed is beautiful," she stammered, looking everywhere but at him, and the steady look in his eyes. It was an antique four-poster, covered in plump white pillows, the comforter as white as snow.

"A present from the Watsons." He smiled. "The neighbor women have been in here all week, clucking at the mess me and Jesse have managed to make. You've never seen so many feather dusters and mops going."

"I would have done it."

"I don't want to turn you into a cleaning woman, Kathleen. I don't want to feel like I'm stealing your life from you."

She laughed shakily. "Oh, Evan. This is what I

want. To be a mom to Jesse and Mac.'' She whispered. ''To be a wife to you.''

''You know you're a woman who could do anything, don't you? You could be an astronaut or a doctor. And here you are on this little farm in Saskatchewan.''

''Evan, it's not about whether I'm an astronaut, or a doctor or a housewife. It's about me being allowed to choose what I really want without feeling ashamed or as if I have to make excuses. Why do women always have to make excuses about everything, the work they do, the books they read? Right now I've got exactly what I want. Do you understand?''

''Yes, ma'am'' he said, his voice low and throaty.

''This dress,'' she said shakily, ''has thirty-eight buttons on the back of it.''

''Really?'' he breathed. ''Then I guess we better get started. We only have six hours until dawn.''

She laughed, as she knew he had intended, and turned around, her heart hammering in her throat, as his hands found their way to the buttons, big hands, strong, but sure on the delicate workings of those buttons.

''Are you scared?'' he asked in her ear, his hands faltering on the last button.

''No.''

''I am.'' He worked the button free.

She looked at him over her shoulder, then turned slowly to face him, the dress loose now. She waited, her eyes on his face. He licked his lips, hesitated, closed his eyes.

''Evan?'' She could have sworn he was praying.

But when he opened his eyes, the anxiety was gone from his steady gaze, and he looked playful and tender and like the Evan she knew.

He moved close to her, looked into her eyes, his hands moved to her shoulders.

She gasped as the dress fell away, and she was standing before him in the lace and silk of her ivory-colored camisole.

"Undo this tie, Kathleen, before it chokes me."

Shaking now, but not from fear, she did as he asked, taking her time, her hands unsteady on the unfamiliar tie. When it was gone, she hazarded a brief look into his eyes, and then she undid his buttons on his shirt. The buttons seemed as if they were too large for the button holes as she fumbled with them, focused on them, her tongue caught between her teeth.

And then the last one was undone and his shirt hung open. She glanced at his chest, and felt her heart pick up tempo.

"Touch me," he whispered, and her heart moved into double time.

She slipped her hands inside his shirt and touched the skin and muscle she had yearned to feel for so long. Without interrupting her, he peeled off the shirt and dropped it to the floor. She gulped, looking at him.

"Don't stop. Touch me all you want. Until you don't want to anymore."

"That will be never," she said, and then blushed.

But he laughed, low in his throat. "We can only hope."

She could feel a faint tremble in him now, as her hands moved over him, over the broadness of his shoulders, the deepness of his chest, down to the hard muscles of his narrow stomach. His skin felt as she knew it would—heated silk wrapped around solid iron. She reached behind him, and ran her hands down the muscled expanse of his back, pulled herself in close to him, and rested her head on his chest.

She could feel his heart beating. Double time.

''Taste me,'' he whispered.

She looked at him, wide-eyed, and then with a sigh of surrender, she touched her lips to his chest. To the place above his heart. To the hollow of his throat. To his ears.

And finally, to his mouth.

It was the invitation he had waited for, and he gathered her to him, pressed her softness into his hard length and took her mouth with his.

She felt then, the kind of power she held over him, and in his kiss felt his absolute and unconditional surrender to it. She felt the desire on his lips, and saw it turn his eyes to smoke.

She gnawed on the sensuous fullness of his bottom lip, and felt the tremble within him deepen. She nipped lightly, and then his hand made its way to the back of her head, pulled her toward him and he took her lips captive. There was no innocence in him. What was in him was male need—powerful, wild, intoxicating.

He demanded more than little light kisses.

She had lit a match.

And he was tinder. And now fire.

His tongue pierced the hollow of her mouth, and the jolt went down deep inside her to a place she was not aware had existed. He took her lips and commanded, without words, that she give back everything that he gave, that she match him, passion for passion.

Tentatively, uncertainly at first, and then with growing boldness and confidence she met him, explored with him, until she was gasping with pleasure and need so great it bordered on pain.

He tumbled her backwards on the bed. Kissed her toes until she shrieked with tortured delight and swelling anticipation. He rained fire as he carved a path up the curve of her leg with his tongue. And then, slowly, his eyes suddenly on her face, he slid her slip upward and touched his lips to the delicate flesh of her inner thigh.

Then, his eyes turned to molten pewter, his intensity showing in the tautness of every muscle in his body, he slipped his fingers under the strap of her camisole, and paused.

"Yes," she whispered.

He slid the silken strap from her shoulder, kissed where it had been.

And then he moved the fabric away from her breastbone, and kissed where it had been. He continued until there were no silken barriers left between her naked skin and his questing lips.

And she did not think she was old. She did not think he was young. She did not think at all. Pure feeling took over, as his lips found the soft mound of her breasts, and he anointed them with his breath and his tongue.

Something wild leaped within her. Wild. Untamed. Primal. As old as the earth. As old as man and woman together.

Her hands slid to the waistband of his trousers, found the button, undid it. Her hands moved to his hips, and slowly, she tugged them off.

His lips claimed hers again, feverish, and she arched against him, begging him with her body to fill her, to fill that part of her that had never been filled.

And then she felt him part her legs, gently, watched as he posed above her on strong arms, trembling from holding himself above her, from holding himself back, but not even seeming to be aware of his own trembling.

"Evan," she called his name across all the time that had separated them in this universe and on this plain of life.

"Evan," she called her welcome to him, as he entered her, filled her, completed her.

"Evan," she called once more, as sensation took her in its mighty grip, shook her, carried her, took her finally, to a place she had never been. To a place where people become as gods, for a few short seconds, where they became heaven and earth, sky and wind and fire, calm and storm.

He lay against her, his head buried in her shoulder, his hair plastered to her skin.

She ran her hands through that hair, nipped his ear with her teeth, then laughed with something that went deeper than pleasure. Joy.

"If I'd have known what I was missing," she finally said huskily, when her breathing had calmed, "I might have tried this sooner."

He lifted his head and looked at her. More than looked. Drank her in, a man who had crossed a desert, dying of thirst, and found life at the fountain of her love.

"If I had known it would be like this with you, I think I would have waited," he said.

And then they cuddled in each other's arms, kissing, exploring, talking, laughing, kissing some more. Dawn was bathing them in its first rosy light when they finally slept in the tangle of their wedding clothes and in the circle of each other's arms.

Chapter Eight

"Darlin', wake up."

Kathleen snuggled deeper under the covers. Then she felt lips on her toes. Her eyes flew open, and she remembered suddenly, deliciously, where she was, who she was—Mrs. Evan Atkins—and what they had spent the night doing.

Evan burrowed under the covers, his head popping out beside hers.

She smiled, looking into the deep, laughter-filled blue of his eyes.

"Good morning, Mrs. Atkins." He kissed her on the cheek.

"Is that supposed to be a step up from ma'am?" she groaned.

"I forgot you're grouchy in the morning. Except it's not morning. We were supposed to leave on our honeymoon three hours ago."

Ma Watson had offered to take the boys for four days so that Evan and Kathleen could slip away to

Cypress Hills, an oasis of earth not far from Medicine Hat that had been missed by the ravaging effects of the glaciers.

"You'll love it there," Evan said, nibbling her ear. "It's exotic, almost like a rain forest in the middle of a desert."

"What you're doing is pretty exotic," she said.

"Innocent. That's called erotic."

And by the time they had finished exploring that, another two hours were gone from their honeymoon.

"I think we better go soon," Evan said, looking at her from one end of the bathtub, mounds of bubbles in between them.

She reached out with her toe and tickled his chin.

"I think we should stay right here."

"What kind of honeymoon is that?"

"I seem to be enjoying it so far," she said. "You know what I'd like to do?"

"Again?" he asked, astounded.

"Besides that. Paint the boys' rooms."

"That sounds romantic."

"You might be surprised."

They spent the rest of the day painting Jesse's room a lovely sky-blue. Evan was a terrible painter, ending up with more paint on him than on the walls.

"Come here," he growled at her, when the last wall was done.

"Are you kidding? I'm not touching you."

He advanced toward her.

"Evan, you're blue!"

"In sickness and in health," he reminded her, moving stealthily toward her, blue-smudged hands reaching.

She dodged. "I don't remember anything about 'in paint.'"

"I do. In sickness and in health, in red or in blue, I swear I will always chase after you." He lunged.

She darted away. He came after her. She ran through the house, shrieking, and right out the back door. He came behind her, breathing down her neck.

She knew he could catch her in an instant. She was not in the same kind of physical condition he was in. He was just enjoying the game, as she was. She felt suddenly awed by the course her life had taken.

When Howard had told her—after their long engagement—she was going to have to pick him or pick Mac, she had been devastated. She felt as if she had invested the best years of her life into her relationship with Howard. They had been engaged for several years, but she had been unable to celebrate a wedding with her sister so ill, needing her, so it had been postponed over and over again.

It occurred to her Evan would have married her anyway.

Hadn't she secretly hoped Howard would insist they marry anyway, that it was the time she most needed support, that he would help her through it, that a large wedding was unnecessary, that it was the vows that mattered and that he would say them to her without fanfare?

But he never had. Looking back, had he actually seemed relieved when the marriage was postponed? And relieved again when she had chosen Mac?

Had he known, somewhere in his heart of hearts, that if they said yes to each other they would miss the opportunity to have exactly what she now had with Evan?

She giggled out loud at the thought, and it slowed her down some.

Because it was really too funny thinking of Howard being passionate. Or playful. What, exactly, had she liked about him?

It had seemed to her he was the most stable of men. Safe.

He was successful at his business, and that had appealed to her, too. In a way her attraction to Howard had been about her own self-esteem, flattered that a man of his stature would even be interested in someone like her.

And in the end, he had not really been safe at all.

As she ran along the well-worn path to the barn, laughter bubbling out of her, it suddenly seemed that that event all those years ago—Howard making her choose—had not been devastating at all, not in light of where it had led her.

That hard choice he had forced her to make had really been a gift from heaven, the very thing that had paved the way to her having the moment she was having now.

She glanced over her shoulder at her husband, still in hot pursuit, then wrenched open the barn door and ran into the cool darkness, up the narrow stairs to the loft, Evan right on her heels.

Finally he took mercy on her and caught her. They tumbled down in loose, sweet-smelling hay, and he put his blue hands all over her until her laughter died in her throat, and she was kissing him with the fever and hunger and passion of a woman making up for lost time.

"I told you you might find painting surprising," she breathed against his neck.

"I love it," he agreed, his lips trailing fire down across her breastbone.

"Tomorrow, Mac's room. Red and black." It came out in gasps.

"I can hardly wait."

"He picked the colors himself."

"I guessed."

"Evan, this isn't even comfortable. I have hay poking into me."

"In sickness and in health, in night and day, in every way *and* in hay."

She laughed. "You're awful."

"Awful good. Say it, or I'll tickle you."

Breathlessly, when his blue hand moved inside her shirt, she said, "Evan, you're awfully good."

He wagged a fiendish eyebrow at her, and then covered her lips with his own. She wrapped her arms around his neck, and somehow couldn't feel that hay poking into her at all anymore, and the last thing on her mind was that her bra had blue handprints all over it.

The next day, while Evan painted Mac's room, Kathleen painted Mickey Mouse and Pluto and Goofy on Jesse's walls.

"Hey, you're good," Evan said, admiring her paintings, but his eyes came back to her and settled there.

She glanced at him, leaning against the door frame, pretty much covered in red and black paint. "Awfully good," she said, and shivered at the look in his eyes. "And don't even think it, until you have that paint off."

"I bet I could have it off in under three minutes."

"You're on," she whispered, and the light that deepened in his eyes made her feel as if she had never lived before.

As if she had slept away her life, until this knight in shining armor, disguised as a humble cowboy, had come along, and literally kissed her awake.

Every day she became a little more certain that she had done exactly the right thing, the only thing. She couldn't touch him enough, look at him enough, be with him enough.

And she knew, beyond a shadow of a doubt, that he felt the same way about her. Evan glowed with happiness.

And then, abruptly, the honeymoon was over. The boys came home.

And it was like sweet torture curbing all the things she felt for Evan, having to wait until no one was looking to run her hand over the curve of a blue-jeaned backside, to kiss him until they both had to come up for air, to hide her burning desire, to haul him down on the rug or the couch or the floor or the grass.

For as much as she practiced perfect decorum, she knew Mac's eyes followed her, bewilderment just beneath the anger.

How dare anyone else make his auntie Kathy so happy?

"I hate my bedroom," Mac announced after his first night in it, pushing his bacon and eggs around on his plate.

"What do you hate about it?" Kathleen asked, helping Jesse up into his chair.

"Red and black are gross. It's manic."

"We'll repaint it," Kathleen told him. Where on earth did Mac get these expressions from? Manic?

"No, we won't," Evan said. "You asked for those

colors, you live with them. Great breakfast, Kathleen. Mac and I will cook it tomorrow. What do you say, Mac?''

''I only know how to make cereal,'' Mac said sullenly.

''Great,'' Evan said. ''That's Jesse's favorite. Captain Crunch.''

''Could you and I talk for a minute?'' Kathleen said to Evan.

She stepped out of the kitchen door and onto the small back porch. She took a deep breath. The air was crisp and clean. In the distance she could hear a calf bawling. ''He doesn't like his room. Why not repaint it?''

''Kathleen, the room isn't what he doesn't like. You're desperate to make him happy and he knows it. He'll have you repainting that room twice a week.''

She knew Evan might be right, but she was not used to having to discuss her decisions with anyone, and she didn't like being called wrong, even when she knew she probably was.

''And isn't it my life?'' she said. ''I can't paint his room twice a week if that's what I want?''

''No.''

She folded her arms over her chest, felt her eyes narrowing. ''You're going to presume to tell me what to do?''

''This isn't even about you, Kathleen, it's about him. He thinks this is what he wants, to get us fighting over him. But it isn't really, and if he succeeds, he'll feel so sick inside he won't know what to do with himself. We have to show solidarity.''

''Then you should have agreed it was okay to paint the bedroom, or at least to discuss it with me in private!

I didn't like being vetoed in front of him, as if you make all the decisions in this house and I just sit back and say, 'Yes, Evan.'"

Looking at him now, she had trouble matching the man he was now with the one who had chased her around the bedroom until the very walls sang with their laughter. He looked hard and stern, and not in the least likely to back down.

"Look, I'm sorry if you didn't like how I handled it. I'm not exactly accustomed to consulting with people about my decisions, either. I'll try to do better next time, but for now that room is being repainted over my dead body."

She saw the set of his jaw and the look in his eyes, and it made him seem like a complete stranger to her. Which he was, really, if she thought about it.

Which maybe she should have done.

"You're very stubborn," she said uneasily.

"As a mule."

"Me, too."

"Well, as long as we're pulling together, that's fine." He sighed. "Kathleen, if he still hates the bedroom in a month, we'll get some more paint. But he'll have to do it himself."

"I want him to be happy," she wailed.

"There aren't any shortcuts to that! You won't make him happy by painting his room or buying him expensive shoes. I'm not sure that you can make him happy at all, if he's decided that he's not going to be."

"I'm afraid I did the wrong thing," she whispered.

And when she saw the pain flash through his eyes, she knew she could not have said a worse thing to her new husband if she had worked at it.

"I didn't mean that the way it sounded." She touched his arm.

But the damage was done. She could see the hurt in his eyes even though he smiled a little bit. "Our first fight, Kathleen. Not counting the day we met. Maybe we did do the wrong thing if we can't even have words without one of us looking for the exit. Did you think we were never going to disagree about anything?"

"It just seems, after the last few days…" Her voice trailed off.

"What's the expression? The honeymoon is over?"

But she didn't want the honeymoon to be over. She wanted it to last forever, and she wanted them to be a perfect family, with everyone happy all the time. She pictured them playing board games together and laughing while they cooked dinners and the whole house filled with a loving glow, the energy of harmony.

"Aw, don't do that, Kathleen."

"What?"

He pressed her forehead. "Don't worry so much. Just don't expect everything to be perfect without giving it some time. Everybody has a few adjustments to make here." He kissed her on the cheek.

But she knew by "everybody" he meant Mac.

He moved past her, back into the house. "Come on, Mac, let's go do those calves."

"Does my room get painted?" Mac asked, looking between them with satisfaction.

"No," Evan said. "It doesn't."

She came in behind him.

"But I hate it!" Mac was looking at her, his big eyes filling with tears, begging her to help him.

She looked at Evan, squared her shoulders. "If you don't like it in a month, you can repaint it yourself."

"That stinks."

"Speaking of stink, let's get at those calves," Evan said calmly.

Mac threw down his napkin, gave her a dirty look and stomped out of the house after Evan.

Jesse looked up at her, with his big brown eyes, and smiled. "Like paint my woom."

"Thanks, sweetie."

He must have sensed her distress, because he added enthusiastically. "Lots!"

She went and picked him up and hugged him close to her. He hugged her back, and whispered "Mommy" in her ear, a word he could not seem to get enough of, and she wondered how she could have thought, even for a second, that she had made a mistake.

Alone that night, in their bedroom, she could still feel it between her and Evan, a wall up where there had not been one before, a subtle tension. She watched from their bed as he stripped off his shirt, felt a familiar heat rising in her.

"Evan, I didn't mean that. About making a mistake. I just feel so responsible for Mac. I can see he's unhappy and I want to fix it."

The rest of his clothes fell in a pool at his feet, and he slid into bed beside her, scooted over to her and gathered her in his arms. "Have you been worrying about that all day?"

"Yes!"

"You've been doing it on your own with Mac for a long time. I probably should have let you handle it. I guess I just feel men handle things differently, and I don't really think Mac needs the gentle approach right now."

"You think I baby him."

"I didn't say that. It's just that you're so damned anxious not to have a confrontation with him. Confrontations don't break people, Kathleen. He's got to know who is the boss in this house, and that it's not him. He'll be relieved to know it's not him."

"And who is the boss in this house?" she asked, feeling her temper rising again.

"I think both of us can be in charge."

"Is that what you really think, or are you avoiding a confrontation?"

"I can think of other things I'd rather do with you." He reached out and touched her hair. Kissed her neck.

She closed her eyes. It seemed like nothing else mattered but this. Nothing. And she felt guilty for feeling that way, and helpless to feel any other.

And by the next morning she did wonder if she worried too much. Mac and Jesse were in Mac's bedroom howling with laughter, obviously happy, just as she had hoped. When they came out for breakfast the happiness lingered as the pair of them mooed, and made other animal noises through breakfast.

Evan looked at her over his coffee and winked.

On his way out the door, a few minutes after Evan had left, Mac spoiled it all by saying to her, "I know you love him better than me. I know it."

"Mac, that's not true. At all. I feel very strongly for Evan. But it's an entirely different kind of love than what I have for you."

Mac gave her a disgusted look and went out the door.

That night, after supper, she and Evan walked on the prairies; the boys watched TV.

"Mac told me today he wants to go see his dad," Evan said.

"What?"

"That's what he told me."

"Oh, Evan, he doesn't even know his dad. I don't even think he knows his name. The man abandoned my sister as soon as he found out she was pregnant."

Very softly, under his breath, Evan said the word that had recently been removed completely and professionally from the side of his truck. "He made it sound like he knew him. He just had to make a phone call and a ticket would be on the way."

"Why would he do that?"

"Maybe that's what he would like to be true. Anything would be better than me, the one who forces him to move manure. And stole a piece of a heart he's had all to himself for a whole long time."

"He's so jealous," she said, feeling sick and torn.

"Your face will freeze like that," Evan said tenderly, touching her forehead. But when she looked at him, she could see he was feeling distressed, too.

"What can we do?"

"I don't think there's a thing we can do, except be as normal as possible. It would be a mistake to pander to him. I'll just keep working with him every day. He seems to really like farm work. And you just keep lovin' him. You have a talent for that."

"I feel like he's begging me to love him, but when I try, it's like he's got a big glass wall around him that just deflects whatever I send to him. I think the work's better for him than my TLC. It helps him blow off some of his teenage angst."

"You know what I feel really awful about? That Mac is so unhappy, and Jesse is just blossoming."

It was true. Jesse followed her around the house like a little puppy, eagerly climbing onto her lap the moment she sat down, chattering away a mile a minute, loving hugs and kisses and "helping" her with everything. Laundry and making cookies, he had to have his little tasks to do right along side her.

Kathleen even thought she detected changes in the way he said *r*. She read him lots of stories and would have him repeat the *r* words after her.

Still, for all his devotion to her, and hers to him, he resisted surrendering his soother and diapers, and his first loyalty, touchingly, was still to his "bwadda" Mac.

The next morning when Kathleen got up, Mac's room was empty. For a heart-stopping moment she thought he had gone, run away, or in a pathetic search for his father.

Then she saw him outside in the driveway. Right beside Evan's truck.

A feeling of trepidation grew in her.

Evan came up behind her, put his arms around her, nuzzled her neck.

"What's Mac doing?"

At that precise moment Mac stepped back from the truck and revealed his handiwork.

The new word was far worse than the first one had been.

"Oh, Evan," Kathleen breathed when she felt his muscles coil with tension and anger when he saw the word. "I'm so sorry."

"You're sorry? Why on earth would you be sorry? Are you out there with a nail?"

She could hear the barely leashed fury in his words, and then he removed his hands from around her waist, and headed for the door.

"Evan, don't deal with it in anger."

"I don't think it will hurt him to know I'm angry!"

"Please?"

"Don't you trust me at all? What the hell do you think I'm going to do? Beat him with a two-by-four? Is that what you think of me, Kathleen? That I'm just a rough cowboy who can't be trusted to deal with a twelve-year-old?"

"I didn't say that."

"It's right there in your eyes that you want to protect him. *From me.* Have I done something to deserve that?"

"He just seems so mixed up right now, so fragile."

"That looks fragile to you? You know what it looks like to me? Like out-and-out belligerence. He's asking for some guidelines, and I intend to give them to him."

He turned on his heel and went out the door.

She fought back the urge to go with him, to supervise, and instead watched from the window as he talked to Mac. And he was right. He had never, right from the very start, given her any reason to believe that he wouldn't handle it just fine.

As far as she could tell he didn't even raise his voice.

What was happening to her? She felt so torn, as if by choosing happiness for herself with Evan, she had let down her sister in her promise to look after Mac. She had really and truly believed that this union would be the right thing for Mac, too.

Or had she? Had she been pulled by a force within her so strong it would have told her any lie to get her into the heaven of Evan's arms?

And what if the two of them couldn't resolve it? Exactly what had those vows meant to her? At what price to Mac was she prepared to go to keep her promises to Evan?

Both her men came back in the house a few seconds later.

"Mac," she said, "Why? I just don't—"

"Kathleen, leave it," Evan snapped. "I have tons of manure. Probably enough to see him through until his eighteenth birthday."

Mac said nothing, and in fact when he glanced at her she saw the oddest expression on his face. It was as if he wanted to hate this man, and could not. Had specifically thought of the worst thing he could do, had tried to infuriate Evan, like a test. Will you hate me back?

And Evan had just answered him.

No.

The answer Mac most needed to hear.

"I guess I'm going to be moving so much manure," Mac said, "you'll probably have to buy more cows."

"That's right, son." Kathleen detected just the slightest smile in Evan's eyes.

Mac didn't even protest being called son.

Trust him, she told herself. Trust your husband. And then she realized it had been a long, long time since she had to trust anyone but herself. And that when she had stood in front of this whole town and said "I do" she had really vowed to learn all kinds of lessons about loving.

Some of them seemed easier than others.

Chapter Nine

It was Evan's favorite time of day. It hadn't always been, but it was now.

The boys were in bed. Mac had actually sought him out tonight, and they had looked at some maps of the area together. Then, when it was time for Jesse's bedtime story, they had all piled on his bed, including Mac, and laughed at the stories of Robert Munsch. Evan had looked at Kathleen and seen so clearly how happy she was, that this was what she dreamed of, and hoped for. A family not at war.

Which is, of course, what he had dreamed of his entire life, too.

Mac just didn't share the dream. Evan had known it was a momentary truce only when he'd gone into the bathroom after the boys. Mac had written his name on the mirror in toothpaste. Evan wiped it off before Kathleen saw it, knowing how quickly it would erase the storytime serenity from her face.

Now, he and Kathleen had put away the last of the dishes, and the star-studded night beckoned.

He held open the back porch door for her, and watched how she walked with her head tilted back, looking at those stars as if she hadn't seen them last night or the night before that.

When they reached their favorite little knoll, he reached inside his shirt and pulled out a long-stemmed rose.

"Evan! What's this for?"

"Two weeks today."

"Did you have to go all the way to town for it?" She held it to her nose and breathed in.

"Yeah."

"And didn't it scratch you, inside your shirt?"

"Yes, it did."

"Was it worth it?"

"Oh, yes, ma'am. It made you smile. That little knot is all but gone."

She looked swiftly away from him, then. "How can I not worry? Evan, he is being so *bad*. He's never behaved like this. As if scratching that new word on the truck wasn't bad enough! Then the 'accidents' started happening. Letting the calves out, driving your four-wheeler through the new garden, throwing that baseball through the bathroom window—"

"What?"

"This afternoon."

"Let me guess, an accident?"

"Didn't you notice?"

"I thought the bathroom window was open." Actually, he'd been completely distracted by the toothpaste, which he decided not to tell her about.

"I just feel so sick, Evan, torn between loyalty and love."

He knew that. Had known it from the first time they'd had words over Mac. He was scared to ask her which of them she felt loyal to and which she loved. They didn't say those words to each other.

It surprised him how much he wanted to hear them from her.

How he woke up every morning and hoped today would be the day Kathleen told him she loved him.

Instead they woke up to some new horror of Mac's and she got that worried look on her face, and the pain in her eyes ripped Evan apart.

He loved her.

He could not believe how it had come to him. How simply this gift had been given to him by the universe.

He watched her with his son, and he could feel the love grow inside his chest.

He came into his house to the smell of cleanliness and fresh cookies and it grew some more.

He watched her plant those flowers, so full of hope, so unrealistic about the challenges of the weather and wind here in Saskatchewan, and the love in him grew.

He went to their bed at night, and she was so full of wonder, so eager, so sexy without having any idea that she was, and his love grew more.

He saw her, after all these years of being on her own, giving her trust to him, slowly, and he took it as a gift he was not always sure he was worthy of.

They walked out here, under these huge mystical skies, and talked, and he came to love the sound of her voice and her quiet insights, her gentleness, her thoughtfulness and his love just kept growing inside him.

As hopeful as those flowers she'd planted.

And maybe, he thought darkly, just as doomed.

How could he love her and keep her when she was feeling ripped up, torn between him and Mac, suffering every single day? This being a decent guy—her knight—was really harder than he had ever believed it could be.

"There's something else," she said.

"Do you have to tell me?" he groaned.

"The Mortimers called this afternoon. They were very nasty. They said they were going to expose our marriage as a sham in court, and that then they would get Jesse for sure."

Forgetting momentarily that he had turned over a new leaf, that he was a gentleman now, he said a word she probably hadn't heard much. She would have seen it though, right there on the side of his truck.

"Evan, would you tell me about Dee? I feel if I understood some things about her I could understand Jesse better. And maybe her parents, too."

He'd never wanted to talk about Dee before, and certainly not to his new wife, but suddenly he realized what Kathleen was offering—not just to understand Jesse better, but to help him heal, too. It reminded him that it was not just Kathleen who had come into this relationship with issues that needed to be dealt with. It was not just Kathleen who needed to learn to trust, to lean on other people. It was him, too.

"I met her at a rodeo. She was a barrel racing queen. Beautiful. Wild. I liked that—that she was as wild as me. She liked life fast. Lots of speed, lots of action. She was unpredictable and unreliable, and at the time, that just added to the whole sense of excitement I felt around her.

"She told me she was protected, so you could have knocked me over with a feather when she announced she was pregnant." He tried to erase the bitterness from his voice, but knew he had not succeeded. "It didn't even bother her to think about getting an abortion.

"I talked her out of it. I thought she'd be as ready and willing to change as I was when that baby came. But I learned a hard lesson about human nature. People tell you right off who they are. And you don't have the chance of a snowball in hell of changing that into what you want it to be.

"She wasn't interested in being nobody's mama. She hated the farm, hated the hard work, and in pretty short order she seemed to hate me.

"Too late, I saw that in the wild no-holds-barred way that she went around a barrel on a horse she simply didn't care if she lived or died. She wanted excitement and lots of it, and there's not too much exciting about farm life in Saskatchewan."

Or at least, he'd believed that until he met Kathleen. Suddenly with Kathleen, who seemed so calm and so quiet, his farm in Saskatchewan had become a pretty exciting place after all. And that didn't even include the hijinks Mac got up to every day!

"It was like there was something wrong with Dee," he continued thoughtfully, giving it words for the first time. "Hidden behind that reckless grin was the fact she didn't care much about anything but Dee. Everything about her got worse after the baby was born. She was more restless and more angry and more resentful.

"I'd come in off the farm, and sometimes she's just start throwing things at me and screaming. She claimed I loved the baby and not her, and that I wanted her to die of boredom and that I was killing her on purpose.

"One day she took the baby and she left. Took the baby, not because she wanted him, but to hurt me. To punish me for all her shattered expectations, I guess, for me not being able to fill that hole inside her, that I don't think anything could have filled. Really, the more I tried to understand her convoluted thinking, the more I failed.

"I tracked her down, caught up to them once or twice, just long enough to see the satisfaction in her eyes that she was causing me such misery. And then she'd be gone again.

"I thank God every day that Jesse wasn't with her the night she died in the car wreck, one party too many, one trip too fast. I suspect she told Jesse all kinds of rotten things about me, because when he first came he seemed terrified of me, suspicious and silent. He's really coming out of it now."

"That poor baby," Kathleen said. "Both of them, poor babies."

"Dee?" he said incredulously.

"Evan, she never grew up. That's why Jesse is so taken with Mac. That's just what Mac acts like. Affectionate to Jess, but not if it's going to interfere with his plans."

"I'm not sorry she died," he said. "Is that awful?"

"It's human. Evan? I think we need to invite her parents here."

"Get real." He thought dealing with Mac every day was quite enough to ask of a man.

"No, I mean it." Her voice was firm, and he was beginning to recognize when she planned to be mulish. "They lost their daughter, and they're full of anger and rage and want to blame someone, but if you let them come here, they'll see it's not you."

"Yeah, right."

"And they'll see, maybe, that they still have a grand-son, and that everything that was best about their daughter goes on in him."

"What if they're the ones who made her like that?"

"I'm not asking you to let them raise Jesse, but to allow them to be a small part of his life. His connection to his mother, and theirs to her."

"I don't want to," he said.

"Just think about it."

"Do I have to?" A true knight would.

"Yes."

And it seemed to him that what he had just said about Dee—that a person let you know right off who they were—applied also to Kathleen.

Right off he had known that she was soft and gentle, but with a core of strength and stubbornness running through her.

Right off he had known in some part of himself that he would be required to be a bigger man than he was if he wanted to keep her—more open, more loving. Yes, even more forgiving. He was going to have to leave that renegade in him behind, the tough guy who could hold a grudge for a long, long time, if he wanted to ever be the man Kathleen thought he was.

"All right," he said gruffly. "I'll call them."

She leaned over and kissed his cheek, and he felt his heart soar as high as those stars up there. Until he re-membered one more thing that she had let him know, right off, and that was that her nephew meant the world to her, and that she would always do what she thought was best for him.

And so he wondered, looking at those stars, if being

a bigger man than he was, would involve letting her go, rather than watching her be ripped up like this.

He hoped not. God, he hoped not.

He would give it more time.

Sometimes time solved things that all a man's pushing and shoving and working and fretting could not solve.

She leaned over and kissed him again, on the mouth this time. And before he knew it they were clothed only in darkness, beneath a gorgeous summer sky, and she wasn't even worried about snakes.

In the pleasant afterglow, when he felt ten feet high and bullet proof, he thought about what he could do to repair his relationship with Mac, to get by the boy's anger. He had a brilliant insight. Brilliant. The kid wanted to find his dad. Why not help him? It was something they could work on together, unite them, make it so Mac didn't see him as the enemy who'd stolen his auntie Kathy's love.

Mac gave him an opportunity first thing in the morning. They were working together, feeding the mix to the calves, when Mac started.

"I'm going to find my dad. If we had the Internet I could find him really fast. Of course, out here in the boonies, we don't have the Internet. How come we don't have a computer? How come—"

"Do you know his name?" Evan interrupted.

"Of course I know my dad's name!" Mac said so furiously that Evan suspected he didn't.

"I'll help you find him," Evan said.

Mac froze, and Evan suddenly wished that he had discussed this with Kathleen, because the look on Mac's face was not one of undying gratitude.

He looked very young and very vulnerable.

And he looked terrified.

He turned swiftly away from Evan's probing gaze. "That would be great," he said. "We'll find my dad and I'll go live with him."

"Whoa, buddy. Nobody said anything about that. I'll help you find him and then we'll talk to your auntie Kathleen about what to do next. Maybe you could write him some letters or something, arrange to meet him later."

Mac didn't say anything.

"Next week, okay? After Jesse's grandparents come on Sunday."

"I can't wait," Mac said, but Evan heard something else, and wished he wouldn't have opened his mouth.

Kathleen looked at the flowers in the vase. Scraggly, her bedding plants were not holding out very well against the ravages of the wind. Still, there had been a few blossoms to pick, and with the long-lasting rose Evan had given her, it looked quite nice.

She glanced at the clock. The Mortimers should be here within the hour.

Evan came in and smiled at her flowers.

"Are they pathetic?" she asked.

"They're pretty."

"Could you go get the boys? Mac took Jesse out to the barn to play with the new kittens. I haven't seen them for a while. Jesse will need a bath."

"The Mortimers sounded so excited to be coming, Kathleen. I think you were right."

"I'll try not to rub it in."

"Very gracious of you."

She wanted to tell him right now. That she loved him. When she got up in the morning the words went through her head, and they went though it all day long. In light of the rather intimate things they were doing, why did the words seem so scary to say?

Maybe it was because Mac was behaving so badly. How long could Evan stand it? How long before he suggested maybe this wasn't working? And what did that say about her? That she was attaching a condition to her love? That he had to keep her in order for her to love him?

Keep her, she thought, as if he could return her to the store and get a new one or something. He would never break those vows he had said. Never. Was it going to be up to her to let him out of this?

"Now what are you worried about?" he said, pressing the line on her forehead.

"I think I'm wrecking your life," she whispered.

"Wrecking my life?"

"If you've had enough of Mac destroying your property, I'll understand."

"Maybe what you're trying to say is that you've had enough of the tension between us," he said softly.

Was he giving her a way out? But the thought of leaving him filled her with such an ache she thought she would cry. She was not even sure she could do that for Mac. What kind of person had she become? Only able to think about herself? Was what she felt for Evan really love if it made her self-centered instead of a better person?

"We'll talk later," she said. "Please, go get the boys."

With one more shrewd look at her, he went out the back door. But when he returned, nearly half an hour later, he looked pale and distraught. "I've looked everywhere, Kathleen. I can't find them."

She stared at him. "You can't find them? But that's impossible. Where would they go?"

They searched the farm together, and then the house. Mac's note was in his room, laying on his pillow.

Poorly spelled and stained with tears, Kathleen picked it up and read it out loud.

Dear Aunt Kathy:

I have been very bad and I'm sorry. I see you are very happy, except for me, and I know you don't want me anymore. Old bowwow already left because of me, and pretty soon Evan will, too. I don't make anybody happy, just mad and sad. I don't know why. I guess I feel mad and sad all the time. My mom died, and my dad never wanted me, and I wonder if it's my fault those things happened, and no wonder nobody wants me around.

Evan said he would help me find my dad. That means he wants to get rid of me, too.

"God," Evan said.

"What's this about his dad?"

"Aw, Kathleen, I thought if I offered to help him with that he wouldn't be so angry with me, wouldn't feel we were on opposite teams. It was a dumb mistake."

"It was a nice thing to do," she said sternly, and then continued to read the letter out loud:

Jesse really likes me, and I like him, too, even if he is a real Stinky Pants. But he has a real dad, and now he calls you Mom, and his real grandma and grandpa are coming to see him. I don't have a grandma and grandpa and nobody will ever come see me. Someday I bet he'll have a real brother or sister. And I won't have that, ever.

Don't worry about me. I am going back to Vancouver. It is warm there and people can live on the streets even in the winter. I can be a squeegee kid just like those ones you always give money to. Don't come looking because I have a secret route planned and you will never find me.

Bye forever. I love you. Mac

P.S. Jesse is in the barn playing with the kittens. I told him not to come with me. You know he listens to me.

"Oh, my God," Kathleen said. She sank into a chair and held the letter, read it again, the tears spilling down her face. "Where could he have gone? And where is Jesse?"

Evan's face looked taut and pained. "I think he decided not to listen to Mac this time."

She looked at Evan, stricken. "Where do you think he would go? He's got to be our first concern. He's smaller."

"I think he's following Mac, wherever Mac is. The question is, does Mac know yet? How long has he been gone?"

She looked at the clock in distress. "At least an hour, closer to two. Why didn't I check on them?"

"You are not to blame. Why would you check on them? They've played in the barn before for hours. I'm going to go saddle a horse. This note is making me wonder if he decided to try to cross-country to the highway. He was asking me about that a few days ago, when I was showing him a map."

"You are not to blame, either."

"Maybe I am, Kathleen. I could see how unhappy that boy was, and how unhappy he was making you."

"It's you he was making unhappy," she said.

"Me? I could handle ten kids just like him with one arm tied behind my back just to be with you. Look, I want you to call the police. And then Ma Watson. Tell her what happened and tell her to get the word out that we need as many people as possible to come out here. They can bring horses or be prepared to search on foot, but no all-terrain vehicles. It's going to get dark, and I don't want anybody running over those kids. After you've called, hop in the truck and drive toward town. Look in the ditches, and go slow by anything they might be hiding behind."

She registered every word he said, but somehow her mind stopped on *just to be with you,* and those words in all their quiet simplicity kept the panic at bay and made her feel stronger than she had ever felt.

"What if all those people come and Mac and Jesse are asleep under a pile of hay?"

"I can't take that chance. The people in this country would rather be called on to help too soon than be on the receiving end of bad news too late."

They heard a car pull up outside the house. Evan looked baffled and then he scowled.

"The Mortimers," he said. "Perfect bloody timing."

"It is perfect timing," she said. "Because I'm going to put them in charge of the command center, and I'm going with you. Saddle two horses."

"Have you ever ridden before?"

"Yes." She didn't tell him it had been a Shetland

pony that went around in a circle at the fair. "Go get the horses ready."

And while he went out the back door, she went to the front.

Briefly she introduced herself, told them what had happened and what she needed done, and was impressed with Ron Mortimer's immediate take-charge attitude.

In no time he was set up at the kitchen table with Evan's address book and photographs of both the boys. After he had hung up from Ma Watson, he asked her the names of the local radio stations.

Fiona Mortimer asked her where her coffeepot was, and supplies to make sandwiches. "We'll need to feed those searchers if the boys aren't found right away."

"Thank you," Kathleen said. "I'm so sorry. I can't imagine the shock this is for you. I have to go—"

"You wait five minutes. Go find warm clothes for you and Evan. And when you come back I'll have sandwiches ready for you. Where's your thermos?"

With that Fiona hustled Kathleen out of the room. In a few minutes, Kathleen was running toward the barn, full thermoses, warm clothes and sandwiches with her.

Evan had two horses ready. They looked huge to her, but she would not allow herself to be timid. Not now. Not with that knowledge tucked inside her that he would do anything to be with her.

He helped her mount, watched critically as she got on. Grimly he said, "I suppose they're in there talking about custody now for sure."

"Evan," she said, "I think you might be surprised."

He swung on his horse, the Mortimers already dismissed from his mind.

"I want to go this way," he said, pointing. "I found a partial print on the ground, and Mac asked all kinds of questions when we looked at that map together. You could eventually join the highway, cross-country, if you went this way. But it's thirty miles of rugged going. A map doesn't show the river coulees between here and there."

Kathleen looked at the prairie and felt overwhelmed by how huge it was. If they went a few steps different than the boys, how were they going to find them? Were the boys even together? She drew in a long, shuddering breath, told herself to be strong.

She suddenly came face-to-face with a fact she had not acknowledged in her entire life. Worrying would solve nothing. Only action would.

And Evan was a man of action.

Chapter Ten

"They've been this way."

Kathleen sat in her saddle, aching with weariness. She looked at Evan, crouched down in front of his horse peering at the ground. Never before had she so appreciated the toughness at his very core. She knew he would not quit until he found their boys.

"What have you found?" she asked. At first she had gotten on and off her horse every time he did, but she had soon found out it was much harder than it looked, and that she needed to conserve her energy.

When she thought she could just weep because she was so frightened for Mac and Jesse, and her muscles ached from the unfamiliar motion of riding, she would think of Jesse's sturdy little legs and wonder how on earth he had walked this far.

Evan had found tracks that suggested both the boys had come this way.

For the first time she'd been very pleased about those expensive runners she had bought for Mac. They left a distinctive name brand anyplace the soil was bare and damp.

"I think this is Jesse. I think he sat down here, from the size of the patch of grass that is flattened." He squinted closer. "It looks like he scuffed around in the dirt with his truck a little bit."

She closed her eyes, seeing Jesse sitting in the grass, singing to himself, tired, playing with his truck. Did he still have Mac in his sights? Was he scared or was he too innocent to know that he had anything to be scared about?

Tracking the boys took an enormous amount of time and patience. Evan rode in a slow serpentine, so as not to miss anything, got off his horse often to look at the ground, at the way grass was flattened, at scuffs in mud—most of which had nothing to do with the boys.

He would also stop his horse frequently, silently scanning the horizon. Seeing him this way, sitting his horse, it was as if Kathleen was seeing what and who Evan really was. Straight-backed, proud, strong, capable, able to take on a rugged, rugged world, and be a victor over its challenges. She was so glad it was Evan looking for these boys. She could not think of one other person on the face of the earth she would have wanted, or trusted, with this task.

She, too, scanned the endless rolling landscape, looking so hard it felt like her eyes were watering all the time, like she was seeing things that were not there.

"Get off your horse for a minute, Kathleen. Stretch your legs. We'll have some of that coffee."

"I can keep going," she said stubbornly. She didn't want him making concessions to her weaknesses that might cost them valuable minutes in their search.

"If we don't look after ourselves, if we start getting

too hungry or too tired or too sore, we won't be as alert as we need to be. We might miss something.''

She got off the horse, thinking maybe that was true of everything in life. That a person had to learn to care for themselves first, before they were any good to anyone else.

''Maybe,'' she said out loud, getting off the horse, hearing her knees crack as her feet touched the ground, ''that's the mistake I made with Mac. I always put him first. When I stopped—'' Her voice choked.

Evan poured a cup of coffee from the thermos, and held it to her lips. She took a deep, shuddering sip of it.

''I don't want you talking like that. As if it's your fault. If anyone's to blame, it's me, trying to play hero, offering to help him find his dad. I thought he would see it for what it was—me trying to tell him how much I cared about him. Instead he thought I was trying to get rid of him. I guess that's what happens when a guy like me tries to be a hero.''

''What do you mean, a guy like you?''

''Kathleen, I've lived pretty close to the edge most of my life. I've been wild and irresponsible and about as devil-may-care as they come. I've looked after myself, and I never got good at seeing another person's point of view. Even with Dee, I could never see what she wanted, only what I wanted. And then when you came along, I thought you deserved something better.'' He laughed, a harsh, self-depreciating sound. ''I thought I could make myself into a knight for you. Maybe Mac could see through all that.''

''You listen to me, Evan,'' she said, her voice low and full of fury. ''I won't listen to you talk about yourself like that. I won't. I've watched you with your son and my nephew, I've seen—'' she blushed thinking of their wedding night ''—the great and uncommon tenderness you are capable of. And yet, when you are called on to be strong and sure, to remain calm in a crisis, you can do that, too. If you are not a knight, then there is no such thing. And if there is no such thing, my heart will be broken.

"I have searched all my life for what I see in you—integrity, strength and tenderness. I looked in those men who are so suave and so sophisticated, who knew what to wear and what fork to use and what wine to order. Not one of those men would be worthy to hold your horse for you, Evan. Not one of them. There is not one man on this earth who I would want here with me more than you.''

"You wouldn't be in this predicament right now if it weren't for me.''

"Really? It seems to me Mac has been a predicament looking for a place to happen for sometime. This was my meaning—that no matter what kind of distress I ever found myself in, it would always be your name I would call. Maybe you don't have a suit of shining armor, but you're real, Evan. You aren't trying to be something you are not, you are trying to uncover what you really are. I knew what you really were from the first moment I looked into your eyes. And I knew you would help me become what I really am, too. That's why I love you. That's why I have loved you from almost the first moment I laid eyes on you.''

He was smiling, a slow, sweet smile that nearly melted her heart.

"You just like the way I fill out a pair of blue jeans,'' he said.

And she smiled back at him. "I'd take blue jeans over armor any day."

And then, as if they had needed a break from the terrible tension they were under, they held each other, and laughed. She laughed until the laughter became tears, and she sobbed helplessly against him as she listened to him say, over and over, that he loved her. That he planned to love her forever. No matter what.

"What do you mean, no matter what?" she asked, stepping back from him, mopping the tears from her eyes with her shirtsleeve.

"I mean if you decide that you have to leave me to give Mac the life you want to give him, I will still love you. I'll wait for you. I promise."

She thought how very different that was than what Howard had said all those years ago.

"That's funny," she said. "I was waiting to say the exact same thing to you, only reversed. That if you couldn't handle Mac anymore, and all the terrible things he does, then I would go."

"Ma'am, I already told you I could handle ten more just like him. Just to be with you. But here's another truth. I love that kid. He's so much like I was at that age it's spooky. That's what I needed to tell him the other day. Not that I would help him find his dad, but that I wanted more than anything on earth to be his dad."

She suddenly had a sense of something relaxing within her, the tension leaving, a river of peace taking its place. Everything was part of the plan. Everything.

Mac had brought her and Evan together, and now he had been the one who had allowed them to finally express their true feelings for each other.

She knew they would find him, and that this moment, searching the prairies, would become the pivotal one in the family history that was just beginning.

That moment when truth made itself known to them.

The simplest of truths, the strongest of truths, the only truth.

Love was everything.

Without it a man could wander forever in his own uncertainties. With it people became strong, discovered who they were and how they fit in the plan. Her place was on these prairies, beside this man, raising their children, those children their link to forever.

"Are you ready to go?"

He helped her back into the saddle. The weariness seemed to be gone from her, but she did notice, uneasily, the light was fading from the sky.

But Evan saw it differently. "Good," he said. "Mac might have matches. I hope he'll light a fire. If he does, it will show up for a long way."

"If he lights a fire," she said, "it will mean he wants us to find him."

Twenty minutes later, the sky still holding sunset, but the earth blanketed in darkness, she heard Evan's yip of triumph, and saw the flicker of the fire in the distance.

Evan pushed his horse into a gallop, and hers followed. Holding the horn, the first stars coming out, feeling as though her heart would burst with joy and completion, she followed Evan at breakneck speed, over uncertain ground toward the future. Her future and his.

They galloped to the fire, Evan pulling his horse to a swift halt, and getting off it in one smooth move, running now. And then out of the circle of the fire she saw Mac, coming toward them, Jesse's hand firmly in his, both boys faces streaked with dirt from tears.

"Evan," Mac said, his voice quavering, "I'm sorry." He was sobbing now, rubbing his eyes with his hands. "I didn't know Jesse would follow me. I didn't know. You must have been so scared when he was gone."

Evan got down on one knee in front of Mac, and Jesse barreled by and jumped into his lap. "Daddy," he said over and over. "Daddy. Mac, I tell you my daddy would come."

Mac drew in a long, shuddering breath and stood, his head hanging, his tears splashing down into the dirt at his feet.

Kathleen managed to get off her horse and came toward them, and Evan stood and put Jesse in her arms, and then turned back to Mac.

"I was scared when both my boys were gone," Evan said. "Scared out of mind. More scared than I have ever been in my life."

"You're not scared of nothing," Mac said. "I know."

"Every man's scared of something, Mac."

"You can hit me," Mac said, still looking at his boots.

"Hit you?" Evan said. He closed the distance between them and wrapped his powerful arms around the broken little boy, pulled him into him. "I'll never hurt you, ever."

Mac's control broke. He wrapped his arms around Evan's neck and sobbed.

Evan picked him up as if he were a baby, rocked him against his chest. "You know, all my life I wanted a family to love. And when God gave me your auntie, he saw how much I needed a boy just like you, too. I should have said that to you sooner. A whole lot sooner.''

"Do you love me?" Mac said. "Me?"

"Yeah, you.''

"After what I just did?''

"Yeah.''

"After your truck, and letting the cows out and wrecking the garden?''

"Don't forget the bathroom window.''

Mac smiled a little crookedly through his tears. "And the bathroom window?''

"Yeah.''

"I love my auntie Kathy more than anybody in the world. That's why I ran away. Even though I didn't show it, all I really want is for her to be happy. I could tell you made her happy, and I didn't. It made me mad and scared, too. I thought the more she loved you, the less she loved me.

"You know what made me think maybe I had it all wrong? When I turned around and saw Jesse behind me. I didn't even know how much he meant to me until I turned around and saw him way behind me. I ran back to him, and he had his stupid truck, and he was so happy I came back for him like it wasn't my stupid fault he was out here in the first place. I went to bring him home, and that's when I got really, really scared.

"Because I didn't know which way home was. I thought I'd been going in a straight line, but when I looked around everything looked the same. I tried to figure out from the sun which way to go back, but I just felt so mixed up and Jesse was so tired. He kept sitting down and crying, and telling me he wanted his daddy. After a while we sat down and I had some matches, and it made Jesse stop crying to find little twigs and pieces of grass to put on the fire. I only had one peanut butter sandwich with me, though, and I gave that to him a long time ago.''

"I hope you had some of it, too, son."

Mac shook his head, vehemently. "That's the part I'm getting to. I wanted him to have it all. I figured out I don't just like the kid, I really love him lots. And I figured out it doesn't make me love Auntie Kathy any less. It kind of makes me feel bigger than I did before. Maybe you'll laugh at me, but like I'm almost a man, now."

"I ain't laughing," Evan said quietly.

"I guess maybe if that's the way things are, I better stand on my own two feet," Mac said.

Evan set him down.

"Me man now, too?" Jesse said hopefully.

"Oh, sure," Mac said. "But no more Mr. Stinky Pants, then. Not ever. Got it?"

"Got it," Jesse responded solemnly, and they all laughed.

Evan looked at the gathering darkness. "I think we're stuck here for the night. I don't want to risk it in the dark. Those horses are done. We'll just sit tight for now. Break out those sandwiches, Kathleen."

"Can you find your way home from here," Mac asked anxiously, "or are we going to be like the Swiss Family Robinson, only lost on the prairie?"

"Even if I couldn't find my way home," Evan said, "those horses could. You could turn them around in a hundred circles and when you were done they'd point their noses for home and go in a straight line right there."

They sat around the campfire. The boys ate every sandwich and Evan made them both drink some coffee.

And then a strange and magical thing happened.

There beneath the stars, they became a family. The family Kathleen had pictured, the family she had dreamed of.

Laughing and telling jokes and singing. As the night got colder, Evan stripped the blankets off the horses, and they squeezed under them, and holding as tight together as they could, they went to sleep.

They woke in the morning to the sound of a helicopter beating over them.

It landed close by.

"Put the boys on it," Kathleen said. "I'll ride back with you."

"No way, Auntie Kathy. You and Jesse go. I'll ride back with Evan."

Kathleen did not miss the authority this was spoken with, like a true man, and so she climbed aboard the helicopter, a wide-eyed Jesse on her lap, and watched as her husband and her boy worked side by side to get their horses ready. Saw Evan clap Mac on the shoulder, and Mac lean into that hand for a moment, gathering strength, before he stood tall.

She watched them standing together on that seemingly endless prairie, until she could see them no more. With a sigh of contentment, she looked ahead.

Later that day, feeling exhausted and exhilarated, she welcomed the two dusty riders home, and said goodbye to the last of the search crews, her friends and neighbors.

"We're going to go now, too," Fiona Mortimer said. "Evan, we owe you an apology."

Kathleen turned to see her holding a sleeping Jesse, looking out the window.

Fiona began to speak, almost to herself. "All we wanted was for Dee to be happy. She was our only child. We gave her too much. I can see that now. We gave her too much stuff, and we gave her too much freedom, and the more we tried to fill her up the emptier she got.

"Evan, either you've changed, or I read you wrong, and I suspect it's a bit of both, but I know you and Kathleen will do a wonderful job of raising our grandson. Jesse is in good hands. We won't bother you again."

She turned from the window and put the sleeping child in Evan's arms. Blinking back tears she walked rapidly to the door.

"Fiona," Evan said. "Thank you. You know you are welcome here, anytime. And it's no bother."

Her husband cleared his throat and spoke. "We read Mac's note while you were out there, and we realized something. We have been so broken by our daughter's death that we forgot there would still be people who needed us, that we could still be of use. When we read Mac's note, we realized there were lots of kids who feel like him. Who would love grandparents just like us. We need someone to dote on. When we get back to Regina we're going to find out if there are some kids who need a granny and a grandpa to love them. Maybe that's how we can say we're sorry to Dee for loving her in all the wrong ways."

"Ron," Evan said slowly, "it seemed to me you got two kids right here that need a grandma and a grandpa to love them."

Looking pretty close to tears himself, Ron nodded, shook Evan's hand and followed his wife out the door.

"Who would have thought?" Evan murmured, watching them drive away.

"Do you ever feel as if we are in the presence of miracles?" Kathleen whispered.

"Well yes, ma'am, I do. A humble cowboy becomes a knight in shining armor. I know a miracle when I see one."

"Love is the miracle. It makes good things grow out of hard ground, it makes tears into diamonds, it makes things that are wrong right again. It gives little boys daddies like you, and a woman like me the husband of her dreams."

"You're just saying that 'cause of the way I fill out my blue jeans."

"Damn right, cowboy."

And she kissed him. It felt as fresh, as exhilarating, as intoxicating, as it had the very first time.

She knew some people were blessed that way.

They went through life as if it were a dance, as if everything were brand-new and magic, as if there were all kinds of things left to explore and to fill them with that feeling of first-time wonder.

She knew, when he returned her kiss, that she had just become one of those people.

Every single day a new opportunity to live, to laugh, to fall in love all over again.

Every single day a first time.

Forever.

Epilogue

"Auntie Kathy, Granny and Grandpa Mortimer are here!"

Kathleen wiped her hands on a tea towel, and went to the door, watching as Mac flung himself into his adopted grandmother's embrace.

"I got my report card," she could hear him saying excitedly. "Straight *A*'s. Know what that means? My dad is going to teach me how to ride bulls. Well, steers. I'm going in a rodeo this summer."

It was nearly six months now since Mac had started calling Evan Dad, and Kathleen still felt the same catch in her throat at the way he said *my dad* with such fierce pride and possessiveness.

Jesse shot out by her.

"Granny. Grandpa!"

Perfect *r*'s she noted, and felt just the faintest sadness at the passing of time, at how quickly little boys became big ones.

Jesse had said good-bye to diapers and his soother

forever after he and Mac had walked onto the prairie that day.

They came through the door, the boys and their grandparents, and Kathleen noticed the soft radiance in Fiona's face.

"How's Adopt-A-Granny going?" she asked after they had exchanged hugs.

"I still think the name is sexist," her husband groused good-naturedly behind her.

"We've had calls from all over North America asking for information. I'm going to be a guest speaker in Los Angeles next month. Me!"

"Fiona and I have sixteen grandchildren now," Ron said, "including these two." He rustled Mac's head affectionately.

"Me going to be in rodeo," Jesse crowed.

"What?" his grandparents said together.

"He's going to be a mutton buster," Mac said. "I'm helping him learn."

Kathleen laughed. "Mac bought some sheep with his 4-H money. I think we're the only farm in Saskatchewan with sheep that are now all broken to ride."

"Yeah," Mac said disgustedly, "not much buck left in them. Hey, did you notice my auntie Kathy looks different?"

She felt herself blush as the Mortimers turned their full attention to her.

"I do not!" she said.

"She's pregnant!" Mac announced officiously. "We're going to have a baby. Jess and me want a boy, but she doesn't. She'd like a girl."

"Me, too," Evan said, coming in the back door. "I want a little girl with big brown eyes and long dark hair. Hi, Fiona, Ron. Good to see you."

Kathleen watched as Ron shook his hand and Fiona hugged him. She could actually feel the love shimmering in the room.

Then he kissed her, as if he hadn't seen her for a year instead of the few hours it had been. He turned back to their guests, his arm around her waist.

"I really appreciate you coming to spend a few days with Jess and Mac. I've been promising to take Kathleen to the Cypress Hills forever. Our first anniversary just seemed like the right time."

Our first anniversary, Kathleen thought. Her thoughts went back over the year, and it seemed as if her mind was a photo album full of snapshots of moments she had once just imagined: Mac and Jesse chasing butterflies through the tall grass, their house brimming over with laughter, Evan looking at her with a tenderness that never went away.

"You're doing us the favor," Fiona said. "What do you guys want to do first?"

"The water slides in Medicine Hat," Mac said.

"I'm too old for that," Fiona said, with mock fear.

"That's what you said about tobogganing," Mac reminded her. "When me and Jesse were cold and wanted to come back in, we couldn't get you off the sled."

"These older women," Evan said solemnly, "just run a man into the ground. They're full of surprises."

Kathleen smacked him on the arm, then looked into his eyes and felt a deep welling of gratitude for all the wonderful surprises life had brought her.

"Come see my room, Grandma," Mac said, tugging on her arm. "I just repainted it."

"Thank the Lord," she said.

"All black," he said gleefully. "Even the ceiling."

"Me want black room, too," Jesse said.

"You have to wait until you're twelve," Mac told him sternly.

They had dinner together, and then Evan and Kathleen were shooed out the door, their suitcases already in the truck.

"The stars are just coming out," she said wistfully, after they had driven for half an hour or so.

"I suppose you want to stop?"

"Could we?"

He stopped the truck and they sat in the silence and looked at the stars. After a long time she reached into her bag and got him out a small square box.

He unwrapped it.

Inside was a belt buckle, engraved with the date and year of their anniversary.

"The silver," she said softly, "was from a real suit of armor, worn by a real knight in the middle ages. The armor was damaged in a fire. It couldn't be fixed."

"How on earth did you find something like that?" he asked, turning the buckle over in his hands.

"The Internet."

He laughed. "Is the world going to leave this old cowboy behind?"

"No. The world will always need cowboys. And knights. Always."

"Come here."

She slid across the seat to him, into the place she loved to be most. His arms. He kissed her until they were both breathless.

"Kathleen, will we ever get to the Cypress Hills?"

She thought of the options. Kissed him again, long and hard, and said, "I certainly hope not."

*   *   *   *   *

Happy Birthday

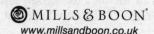

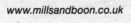

...International affairs, seduction and passion guaranteed

Volume 1 – July 2007
The Future King's Pregnant Mistress by Penny Jordan

Volume 2 – August 2007
Surgeon Prince, Ordinary Wife by Melanie Milburne

Volume 3 – September 2007
Bought by the Billionaire Prince by Carol Marinelli

Volume 4 – October 2007
The Tycoon's Princess Bride by Natasha Oakley

8 volumes in all to collect!

THE ROYAL HOUSE OF NIROLI

...International affairs, seduction and passion guaranteed

Volume 5 – November 2007
Expecting His Royal Baby by Susan Stephens

Volume 6 – December 2007
The Prince's Forbidden Virgin by Robyn Donald

Volume 7 – January 2008
Bride by Royal Appointment by Raye Morgan

Volume 8 – February 2008
A Royal Bride at the Sheikh's Command by Penny Jordan

8 volumes in all to collect!

Medieval
LORDS & LADIES
COLLECTION

When courageous knights risked all to win the hand of their lady!

Volume 1: Conquest Brides – July 2007
Gentle Conqueror by Julia Byrne
Madselin's Choice by Elizabeth Henshall

Volume 2: Blackmail & Betrayal – August 2007
A Knight in Waiting by Juliet Landon
Betrayed Hearts by Elizabeth Henshall

Volume 3: The War of the Roses – September 2007
Loyal Hearts by Sarah Westleigh
The Traitor's Daughter by Joanna Makepeace

6 volumes in all to collect!

www.millsandboon.co.uk   M&B

Medieval
LORDS & LADIES
COLLECTION

When courageous knights risked all to win the hand of their lady!

Volume 4: Christmas Knights – October 2007
King's Pawn by Joanna Makepeace
The Alchemist's Daughter by Elaine Knighton

Volume 5: Exotic East – November 2007
Captive of the Harem by Anne Herries
Pearl Beyond Price by Claire Delacroix

Volume 6: Mediterranean Heroes – December 2007
Honeyed Lies by Claire Delacroix
Rinaldi's Revenge by Paula Marshall

6 volumes in all to collect!

M&B